THE BERLIN STORIES

By Christopher Isherwood

AVAILABLE FROM NEW DIRECTIONS

•

All the Conspirators

The Berlin Stories

Goodbye to Berlin

Mr Norris Changes Trains

THE BERLIN STORIES

CHRISTOPHER ISHERWOOD

Introduction by Armistead Maupin

Preface by Christopher Isherwood

A NEW DIRECTIONS BOOK

Manufactured in the United States of America
First published as NDP134 in 1963; reissued as NDP1120 in 2008 with an introduction by Armistead Maupin.
This volume comprises the 1935 edition of *Mr Norris Changes Trains* and the 1939 edition of *Goodbye to Berlin.*
Published simultaneously in Canada by Penguin Books Canada Limited
New Directions Books are printed on acid-free paper.
Design by Erik Rieselbach

Isherwood, Christopher, 1904–1986.
[Mr Norris Changes Trains]
Berlin stories / Christopher Isherwood ; introduction by Armistead Maupin.
p. cm.
ISBN 978-0-8112-1804-7 (pbk. : alk. paper)
1. Berlin (Germany)—Social life and customs—Fiction.
I. Isherwood, Christopher, 1904–1986. Goodbye to Berlin. II. Title.
III. Title: Mr Norris Changes Trains. IV. Title: Goodbye to Berlin.
PR6017.S5L37 2008
823'.912—dc22

2008023325

10 9 8 7 6 5 4 3

New Directions Books are published for James Laughlin
by New Directions Publishing Corporation
80 Eighth Avenue, New York 10011

Contents

Introduction

SEVERAL YEARS AGO, on a break from the Berlin Film Festival, my husband Christopher and I took our friend Ian McKellen on a pilgrimage to Nollendorfstrasse 17, the address made mythic by Christopher Isherwood's *Berlin Stories*. It was a bitter winter night, stinging with sleet, but we were heartened to find the street much as the writer had described it: "Cellar-shops ... under the shadow of top-heavy balconied façades ... houses like shabby monumental safes crammed with the tarnished valuables and second-hand furniture of a bankrupt middle class." A brass plaque, rendered in German and tagged with graffiti, marked the apartment house where Isherwood had lived in the early 1930s, sometimes down the hall from the model for his best-known creation, Sally Bowles. Across the street, on the side of another house, a pink neon sign was bleeding its message into the black-and-white landscape—GAY INTERNET CAFÉ—prompting Ian to smile in tender appreciation. "Perfect," he murmured. "Absolutely perfect."

I knew what he meant. It was lovely to see that seventy-five years after Isherwood had lived on this "deep solemn massive street," young men were still coming here to tell stories and look for love. The writer had come here himself because "Berlin meant boys," all those decades ago, and the boys were back in town, proclaiming their desires in unapologetic neon. In the course of Isherwood's life two holocausts—one brought on by fascism, the other by a deadly virus—had decimated the people he called his tribe, yet we were still here, still riding a wave of change that Isherwood himself had helped to set in motion. That neon sign was as much his legacy as his writing.

A small confession: I found my way to *The Berlin Stories* the way many readers of my generation did—through the 1972 movie musical *Cabaret*. (Isherwood, unlike his less cheeky Berlin compatriots Stephen Spender and W. H. Auden, was not widely taught in American schools in the 1960's, especially in the South.) As a young gay man who'd recently defected to San Francisco, I was stunned to find echoes of my new life in this film about another city and another time. Liza Minnelli's Sally Bowles reminded me of some my own new women friends: daffy and wounded and falsely naughty and refreshingly nonchalant about homosexuality. And the Michael York character—the Isherwood figure, I learned—was so winsome and virile and gorgeous that I wanted to *be* him, going so far as to buy a sleeveless sweater like the one he wore in the movie.

So I went straight to the source and plunged into the old New Directions "paperbook" of *The Berlin Stories*—that black-and-white cover with the Brechtian piano player—where I was willingly led astray by Isherwood's cast of charlatans and rent boys and all-seeing landladies in the last days of the Weimar Republic. The novel, as it turned out, was actually two novels, both told in the first person. The first of them, *The Last of Mr. Norris* (1935)*, was narrated by a young writer named William Bradshaw—Isherwood's two middle names, unsubtly enough. The second novel, *Goodbye to Berlin* (1939), while still presented as a work of fiction, was told in the voice of someone

*The title given to *Mr Norris Changes Trains* on its American publication. [Ed.]

called Christopher Isherwood. This was perhaps the first step in a long journey toward ever more candid self-disclosure that would occupy Isherwood for the rest of his days. The well-examined life would become his obsession—and, some would say, his great gift to literature.

I admit to a certain frustration upon encountering the Bradshaw/Isherwood narrator in *The Berlin Stories*. While his voice was seductive in its elegant economy, his eye was always turned towards the Others; his own life, particularly his sex life, was a blank. "I am a camera with its shutter open," he tells us, "quite passive, recording, not thinking." He meant simply that he was new in town and absorbing everything around him, but he would come to think of those first four words as "infamous" after they were popularized as the title of John van Druten's stage adaptation of the novel. From that point on, lazy critics would have a far-too-handy shorthand for analyzing his work.

Isherwood was not, as the camera metaphor suggested, a detached or clinical observer; he was as fully engaged as a writer could be, both with his work and his readers. The problem for him was an ethical one: the need not to lie. Time spent with Magnus Hirschfeld at the Institute for Sexual Research (not to mention in bed with working-class boys) had radicalized the young Christopher about his newfound identity. It would have stuck in his craw, he later explained, to make Bradshaw/Isherwood heterosexual. On the other hand, a homosexual narrator would have been unthinkable in those days and would have distracted severely from the other portraits of Berliners on the fringes of society. So our hero ends up a neutered observer, alone in his room at night while randy youths in the street whistle up to their girlfriends to throw down their keys. In real life, of course, some of those whistles were meant for Isherwood.

The author examines all of this and more in *Christopher and His Kind*, a 1976 memoir that serves as a fascinating companion volume to *The Berlin Stories*. Here, through the eyes of a wry and self-effacing septuagenarian, we learn the full story of

Isherwood's four years in Berlin. He tells us, for instance, that his reasons for moving in with strapping, young Otto Nowak and his family in *Goodbye to Berlin* were not financial but romantic and that Otto's mother knew of their relationship and was not in the least shocked. This revisionist approach to his own material, far from diminishing the power of the original, offers a singular glimpse into the working process of a novelist, the ways in which remembered events are altered or erased altogether in service of privacy or vanity or the story itself. Few writers have ever been so generous with their trade secrets, so willing to undercut their own well-honed mythology in the name of telling the truth.

In the end, *The Berlin Stories* can withstand anyone's scrutiny, even Isherwood's. These trenchant, funny, heartbreaking vignettes of a city already doomed to fascism still dazzle us today, thanks to the author's abiding fascination with the particular and the personal. He is also that rarest of creatures, an esteemed "literary" writer who refuses to inflict upon his readers a single word he does not need or mean. Make no mistake, the raw simplicity of these pages took work, but Isherwood was always too much of an artist—and a gentleman—to let it show. He understood instinctively that crisp, unhysterical prose would best contain the horrors unfolding around him, that understatement, in such a brash and gaudy setting, would pack a more powerful punch.

I met Christopher Isherwood by chance at a Hollywood cocktail party in 1978 when he was in his mid seventies. My first novel was only months away from publication, so I screwed up my courage and asked him to read it. The blurb he so graciously provided likened my work to that of Dickens, though he could not have overlooked how strongly I'd been influenced by *The Berlin Stories*. While set in San Francisco in the seventies, my story also involved an apartment house with a motherly landlady and her one-of-everything tenants, a microcosm of the freewheeling society that contained it. What's more, my title—*Tales of the City*—intentionally echoed *The*

Berlin Stories in its suggestion that the city itself was the main character of the piece. I'd even been so brazen as to name one of my characters Bradshaw—just for luck, I suppose.

Once I'd come to know him, Isherwood proved as vivid in life as he had been on the page. I still picture him in blue jeans and loafers, bouncing on his heels like a schoolboy, his brambled eyebrows cavorting as he tells a story. Like many young queers of that era, I regarded him as a sort of spiritual grandfather. (He used the term queer himself, way back then, explaining with a conspiratorial wink that "it embarrasses our oppressors.") He'd been officially out of the closet for at least five years—ever since a memoir called *Kathleen and Frank*—and had landed on the shores of his happy ending in Santa Monica with the artist Don Bachardy, thirty years his junior. This was the man he'd described in the closing paragraph of *Christopher and His Kind*, "the ideal companion to whom you can reveal yourself totally and yet be loved for what you are, not what you pretend to be." To see those two together, still blissful after twenty-five years in their house above the sea, was to imagine a happy ending for yourself.

In 1985, for the *Village Voice*, I spoke to Isherwood and Bachardy for what would prove to be the writer's last interview. Though struggling with cancer himself, he offered fighting words to the legions of young men already dying of AIDS. "They're told by their relatives that it's God's will and all that sort of thing. And I think they have to be very tough with themselves and really decide which side they're on. You know, fuck God's will. God's will must be circumvented if that's what it is." It was just that kind of straight talk that made Isherwood so loved. It embarrassed some of his more "discreet" Hollywood friends (most of them younger than he) but it was a battle cry for some of us—and for once, miraculously, it was coming from an elder. More than anyone of his generation, Isherwood reminded us that gay self-respect came with its own noble lineage.

I felt the tug of that lineage just this morning when I asked

Don Bachardy about the dolphin clock that Isherwood mentions on the second page of *Goodbye to Berlin*. Contemplating his landlady's "unnecessarily solid, abnormally heavy" knick-knacks, the writer asks slyly: "What becomes of such things? How could they ever be destroyed? They will probably remain intact for thousands of years; people will treasure them in museums. Or perhaps they will merely be melted down for munitions in a war." The clock, as irony would have it, eventually survived a bomb blast with barely a scratch and, even more ironically, ended up in Isherwood's hands. He tells us in his 1954 preface to *The Berlin Stories* that his former landlady— by then in her seventies—had presented this sturdy object to her famous tenant on a recent visit to Nollendorfstrasse. "It stands now on my writing table in a Californian garden—and I like to think it will survive me, and anything that may be dropped on this neighborhood, in the near or distant future."

"So what did you want to know about it?" Bachardy asked when I spoke to him this morning.

"Is it still there?" I asked. "Do you still have it?"

"Oh, yes. It's on Chris's desk. I'm looking at it now." He paused as if to emphasize the final irony. "It will probably end up at the Huntington."

That joke about museums had been right on the nose.

ARMISTEAD MAUPIN
San Francisco
California
June, 2008

About This Book

FROM 1929 TO 1933, I lived almost continuously in Berlin, with only occasional visits to other parts of Germany and to England. Already, during that time, I had made up my mind that I would one day write about the people I'd met and the experiences I was having. So I kept a detailed diary, which in due course provided raw material for all my Berlin stories.

My first idea, immediately after leaving Berlin in 1933, was to transform this material into one huge tightly constructed melodramatic novel, in the manner of Balzac. I wanted to call it *The Lost*. This title, or rather its German equivalent, *Die Verlorenen*, seemed to me wonderfully ominous. I stretched it to mean not only The Astray and The Doomed—referring tragically to the political events in Germany and our epoch—but also "The Lost" in quotation marks—referring satirically to those individuals whom respectable society shuns in horror: an Arthur Norris, a von Pregnitz, a Sally Bowles.

Maybe Balzac himself could have devised a plot-structure which would plausibly contain the mob of characters I wanted to introduce to my readers. The task was quite beyond my powers. What I actually produced was an absurd jumble of subplots and coincidences which defeated me whenever I tried to straighten it out on paper. Thank Goodness I never did write *The Lost*!

Just the same, all of these characters had grown together, like a nest of Siamese twins, in my head, and I could only separate them by the most delicate operations. There was a morning of acute nervous tension throughout which I paced up and down the roof of an hotel in the Canary Islands, shaping the plot of *Mr Norris* and discarding everybody and everything that didn't belong in it. This was in May, 1934. A few days later, I set to work on the novel, sitting in the garden of a pension at Orotava on Tenerife. The pension was run by a happy-go-lucky Englishman, who used to laugh at my industry and tell me I ought to go swimming, while I was still young. "After all, old boy, I mean to say, will it matter a hundred years from now if you wrote that yarn or not?" Relentlessly, at four o'clock every afternoon, he would start playing records at full blast through the loudspeaker on the patio, hoping to attract wandering tourists in for a drink. They seldom came, but the jazz tunes always put an end to my day's work. On August 12, I noted in my diary: "Finished *Mr Norris*. The gramophone keeps repeating a statement about Life with which I do not agree." I remember how I raced through that last chapter with one eye on my watch, determined to get finished before the racket started.

Mr Norris was published in 1935. In England, the book bore its correct name: *Mr Norris Changes Trains*; but the American publisher, William Morrow, found this obscure—so I changed it to *The Last of Mr. Norris*, a title which should be followed by a very faint question mark.*

Next I wrote the story of *Sally Bowles*, and it appeared as a small separate volume in 1937. Three other pieces—*The Nowaks*, *The Landauers* and *Berlin Diary: Autumn 1930*—were published in issues of John Lehmann's *New Writing*. Finally, the complete *Goodbye to Berlin* was published in 1939.

Goodbye indeed! During those years that followed, the

* With this edition, we return to Isherwood's original title. [Ed.]

Berlin I'd known seemed as dead as ancient Carthage. But 1945 came at last, and V-E Day. That summer, New Directions was getting ready to republish *Mr Norris* and *Goodbye to Berlin* in one volume, *The Berlin Stories*. While I was correcting the proofs, a letter, the first in seven years, reached me from Heinz, my closest "enemy" friend, telling how he had fought in Russia and later been taken prisoner by the Americans. After the fighting was over, the authorities at his POW camp had more or less allowed him, and a number of others, to run away, and had later forwarded his mail to his home address, marked "Escaped"! As I read and reread this letter, the feeling began to work through me painfully and joyfully, like blood through a numbed leg, that Berlin—or, at any rate, the Berliners—still existed, after all.

Then, in the summer of 1951, John van Druten decided that he could make a play out of *Sally Bowles*. His adaptation, *I Am a Camera*, was written with his usual skilled speed, and was ready for production that fall. When I arrived in New York to sit in on rehearsals, I had first to go to a studio and be photographed, for publicity, with our leading lady, Julie Harris. I had never met Miss Harris before. I hadn't even seen her famous performance in *The Member of the Wedding*.

Now, out of the dressing-room, came a slim sparkling-eyed girl in an absurdly tart-like black satin dress, with a little cap stuck jauntily on her pale flame-colored hair, and a silly naughty giggle. This was Sally Bowles in person. Miss Harris was more essentially Sally Bowles than the Sally of my book, and much more like Sally than the real girl who long ago gave me the idea for my character.

I felt half hypnotized by the strangeness of the situation. "This is terribly sad," I said to her. "You've stayed the same age while I've gotten twenty years older." We exchanged scraps of dialogue from the play, ad-libbed new lines, laughed wildly, hammed and hugged each other, while the photographer's camera clicked. I couldn't take my eyes off her. I was dumbfounded, infatuated. Who was she? What was she? How much was there in her of Miss Harris, how much of van Druten, how much of the girl I used to know in Berlin, how much of myself? It was no longer possible to say. I only knew that she was lovable in a way that no human could ever quite be, since, being a creature of art, she had been created out of pure love.

As I watched those rehearsals, I used to think a good deal—sometimes comically, sometimes sentimentally—about the relation of art to life. In writing *Goodbye to Berlin*, I destroyed a certain portion of my real past. I did this deliberately, because I preferred the simplified, more creditable, more exciting fictitious past which I'd created to take its place. Indeed, it had now become hard for me to remember just how things really had happened. I only knew how I would like them to have happened—that is to say, how I had made them happen in my stories. And so, gradually, the real past had disappeared, along with the real Christopher Isherwood of twenty years ago. Only the Christopher Isherwood of the stories remained.

I'd never thought about this situation before, because it had never seemed to have any particular significance. If my past was artificial, at least it had been entirely my own—until now. Now John, Julie and the rest of them had suddenly swooped down on it, and carried bits of it away with them for their artistic use. Watching my past being thus reinterpreted, revised and transformed by all these talented people upon the stage, I said to myself: "I am no longer an individual. I am a collaboration. I am in the public domain."

After the play had opened successfully on Broadway, I went to England. This was my third visit since the end of the war; and this time, I knew, I must go over to Germany as well. It was a definite obligation—but how I dreaded it! I dreaded meeting the people I'd known and facing the fact that there was practically nothing I could do to help them. I dreaded seeing familiar places in ruins. Though my mind was made up, my unconscious still protested: I developed symptoms of duodenal ulcer, and nearly broke my leg on a staircase. Throughout the flight from London, I expected a crash, and was almost disappointed when we landed safe at Tempelhofer Feld in a mild snowstorm—"a psychosomatic snowstorm, obviously," one of my friends commented, later.

I had arrived prepared—overprepared—for a shock; and the drive through the streets wasn't as depressing as I'd anticipated. As it was night, you couldn't see much, anyhow, and it so happened that the houses along our route were less badly damaged than elsewhere. Indeed, the end of the drive brought a shock of a different kind; for I found myself among the new neon-lighted shops and bars of the Kurfuerstendamm, and entered a modernistic hotel where I was surrounded by thick-necked cigar-smoking businessmen who might have stepped right out of the cartoons of Georg Grosz. It was I, not these people, who had changed; for now I could afford to live with them. During my former Berlin existence as a down-at-heel English teacher, I used to know such places only from the outside, peering into them as I passed along the sidewalk with disapproval, moral superiority and envy.

But in those days (February, 1952) the Kurfuerstendamm was one of the still few areas of relatively intact prosperity. At the end of it, the nineteenth-century-Gothic Memorial Church looked more Gothic than ever in its jaggedly pinnacled ruins. The Tauentzienstrasse beyond was like an avenue of shattered monuments. Through wide gaps between formless mounds of rubble, you got views over the great central desert of destruction, and saw the Sieges Saeule rising forlornly from the treeless, snow-covered plain of the Tiergarten, which was dotted with bizarre remnants of statuary: a uniformed general, a naked nymph on a horse. In the background, the skeleton of a railroad station showed up starkly; and against the blue winter sky, a red flag fluttered from the Brandenburger Tor, entrance to the Soviet sector. There was something doubly strange about this landscape. It is strange enough to see a vast city shattered and dead. It is far stranger to see one that is briskly and teemingly inhabited, amidst its ruins. Berlin seemed convinced that it was alive; and, after a few hours there, you began to agree that it certainly was.

The street where I used to live is behind the Nollendorfplatz, about ten minutes' walk from the hotel where I was staying. I knew that my old landlady, "Frl. Schroeder," was still there; we had been corresponding, but I hadn't told her that I was coming to Berlin for fear of a last-minute disappointment. Even before the war, this was a decayed and forbidding district; but when I saw it again I was really awestruck. The fronts of the buildings were pitted with shrapnel and eaten by rot and weather, so that they had that curiously blurred, sightless look you see on the face of the Sphinx.

Only a very young and frivolous foreigner, I thought, could have lived in such a place and found it amusing. Hadn't there been something youthfully heartless in my enjoyment of the spectacle of Berlin in the early thirties, with its poverty, its political hatred and its despair? I felt extremely middle-aged, that morning. The house next to ours had been hit: on the third floor, a handsome tiled stove still stood in the corner of a half-room which jutted out over the abyss. With reverent feet, I entered the deep dank courtyard, whose floor the sun never strikes, and climbed the musty stairs, dark even in the daytime, to Frl. Schroeder's door. The scream she uttered on recognizing me must have been heard all over the building.

She looked wonderful; better, now, in her seventies than in her fifties, and considerably slimmer. (Her only objection to my description of her in my stories was that I'd said she "waddled.") Yet she had been through as bad a time as any average Berliner: serious illness, poverty—forcing her to move to this much smaller flat, where she nevertheless had to have one lodger in the only spare bedroom and another sleeping in the kitchen—then the war, and the last awful year of bombing, when she and the other tenants lived almost continuously in the cellar. "There were forty or fifty of us down there. We used to hold each other in our arms and say at least we'd all die together. I can tell you, Herr Issyvoo, we prayed so much we got quite religious."

And then, with the fall of Berlin, came the Russian soldiers, searching the houses for arms. Frl. Schroeder thought she had nothing to fear until, at the last moment, she discovered to her horror that an Italian lodger, who had run away, had left a sporting rifle in his room. Caught with it, she would certainly have been shot; probably the whole building would have been burned down. So she and a woman friend took the rifle apart, hid the pieces under their clothes and set out for the canal, into which they planned to drop them. This they finally succeeded in doing, but only after a hair-raising encounter with some more Russians, who chased them with erotic intentions.

"Every time I went out on the street, they'd be after me," said Frl. Schroeder, not without a certain complacency. "So I used to screw up my eyes—like this—and make a hump in my back, and limp. You ought to have seen me, Herr Issyvoo! Even those Russians didn't want me any more. I looked like a regular old hag!"

By the time she had finished her stories, we were both quite exhausted with laughing and crying, and had drunk a whole bottle of Liebfraumilch.

Frl. Schroeder could only give me news of two of my old friends. Bobby the bartender had come through the war without a scratch, and had gotten married. Otto Nowak, now a black-market operator, had shown up recently at the flat, wanting to buy some carpets.

"He hadn't changed one bit. He was very well dressed—quite the fine gentleman. There's a rich woman somewhere in the background, I shouldn't wonder. Oh, you can rely on him to look after himself! And he's as fresh as ever. I soon sent him about his business."

As I listened to all this, I marveled, as one always does, at the individual's ability to be himself and survive, amidst a huge undifferentiated military mess. This was Frl. Schroeder's History of World War II—and its only moral was: "Somehow or other, life goes on in spite of everything."

When we said Goodbye, she gave me the brass dolphin-clock

which is referred to on the second page of *Goodbye to Berlin*, where I ask, prophetically, how it could ever be destroyed. It couldn't, apparently—for a bomb-blast had hurled it across the room and only slightly scratched its green marble base. It stands now on my writing table in a Californian garden—and I like to think that it will survive me, and anything that may be dropped on this neighborhood, in the near or distant future. Meanwhile, I treasure it, as a souvenir of my dear friend and as a symbol of that indestructible something in a place and an environment that resists all outward change.

The indestructible something—that, I soon realized, was what I had had to come back to Berlin to look for. And I seemed to sense it almost at once, in the very air of the city and in the sound of its inhabitants' voices. Berlin in winter, like New York, has an atmosphere that is immensely exhilarating. Evening after evening, I left the hotel and wandered from bar to bar, overstimulated and sleepless. And all I wanted was to speak and hear German. I felt I could never tire of the rich, confident, well-remembered tones of the Berliner accent; and I was surprised and pleased to discover how little the idiom and the slang had altered. Berliners love to talk—with a blunt directness which is both rude and friendly—and even in their grumbling there is a note of pleasure.

Comparing the two cities—the Berlin I knew in the early thirties and the Berlin I revisited in the early fifties—I have to admit that the latter is, in many respects, a far more exciting setting for a novel or a sequence of stories. Life in the Berlin of 1952 had an intensely dramatic doubleness. Here was a shadow-line cutting a city in half—a frontier between two worlds at war—across which people were actually being kidnapped, to disappear into prisons or graves. And yet this shadow-frontier was being freely crossed in the most humdrum manner every day, on foot, in buses, or in electric trains, by thousands of Berliners commuting back and forth between their work and their homes. Many men and women who lived in West Berlin were on the black list of the East German police;

and, if the Russians had suddenly marched in, they couldn't have hoped to escape. Yet, in this no man's land between the worlds, you heard the usual talk about business and sport, the new car, the new apartment, the new lover. "My God," I exclaimed to one of my acquaintances, after he had been holding forth on such topics for an hour or more, "one would think you lived in Minneapolis!" This was said, and taken, as a compliment. Berliners, in those days, were justifiably a little proud of their sang-froid. They still have reason to be.

How would Mr Norris have thrived in these troubled waters? Would he, perhaps, have found the fish rather too large and the current too strong for him? Would Sally Bowles have set her cap at the New Rich of the reconstruction period, or preferred the American, British and French officers? Would Otto Nowak have stuck to the black market, or entered the circles of the neo-Nazis? Could Bernhard Landauer have rebuilt his firm amidst the wreckage—and would he have cared to? All that is not for me to say. The ways of my own life have led me elsewhere. But I hope that some young foreigner has fallen in love with this later city, and is writing what happened or might have happened to him there.

CHRISTOPHER ISHERWOOD
Santa Monica
California
July, 1954

MR NORRIS CHANGES TRAINS

for W. H. Auden

Chapter One

MY FIRST IMPRESSION was that the stranger's eyes were of an unusually light blue. They met mine for several blank seconds, vacant, unmistakably scared. Startled and innocently naughty, they half reminded me of an incident I couldn't quite place; something which had happened a long time ago, to do with the upper fourth form classroom. They were the eyes of a schoolboy surprised in the act of breaking one of the rules. Not that I had caught him, apparently, at anything except his own thoughts: perhaps he imagined I could read them. At any rate, he seemed not to have heard or seen me cross the compartment from my corner to his own, for he started violently at the sound of my voice; so violently, indeed, that his nervous recoil hit me like repercussion. Instinctively I took a pace backwards.

It was exactly as though we had collided with each other bodily in the street. We were both confused, both ready to be apologetic. Smiling, anxious to reassure him, I repeated my question:

"I wonder, sir, if you could let me have a match?"

Even now, he didn't answer at once. He appeared to be engaged in some sort of rapid mental calculation, while his fingers, nervously active, sketched a number of flurried gestures round his waistcoat. For all they conveyed, he might equally have been going to undress, to draw a revolver, or merely to make sure that I hadn't stolen his money. Then the moment of agitation passed from his gaze like a little cloud, leaving a clear blue sky. At last he had understood what it was that I wanted:

"Yes, yes. Er—certainly. Of course."

As he spoke he touched his left temple delicately with his finger-tips, coughed, and suddenly smiled. His smile had great charm. It disclosed the ugliest teeth I had ever seen. They were like broken rocks.

"Certainly," he repeated. "With pleasure."

Delicately, with finger and thumb, he fished in the waistcoat pocket of his expensive-looking soft grey suit, extracted a gold spirit-lighter. His hands were white, small, and beautifully manicured.

I offered him my cigarettes.

"Er—thank you. Thank you."

"After you, sir."

"No, no. Please."

The tiny flame of the lighter flickered between us, as perishable as the atmosphere which our exaggerated politeness had created. The merest breath would have extinguished the one, the least incautious gesture or word would have destroyed the other. The cigarettes were both lighted now. We sat back in our respective places. The stranger was still doubtful of me. He was wondering whether he hadn't gone too far, delivered himself to a bore or a crook. His timid soul was eager to retire. I, on my side, had nothing to read. I foresaw a journey of utter silence, lasting seven or eight hours. I was determined to talk.

"Do you know what time we arrive at the frontier?"

Looking back on the conversation, this question does not seem to me to have been particularly unusual. It is true that I had no interest in the answer; I wanted merely to ask something which might start us chatting, and which wasn't, at the same time, inquisitive or impertinent. Its effect on the stranger was remarkable. I had certainly succeeded in arousing his interest.

He gave me a long, odd glance, and his features seemed to stiffen a *little.* It was the glance of a poker-player who guesses suddenly that his opponent *holds* a straight flush and that he had better be careful. At length he answered, speaking slowly and with caution:

"I'm afraid I couldn't tell you *exactly.* In about an hour's time, I believe."

His glance, now vacant for a *moment,* was clouded again. An unpleasant thought seemed to tease him like a wasp; he moved his head slightly to avoid it. Then he added, with surprising petulance:

"All these frontiers ... such a horrible nuisance."

I wasn't quite sure how to take this. The thought crossed my mind that he was perhaps some kind of mild internationalist; a member of the League of Nations Union. I ventured encouragingly:

"They ought to be done away with."

"I quite agree with you. They ought, indeed."

There was no mistaking his warmth. He had a large blunt fleshy nose and a chin which seemed to have slipped sideways. It was like a broken concertina. When he spoke, it jerked crooked in the most curious fashion and a deep cleft dimple like a wound surprisingly appeared in the side of it. Above his ripe red cheeks, his forehead was sculpturally white, like marble. A queerly cut fringe of dark grey hair lay across it, *compact, thick,* and heavy. After a moment's examination, I realized, with extreme interest, that he was wearing a wig.

"Particularly," I followed up my success, "all these red-tape formalities; the passport examination, and so forth."

But now. This wasn't right. I saw at once from his expression that I'd somehow managed to strike a new, disturbing note. We were speaking similar but distinct languages. This time, however, the stranger's reaction was not mistrust. He asked, with a puzzling air of frankness and unconcealed curiosity:

"Have you ever had trouble here yourself?"

It wasn't so much the question which I found odd, as the

tone in which he asked it. I smiled to hide my mystification.

"Oh, no. Quite the reverse. Often they don't bother to open anything; and as for your passport, they hardly look at it."

"I'm so glad to hear you say that."

He must have seen from my face what I was thinking, for he added hastily: "It may seem absurd, but I do so hate being fussed and bothered."

"Of course. I quite understand."

I grinned, for I had just arrived at a satisfactory explanation of his behaviour. The old boy was engaged in a little innocent private smuggling. Probably a piece of silk for his wife or a box of cigars for a friend. And now, of course, he was beginning to feel scared. Certainly he looked prosperous enough to pay any amount of duty. The rich have strange pleasures.

"You haven't crossed this frontier before, then?" I felt kindly and protective and superior. I would cheer him up, and, if things came to the worst, prompt him with some plausible lie to soften the heart of the customs officer.

"Of recent years, no. I usually travel by Belgium. For a variety of reasons. Yes." Again he looked vague, paused, and solemnly scratched his chin. All at once, something seemed to rouse him to awareness of my presence: "Perhaps, at this stage in the proceedings, I ought to introduce myself. Arthur Norris, Gent. Or shall we say: Of independent means?" He tittered nervously, exclaimed in alarm: "Don't get up, I beg."

It was too far to shake hands without moving. We compromised by a polite seated bow from the waist.

"My name's William Bradshaw," I said.

"Dear me, you're not by any chance one of the Suffolk Bradshaws?"

"I suppose I am. Before the War we used to live near Ipswich."

"Did you really, now? I used at one time to go and stay with a Mrs Hope-Lucas. She had a lovely place near Matlock. She was a Miss Bradshaw before her marriage."

"Yes, that's right. She was my great-aunt Agnes. She died about seven years ago."

"Did she? Dear, dear. I'm very sorry to hear that … Of course, I knew her when I was quite a young man; and she was a middle-aged lady then. I'm speaking now, mind you, of 'ninety-eight."

All this time I was covertly studying his wig. I had never seen one so cleverly made before. At the back of the skull, where it was brushed in with his own hair, it was wonderfully matched. Only the parting betrayed it at once, and even this would have passed muster at the distance of three or four yards.

"Well, well," observed Mr Norris. "Dear me, what a very small place the world is."

"You never met my mother, I suppose? Or my uncle, the admiral?"

I was quite resigned, now, to playing the relationships game. It was boring but exacting, and could be continued for hours. Already I saw a whole chain of easy moves ahead of me—uncles, aunts, cousins, their marriages and their properties, death duties, mortgages, sales. Then on to public school and university, comparing notes on food, exchanging anecdotes about masters, famous matches, and celebrated rows. I knew the exact tone to adopt.

But, to my surprise, Mr Norris didn't seem to want to play this game after all. He answered hurriedly:

"I'm afraid not. No. Since the War, I've rather lost touch with my English friends. My affairs have taken me abroad a good deal."

The word "abroad" caused both of us naturally to look out of the window. Holland was slipping past our viewpoint with the smooth somnolence of an afterdinner dream: a placid swampy landscape bounded by an electric tram travelling along the wall of a dike.

"Do you know this country well?" I asked. Since I had noticed the wig, I found myself somehow unable to go on calling him sir. And, anyhow, if he wore it to make himself look younger, it was both tactless and unkind to insist thus upon the difference between our ages.

"I know Amsterdam pretty well." Mr Norris rubbed his chin with a nervous, furtive movement. He had a trick of doing this and of opening his mouth in a kind of snarling grimace quite without ferocity, like an old lion in a cage. "Pretty well, yes."

"I should like to go there very much. It must be so quiet and peaceful."

"On the contrary, I can assure you that it's one of the most dangerous cities in Europe."

"Indeed?"

"Yes. Deeply attached as I am to Amsterdam, I shall always maintain that it has three fatal drawbacks. In the first place, the stairs are so steep in many of the houses that it requires a professional mountaineer to ascend them without risking heart failure or a broken neck. Secondly, there are the cyclists. They positively overrun the town, and appear to make it a point of honour to ride without the faintest consideration for human life. I had an exceedingly narrow escape only this morning. And, thirdly, there are the canals. In summer, you know ... most insanitary. Oh, most insanitary. I can't tell you what I've suffered. For weeks on end I was never without a sore throat."

By the time we had reached Bentheim, Mr Norris had delivered a lecture on the disadvantages of most of the chief European cities. I was astonished to find how much he had travelled. He had suffered from rheumatics in Stockholm and draughts in Kaunas; in Riga he had been bored, in Warsaw treated with extreme discourtesy, in Belgrade he had been unable to obtain his favourite brand of toothpaste. In Rome he had been annoyed by insects, in Madrid by beggars, in Marseilles by taxi-horns. In Bucharest he had had an exceedingly unpleasant experience with a water-closet. Constantinople he had found expensive and lacking in taste. The only two cities of which he greatly approved were Paris and Athens. Athens particularly. Athens was his spiritual home.

By now the train had stopped. Pale stout men in blue uniforms strolled up and down the platform with that faintly sinister air of leisure which invests the movements of officials at frontier stations. They were not unlike prison warders. It was as if we might none of us be allowed to travel any farther. Far down the corridor of the coach a voice echoed: *"Deutsche Passkontrolle."*

"I think," said Mr Norris, smiling urbanely at me, "that one of my pleasant memories is of the mornings I used to spend pottering about those quaint old streets behind the Temple of Theseus."

He was extremely nervous. His delicate white hand fiddled incessantly with the signet ring on his little finger; his uneasy blue eyes kept squinting rapid glances into the corridor. His voice rang false; high-pitched in archly forced gaiety, it resembled the voice of a character in a pre-war drawing-room comedy. He spoke so loudly that the people in the next compartment must certainly have been able to hear him.

"One comes, quite unexpectedly, upon the most fascinating little corners. A single column standing in the middle of a rubbish-heap …"

"Deutsche Passkontrolle. All passports, please."

An official had appeared in the doorway of our compartment. His voice made Mr Norris give a slight but visible jump. Anxious to allow him time to pull himself together, I hastily offered my own passport. As I had expected, it was barely glanced at.

"I am travelling to Berlin," said Mr Norris, handing over his passport with a charming smile; so charming, indeed, that it seemed a little overdone. The official did not react. He merely grunted, turned over the pages with considerable interest, and then, taking the passport out into the corridor, held it up to the light of the window.

"It's a remarkable fact," said Mr Norris, conversationally, to me, "that nowhere in classical literature will you find any reference to the Lycabettos Hill."

I was amazed to see what a state he was in; his fingers twitched and his voice was scarcely under control. There were actually beads of sweat on his alabaster forehead. If this was what he called "being fussed," if these were the agonies he suffered whenever he broke a by-law, it was no wonder that his nerves had turned him prematurely bald. He shot an instant's glance of acute misery into the corridor. Another official had arrived. They were examining the passport together, with their backs turned towards us. By what was obviously an heroic effort Mr Norris managed to maintain his chattily informative tone.

"So far as we know, it appears to have been overrun with wolves."

The other official had got the passport now. He looked as though he was going to take it away with him. His colleague was referring to a *small* black shiny notebook. Raising his head, he asked abruptly:

"You are at present residing at Courbierestrasse 168?"

For a moment I thought Mr Norris was going to *faint.*

"Er—yes ... I am ..."

Like a bird with a cobra, his eyes were fastened upon his interrogator in helpless fascination. One might have supposed that he expected to be arrested on the spot. Actually, all that happened was that the official made a note in his book, grunted again, and turning on his heel went on to the next compartment. His colleague handed the passport back to Mr Norris and said: "Thank you, sir," saluted *politely* and followed him.

Mr Norris sank back against the hard wooden seat with a deep sigh. For a moment he seemed incapable of speech. Taking out a big white silk handkerchief, he began to dab at his forehead, being careful not to disarrange his wig.

"I wonder if you'd be so very kind as to open the window," he said at length in a faint voice. "It seems to have got dreadfully stuffy in here all of a sudden."

I hastened to do so.

"Is there anything I can fetch you?" I asked. "A glass of water?"

He feebly waved the offer aside. "Most good of you ... No.

I shall be all right in a moment. My heart isn't quite what it was." He sighed: "I'm getting too old for this sort of thing. All this travelling ... very bad for me."

"You know, you really shouldn't upset yourself so." I felt more than ever protective towards him at that moment. This affectionate protectiveness, which he so easily and dangerously inspired in me, was to colour all our future dealings. "You let yourself be annoyed by trifles."

"You call that a trifle!" he exclaimed in rather pathetic protest.

"Of course. It was bound to have been put right in a few minutes, anyhow. The man simply mistook you for somebody else of the same name."

"You really think so?" He was childishly eager to be reassured.

"What other possible explanation is there?"

Mr Norris didn't seem so certain of this. He said dubiously: "Well—er—none, I suppose."

"Besides, it often happens, you know. The most innocent people get mistaken for famous jewel thieves. They undress them and search them all over. Fancy if they'd done that to you!"

"Really!" Mr Norris giggled. "The mere thought brings a blush to my modest cheek."

We both laughed. I was glad that I had managed to cheer him up so successfully. But what on earth, I wondered, would happen when the customs examiner arrived? For this, if I was right about the smuggled presents, was the real cause of all his nervousness. If the little misunderstanding about the passport had upset him so much, the customs officer would most certainly give him a heart attack. I wondered if I hadn't better mention this straight out and offer to hide the things in my own suitcase; but he seemed so blissfully unconscious of any approaching trouble that I hadn't the heart to disturb him.

I was quite wrong. The customs examination, when it came, seemed positively to give Norris pleasure. He showed not the slightest signs of uneasiness; nor was anything dutiable discovered in his luggage. In fluent German he laughed and joked with the official over a large bottle of Coty perfume: "Oh, yes, it's for my personal use, I can assure you. I wouldn't part with it for the world. Do let me give you a drop on your handkerchief. It's so deliciously refreshing."

At length it was all over. The train cranked slowly forward into Germany. The dining-car attendant came down the corridor, sounding his little gong.

"And now, my dear boy," said Mr Norris, "after these alarms and excursions and your most valuable moral support, for which I'm more grateful than I can tell you, I hope you'll do me the honour of being my guest at lunch."

I thanked him and said that I should be delighted.

When we were seated comfortably in the restaurant car, Mr Norris ordered a small cognac:

"I have made it a general rule never to drink before meals, but there are times when the occasion seems to demand it."

The soup was served. He took one spoonful, then called the attendant and addressed him in a tone of mild reproach.

"Surely you'll agree that there's too much onion?" he asked anxiously. "Will you do me a personal favour? I should like you to taste it for yourself."

"Yes, sir," said the attendant, who was extremely busy, and whisked away the plate with faintly insolent deference. Mr Norris was pained.

"Did you see that? He wouldn't taste it. He wouldn't admit there was anything wrong. Dear me, how very obstinate some people are!"

He forgot this little disappointment in human nature within a few moments, however. He had begun to study the wine list with great care.

"Let me see … Let me see … Would you be prepared to contemplate a hock? You would? It's a lottery, mind you. On a train one must always be prepared for the worst. I think we'll risk it, shall we?"

The hock arrived and was a success. Mr Norris had not tasted such good hock, he told me, since his lunch with the Swedish Ambassador in Vienna last year. And there were kidneys, his favourite dish. "Dear me," he remarked with pleasure, "I find I've got quite an appetite ... If you want to get kidneys perfectly cooked you should go to Budapest. It was a revelation to me ... I must say these are really delicious, don't you agree? Really quite delicious. At first I thought I tasted that odious red pepper, but it was merely my overwrought imagination." He called the attendant: "Will you please give the chef my compliments and say that I should like to congratulate him on a most excellent lunch? Thank you. And now bring me a cigar." Cigars were brought, sniffed at, weighed between the finger and thumb. Mr Norris finally selected the largest on the tray: "What, my dear boy, you don't smoke them? Oh, but you should. Well, well, perhaps you have other vices?"

By this time he was in the best of spirits.

"I must say the older I get the more I come to value the little comforts of this life. As a general rule, I make a point of travelling first class. It always pays. One gets treated with so much more consideration. Take today, for instance. If I hadn't been in a third-class compartment, they'd never have dreamed of bothering me. There you have the German official all over. 'A race of non-commissioned officers,' didn't somebody call them? How very good that is! How true ..."

Mr Norris picked his teeth for a few moments in thoughtful silence.

"My generation was brought up to regard luxury from an aesthetic standpoint. Since the War, people don't seem to feel that any more. Too often they are merely gross. They take their pleasures coarsely, don't you find? At times, one feels guilty, oneself, with so much unemployment and distress everywhere. The conditions in Berlin are very bad. Oh, very bad ... as no doubt you yourself know. In my small way I do what I can to help, but it's such a drop in the ocean." Mr Norris sighed and touched his napkin with his lips.

"And here we are, riding in the lap of luxury. The social reformers would condemn us, no doubt. All the same, I suppose if somebody didn't use this dining-car, we should have all these employees on the dole as well ... Dear me, dear me. Things are so very complex nowadays."

We parted at the Zoo Station. Mr Norris held my hand for a long time amidst the jostle of arriving passengers.

"Auf Wiedersehen, my dear boy. *Auf Wiedersehen. I* won't say goodbye because I hope that we shall be seeing each other in the very near future. Any little discomforts I may have suffered on that odious journey have been amply repaid by the great pleasure of making your acquaintance. And now I wonder if you'd care to have tea with me at my flat one day this week? Shall we make it Saturday? Here's my card. Do please say you'll come."

I promised that I would.

Chapter Two

MR NORRIS HAD two front doors to his flat. They stood side by side. Both had little round peep-holes in the centre panel and brightly polished knobs and brass name-plates. On the left-hand plate was engraved: *Arthur Norris. Private.* And on the right hand: *Arthur Norris. Export and Import.*

After a moment's hesitation, I pressed the button of the left-hand bell. The bell was startlingly loud; it must have been clearly audible all over the flat. Nevertheless, nothing happened. No sound came from within. I was just about to ring again when I became aware that an eye was regarding me through the peep-hole in the door. How long it had been there, I didn't know. I felt embarrassed and uncertain whether to stare the eye out of its hole or merely pretend that I hadn't seen it. Ostentatiously, I examined the ceiling, the floor, the walls; then ventured a furtive glance to make sure that it had gone. It hadn't. Vexed, I turned my back on the door altogether. Nearly a minute passed.

When, finally, I did turn round it was because the other door, the Export and Import door, had opened. A young man stood on the threshold.

"Is Mr Norris in?" I asked.

The young man eyed me suspiciously. He had watery light yellow eyes and a blotched complexion the colour of porridge. His head was huge and round, set awkwardly on a short plump body. He wore a smart lounge suit and patent-leather shoes. I didn't like the look of him at all.

"Have you an appointment?"

"Yes." My tone was extremely curt.

At once, the young man's face curved into oily smiles. "Oh, it's Mr Bradshaw? One moment, if you please."

And, to my astonishment, he closed the door in my face, only to reappear an instant later at the left-hand door, standing aside for me to enter the flat. This behaviour seemed all the more extraordinary because, as I noticed immediately I was inside, the Private side of the entrance hall was divided from the Export side only by a thick hanging curtain.

"Mr Norris wished me to say that he will be with you in one moment," said the big-headed young man, treading delicately across the thick carpet on the toes of his patent-leather shoes. He spoke very softly, as if he were afraid of being overheard. Opening the door of a large sitting-room, he silently motioned me to take a chair and withdrew.

Left alone, I looked around me, slightly mystified. Everything was in good taste, the furniture, the carpet, the colour scheme. But the room was curiously without character. It was like a room on the stage or in the window of a high-class furnishing store; elegant, expensive, discreet. I had expected Mr Norris's background to be altogether more exotic; something Chinese would have suited him, with golden and scarlet dragons.

The young man had left the door ajar. From somewhere just outside I heard him say, presumably into a telephone: "The gentleman is here, sir." And now, with even greater distinctness, Mr Norris's voice was audible as he replied, from behind a door in the opposite wall of the sitting-room: "Oh, is he? Thank you."

I wanted to laugh. This little comedy was so unnecessary as

to seem slightly sinister. A moment later Mr Norris himself came into the room, nervously rubbing his manicured hands together.

"My dear boy, this is indeed an honour! Delighted to welcome you under the shadow of my humble roof-tree."

He didn't look well, I thought. His face wasn't so rosy today, and there were rings under his eyes. He sat down for a moment in an armchair, but rose again immediately, as if he were not in the mood for sitting still. He must have been wearing a different wig, for the joins in this one showed as plain as murder.

"You'd like to see over the flat, I expect?" he asked, nervously touching his temples with the tips of his fingers.

"I should, very much." I smiled, puzzled because Mr Norris was obviously in a great hurry about something. With fussy haste, he took me by the elbow, steering me towards the door in the opposite wall, from which he himself had just emerged.

"We'll go this way first, yes."

But hardly had we taken a couple of steps when there was a sudden outburst of voices from the entrance hall.

"You can't. It's impossible," came the voice of the young man who had ushered me into the flat. And a strange, loud, angry voice answered: "That's a dirty lie! I tell you he's here!"

Mr Norris stopped as suddenly as if he'd been shot. "Oh dear!" he whispered, hardly audible. "Oh dear!" Stricken with indecision and alarm, he stood still in the middle of the room, as though desperately considering which way to turn. His grip on my arm tightened, either for support or merely to implore me to keep quiet.

"Mr Norris will not be back until late this evening." The young man's voice was no longer apologetic, but firm. "It's no good your waiting."

He seemed to have shifted his position and to be just outside, perhaps barring the way into the sitting-room. And, the next moment, the sitting-room door was quietly shut, with a click of a key being turned. We were locked in.

"He's in there!" shouted the strange voice, loud and menacing. There was a scuffling, followed by a heavy thud, as if the young man had been flung violently against the door. The thud roused Mr Norris to action. With a single, surprisingly agile movement, he dragged me after him into the adjoining room. We stood there together in the doorway, ready, at any moment, for a further retreat. I could hear him panting heavily at my side.

Meanwhile, the stranger was rattling the sitting-room door as if he meant to burst it open: "You damned swindler!" he shouted in a terrible voice. "You wait till I get my hands on you!"

It was all so very extraordinary that I quite forgot to feel frightened, although it might well be supposed that the person on the other side of the door was either raving drunk or insane. I cast a questioning glance at Mr Norris, who whispered reassuringly: "He'll go away in a minute, I think." The curious thing was that, although scared, he didn't seem at all surprised by what was taking place. It might have been imagined, from his tone, that he was referring to an unpleasant but frequently recurring natural phenomenon: a violent thunder-storm, for instance. His blue eyes were warily, uneasily alert. His hands rested on the door handle, prepared to slam it shut at an instant's notice.

But Mr Norris had been right. The stranger soon got tired of rattling the sitting-room door. With an explosion of Berlin curses, his voice retreated. A moment later, we heard the outside door of the flat close with a tremendous bang.

Mr Norris drew a long breath of relief. "I knew it couldn't last long," he remarked with satisfaction. Abstractedly pulling an envelope out of his pocket, he began fanning himself with it. "So upsetting," he murmured. "Some people seem to be utterly lacking in consideration … My dear boy, I really must apologize for this disturbance. Quite unforeseen, I assure you."

I laughed. "That's all right. It was rather exciting."

Mr Norris seemed pleased. "I'm glad you take it so lightly.

It's so rare to find anyone of your age who's free from these ridiculous bourgeois prejudices. I feel that we have a great deal in common."

"Yes, I think we have," I said, without, however being quite clear as to which particular prejudices he found ridiculous or how they applied to the angry visitor.

"In the course of my long and not uneventful life, I can truthfully say that for sheer stupidity and obstructiveness, I have never met anyone to equal the small Berlin tradesman. I'm not speaking, now, mind you, of the larger firms. They're always reasonable: more or less ..."

He was evidently in a confidential mood and might have imparted a good deal of interesting information, had not the sitting-room door now been unlocked and the young man with the large head reappeared on the threshold. The sight of him seemed to disconnect instantly the thread of Mr Norris's ideas. His manner became at once apologetic, apprehensive, and vague, as though he and I had been caught doing something socially ridiculous which could only be passed off by an elaborate display of etiquette.

"Allow me to introduce: Herr Schmidt—Mr Bradshaw. Herr Schmidt is my secretary and my right hand. Only, in this case," Mr Norris tittered nervously, "I can assure you that the right hand knows perfectly well what the left hand doeth."

With several small nervous coughs he attempted to translate this joke into German. Herr Schmidt, who clearly didn't understand it, did not even bother to pretend to be amused. He gave me a private smile, however, which invited me to join him in tolerant contemptuous patronage of his employer's attempts at humour. I didn't respond. I had taken a dislike to Schmidt already. He saw this, and at the moment I was pleased that he saw it.

"Can I speak to you alone?" he said to Mr Norris, in a tone which was obviously intended to insult me. His tie, collar, and lounge suit were as neat as ever. I could see no sign whatever of the violent handling he had apparently just received.

"Yes. Er—yes. Certainly. Of course." Mr Norris's tone was petulant but meek. "You'll excuse me, my dear boy, a moment? I hate to keep my guests waiting, but this little matter is rather urgent."

He hurried across the sitting-room and disappeared through a third door, followed by Schmidt. Schmidt was going to tell him the details of the row, of course. I considered the possibility of eavesdropping, but decided that it would be too risky. Anyhow, I should be able to get it out of Mr Norris one day, when I knew him better. Mr Norris did not give one the impression of being a discreet man.

I looked around me and found that the room in which I had all this time been standing was a bedroom. It was not very large, and the available space was almost entirely occupied by a double bed, a bulky wardrobe and an elaborate dressing-table with a winged mirror, on which were ranged bottles of perfume, lotions, antiseptics, pots of face cream, skin food, powder, and ointment enough to stock a chemist's shop. I furtively opened a drawer in the table. I found nothing in it but two lipsticks and an eyebrow pencil. Before I could investigate further, I heard the door into the sitting-room open.

Mr Norris re-entered fussily. "And now, after this most regrettable interlude, let us continue our personally conducted tour of the royal apartments. Before you, you behold my chaste couch; I had it specially made for me in London. German beds are so ridiculously small, I always think. It's fitted with the best spiral springs. As you observe, I'm conservative enough to keep to my English sheets and blankets. The German feather-bags give me the most horrible nightmares."

He talked rapidly with a great show of animation, but I saw at once that the conversation with his secretary had depressed him. It seemed more tactful not to refer again to the stranger's visit. Mr Norris evidently wanted the subject to be dropped. Fishing a key out of his waistcoat pocket, he unlocked and threw open the door of the wardrobe.

"I've always made it a rule to have a suit for every day of the week. Perhaps you'll tell me I'm vain, but you'd be surprised if you knew what it had meant to me, at critical moments of my life, to be dressed exactly in accordance with my mood. It gives one such confidence, I think."

Beyond the bedroom was a dining-room.

"Please admire the chairs," said Mr Norris, and added—rather strangely, as I thought at the time: "I may tell you that this suite has been valued at four thousand marks."

From the dining-room, a passage led to the kitchen, where I was introduced to a dour-faced young man who was busy preparing the tea.

"This is Hermann, my major-domo. He shares the distinction, with a Chinese boy I had years ago in Shanghai, of being the best cook I have ever employed."

"What were you doing in Shanghai?"

Mr Norris looked vague. "Ah. What is one ever doing anywhere? Fishing in troubled waters, I suppose one might call it. Yes ... I'm speaking now, mind you, of nineteen hundred and three. Things are very different nowadays, I'm told."

We returned to the sitting-room, followed by Hermann with the tray.

"Well, well," observed Mr Norris, taking his cup, "we live in stirring times; tea-stirring times."

I grinned awkwardly. It was only later, when I knew him better, that I realized that these aged jokes (he had a whole repertoire of them) were not even intended to be laughed at. They belonged merely to certain occasions in the routine of his day. Not to have made one of them would have been like omitting to say a grace.

Having thus performed his ritual, Mr Norris relapsed into silence. He must be worrying about the noisy caller again. As usual, when left to my own devices, I began studying his wig. I must have been staring very rudely, for he looked up suddenly and saw the direction of my gaze. He startled me by asking simply:

"Is it crooked?"

I blushed scarlet. I felt terribly embarrassed.

"Just a tiny bit, perhaps."

Then I laughed outright. We both laughed. At that moment I could have embraced him. We had referred to the thing at last, and our relief was so great that we were like two people who have just made a mutual declaration of love.

"It wants to go a shade more to the left," I said, reaching out a helpful hand. "May I . . ."

But this was going too far. "My God, no!" cried Mr Norris, drawing back with involuntary dismay. An instant later he was himself again, and smiled ruefully.

"I'm afraid that this is one of those—er—mysteries of the toilet which are best performed in the privacy of the boudoir. I must ask you to excuse me."

"I'm afraid this one doesn't fit very well," he continued, returning from his bedroom some minutes later. "I've never been fond of it. It's only my second best."

"How many have you got, then?"

"Three altogether." Mr Norris examined his fingernails with a modest proprietary air.

"And how long do they last?"

"A very short time, I'm sorry to say. I'm obliged to get a new one every eighteen months or so, and they're exceedingly expensive."

"How much, roughly?"

"Between three and four hundred marks." He was seriously informative. "The man who makes them for me lives in Köln and I'm obliged to go there myself to get them fitted."

"How tiresome for you."

"It is indeed."

"Tell me just one more thing. However do you manage to make it stay on?"

"There's a small patch with glue on it." Mr Norris lowered his voice a little, as though this were the greatest secret of all: "Just here."

"And you find that's sufficient?"

"For the ordinary wear and tear of daily life, yes. All the same, I'm bound to admit that there have been various occasions in my chequered career, occasions which I blush to think of, when all has been lost."

After tea, Mr Norris showed me his study, which lay behind the door on the other side of the sitting-room.

"I've got some very valuable books here," he told me. "Some very *amusing* books." His tone coyly underlined the words. I stopped to read the titles: *The Girl with the Golden Whip. Miss Smith's Torture-Chamber. Imprisoned at a Girls' School, or The Private Diary of Montague Dawson, Flagellant.* This was my first glimpse of Mr Norris's sexual tastes.

"One day I'll show you some of the other treasures of my collection," he added archly, "when I feel I know you well enough."

He led the way through into a little office. This, I realized, was where the unwelcome visitor must have been waiting at the time of my own arrival. It was strangely bare. There was a chair, a table, a filing cabinet, and, on the wall, a large map of Germany. Schmidt was nowhere to be seen.

"My secretary has gone out," Mr Norris explained, his uneasy eyes wandering over the walls with a certain distaste, as if this room had unpleasant associations for him. "He took the typewriter to be cleaned. This was what he wanted to see me about, just now."

This lie seemed so entirely pointless that I felt rather offended. I didn't expect him to confide in me yet; but he needn't treat me like an imbecile. I felt absolved from any lingering scruples about asking pointed questions, and said, with frank inquisitiveness:

"What is it, exactly, that you export and import?"

He took it quite calmly. His smile was disingenuous and bland.

"My dear boy, what in my time, have I not exported? I think I may claim to have exported everything which is—er—exportable."

He pulled out one of the drawers of the filing cabinet with the gesture of a house agent. "The latest model, you see."

The drawer was quite empty. "Tell me one of the things you export," I insisted, smiling.

Mr Norris appeared to consider.

"Clocks," he said at length.

"And where do you export them to?"

He rubbed his chin with a nervous, furtive movement. This time my teasing had succeeded in its object. He was flustered and mildly vexed.

"Really, my dear boy, if you want to go into a lot of technical explanations, you must ask my secretary. I haven't the time to attend to them. I leave all the more—er—sordid details entirely in his hands. Yes …"

Chapter Three

A FEW DAYS AFTER Christmas I rang up Arthur (we called each other by our Christian names now) and suggested that we should spend *Silvesterabend* together.

"My dear William, I shall be delighted, of course. Most delighted ... I can imagine no more charming or auspicious company in which to celebrate the birth of this peculiarly ill-omened New Year. I'd ask you to have dinner with me, but unfortunately I have a previous engagement. Now where do you suggest we shall meet?"

"What about the Troika?"

"Very well, my dear boy. I put myself in your hands entirely. I fear I shall feel rather out of place amidst so many young faces. A greybeard with one foot in the tomb ... Somebody say No, no! Nobody does. How cruel Youth is. Never mind. Such is Life ..."

When once Arthur had started telephoning it was difficult to stop him. I used often to lay the receiver on the table for a few minutes knowing that when I picked it up again he would still be talking away as fast as ever. Today, however, I had a pupil waiting for an English lesson and had to cut him short.

"Very well. In the Troika. At eleven."

"That will suit me admirably. In the meantime, I shall be

careful what I eat, go to bed early, and generally prepare myself to enjoy an evening of *Wein, Weib, und Gesang.* More particularly *Wein.* Yes. God bless you, dear boy. Goodbye."

On New Year's Eve I had supper at home with my landlady and the other lodgers. I must have been already drunk when I arrived at the Troika, because I remember getting a shock when I looked into the cloakroom mirror and found that I was wearing a false nose. The place was crammed. It was difficult to say who was dancing and who was merely standing up. After hunting about for some time, I came upon Arthur in a corner. He was sitting at a table with another rather younger gentleman who wore an eyeglass and had sleek dark hair.

"Ah, here you are, William. We were beginning to fear that you'd deserted us. May I introduce two of my most valued friends, to each other? Mr Bradshaw—Baron von Pregnitz."

The Baron, who was fishy and suave, inclined his head. Leaning towards me, like a cod swimming up through water, he asked:

"Excuse me. Do you know Naples?"

"No. I've never been there."

"Forgive me. I'm sorry. I had the feeling that we'd met each other before."

"Perhaps so," I said politely, wondering how he could smile without dropping his eyeglass. It was rimless and ribbonless and looked as though it had been screwed into his pink, well-shaven face by means of some horrible surgical operation.

"Perhaps you were at Juan-les-Pins last year?"

"No, I'm afraid I wasn't?"

"Yes, I see." He smiled in polite regret. "In that case I must beg your pardon."

"Don't mention it," I said. We both laughed very heartily. Arthur, evidently pleased that I was making a good impression on the Baron, laughed too. I drank a glass of champagne off at a gulp. A three-man band was playing: *Grüss' mir mein Hawai, ich bleib' Dir treu, ich hab' Dich gerne.* The dancers, locked frigidly together, swayed in partial-paralytic rhythms under a huge sunshade suspended from the ceiling and oscillating gently through cigarette smoke and hot rising air.

"Don't you find it a trifle stuffy in here?" Arthur asked anxiously.

In the windows were bottles filled with coloured liquids brilliantly illuminated from beneath, magenta, emerald, vermilion. They seemed to be lighting up the whole room. The cigarette smoke made my eyes smart till the tears ran down my face. The music kept dying away, then surging up fearfully loud. I passed my hand down the shiny black oil-cloth curtains in the alcove behind my chair. Oddly enough, they were quite cold. The lamps were like alpine cowbells. And there was a fluffy white monkey perched above the bar. In another moment, when I had drunk exactly the right amount of champagne, I should have a vision. I took a sip. And now, with extreme clarity, without passion or malice, I saw what Life really is. It had something, I remember, to do with the revolving sunshade. Yes, I murmured to myself, let them dance. They are dancing. I am glad.

"You know, I like this place. Extraordinarily," I told the Baron with enthusiasm. He did not seem surprised.

Arthur was solemnly stifling a belch.

"Dear Arthur, don't look so sad. Are you tired?"

"No, not tired, William. Only a little contemplative, perhaps. Such an occasion as this is not without its solemn aspect. You young people are quite right to enjoy yourselves. I don't blame you for a moment. One has one's memories."

"Memories are the most precious things we have," said the Baron with approval. As intoxication proceeded, his face seemed slowly to disintegrate. A rigid area of paralysis formed round the monocle. The monocle was holding his face together. He gripped it desperately with his facial muscles, cocking his disengaged eyebrow, his mouth sagging slightly at the corners, minute beads of perspiration appearing along the parting of his thin, satin-smooth dark hair. Catching my eye, he swam up towards me, to the surface of the element which seemed to separate us.

"Excuse me, please. May I ask you something?"

"By all means."

"Have you read *Winnie the Pooh,* by A. A. Milne?"

"Yes, I have."

"And tell me, please, how did you like it?"

"Very much indeed."

"Then I am very glad. Yes, so did I. Very much."

And now we were all standing up. What had happened? It was midnight. Our glasses touched.

"Cheerio," said the Baron with the air of one who makes a particularly felicitous quotation.

"Allow me," said Arthur, "to wish you both every success and happiness in nineteen thirty-one. Every success …" His voice trailed off uneasily into silence. Nervously he fingered the heavy fringe of hair. A tremendous crash exploded from the band. Like a car which has slowly, laboriously reached the summit of the mountain railway, we plunged headlong downwards into the New Year.

The events of the next two hours were somewhat confused. We were in a small bar, where I remember only the ruffled plumes of a paper streamer, crimson, very beautiful, stirring like seaweed in the draught from an electric fan. We wandered through streets crowded with girls who popped teasers in our faces. We ate ham and eggs in the first-class restaurant of the Friedrichstrasse Station. Arthur had disappeared. The Baron was rather mysterious and sly about this; though I couldn't understand why. He had asked me to call him Kuno, and explained how much he admired the character of the English upper class. We were driving in a taxi, alone. The Baron told me about a friend of his, a young Etonian. The Etonian had been in India for two years. On the morning after his return he had met his oldest school friend in Bond Street. Although they hadn't seen each other for so long, the school friend had merely said: "Hello. I'm afraid I can't talk to you now. I have to go shopping with my mother." "And I find this so very nice," the Baron concluded. "It is your English self-control, you see." The taxi crossed several bridges and passed a gas-works. The Baron pressed my hand and made me a long speech about how wonderful it is to be young. He had become rather indistinct and his English was rapidly deteriorating. "You see, excuse me, I've been watching your reactions the whole evening. I hope you are not offended?" I found my false nose in my pocket and put it on. It had got a bit crumpled. The Baron seemed impressed. "This is all so very interesting for me, you see." Soon after this I had to stop the taxi under a lamp-post in order to be sick.

We were driving along a street bounded by a high dark wall. Over the top of the wall I suddenly caught sight of an ornamental cross. "Good God!" I said. "Are you taking me to the cemetery?"

The Baron merely smiled. We had stopped; having arrived, it seemed, at the blackest corner of the night. I stumbled over something, and the Baron obligingly took my arm. He seemed to have been here before. We passed through an archway and into the courtyard. There was light here from several windows, and snatches of gramophone music and laughter. A silhouetted head and shoulders leant out of one of the windows, shouted: "*Prosit Neujahr!*" and spat vigorously. The spittle landed with a soft splash on the paving-stone just beside my foot. Other heads emerged from other windows. "Is that you Paul, you sow?" someone shouted. "Red Front!" yelled a voice, and a louder splash followed. This time, I think, a beer-mug had been emptied.

Here one of the anaesthetic periods of my evening supervened. How the Baron got me upstairs, I don't know. It was quite painless. We were in a room full of people dancing, shouting, singing, drinking, shaking our hands, and thumping us on the back. There was an immense ornamental gasolier, converted to hold electric bulbs and enmeshed in paper festoons. My glance reeled about the room, picking out large or minute objects, a bowl of claret-cup in which floated an empty match-box, a broken bead from a necklace, a bust of Bismarck on the top of a Gothic dresser—holding them for an instant, then losing them again in general coloured chaos. In this manner I caught a sudden startling glimpse of Arthur's head, its mouth open, the wig jammed down over its left eye. I stumbled about looking for the body and collapsed comfortably on to a sofa, holding the upper half of a girl. My face was buried in dusty-smelling lace cushions. The noise of the party burst over me in thundering waves, like the sea. It was strangely soothing. "Don't go to sleep, darling," said the girl I was holding. "No, of course I won't," I replied, and sat up, tidying my hair. I felt suddenly quite sober.

Opposite me, in a big arm-chair, sat Arthur, with a thin, dark, sulky-looking girl on his lap. He had taken off his coat and waistcoat and looked most domestic. He wore gaudily-striped braces. His shirt-sleeves were looped up with elastic bands. Except for a little hair round the base of the skull, he was perfectly bald.

"What on earth have you done with it?" I exclaimed. "You'll catch cold."

"The idea was not mine, William. Rather a graceful tribute, don't you think, to the Iron Chancellor?"

He seemed in much better spirits now than earlier in the evening, and, strangely enough, not at all drunk. He had a remarkably strong head. Looking up, I saw the wig perched rakishly on Bismarck's helmet. It was too big for him.

Turning, I saw the Baron sitting beside me on the sofa. "Hullo, Kuno," I said. "How did you get here?"

He didn't answer, but smiled his bright, rigid smile and desperately cocked an eyebrow. He seemed on the very point of collapse. In another moment his monocle would fall out.

The gramophone burst into loud braying music. Most of the people in the room began to dance. They were nearly all young. The boys were in shirt-sleeves; the girls had unhooked their dresses. The atmosphere of the room was heavy with dust and perspiration and cheap scent. An enormous woman elbowed her way through the crowd, carrying a glass of wine in each hand. She wore a pink silk blouse and a very short pleated white skirt; her feet were jammed into absurdly small high-heeled shoes, out of which bulged pads of silk-stockinged flesh. Her cheeks were waxy pink and her hair dyed tinsel-golden, so that it matched the glitter of the half-dozen bracelets on her powdered arms. She was as curious and sinister as a life-size doll. Like a doll, she had staring china-blue eyes which did not laugh, although her lips were parted in a smile revealing several gold teeth.

"This is Olga, our hostess," Arthur explained.

"Hullo, Baby!" Olga handed me a glass. She pinched Arthur's cheek: "Well, my little turtle-dove?"

The gesture was so perfunctory that it reminded me of a vet with a horse. Arthur giggled: "Hardly what one would call a strikingly well-chosen epithet, is it? A turtle-dove. What do you say to that, Anni?" He addressed the dark girl on his knee. "You're very silent, you know. You don't sparkle this evening. Or does the presence of the extremely handsome young man opposite distract your thoughts? William, I believe you've made a conquest. I do indeed."

Anni smiled at this, a slight self-possessed whore's smile.

Then she scratched her thigh and yawned. She wore a smartly-cut little black jacket and a black skirt. On her legs were a pair of long black boots, laced up to the knee. They had a curious design in gold running round the tops. They gave to her whole costume the effect of a kind of uniform.

"Ah, you're admiring Anni's boots," said Arthur with satisfaction. "But you ought to see her other pair. Scarlet leather with black heels. I had them made for her myself. Anni won't wear them in the street; she says they make her look too conspicuous. But sometimes, if she's feeling particularly *energetic*, she puts them on when she comes to see me."

Meanwhile, several of the girls and boys had stopped dancing. They stood round us, their arms interlaced, their eyes fixed on Arthur's mouth with the naïve interest of savages, as though they expected to see the words jump visibly out of his throat. One of the boys began to laugh. "Oh, yes," he mimicked. "I spik you Englisch, no?"

Arthur's hand was straying abstractedly over Anni's thigh. She raised herself and smacked it sharply, with the impersonal viciousness of a cat.

"Oh, dear, I'm afraid you're in a very *cruel* mood this evening! I see I shall be *corrected* for this. Anni is an exceedingly *severe* young lady." Arthur sniggered loudly: continued conversationally in English: "Do you think it's an exquisitely beautiful face? Quite perfect in its way. Like a Raphael Madonna. The other day I made an epigram. I said, Anni's beauty is only *sin*-deep. I hope that's original? Is it? Please laugh."

"I think it's very good indeed."

"Only *sin*-deep. I'm glad you like it. My first thought was, I must tell that to William. You positively inspire me, you know. You make me sparkle. I always say that I only wish to have three sorts of people as my friends, those who are very rich, those who are very witty, and those who are very beautiful. You may, my dear William, belong to the second category."

I could guess to which category Baron von Pregnitz belonged, and looked round to see whether he had been listening. But the Baron was otherwise engaged. He reclined upon the farther end of the sofa in the embrace of a powerful youth in a boxer's sweater, who was gradually forcing a mugful of beer down his throat. The Baron protested feebly; the beer was spilling all over him.

I became aware that I had my arm round a girl. Perhaps she had been there all the time. She snuggled against me, while from the other side a boy was amateurishly trying to pick my pocket. I opened my mouth to protest, but thought better of it. Why make a scene at the end of such an enjoyable evening? He was welcome to my money. I only had three marks left at the most. The Baron would pay for everything, anyhow. At that moment I saw his face with almost microscopic distinctness. He had, as I noticed now for the first time, been taking artificial sunlight treatment. The skin round his nose was just beginning to peel. How nice he was! I raised my glass to him. His fish-eye gleamed faintly over the boxer's arm and he made a slight movement of his head. He was beyond speech. When I turned round, Arthur and Anni had disappeared.

With the vague intention of going to look for them, I staggered to my feet, only to become involved in the dancing which had broken out again with renewed vigour. I was seized round the waist, round the neck, kissed, hugged, tickled, half undressed; I danced with girls, with boys, with two or three people at the same time. It may have been five or ten minutes before I reached the door at the further end of the room. Beyond the door was a pitch-dark passage with a crack of light at the end of it. The passage was crammed so full of furniture that one could only edge one's way along it sideways. I had wriggled and shuffled about half the distance when an agonized cry came from the lighted room ahead of me.

"*Nein, nein!* Mercy! Oh dear! *Hilfe! Hilfe!*"

There was no mistaking the voice. They had got Arthur in there, and were robbing him and knocking him about, I might have known it. We were fools ever to have poked our noses into a dark place like this. We had only ourselves to thank. Drink made me brave. Struggling forward to the door, I pushed it open.

The first person I saw was Anni. She was standing in the middle of the room. Arthur cringed on the floor at her feet. He had removed several more of his garments, and was now dressed, lightly but with perfect decency, in a suit of mauve silk underwear, a rubber abdominal belt and a pair of socks. In one hand he held a brush and in the other a yellow shoe-rag. Olga towered behind him, brandishing a heavy leather whip.

"You call that clean, you swine!" she cried in a terrible voice. "Do them again this minute! And if I find a speck of dirt on them I'll thrash you till you can't sit down for a week."

As she spoke she gave Arthur a smart cut across the buttocks. He uttered a squeal of pain and pleasure, and began to brush and polish Anni's boots with feverish haste.

"Mercy! Mercy!" Arthur's voice was shrill and gleeful, like a child's when it is shamming. "Stop! You're killing me."

"Killing's too good for you," retorted Olga, administering another cut. "I'll skin you alive!"

"Oh! Oh! Stop! Mercy! Oh!"

They were making such a noise that they hadn't heard me bang open the door. Now they saw me, however. My presence did not seem to disconcert any of them in the least. Indeed, it appeared to add spice to Arthur's enjoyment.

"Oh dear! William, save me! You won't? You're as cruel as the rest of them. Anni, my love! Olga! Just look how she treats me. Goodness knows what they won't be making me do in a minute!"

"Come in, Baby," cried Olga with tigerish jocularity. "Just you wait! It's your turn next. I'll make you cry for Mummy!"

She made a playful slash at me with the whip which sent me in headlong retreat down the passage, pursued by Arthur's delighted and anguished cries.

Several hours later I woke to find myself lying curled up on the floor, with my face pressed against the leg of the sofa. I had a head like a furnace, and pains in every bone. The party was over. Half a dozen people lay insensible about the dismantled room, sprawling in various attitudes of extreme discomfort. Daylight gleamed through the slats of the venetian blinds.

After making sure that neither Arthur nor the Baron were among the fallen, I picked my way over their bodies, out of the flat, downstairs, across the courtyard and into the street. The whole building seemed to be full of dead drunks. I met nobody.

I found myself in one of the back streets near the canal, not far from the Möckernbrücke Station, about half an hour from my lodgings. I had no money for the electric train. And, anyhow, a walk would do me good. I limped home, along dreary streets where paper streamers hung from the sills of damp, blank houses, or were entangled in the clammy twigs of the trees. When I arrived, my landlady greeted me with the news that Arthur had rung up already three times to know how I was.

"Such a nice-spoken gentleman, I always think. And so considerate."

I agreed with her, and went to bed.

Chapter Four

FRL. SCHROEDER, MY landlady, was very fond of Arthur. Over the telephone she always addressed him as *Herr Doktor*, her highest mark of esteem.

"Ah, is that you, *Herr Doktor?* But of course I recognize your voice; I should know it in a million. You sound very tired this morning. Another of your late nights? *Na, Na,* you can't expect an old woman like me to believe that; I know what gentlemen are when you go out on the spree ... What's that you say? Stuff and nonsense! You flatterer! Well, well, you men are all alike; from seventeen to seventy ... *Pfui!* I'm surprised at you ... No, I most certainly shall not! Ha, ha! You want to speak to Herr Bradshaw? Why, of course, I'd forgotten. I'll call him at once."

When Arthur came to tea with me, Frl. Schroeder would put on her black velvet dress, which was cut low at the neck, and her string of Woolworth pearls. With her cheeks rouged and her eyelids darkened, she would open the door to him, looking like a caricature of Mary Queen of Scots. I remarked on this to Arthur, who was delighted.

"Really, William, you're most unkind. You say such sharp things. I'm beginning to be afraid of your tongue. I am indeed."

After this he usually referred to Frl. Schroeder as Her Majesty. *La divine* Schroeder was another favourite epithet.

No matter how much of a hurry he was in, he always found time for a few minutes' flirtation with her, brought her flowers, sweets, cigarettes, and sympathized with every fluctuation in the delicate health of Hanns, her canary. When Hanns finally died and Frl. Schroeder shed tears, I thought Arthur was going to cry, too. He was genuinely upset. "Dear, dear," he kept repeating. "Nature is really very cruel."

My other friends were less enthusiastic about Arthur. I introduced him to Helen Pratt, but the meeting was not a success. At that time Helen was Berlin correspondent to one of the London political weeklies, and supplemented her income by making translations and giving English lessons. We sometimes passed on pupils to each other. She was a pretty, fair-haired, fragile-looking girl, hard as nails, who had been educated at the University of London and took Sex seriously. She was accustomed to spending her days and nights in male society and had little use for the company of other girls. She could drink most of the English journalists under the table, and sometimes did so, but more as a matter of principle than because she enjoyed it. The first time she met you, she called you by your Christian name and informed you that her parents kept a tobacco and sweet shop in Shepherd's Bush. This was her method of "testing" character; your reaction to the news damned or saved you finally in her estimation. Above all else, Helen loathed being reminded that she was a woman; except in bed.

Arthur, as I saw too late, had no technique whatsoever for dealing with her sort. From the first moment he was frankly scared of her. She brushed aside all the little polished politenesses which shielded his timid soul. "Hullo, you two," she said, casually reaching out a hand over the newspaper she was reading. (We had met by appointment in a small restaurant behind the Memorial Church.)

Arthur gingerly took the hand she offered. He lingered uneasily beside the table, fidgeted, awaiting the ritual to which he was accustomed. Nothing happened. He cleared his throat, coughed:

"Will you allow me to take a seat?"

Helen, who was about to read something aloud from the newspaper, glanced up at him as though she'd forgotten his existence and was surprised to find him still there.

"What's the matter?" she asked. "Aren't there enough chairs?"

We got talking, somehow, about Berlin night life. Arthur giggled and became arch. Helen, who dealt in statistics and psycho-analytical terms, regarded him in puzzled disapproval. At length Arthur made a sly reference to "the speciality of the Kaufhaus des Westens."

"Oh, you mean those whores on the corner there," said Helen in the bright matter-of-fact tone of a schoolmistress giving a biology lesson, "who dress up to excite the boot-fetishists?"

"Well, upon my soul, ha ha, I must say," Arthur sniggered, coughed and rapidly fingered his wig, "seldom have I met such an extremely, if you'll allow me to say so, er—*advanced,* or shall I say, er—*modern* young lady..."

"My God!" Helen threw back her head and laughed unpleasantly. "I haven't been called a young lady since the days when I used to help mother with the shop on Saturday afternoons."

"Have you—er—been in this city long?" asked Arthur hastily. Vaguely aware that he had made a mistake, he imagined that he ought to change the subject. I saw the look Helen gave him and knew that all was over.

"If you take my advice, Bill," she said to me, the next time we met, "you won't trust that man an inch."

"I don't," I said.

"Oh, I know you. You're soft, like most men. You make up romances about people instead of seeing them as they are. Have you noticed his mouth?"

"Frequently."

"Ugh, it's disgusting. I could hardly bear to look at it. Beastly and flabby like a toad's."

"Well," I said, laughing, "I suppose I've got a weakness for toads."

Not daunted by this failure, I tried Arthur on Fritz Wendel. Fritz was a German-American, a young man about town, who spent his leisure time dancing and playing bridge. He had a curious passion for the society of painters and writers, and had acquired a status with them by working at a fashionable art dealer's. The art dealer didn't pay him anything, but Fritz could afford this hobby, being rich. He had an aptitude for gossip which amounted to talent, and might have made a first-class private detective.

We had tea together in Fritz's flat. He and Arthur talked New York, impressionist painting, and the unpublished works of the Wilde group. Arthur was witty and astonishingly informative. Fritz's black eyes sparkled as he registered the epigrams for future use, and I smiled, feeling pleased and proud. I felt myself personally responsible for the success of the interview. I was childishly anxious that Arthur should be approved of; perhaps because I, too, wanted to be finally, completely convinced.

We said goodbye with mutual promises of an early future meeting. A day or two later, I happened to see Fritz in the street. From the pleasure with which he greeted me, I knew at once that he had something extra spiteful to tell me. For a quarter of an hour he chatted gaily about bridge, night clubs, and his latest flame, a well-known sculptress; his malicious smile broadening all the while at the thought of the tit-bit which he had in reserve. At length he produced it.

"Been seeing any more of your friend Norris?"

"Yes," I said. "Why?"

"Nothing," drawled Fritz, his naughty eyes on my face. "Eventually I'd watch your step, that's all."

"Whatever do you mean?"

"I've been hearing some queer things about him."

"Oh, indeed?"

"Maybe they aren't true. You know how people talk."

"And I know how you listen, Fritz."

He grinned; not in the least offended: "There's a story going round that eventually Norris is some kind of cheap crook."

"I must say, I should have thought that cheap was hardly a word one could apply to him."

Fritz smiled, a superior, indulgent smile.

"I dare say it would surprise you to know that he's been in prison?"

"What you mean is, it'd surprise me to know that your friends *say* he's been in prison. Well, it doesn't in the least. Your friends would say anything."

Fritz didn't reply. He merely continued to smile.

"What's he supposed to have been in prison for?" I asked.

"I didn't hear," Fritz drawled. "But maybe I can guess."

"Well, I can't."

"Look, Bill, excuse me a moment." He had changed his tone now. He was serious. He laid his hand on my shoulder. "What I mean to say, the thing is this. Eventually, we two, we don't give a damn, hell, for goodness' sake. But we've got other people to consider besides ourselves, haven't we? Suppose Norris gets hold of some kid and plucks him of his last cent?"

"How dreadful that would be."

Fritz gave me up. His final shot was: "Well, don't say I didn't warn you, that's all."

"No, Fritz. I most certainly won't."

We parted pleasantly.

Perhaps Helen Pratt had been right about me. Stage by stage I was building up a romantic background for Arthur, and was jealous lest it should be upset. Certainly, I rather enjoyed playing with the idea that he was, in fact, a dangerous criminal; but I am sure that I never seriously believed in it for a moment. Nearly every member of my generation is a crime-snob. I was fond of Arthur with an affection strengthened by obstinacy. If my friends didn't like him because of his mouth or his past, the loss was theirs; I was, I flattered myself, more profound, more humane, an altogether subtler connoisseur of human nature than they. And if, in my letters to England, I sometimes referred to him as "a most amazing old crook," I only meant by this that I wanted to imagine him as a glorified being; audacious and self-reliant, reckless and calm. All of which, in reality, he only too painfully and obviously wasn't.

Poor Arthur! I have seldom known anybody with such weak nerves. At times, I began to believe he must be suffering from a mild form of persecution mania. I can see him now as he used to sit waiting for me in the most secluded corner of our favourite restaurant, bored, abstracted, uneasy; his hands folded with studied nonchalance in his lap, his head held at an awkward, listening angle, as though he expected, at any moment, to be startled by a very loud bang. I can hear him at the telephone, speaking cautiously, as close as possible to the mouthpiece and barely raising his voice above a whisper.

"Hullo. Yes, it's me. So you've seen that party? Good. Now when can we meet? Let's say at the usual time, at the house of the person who is interested. And please ask that other one to be there, too. No no. Herr D. It's particularly important. Goodbye."

I laughed. "One would think, to hear you, that you were an arch-conspirator."

"A very arch conspirator," Arthur giggled. "No, I assure you, my dear William, that I was discussing nothing more desperate than the sale of some old furniture in which I happen to be—er—financially interested."

"Then why on earth all this secrecy?"

"One never knows who may be listening."

"But, surely, in any case, it wouldn't interest them very much?"

"You can't be too careful nowadays," said Arthur vaguely.

By this time, I had borrowed and read nearly all his "amusing" books. Most of them were extremely disappointing. Their authors adopted a curiously prudish, snobby, lower-middle-class tone and despite their sincere efforts to be pornographic, became irritatingly vague in the most important passages. Arthur had a signed set of volumes of *My Life and Loves.* I asked him if he had known Frank Harris.

"Slightly, yes. It's some years ago now. The news of his death came as a great shock to me. He was a genius in his own way. So witty. I remember his saying to me, once, in the Louvre: 'Ah, my dear Norris, you and I are the last of the gentleman adventurers.' He could be very caustic, you know. People never forgot the things he said about them.

"And that reminds me," continued Arthur meditatively, "of a question once put to me by the late Lord Disley. 'Mr Norris,' he asked me, 'are you an adventurer?'"

"What an extraordinary question. I don't call *that* witty. It was damned rude of him."

"I replied: 'We are all adventurers. Life is an adventure.' Rather neat, don't you think?"

"Just the sort of answer he deserved."

Arthur modestly regarded his fingernails.

"I'm generally at my best in the witness-box."

"Do you mean that this was during a trial?"

"Not a trial, William. An action. I was suing the *Evening Post* for libel."

"Why, what had they said about you?"

"They had made certain insinuations about the conduct of a public fund with which I had been entrusted."

"You won, of course?"

Arthur carefully stroked his chin. "They were unable to make good their accusations. I was awarded five hundred pounds damages."

"Have you often brought libel actions?"

"Five times," Arthur modestly admitted. "And on three other occasions the matter was settled out of court."

"And you've always got damages?"

"Something. A mere bagatelle. Honour was satisfied."

"It must be quite a source of income."

Arthur made a deprecatory gesture. "I should hardly go so far as to say that."

This, at last, seemed the moment for my question.

"Tell me, Arthur. Have you ever been in prison?"

He rubbed his chin slowly, baring his ruined teeth. Into his vacant blue eyes came a curious expression. Relief, perhaps. Or even, I fancied, a certain gratified vanity.

"So you heard of the case?"

"Yes," I lied.

"It was very widely reported at the time." Arthur modestly arranged his hands upon the crook of his umbrella. "Did you, by any chance, read a full account of the evidence?"

"No. Unfortunately not."

"That's a pity. I should have had great pleasure in lending you the Press cuttings, but unfortunately they were lost in the course of one of my many moves. I should have liked to hear your impartial opinion ... I consider that the jury was unfairly prejudiced against me from the start. Had I had the experience which I have now I should have undoubtedly been acquitted. My counsel advised me quite wrongly. I should have pleaded justification, but he assured me that it would be quite impossible to obtain the necessary evidence. The judge was very hard on me. He even went so far as to insinuate that I had been engaged in a form of blackmail."

"I say! That was going a bit far, wasn't it?"

"It was indeed." Arthur shook his head sadly. "The English legal mind is sometimes unfortunately unsubtle. It is unable to distinguish between the finer shades of conduct."

"And how much ... how long did you get?"

"Eighteen months in the second division. At Wormwood Scrubs."

"I hope they treated you properly?"

"They treated me in accordance with the regulations. I can't complain ... Nevertheless, since my release, I have felt a lively interest in penal reform. I make a point of subscribing to the various societies which exist for that purpose."

There was a pause, during which Arthur evidently indulged in painful memories. "I think," he continued at length, "I may safely claim that in the course of my whole career I have very seldom, if ever, done anything which I knew to be contrary to the law ... On the other hand, I do and always shall maintain that it is the privilege of the richer but less mentally endowed members of the community to contribute to the upkeep of people like myself. I hope you're with me there?"

"Not being one of the richer members," I said, "yes."

"I'm so glad. You know, William, I feel that we might come, in time, to see eye to eye upon many things ... It's quite extraordinary what a lot of good money is lying about, waiting to be picked up. Yes, positively picked up. Even nowadays. Only one must have the eyes to see it. And capital. A certain amount of capital is absolutely essential. One day I think I really must tell you about my dealings with an American who believed himself to be a direct descendant of Peter the Great. It's a most instructive story."

Sometimes Arthur talked about his childhood. As a boy he was delicate and had never been sent to school. An only son, he lived alone with his widowed mother, whom he adored. Together they studied literature and art; together they visited Paris, Baden-Baden, Rome, moving always in the best society, from *Schloss* to château, from château to palace, gentle, charming, appreciative; in a state of perpetual tender anxiety about each other's health. Lying ill in rooms with a connecting door, they would ask for their beds to be moved so that they could talk without raising their voices. Telling stories, making gay little jokes, they kept up each other's spirits through weary sleepless nights. Convalescent, they were propelled, side by side, in bathchairs, through the gardens of Lucerne.

This invalid idyll was doomed, by its very nature, soon to end. Arthur had to grow up; to go to Oxford. His mother had to die. Sheltering him with her love to the very last, she refused to allow the servants to telegraph to him as long as she remained conscious. When at length they disobeyed her, it was too late. Her delicate son was spared, as she had intended, the strain of a death-bed farewell.

After her death, his health improved greatly, for he had to stand on his own feet. This novel and painful attitude was considerably eased by the small fortune he had inherited. He had money enough to last him, according to the standards of social London in the nineties, for at least ten years. He spent it in rather less than two. "It was at that time," said Arthur, "that I first learnt the meaning of the word 'luxury.' Since then, I am sorry to say, I have been forced to add others to my vocabulary; horrid ugly ones, some of them." "I wish," he remarked simply, on another occasion, "I had the money now, I should know what to do with it." In those days he was only twenty-two and didn't know. It disappeared with magic speed into the mouths of horses and the stockings of ballet girls. The palms of servants closed on it with an oily iron grip. It was transformed into wonderful suits of clothes which he presented after a week or two, in disgust, to his valet; into oriental knick-knacks which somehow, when he got them back to his flat, turned out to be rusty old iron pots; into landscapes of the latest Impressionist genius which by daylight next morning were childish daubs. Well-groomed and witty, with money to burn, he must have been one of the most eligible young bachelors of his large circle; but it was the Jews, not the ladies, who got him in the end.

A stern uncle, appealed to, grudgingly rescued him, but imposed conditions. Arthur was to settle down to read for the Bar. "And I can honestly say that I did try. I can't tell you the agonies I suffered. After a month or two I was compelled to take steps." When I asked what the steps were, he became uncommunicative. I gathered that he had found some way of putting his social connexions to good use. "It seemed very sordid at the time," he added cryptically. "I was such a very sensitive young man, you know. It makes one smile to think of it now.

"From that moment I date the beginning of my career; and, unlike Lot's wife, I have never looked back. There have been ups and downs ... ups and downs. The ups are a matter of European history. The downs I prefer not to remember. Well, well. As the proverbial Irishman said, I have put my hand to the plough and now I must lie on it."

During that spring and early summer Arthur's ups and downs were, I gathered, pretty frequent. He was never very willing to discuss them; but his spirits always sufficiently indicated the state of his finances. The sale of the "old furniture" (or whatever it really was) seemed to provide a temporary respite. And, in May, he returned from a short trip to Paris very cheerful, having, as he guardedly said, "several little irons in the fire."

Behind all these transactions moved the sinister, pumpkin-headed figure of Schmidt. Arthur was quite frankly afraid of his secretary, and no wonder. Schmidt was altogether too useful; he had made his master's interests identical with his own. He was one of those people who have not only a capacity, but a positive appetite for doing their employer's dirty work. From chance remarks made by Arthur in less discreet moments, I was gradually able to form a fair idea of the secretary's duties and talents. "It is very painful for anyone of our own class to say certain things to certain individuals. It offends our delicate sensibilities. One has to be so very crude." Schmidt, it seemed, experienced no pain. He was quite prepared to say anything to anybody. He confronted creditors with the courage and technique of a bull-fighter. He followed up the results of Arthur's wildest shots, and returned with money like a retriever bringing home a duck.

Schmidt controlled and doled out Arthur's pocket-money. Arthur wouldn't, for a long time, admit this; but it was obvious. There were days when he hadn't enough to pay his bus fare; others when he would say: "Just a moment, William. I shall have to run up to my flat to fetch something I'd forgotten. You won't mind waiting down here a minute, will you?"

On such occasions, he would rejoin me, after a quarter of an hour or so, in the street; sometimes deeply depressed, sometimes radiant, like a schoolboy who had received an unexpectedly large tip.

Another phrase to which I became accustomed was: "I'm afraid I can't ask you to come up just now. The flat's so untidy." I soon discovered this to mean that Schmidt was at home. Arthur, who dreaded scenes, was always at pains to prevent our meeting; for, since my first visit, our mutual dislike had considerably increased. Schmidt, I think, not only disliked me, but definitely disapproved of me as a hostile and unsettling influence on his employer. He was never exactly offensive. He merely smiled his insulting smile and amused himself by coming suddenly into the room on his noiseless shoes. He would stand there a few seconds, unnoticed, and then speak, startling Arthur into a jump and a little scream. When he had done this two or three times in succession, Arthur's nerves would be in such a state that he could no longer talk coherently about anything and we had to retire to the nearest café to continue our conversation. Schmidt would help his master on with his overcoat and bow us out of the flat with ironic ceremony, slyly content that his object had been achieved.

In June, we went to spend a long week-end with Baron von Pregnitz; he had invited us to his country villa, which stood on the shore of a lake in Mecklenburg. The largest room in the villa was a gymnasium fitted with the most modern apparatus, for the Baron made a hobby of his figure. He tortured himself daily on an electric horse, a rowing-machine, and a rotating massage belt. It was very hot and we all bathed, even Arthur. He wore a rubber swimming-cap, carefully adjusted in the privacy of his bedroom. The house was full of handsome young men with superbly developed brown bodies which they smeared in oil and baked for hours in the sun. They ate like wolves and had table manners which pained Arthur deeply; most of them spoke with the broadest Berlin accents.

They wrestled and boxed on the beach and did somersault dives from the spring-board into the lake. The Baron joined in everything and often got severely handled. With good-humoured brutality the boys played practical jokes on him which smashed his spare monocles and might easily have broken his neck. He bore it all with his heroic frozen smile.

On the second evening of our visit, he escaped from them and took a walk with me in the woods, alone. That morning they had tossed him in a blanket and he had landed on the asphalt pavement; he was still a bit shaky. His hand rested heavily on my arm. "When you get to my age," he told me sadly, "I think you will find that the most beautiful things in life belong to the Spirit. The Flesh alone cannot give us happiness." He sighed and gave my arm a faint squeeze. "Our friend Kuno is a remarkable man," observed Arthur, as we sat together in the train on our way back to Berlin. "Some people believe that he has a great career ahead of him. I shouldn't be at all surprised if he were to be offered an important post under the next Government."

"You don't say so?"

"I think," Arthur gave me a discreet, sideways glance, "that he's taken a great fancy to you."

"Do you?"

"I sometimes feel, William, that with your talents, it's a pity you're not more ambitious. A young man should make use of his opportunities. Kuno is in a position to help you in all sorts of ways."

I laughed. "To help both of us, you mean?"

"Well, if you put it in that way, yes. I quite admit that I foresee certain advantages to myself from the arrangement. Whatever my faults, I hope I'm not a hypocrite. For instance, he might make you his secretary."

"I'm sorry, Arthur," I said, "but I'm afraid I should find my duties too heavy."

Chapter Five

TOWARDS THE END of August, Arthur left Berlin. An air of mystery surrounded his departure; he hadn't even told me that he was thinking of going. I rang up the flat twice, at times when I was pretty sure Schmidt would not be there. Hermann, the cook, knew only that his master was away for an indefinite period. On the second occasion, I asked where he had gone, and was told London. I began to be afraid that Arthur had left Germany for good. No doubt he had the best of reasons for doing so.

One day, however, during the second week in September, the telephone rang. Arthur himself was on the line.

"Is that you, dear boy? Here I am, back at last! I've got such a lot to tell you. Please don't say you're engaged this evening. You aren't? Then will you come round here about half past six? I think I may add that I've got a little surprise in store for you. No, I shan't tell you anything more. You must come and see for yourself. *Au revoir.*"

I arrived at the flat to find Arthur in the best of spirits.

"My dear William, what a pleasure to see you again! How have you been getting on? Getting on and getting off?"

Arthur tittered, scratched his chin and glanced rapidly and

uneasily round the room as though he were not yet quite convinced that all the furniture was still in its proper place.

"What was it like in London?" I asked. In spite of what he had said over the telephone, he didn't seem in a particularly communicative mood.

"In London?" Arthur looked blank. "Ah yes. London ... To be perfectly frank with you, William, I was not in London. I was in Paris. Just at present, it is desirable that a slight uncertainty as to my whereabouts should exist in the minds of certain persons here." He paused, added impressively: "I suppose I may tell you, as a very dear and intimate friend, that my visit was not unconnected with the Communist Party."

"Do you mean to say that you've become a communist?"

"In all but name, William, yes. In all but name."

He paused for a moment, enjoying my astonishment. "What is more, I asked you here this evening to witness what I may call my Confessio Fidei. In an hour's time I am due to speak at a meeting held to protest against the exploitation of the Chinese peasantry. I hope you'll do me the honour of coming."

"Need you ask?"

The meeting was to be held in Neukölln. Arthur insisted on taking a taxi all the way. He was in an extravagant mood.

"I feel," he remarked, "that I shall look back on this evening as one of the turning-points of my career."

He was visibly nervous and kept fingering his bunch of papers. Occasionally he cast an unhappy glance out of the taxi window, as though he would have liked to ask the driver to stop.

"I should think your career has had a good many turning-points," I said, to distract his thoughts.

Arthur brightened at once at the implied flattery.

"It has, William. It has, indeed. If my life were going to end tonight (which I sincerely hope it won't) I could truthfully say: 'At any rate, I have lived' ... I wish you had known me in the old days, in Paris, just before the War. I had my own car and an apartment on the Bois. It was one of the show places of its kind. The bedroom I designed myself, all in crimson and black. My collection of whips was probably unique." Arthur sighed. "Mine is a sensitive nature. I react immediately to my surroundings. When the sun shines on me, I expand. To see me at my best, you must see me in my proper setting. A good table. A good cellar. Art. Music. Beautiful things. Charming and witty society. Then I begin to sparkle. I am transformed."

The taxi stopped. Arthur fussily paid the driver, and we passed through a large beer-garden, now dark and empty, into a deserted restaurant, where an elderly waiter informed us that the meeting was being held upstairs. "Not the first door," he added. "That's the Skittles Club."

"Oh dear," exclaimed Arthur. "I'm afraid we must be very late."

He was right. The meeting had already begun. As we climbed the broad rickety staircase, we could hear the voice of a speaker echoing down the long shabby corridor. Two powerfully built youths wearing hammer-and-sickle armlets kept guard at the double doors. Arthur whispered a hurried explanation, and they let us pass. He pressed my hand nervously. "I'll see you later, then." I sat down on the nearest available chair.

The hall was large and cold. Decorated in tawdry baroque, it might have been built about thirty years ago and not repainted since. On the ceiling, an immense pink, blue, and gold design of cherubim, roses and clouds was peeled and patched with damp. Round the walls were draped scarlet banners with white lettering: "*Arbeiterfront gegen Faschismus und Krieg.*" "*Wir fordern Arbeit und Brot.*" "*Arbeiter aller Länder, vereinigt euch.*"

The speaker sat at a long table on the stage facing the audience. Behind them, a tattered backcloth represented a forest glade. There were two Chinese, a girl who was taking shorthand notes, a gaunt man with fuzzy hair who propped his head in his hands, as if listening to music. In front of them, dangerously near the edge of the platform, stood a short, broad-shouldered, red-haired man, waving a piece of paper at us like a flag.

"Those are the figures, comrades. You've heard them. They speak for themselves, don't they? I needn't say any more. Tomorrow you'll see them in print in the *Welt am Abend.* It's no good looking for them in the capitalist Press, because they won't be there. The bosses will keep them out of their newspapers, because, if they were published, they might upset the stock exchanges. Wouldn't that be a pity? Never mind. The workers will read them. The workers will know what to think of them. Let's send a message to our comrades in China: The workers of the German Communist Party protest against the outrages of the Japanese murderers. The workers demand assistance for the hundreds of thousands of Chinese peasants now rendered homeless. Comrades, the Chinese section of the I.A.H. appeals to us for funds to fight Japanese imperialism and European exploitation. It's our duty to help them. We're going to help them."

The red-haired man smiled as he spoke, a militant, triumphant smile; his white, even teeth gleamed in the lamplight. His gestures were slight but astonishingly forceful. At moments it seemed as if the giant energy stored up in his short, stocky frame would have flung him bodily from the platform, like an over-powerful motor-bicycle. I had seen his photograph two or three times in the newspaper, but couldn't remember who he was. From where I sat it was difficult to hear everything he said. His voice drowned itself, filling the large, damp hall with thundering echoes.

Arthur now appeared upon the stage, shaking hands hastily with the Chinese, apologizing, fussing to his chair. A burst of applause which followed the red-haired man's last sentence visibly startled him. He sat down abruptly.

During the clapping I moved up several rows in order to hear better, squeezing into a place I had seen was empty in front of me. As I sat down I felt a tug at my sleeve. It was Anni, the girl with the boots. Beside her, I recognized the boy who had poured the beer down Kuno's throat at Olga's on New Year's Eve. They both seemed pleased to see me. The boy shook hands with a grip which nearly made me yell out loud.

The hall was very full. The audience sat there in their soiled everyday clothes. Most of the men wore breeches with coarse woollen stockings, sweaters and peaked caps. Their eyes followed the speaker with hungry curiosity. I had never been to a communist meeting before, and what struck me most was the fixed attention of the upturned rows of faces; faces of the Berlin working class, pale and prematurely lined, often haggard and ascetic, like the heads of scholars with thin, fair hair brushed back from their broad foreheads. They had not come here to see each other or to be seen, or even to fulfil a social duty. They were attentive, but not passive. They were not spectators. They participated, with a curious, restrained passion, in the speech made by the red-haired man. He spoke for them, he made their thoughts articulate. They were listening to their own collective voice. At intervals they applauded it, with sudden, spontaneous violence. Their passion, their strength of purpose elated me. I stood outside it. One day, perhaps, I should be with it, renegade from my own class, my feelings muddled by anarchism talked at Cambridge, by slogans from the confirmation service, by the tunes the band played when my father's regiment marched to the railway station, seventeen years ago. And the little man finished his speech and went back to his place at the table amidst thunders of clapping.

"Who is he?" I asked.

"Why, don't you know?" exclaimed Anni's friend in surprise. "That's Ludwig Bayer. One of the best men we've got."

The boy's name was Otto. Anni introduced us and I got another crushing hand-squeeze. Otto changed places with her so that he could talk to me.

"Were you at the Sport Palace the other night? Man, you ought to have heard him! He spoke for two hours and a half without so much as a drink of water."

A Chinese delegate now stood up and was introduced. He spoke careful, academic German. In sentences which were like the faint, plaintive twanging of an Asiatic musical instrument, he told us of the famine, of the great floods, of the Japanese air-raids on helpless towns. "German comrades, I bring you a sad message from my unhappy country."

"My word!" whispered Otto, impressed. "It must be worse there than at my aunt's in the Simeonstrasse."

It was already a quarter past nine. The Chinese was followed by the man with fuzzy hair. Arthur was becoming impatient. He kept glancing at his watch and furtively touching his wig. Then came the second Chinese. His German was inferior to that of his colleague, but the audience followed the speeches as eagerly as ever. Arthur, I could see, was nearly frantic. At length he got up and went round to the back of Bayer's chair. Bending over, he began speaking in an agitated whisper. Bayer smiled and made a friendly, soothing gesture. He seemed amused. Arthur returned dubiously to his place, where he soon began to fidget again.

The Chinese finished at last. Bayer at once stood up, took Arthur encouragingly by the arm, as though he were a mere boy, and led him to the front of the stage.

"This is the Comrade Arthur Norris, who has come to speak to us about the crimes of British Imperialism in the Far East."

It seemed so absurd to me to see him standing there that I could hardly keep a straight face. Indeed, it was difficult for me to understand why everybody in the hall didn't burst out laughing. But no, the audience evidently didn't find Arthur in the least funny. Even Anni, who had more reason than anyone present to regard him from a comic angle, was perfectly grave.

Arthur coughed, shuffled his papers. Then he began to speak in his fluent, elaborate German, a little too fast:

"Since that day on which the leaders of the allied governments saw fit, in their infinite wisdom, to draw up that, no doubt, divinely inspired document known as the Treaty of Versailles; since that day, I repeat …"

A slight stir, as if of uneasiness, passed over the rows of listeners. But the pale, serious, upturned faces were not ironic.

They accepted without question this urbane bourgeois gentleman, accepted his stylish clothes, his graceful *rentier* wit. He had come to help them. Bayer had spoken for him. He was their friend.

"British Imperialism has been engaged, during the last two hundred years, in conferring upon its victims the dubious benefits of the Bible, the Bottle, and the Bomb. And of these three, I might perhaps venture to add, the Bomb has been infinitely the least noxious."

There was applause at this; delayed, hesitant clapping, as if Arthur's hearers approved his matter, but were still doubtful of his manner. Evidently encouraged, he continued: "I am reminded of the story of the Englishman, the German, and the Frenchman who had a wager as to which of them could cut down the most trees in one day. The Frenchman was the first to try ..."

At the end of this story there was laughter and loud applause. Otto thumped me violently on the back in his delight. *"Mensch! Der spricht prima, nicht wahr?"* Then he bent forward again to listen, his eyes intent upon the platform, his arm round Anni's shoulder. Arthur, exchanging his graceful bantering tone for an oratorical seriousness, was approaching his climax:

"The cries of the starving Chinese peasantry are ringing in our ears as we sit in this hall tonight. They have come to us across the breadth of the world. Soon, we hope, they will sound yet more loudly, drowning the futile chatter of diplomatists and the strains of dance bands in luxurious hotels, where the wives of armament manufacturers finger the pearls which have been bought with the price of the blood of innocent children. Yes, we must see to it that those cries are clearly heard by every thinking man and woman in Europe and in America. For then, and only then, will a term be set to this inhuman exploitation, this traffic in living souls ..."

Arthur concluded his speech with an energetic flourish. His face was quite flushed. Salvo upon salvo of clapping rattled over the hall. Many of the audience cheered. While the applause was still at its height, Arthur came down from the platform and joined me at the doors. Heads were turned to watch us go out. Otto and Anni had left the meeting with us. Otto wrung Arthur's hand and dealt him terrific blows on the shoulder with his heavy palm: "Arthur, you old horse! That was fine!"

"Thank you, my dear boy. Thank you." Arthur winced. He was feeling very pleased with himself. "How did they take it, William? Well, I think? I hope I made my points quite clearly? Please say I did."

"Honestly, Arthur, I was astounded."

"How charming of you: praise from such a severe critic as yourself is indeed music to my ears."

"I'd no idea you were such an old hand at it."

"In my time," admitted Arthur modestly, "I've had occasion to do a good deal of public speaking, though hardly quite of this kind."

We had cold supper at the flat. Schmidt and Hermann were both out: Otto and Anni made tea and laid the table. They seemed quite at home in the kitchen and knew where everything was kept.

"Otto is Anni's chosen protector," Arthur explained while they were out of the room. "In another walk of life, one would call him her impresario. I believe he takes a certain percentage of her earnings. I prefer not to inquire too closely. He's a nice boy, but excessively jealous. Luckily, not of Anni's customers. I should be very sorry indeed to get into his bad books. I understand that he's the middle-weight champion of his boxing club."

At length the meal was ready. He fussed round, giving directions.

"Will the Comradess Anni bring us some glasses? How nice of her. I should like to celebrate this evening. Perhaps, if Comrade Otto would be so kind, we might even have a little brandy. I don't know whether Comrade Bradshaw drinks brandy. You'd better ask him."

"At such an historic moment, Comrade Norris, I drink anything."

Otto came back to report that there was no more brandy.

"Never mind," said Arthur, "brandy is not a proletarian drink. We'll drink beer." He filled our glasses. "To the world revolution."

"To the world revolution."

Our glasses touched. Anni sipped daintily, holding the glass-stem between finger and thumb, her little finger mincingly crooked. Otto drained his at a gulp, banging down the tumbler heavily on to the table. Arthur's beer went the wrong way and choked him. He coughed, spluttered, dived for his napkin.

"I'm afraid that's an evil omen," I said jokingly. He seemed quite upset.

"Please don't say that, William. I don't like people to say things of that kind, even in jest."

This was the first time I had ever known Arthur to be superstitious. I was amused and rather impressed. He appeared to have got it badly. Could he really have undergone a sort of religious conversion? It was difficult to believe.

"Have you been a communist long, Arthur?" I asked in English as we began to eat.

He cleared his throat slightly, shot an uneasy glance in the direction of the door.

"At heart, William, yes. I think I may say that I have always felt that, in the deepest sense, we are all brothers. Class distinctions have never meant anything to me; and hatred of tyranny is in my blood. Even as a small child I could never bear injustice of any kind. It offends my sense of the beautiful. It is so stupid and unaesthetic. I remember my feelings when I was first unjustly punished by my nurse. It wasn't the punishment itself which I resented; it was the clumsiness, the lack of imagination behind it. That, I remember, pained me very deeply."

"Then why didn't you join the Party long ago?"

Arthur looked suddenly vague; stroked his temples with his finger-tips.

"The time was not ripe. No."

"And what does Schmidt say to all this?" I asked mischievously.

Arthur gave the door a second hurried glance. As I had suspected, he was in a state of suspense lest his secretary should suddenly walk in upon us.

"I'm afraid Schmidt and I don't quite see eye to eye on the subject just at present."

I grinned. "No doubt you'll convert him in time."

"Shut up talking English, you two," cried Otto, giving me a vigorous jog in the ribs. "Anni and I want to hear the joke."

During supper we drank a good deal of beer. I must have been rather unsteady on my feet, because, when I stood up at the end of the meal, I knocked over my chair. On the underside of the seat was pasted a ticket with the printed number 69.

"What's this for?" I asked.

"Oh, that?" said Arthur hastily; he seemed very much disconcerted. "That's merely the catalogue number from the sale where I originally bought it. It must have been there all the time ... Anni, my love, do you think you and Otto would be so very kind as to carry some of the things into the kitchen and put them in the sink? I don't like to leave Hermann too much to do in the morning. It makes him cross with me for the rest of the day."

"What is that ticket for?" I repeated gently as soon as they were outside. "I want to know."

Arthur sadly shook his head.

"Ah, my dear William, nothing escapes your eye. Yet another of our domestic secrets is laid bare."

"I'm afraid I'm very dense. What secret?"

"I rejoice to see that your young life has never been sullied by such sordid experiences. At your age, I regret to say, I had already made the acquaintance of the gentleman whose sign-manual you will find upon every piece of furniture in this room."

"Good God, do you mean the bailiff?"

"I prefer the word *Gerichtsvollzieher.* It sounds so much nicer."

"But, Arthur, when is he coming?"

"He comes, I'm sorry to say, almost every morning. Sometimes in the afternoon as well. He seldom finds me at home, however. I prefer to let Schmidt receive him. From what I have seen of him, he seems a person of little or no culture. I doubt if we should have anything in common."

"Won't he soon be taking everything away?"

Arthur seemed to enjoy my dismay. He puffed at his cigarette with exaggerated nonchalance.

"On Monday next, I believe."

"How frightful! Can't anything be done about it?"

"Oh, undoubtedly something can be done about it. Something *will* be done about it. I shall be compelled to pay another visit to my Scotch friend, Mr Isaacs. Mr Isaacs assures me that he comes of an old Scotch family, the Inverness Isaacs. The first time I had the pleasure of meeting him he nearly embraced me. 'Ah, my dear Mr Norris,' he said, 'you are a countryman of mine.'"

"But, Arthur, if you go to a moneylender you'll only get into worse trouble still. Has this been going on for long? I always imagined that you were quite rich."

Arthur laughed.

"I am rich, I hope, in the things of the Spirit ... My dear boy, please don't alarm yourself on my account. I've been living on my wits for nearly thirty years now, and I propose to continue doing so until such time as I am called into the, I'm afraid, not altogether approving company of my fathers."

Before I could ask any more questions, Anni and Otto returned from the kitchen. Arthur greeted them gaily and soon Anni was sitting on his knee, resisting his advances with slaps and bites, while Otto, having taken off his coat and rolled up his sleeves, was absorbed in trying to repair the gramophone. There seemed no place for myself in this domestic tableau and I soon said that I must be going.

Otto came downstairs with a key to let me out of the house door. In parting, he gravely raised his clenched fist in salute:

"Red Front."

"Red Front," I answered.

Chapter Six

One morning, not long after this, Frl. Schroeder came shuffling into my room in great haste, to tell me that Arthur was on the telephone.

"It must be something very serious. Herr Norris didn't even say good morning to me." She was impressed and rather hurt.

"Hullo, Arthur. What's the matter?"

"For heaven's sake, my dear boy, don't ask me any questions now." His tone was nervously irritable and he spoke so rapidly that I could barely understand him. "It's more than I can bear. All I want to know is, can you come here at once?"

"Well ... I've got a pupil coming at ten o'clock."

"Can't you put him off?"

"Is it as important as all that?"

Arthur uttered a little cry of peevish exasperation: "Is it important? My dear William, do please endeavour to exercise your imagination. Should I be ringing you up at this unearthly hour if it wasn't important? All I beg of you is a plain answer: Yes or No. If it's a question of money, I shall be only too glad to pay you your usual fee. How much do you charge?"

"Shut up, Arthur, and don't be absurd. If it's urgent, of course I'll come. I'll be with you in twenty minutes."

I found all the doors of the flat standing open, and walked in unannounced. Arthur, it appeared, had been rushing wildly from room to room like a flustered hen. At the moment, he was in the sitting-room, dressed ready to go out, and nervously pulling on his gloves. Hermann, on his knees, rummaged sulkily in a cupboard in the hall. Schmidt lounged in the doorway of the study, a cigarette between his lips. He did not make the least effort to help and was evidently enjoying his employer's distress.

"Ah, here you are, William, at last!" cried Arthur, on seeing me. "I thought you were never coming. Oh, dear, oh dear! Is it as late as that already? Never mind about my grey hat. Come along, William, come along. I'll explain everything to you oil the way."

Schmidt gave us an unpleasant, sarcastic smile as we went out.

When we were comfortably settled on the top of a bus, Arthur became calmer and more coherent.

"First of all," he fumbled rapidly in all his pockets and produced a folded piece of paper: "Please read that."

I looked at it. It was a *Vorladung* from the Political Police. Herr Arthur Norris was requested to present himself at the Alexanderplatz that morning before one o'clock. What would happen should he fail to do so was not stated. The wording was official and coldly polite.

"Good God, Arthur," I said, "whatever does this mean? What have you been up to now?"

In spite of his nervous alarm, Arthur displayed a certain modest pride.

"I flatter myself that my association with," he lowered his voice and glanced quickly at our fellow passengers, "the representatives of the Third International has not been entirely unfruitful. I am told that my efforts have even excited favourable comment in certain quarters in Moscow ... I told you, didn't I, that I'd been in Paris? Yes, yes, of course ... Well, I had a little mission there to fulfil. I spoke to certain highly placed individuals and brought back certain instructions ... Never mind that now. At all events, it appears that the authorities here are better informed than we'd supposed. That is what I have to find out. The whole question is extremely delicate. I must be careful not to give anything away."

"Perhaps they'll put you through the third degree."

"Oh, William, how can you say anything so dreadful? You make me feel quite faint."

"But, Arthur, surely that would be ... I mean, wouldn't you rather enjoy it?"

Arthur giggled: "Ha, ha. Ha, ha. I must say this, William, that even in the darkest hour your humour never fails to restore me ... Well, well, perhaps if the examination were to be conducted by Frl. Anni, or some equally charming young lady, I might undergo it with—er—very mixed feelings. Yes." Uneasily he scratched his chin. "I shall need your moral support. You must come and hold my hand. And if this," he glanced nervously over his shoulder, "interview should terminate unpleasantly, I shall ask you to go to Bayer and tell him exactly what has happened."

"Yes, I will. Of course."

When we had got out of the bus on the Alexanderplatz, poor Arthur was so shaky that I suggested going into a restaurant and drinking a glass of cognac. Seated at a little table we regarded the immense drab mass of the Praesidium buildings from the opposite side of the roadway.

"The enemy fortress," said Arthur, "into which poor little I have got to venture, all alone."

"Remember David and Goliath."

"Oh, dear, I'm afraid the Psalmist and I have very little in common this morning. I feel more like a beetle about to be squashed by a steam-roller ... It's a curious fact that, since my earliest years, I have had an instinctive dislike of the police. The very cut of their uniforms offends me, and the German helmets are not only hideous but somehow rather sinister. Merely to see one of them filling in an official form in that inhuman copy-book handwriting gives me a sinking feeling in the stomach."

"Yes, I know what you mean."

Arthur brightened a little.

"I'm very glad I've got you with me, William. You have such a sympathetic manner. I could wish for no better companion on the morning of my execution. The very opposite of that odious Schmidt, who simply gloats over my misfortune. Nothing makes him happier than to be in a position to say—I told you so."

"After all, there's nothing very much they can do to you in there. They only knock workmen about. Remember, you belong to the same class as their masters. You must make them feel that."

"I'll try," said Arthur doubtfully.

"Have another cognac?"

"Perhaps I will, yes."

The second cognac worked wonders. We emerged from the restaurant into the still, clammy autumn morning, laughing arm in arm.

"Be brave, Comrade Norris. Think of Lenin."

"I'm afraid, ha, ha, I find more inspiration in the Marquis de Sade."

But the atmosphere of the police headquarters sobered him considerably. Increasingly apprehensive and depressed, we wandered along vistas of stone passages with numbered doors, were misdirected up and down flights of stairs, collided with hurrying officials who carried bulging dossiers of crimes. At length we came out into a courtyard, overlooked by windows with heavy iron bars.

"Oh dear, oh dear!" moaned Arthur. "We've put our heads into the trap this time, I'm afraid."

At this moment a piercing whistle sounded from above.

"Hullo, Arthur!"

Looking down from one of the barred windows high above was Otto.

"What did they get you for?" he shouted jocularly. Before either of us could answer, a figure in uniform appeared beside him at the window and hustled him away. The apparition was as brief as it was disconcerting.

"They seem to have rounded up the whole gang," I said, grinning.

"It's certainly very extraordinary," said Arthur, much perturbed. "I wonder if . . ."

We passed under an archway, up more stairs, into a honeycomb of little rooms and dark passages. On each floor were wash-basins, painted a sanitary green. Arthur consulted his *Vorladung* and found the number of the room in which he was to present himself. We parted in hurried whispers.

"Goodbye, Arthur. Good luck. I'll wait for you here."

"Thank you, dear boy . . . And supposing the worst comes to the worst, and I emerge from this room in custody, don't speak to me or make any sign that you know me unless I speak to you. It may be advisable not to involve you . . . Here's Bayer's address; in case you have to go there alone."

"I'm certain I shan't."

"There's one more thing I wanted to say to you." Arthur had the manner of one who mounts the steps of the scaffold. "I'm sorry if I was a little hasty over the telephone this morning. I was very much upset . . . If this were to be our last meeting for some time, I shouldn't like you to remember it against me."

"What rubbish, Arthur. Of course I shan't. Now run along, and let's get this over."

He pressed my hand, knocked timidly at the door and went in.

I sat down to wait for him, under a blood-red poster advertising the reward for betraying a murderer. My bench was shared by a fat Jewish slum-lawyer and his client, a tearful little prostitute.

"All you've got to remember," he kept telling her, "is that you never saw him again after the night of the sixth."

"But they'll get it out of me somehow," she sobbed. "I know they will. It's the way they look at you. And then they ask you a question so suddenly. You've no time to think."

It was nearly an hour before Arthur reappeared. I could see at once from his face that the interview hadn't been so bad as he'd anticipated. He was in a great hurry.

"Come along, William. Come along. I don't care to stay here any longer than I need."

Outside in the street, he hailed a taxi and told the chauffeur to drive to the Hotel Kaiserhof, adding, as he nearly always did:

"There's no need to drive too fast."

"The Kaiserhof!" I exclaimed. "Are we going to pay a call on Hitler?"

"No, William. We are not ... although, I admit, I derive a certain pleasure from dallying in the camp of the enemy. Do you know, I have lately made a point of being manicured there? They have a very good man. Today, however, I have a quite different object. Bayer's office is also in the Wilhelmstrasse. It didn't seem altogether discreet to drive directly from here to there."

Accordingly, we performed the comedy of entering the hotel, drinking a cup of coffee in the lounge and glancing through the morning papers. To my disappointment, we didn't see Hitler or any of the other Nazi leaders. Ten minutes later, we came out again into the street. I found myself squinting rapidly to right and left, in search of possible detectives. Arthur's police obsession was exceedingly catching.

Bayer inhabited a large untidy flat on the top floor of one of the shabbier houses beyond the Zimmerstrasse. It was certainly a striking enough contrast to what Arthur called "the camp of the enemy," the padded, sombre luxurious hotel we had just left. The door of the flat stood permanently ajar. Inside, the walls were hung with posters in German and Russian, notices of mass meetings and demonstrations, anti-war cartoons, maps of industrial areas and graphs to illustrate the dimensions and progress of strikes. There were no carpets on the bare unpainted floor-boards. The rooms echoed to the rattle of typewriters. Men and women of all ages wandered in and out or sat chatting on upturned sugar-boxes waiting for interviews; patient, good-humoured, quite at home. Everybody seemed to know everybody; a new-comer was greeted almost invariably by his or her Christian name. Even strangers were addressed as Thou. Cigarette smoking was general. The floors were littered with crushed-out stubs.

In the midst of this informal, cheerful activity, we found Bayer himself, in a tiny shabby room, dictating a letter to the girl whom I had seen on the platform at the meeting in Neukölln. He seemed pleased but not especially surprised to see Arthur.

"Ah, my dear Norris. And what can I do for you?"

He spoke English with great emphasis and a strong foreign accent. I thought I had never seen anybody with such beautiful teeth. Indeed, his teeth and Arthur's were both, in their different ways, so remarkable that the two sets might have been placed side by side, as classic contrasts, in a dental museum.

"You have been already to see them?" he added.

"Yes," said Arthur. "We've just come from there."

The girl secretary got up and went out, closing the door behind her. Arthur, his elegantly gloved hands resting demurely in his lap, began to describe his interview with the officials at the Polizeipraesidium. Bayer sat back in his chair and listened. He had extraordinarily vivid animal eyes of a dark reddish brown. His glance was direct, challenging, brilliant as if with laughter, but his lips did not even smile. Listening to Arthur, his face and body became quite still. He did not once nod, or shift his position, or fidget with his hands. His mere repose suggested a force of concentration which was hypnotic in its intensity. Arthur, I could see, felt this also; he squirmed uneasily on his seat and carefully avoided looking Bayer in the eyes. Arthur began by assuring us that the officials had treated him most politely. One of them had helped him off with his coat and hat, the other had offered him a chair and a cigar. Arthur had taken the chair, the cigar he had refused; he made a considerable point of this, as though it were a proof of his singular strong-mindedness and integrity. Thereupon, the official, still courteous, had asked permission to smoke. This Arthur had granted. There had followed a discussion, cross-examination, disguised as chat, about Arthur's business activities in Berlin. Arthur was careful not to go into details here. "It wouldn't interest you," he told Bayer. I gathered, however, that the officials had politely succeeded in frightening him a good deal. They were far too well informed. These preliminaries over, the real questioning began. "We understand, Mr Norris, that you have recently made a journey to Paris. Was this visit in connexion with your private business?"

Arthur had been ready for this, of course. Perhaps too ready. His explanations had been copious. The official had punctured them with a single affable inquiry. He had named a name and an address which Mr Norris had twice visited, on the evening of his arrival and on the morning of his departure. Was this, also, a private business interview? Arthur didn't deny that he had had a nasty shock. Nevertheless, he had been, he claimed, exceedingly discreet. "I wasn't so silly as to deny anything, of course. I made light of the whole matter. I think I impressed them favourably. They were shaken, I could see that, distinctly shaken."

Arthur paused, added modestly: "I flatter myself that I know how to handle that particular kind of situation pretty well. Yes."

His tone appealed for a word of encouragement, of confirmation, here. But Bayer didn't encourage, didn't condemn, didn't speak or move at all. His dark brown eyes continued to regard Arthur with the same brilliant attention, smiling and alert. Arthur uttered a short nervous cough.

Anxious to interest that impersonal, hypnotic silence, he made a great deal of his narrative. He must have talked for nearly half an hour. Actually, there wasn't much to tell. The police, having displayed the extent of their knowledge, had hastened to assure Mr Norris that his activities did not interest them in the least, provided that these activities were confined to foreign countries. As for Germany itself, that, of course, was a different matter. The German Republic welcomes all foreign guests, but requires them to remember that certain laws of hospitality govern guest as well as host. In short it would be a great pity if the German Republic were ever to be deprived of the pleasure of Mr Norris's society. The official felt sure that Mr Norris, as a man of the world, would appreciate his point of view.

Finally, just as Arthur was making for the door, having been helped on with his overcoat and presented with his hat, came a last question asked in a tone which suggested that it hadn't the remotest connexion with anything which had previously been said:

"You have recently become a member of the Communist Party?"

"I saw the trap at once, of course," Arthur told us. "It was simply a trap. But I had to think quickly; any hesitation in answering would have been fatal. They're so accustomed to notice these details ... I am not a member of the Communist Party, nor of any other Left Wing organization. I merely sympathize with the attitude of the K.P.D. to certain non-political problems ... I think that was the right answer? I think so. Yes."

At last Bayer both smiled and spoke. "You have acted quite right, my dear Norris." He seemed subtly amused.

Arthur was as pleased as a stroked cat.

"Comrade Bradshaw was of great assistance to me."

"Oh yes?"

Bayer didn't ask how.

"You have interest in our movement?"

His eyes measured me for the first time. No, he was not impressed. Equally, he did not condemn. A young bourgeois intellectual, he thought. Enthusiastic, within certain limits. Educated, within certain limits. Capable of response if appealed to in terms of his own class-language. Of some small use: everybody can do something. I felt myself blushing deeply.

"I'd like to help you if I could," I said.

"You speak German?"

"He speaks excellent German," put in Arthur, like a mother recommending her son to the notice of the headmaster. Smilingly Bayer considered me once more.

"So?"

He turned over the papers on his desk.

"Here is some translation which you could be so kind as to do for us. Will you please translate this in English? As you will see, it is a report of our work during the past year. From it you will learn a little about our aims. It should interest you, I think."

He handed me a thick wad of manuscript, and rose to his feet. He was even smaller and broader than he had seemed on the platform. He laid a hand on Arthur's shoulder.

"This is most interesting, what you have told me." He shook hands with both of us, gave a brilliant parting smile: "And you will please," he added comically to Arthur, "avoid to entangle this young Mr Bradshaw in your distress."

"Indeed, I assure you, I shouldn't dream of such a thing. His safety is almost, if not quite, as dear to me as my own … Well, ha ha, I won't waste any more of your valuable time. Goodbye."

The interview with Bayer had quite restored Arthur's spirits.

"You made a good impression on him, William. Oh yes, you did. I could see that at once. And he's a very shrewd judge of character. I think he was pleased with what I said to them at the Alexanderplatz, wasn't he?"

"I'm sure he was."

"I think so, yes."

"Who is he?" I asked.

"I know very little about him, myself, William. I've heard that he began life as a research chemist. I don't think his parents were working people. He doesn't give one that impression, does he? In any case, Bayer isn't his real name."

Chapter Six

•

After this meeting, I felt anxious to see Bayer again. I did the translation as quickly as I could, in the intervals of giving lessons. It took me two days. The manuscript was a report on the aims and progress of various strikes, and the measures taken to supply food and clothing to the families of the strikers. My chief difficulty was with the numerous and ever-recurring groups of initial letters which represented the names of the different organizations involved. As I did not know what most of these organizations were called in English, I didn't know what letters to substitute for those in the manuscript.

"It is not so important," replied Bayer, when I asked him about this. "We will attend to this matter ourselves."

Something in his tone made me feel humiliated. The manuscript he had given me to translate was simply not important. It would probably never be sent to England at all. Bayer had given it me, like a toy, to play with, hoping, no doubt, to be rid of my tiresome, useless enthusiasm for a week at least.

"You find this work interesting?" he continued. "I am glad. It is necessary for every man and woman in our days to have knowledge of this problem. You have read something from Marx?"

I said that I had once tried to read *Das Kapital.*

"Ah, that is too difficult, for a beginning. You should try the *Communist Manifesto.* And some of Lenin's pamphlets. Wait, I will give you …"

He was amiability itself. He seemed in no hurry to get rid of me. Could it really be that he had no more important way of spending the afternoon? He asked about the living conditions in the East End of London and I tried to eke out the little knowledge I had collected in the course of a few days' slumming, three years before. His mere attention was flattery of the most stimulating kind. I found myself doing nearly all the talking. Half an hour later, with books and more papers to translate under my arm, I was about to say goodbye when Bayer asked:

"You have known Norris a long time?"

"More than a year, now," I replied, automatically, my mind registering no reaction to the question.

"Indeed? And where did you meet?"

This time I did not miss the tone in his voice. I looked hard at him. But his extraordinary eyes were neither suspicious, nor threatening, nor sly. Smiling pleasantly, he simply waited in silence for my answer.

"We got to know each other in the train, on the way to Berlin."

Bayer's glance became faintly amused. With disarming bland directness, he asked:

"You are good friends? You go to see him often?"

"Oh yes. Very often."

"You have not many English friends in Berlin, I think?"

"No."

Bayer nodded seriously. Then he rose from his chair and shook my hand. "I have to go now and work. If there is anything you wish to say to me, please do not hesitate to come and see me at any time."

"Thank you very much."

So that was it, I thought, on my way down the shabby staircase. None of them trusted Arthur. Bayer didn't trust him but he was prepared to make use of him, with all due precautions. And to make use of me, too, as a convenient spy on Arthur's movements. It wasn't necessary to let me into the secret. I could so easily be pumped. I felt angry, and at the same time rather amused.

After all, one couldn't blame them.

Chapter Seven

OTTO TURNED UP at Arthur's about a week later, unshaved and badly in need of a meal. They had let him out of prison the day before. When I went round to the flat that evening, I found him with Arthur in the dining-room, having just finished a substantial supper.

"And what did they use to give you on Sundays?" he was asking as I came in. "We got pea-soup with a sausage in it. Not so bad."

"Let me see now," Arthur reflected. "I'm afraid I really can't remember. In any case, I never had much appetite ... Ah, my dear William, here you are! Please take a chair. That is, if you don't disdain the company of two old gaol-birds. Otto and I were just comparing notes."

The day before Arthur and I visited the Alexanderplatz, Otto and Anni had had a quarrel. Otto had wanted to give fifteen pfennigs to a man who came round collecting for a strike fund of the I.A.H. Anni had refused to agree to this, "on principle." "Why should the dirty communists have my money?" she had said. "I have to work hard enough to earn it." The possessive pronoun challenged Otto's accepted status and rights; he generously disregarded it. But the adjective had really shocked him. He had slapped her face, "not hard" he assured us, but violently enough to make her turn a somersault over the bed and land with her head against the wall; the bump had dislodged a framed photograph of Stalin, which had fallen to the ground and smashed its glass. Anni had begun to curse him and cry. "That'll teach you not to talk about things you don't understand," Otto had told her, not unkindly. Communism had always been a delicate subject between them. "I'm sick of you," cried Anni, "and all your bloody Reds. Get out of here!" She had thrown the photograph-frame at him and missed.

Thinking all this over carefully, in the neighbouring *Lokal*, Otto had come to the conclusion that he was the injured party. Pained and angry, he began drinking *Korn*. He drank a good deal. He was still drinking at nine o'clock in the evening, when a boy named Erich, whom he knew, came in, selling biscuits. Erich, with his basket, went the round of the cafés and restaurants in the whole district, carrying messages and picking up gossip. He told Otto that he had just seen Anni in a Nazi *Lokal* on the Kreuzberg, with Werner Baldow.

Werner was an old enemy of Otto's, both political and private. A year ago, he had left the communist cell to which Otto belonged and joined the local Nazi storm-troop. He had always been sweet on Anni. Otto, who was pretty drunk by this time, did what even he would never have dared when sober; he jumped up and set off for the Nazi *Lokal* alone. Two policemen who happened to pass the place a minute or two after he entered it probably saved him from getting broken bones. He had just been flung out for the second time and wanted to go in again. The policemen removed him with difficulty; he bit and kicked on the way to the station. The Nazis, of course, were virtuously indignant. The incident featured in their newspapers next day as "an unprovoked and cowardly attack on a National-Socialist *Lokal* by ten armed communists, nine of whom made a successful escape." Otto had the cutting in his pocket-book and showed it to us with pride. He had been unable to get at Werner himself. Werner had retreated with Anni into a room at the back of the *Lokal* as soon as he had come in.

"And he can keep her, the dirty bitch," added Otto violently. "I wouldn't have her again if she came to me on her knees."

"Well, well," Arthur began to murmur automatically, "we live in stirring times ..."

He pulled himself up abruptly. Something was wrong. His eyes wandered uneasily over the array of plates and dishes, like an actor deprived of his cue. There was no teapot on the table.

Not many days after this, Arthur telephoned to tell me that Otto and Anni had made it up.

"I felt sure you'd be glad to hear. I may say that I myself was to some extent instrumental in the good work. Yes ... Blessed are the peacemakers ... As a matter of fact, I was particularly interested in effecting a reconciliation just now, in view of a little anniversary which falls due next Wednesday ... You didn't know? Yes, I shall be fifty-three. Thank you, dear boy. Thank you. I must confess I find it difficult to become accustomed to the thought that the yellow leaf is upon me ... And now, may I invite you to a trifling banquet? The fair sex will be represented. Besides the reunited pair, there will be Madame Olga and two other of my more doubtful and charming acquaintances. I shall have the sitting-room carpet taken up, so that the younger members of the party can dance. Is that nice?"

"Very nice indeed."

On Wednesday evening I had to give an unexpected lesson and arrived at Arthur's flat later than I intended. I found Hermann waiting downstairs at the house door to let me in.

"I'm so sorry," I said. "I hope you haven't been standing here long?"

"It's all right," Hermann answered briefly. He unlocked the door and led the way upstairs. What a dreary creature he is, I thought. He can't even brighten up for a birthday party.

I discovered Arthur in the sitting-room. He was reclining on the sofa in his shirt-sleeves, his hands folded in his lap.

"Here you are, William."

"Arthur, I'm most terribly sorry. I hurried as much as I

could. I thought I should never get away. That old girl I told you about arrived unexpectedly and insisted on having a two-hour lesson. She merely wanted to tell me about the way her daughter had been behaving. I thought she'd never stop ... Why, what's the matter? You don't look well."

Arthur sadly scratched his chin.

"I'm very depressed, dear boy."

"But why? What about? ... I say, where are your other guests? Haven't they come yet?"

"They came. I was obliged to send them away."

"Then you *are* ill?"

"No, William. Not ill. I fear I'm getting old. I have always hated scenes and now I find them altogether too much for me."

"Who's been making a scene?"

Arthur raised himself slowly from his chair. I had a sudden glimpse of him as he would be in twenty years' time; shaky and rather pathetic.

"It's a long story, William. Shall we have something to eat first? I'm afraid I can only offer you scrambled eggs and beer; if, indeed, there is any *beer.*"

"It doesn't matter if there isn't. I've brought you a little present."

I produced a bottle of cognac which I had been holding behind my back.

"My dear boy, you overwhelm me. You shouldn't, you know. You really shouldn't. Are you sure you can afford it?"

"Oh, yes, easily. I'm saving quite a lot of money nowadays."

"I always," Arthur shook his head sadly, "look upon the capacity to save money as little short of miraculous."

Our footsteps echoed loudly through the flat as we crossed the bare boards where the carpet had been.

"All was prepared for the festivities, when the spectre appeared to forbid the feast." Arthur chuckled nervously and rubbed his hands together.

> "Ah, but the Apparition, the dumb sign,
> The beckoning finger bidding me forgo

The fellowship, the converse, and the wine,
The songs, the festal glow!

"Rather apt here, I think. I hope you know your William Watson? I have always regarded him as the greatest of the moderns."

The dining-room was draped with paper festoons in preparation for the party; Chinese lanterns were suspended above the table. On seeing them, Arthur shook his head.

"Shall we have these things taken down, William? Will they depress you too much, do you think?"

"I don't see why they should," I said. "On the contrary, they ought to cheer us up. After all, whatever has happened, it's still your birthday."

"Well, well. You may be right. You're always so philosophical. The blows of fate are indeed cruel."

Hermann gloomily brought in the eggs. He reported, with rather bitter satisfaction, that there was no butter.

"No butter," Arthur repeated. "No butter. My humiliation as a host is complete ... Who would think, to see me now, that I have entertained more than one member of a royal family under my own roof? This evening I had intended to set a sumptuous repast before you. I won't make your mouth water by reciting the menu."

"I think the eggs are very nice. I'm only sorry that you had to send your guests away."

"So am I, William. So am I. Unfortunately, it was impossible to ask them to stay. I shouldn't have dared face Anni's displeasure. She was naturally expecting to find a groaning board ... And, in any case, Hermann told me there weren't enough eggs in the house."

"Arthur, do tell me now what has happened."

He smiled at my impatience, enjoying a mystery, as always. Thoughtfully he squeezed his collapsed chin between finger and thumb.

"Well, William, the somewhat sordid story which I am about to relate to you centres on the sitting-room carpet."

"Which you had taken up for the dancing?" Arthur shook his head.

"It was not, I regret to say, taken up for the dancing. That was merely *façon de parler.* I didn't wish to distress one of your sympathetic nature unnecessarily."

"You mean, you've sold it?"

"Not sold, William. You should know me better. I never sell if I can pawn."

"I'm sorry. It was a nice carpet."

"It was indeed ... And worth very much more than the two hundred marks I got for it. But one mustn't expect too much these days ... At all events, it would have covered the expenses of the little celebration I had planned. Unfortunately," here Arthur glanced towards the door, "the eagle, or, shall I say, the vulture eye of Schmidt lighted upon the vacant space left by the carpet, and his uncanny acumen rejected almost immediately the very plausible explanation which I gave for its disappearance. He was very cruel to me. Very firm ... To cut a long story short, I was left, at the end of our most unpleasant interview, with the sum of four marks, seventy-five pfennigs. The last twenty-five pfennigs were an unfortunate afterthought. He wanted them for his bus-fare home."

"He actually took away your money?"

"Yes, it *was* my money, wasn't it?" said Arthur eagerly, seizing this little crumb of encouragement. "That's just what I told him. But he only shouted at me in the most dreadful way."

"I never heard anything like it. I wonder you don't sack him."

"Well, William, I'll tell you. The reason is very simple. I owe him nine months' wages."

"Yes, I supposed there was something like that. All the same, it's no reason why you should allow yourself to be shouted at. I wouldn't have put up with it."

"Ah, my dear boy, you're always so firm. I only wish I'd had you there to protect me. I feel sure you would have been able to deal with him. Although I must say," Arthur added doubtfully, "Schmidt can be terribly firm when he likes."

"But, Arthur, do you seriously mean to tell me that you intended spending two hundred marks on a dinner for seven people? I never heard anything so fantastic."

"There were to have been little presents," said Arthur meekly. "Something for each of you."

"It would have been lovely, of course ... But such extravagance ... You're so hard up that you can only eat eggs, and yet, when you do get some cash, you propose to blow it immediately."

"Don't *you* start lecturing me, too, William, or I shall cry. I can't help my little weaknesses. Life would be drab indeed if we didn't sometimes allow ourselves a treat."

"All right," I said, laughing. "I won't lecture you. In your place, I'd probably have done just the same."

After supper, when we had returned with the cognac into the denuded sitting-room, I asked Arthur if he had seen Bayer lately. The change which came over his face at the mention of the name surprised me. His soft mouth pursed peevishly. Avoiding my glance, he frowned and abruptly shook his head.

"I don't go there more than I can help."

"Why?"

I had seldom seen him like this. He seemed, indeed, annoyed with me for having asked the question. For a moment he was silent. Then he broke out, with childish petulance:

"I don't go there because I don't like to go. Because it upsets me to go. The disorder in that office is terrible. It depresses me. It offends a person of my sensibilities to see such entire lack of method ... Do you know, the other day Bayer lost a most important document, and where do you think it was found? In the waste-paper basket. Actually ... to think that those people's wages are paid out of the hard-earned savings of the workers. It makes one's blood boil ... And, of course, the whole place is infested with spies. Bayer even knows their names ... And what does he do about it? Nothing. Absolutely nothing. He doesn't seem to care. That's what so infuriates me; that happy-go-lucky way of doing things. Why, in Russia, they'd simply be put against the wall and shot."

I grinned. Arthur as the militant revolutionary was a little too good to be true.

"You used to admire him so much."

"Oh, he's an able enough man in his way. No doubt about that." Arthur furtively rubbed his chin. His teeth were bared in a snarl of an old lion. "I've been very much disappointed in Bayer," he added.

"Indeed?"

"Yes." Some last vestiges of caution visibly held him back. But no. The temptation was too exquisite. "William, if I tell you something you must promise on all you hold sacred that it will go no farther."

"I promise."

"Very well. When I threw in my lot with the Party, or, rather, promised it my help (and though I say it who shouldn't, I am in a position to help them in many quarters to which they have not hitherto had access)—"

"I'm sure you are."

"I stipulated, very naturally I think, for a (how shall I put it?)—let us say–a *quid pro quo*." Arthur paused and glanced at me anxiously. "I hope, William, that that doesn't shock you?"

"Not in the least."

"I'm very glad. I might have known that you'd look at the thing in a sensible light ... After all, one's a man of the world. Flags and banners and catchwords are all very well for the rank and file, but the leaders know that a political campaign can't be carried on without money. I talked this over with Bayer at the time when I was considering taking the plunge, and, I must say, he was very reasonable about it. He quite saw that, crippled as I am with five thousand pounds' worth of debts ..."

"My God, is it as much as that?"

"It is, I'm sorry to say. Of course, not all my engagements are equally pressing ... Where was I? Yes. Crippled as I am with debts I am hardly in a position to be of much service to the Cause. As you know yourself, I am subject to all sorts of vulgar embarrassments."

"And Bayer agreed to pay some of them?"

"You put things with your usual directness, William. Well, yes, I may say that he hinted, most distinctly hinted, that Moscow would not be ungrateful if I fulfilled my first mission successfully. I did so. Bayer would be the first to admit that. And what has happened? Nothing. Of course, I know it's not altogether his fault. His own salary and that of the typists and clerks in his office is often months overdue. But it's nonetheless annoying for that. And I can't help feeling that he doesn't press my claim as much as he might. He even seems to regard it as rather funny when I come to him and complain that I've barely enough money for my next meal ... Do you know, I'm still owed for my trip to Paris? I had to pay the fare out of my own pocket; and imagining, naturally enough, that the expenses, at least, would be defrayed, I travelled first class."

"Poor Arthur!" I had some trouble to avoid laughing. "And what shall you do now? Is there any prospect of this money coming after all?"

"I should think none," said Arthur gloomily.

"Look here, let me lend you some. I've got ten marks."

"No, thank you, William. I appreciate the thought, but I couldn't borrow from you. I feel that it would spoil our beautiful friendship. No, I shall wait two days more; then I shall take certain steps. And, if these are not successful, I shall know what to do."

"You're very mysterious." For an instant the thought even passed through my mind that Arthur was perhaps meditating suicide. But the very idea of his attempting to kill himself was so absurd that it made me begin to smile. "I hope everything will go off all right," I added, as we said goodbye.

"So do I, my dear William. So do I." Arthur glanced cautiously down the staircase. "Please give my regards to the divine Schroeder."

"You really must come and visit us some day soon. It's such a long time since you've been. She's pining away without you."

"With the greatest pleasure, when all these troubles are over. If they ever are." Arthur sighed deeply. "Good night, dear boy. God bless you."

Chapter Eight

THE NEXT DAY, Thursday, I was busy with lessons. On Friday I tried three times to ring up Arthur's flat, but the number was always engaged. On Saturday I went away for the week-end to see some friends in Hamburg. I didn't get back to Berlin until late Monday afternoon. That evening I dialled Arthur's number, wanting to tell him about my visit; again there was no reply. I rang four times, at intervals of half an hour, and then complained to the operator. She told me, in official language, that "the subscriber's instrument' was "no longer in use."

I wasn't particularly surprised. In the present state of Arthur's finances, it was hardly to be expected that he would have settled his telephone bill. All the same, I thought, he might have come to see me or sent a note. But no doubt he was busy, too.

Three more days went by. It was seldom that we had ever let a whole week pass without a meeting or, at any rate, a telephone conversation. Perhaps Arthur was ill. Indeed, the more I thought about it, the surer I felt that this must be the explanation of his silence. He had probably worried himself into a nervous breakdown over his debts. And, all this while,

I had been neglecting him. I felt suddenly very guilty. I would go round and see him, I decided, that same afternoon.

Some premonition or pang of conscience made me hurry. I reached the Courbierestrasse in record time, ran quickly upstairs, and, still panting, rang the bell. After all, Arthur was no longer young. The life he had been leading was enough to break anybody down; and he had a weak heart. I must be prepared to hear serious news. Supposing ... hullo, what was this? In my haste, I must have miscounted the number of floors. I was standing in front of a door without a name-plate: the door of a strange flat. It was one of those silly embarrassing things which always happen when one lets oneself get flustered. My first impulse was to run away, up or down stairs, I wasn't quite sure which. But, after all, I had rung these people's bell. The best thing would be to wait until somebody answered it, and then explain my mistake.

I waited; one minute, two, three. The door didn't open. There was nobody home, it seemed. I had been saved from making a fool of myself after all.

But now I noticed something else. On both the doors which faced me were little squares of paint which were darker than the rest of the woodwork. There was no doubt about it; they were the marks left by recently removed name-plates. I could even see the tiny holes where the screws had been.

A kind of panic seized me. Within half a minute I had run up the stairs to the top of the house, then down again to the bottom; very quickly and lightly, as one sometimes runs in a nightmare. Arthur's two name-plates were nowhere to be found. But wait: perhaps I was in the wrong house altogether. I had done stupider things before now. I went out into the street and looked at the number over the entrance. No, there was no mistake there.

I don't know what I mightn't have done, at that moment, if the portress herself hadn't appeared. She knew me by sight and nodded ungraciously. She plainly hadn't much use for Arthur's callers. No doubt the visits of the bailiff had got the house a bad name.

"If you're looking for your friend," she maliciously emphasized the word, "you're too late. He's gone."

"Gone?"

"Yes. Two days ago. The flat's to let. Didn't you know?"

I suppose my face was a comic picture of dismay, for she added unpleasantly: "You aren't the only one he didn't tell. There've been a dozen round here already. Owed you some money, did he?"

"Where's he gone to?" I asked dully.

"I'm sure I don't know, or care. That cook of his comes round here and collects the letters. You'd better ask him."

"I can't. I don't know where he lives."

"Then I can't help you," said the portress with a certain vicious satisfaction. Arthur must have neglected to tip her. "Why don't you try the police?"

With this parting shot she went into her lodge and slammed the door. I walked slowly away down the street, feeling rather dazed.

My question was soon answered, however. The next morning I got a letter, dated from a hotel in Prague:

> MY DEAR WILLIAM,
>
> Do forgive me. I was compelled to leave Berlin at very short notice and under conditions of secrecy which made it impossible for me to communicate with you. The little *operation* about which I spoke to you was, alas, the reverse of successful, and the doctor ordered an immediate *change of air.* So *unhealthy,* indeed, had the atmosphere of Berlin become for one of my peculiar constitution, that, had I remained another week, *dangerous complications* would almost certainly have arisen.
>
> My *lares and penates* have all been sold and the proceeds largely swallowed up by the demands of my various satellites. I don't complain of that. They

have, with *one* exception, served me faithfully, and the labourer is worthy of his hire. As for that *one*, I shall not permit his odious name to pass my lips again. Suffice it to say that he was and is a scoundrel of the *deepest dye* and has behaved as such.

I find life here very pleasant. The cooking is good, not so good as in my beloved incomparable Paris, whither I hope, next Wednesday, to wend my weary steps, but still far better than anything which barbarous Berlin could provide. Nor are the consolations of the fair and *cruel* sex absent. Already, under the grateful influence of civilized comfort, I put forth my leaves, I expand. To such an extent, indeed, have I already expanded that I fear I shall arrive in Paris almost devoid of means. Never mind. The Mammon of Unrighteousness will, no doubt, be ready to receive me into habitations which, if not everlasting, will at least give me time to look round.

Please convey to our mutual friend my most fraternal greetings and tell him that I shall not fail, on arriving, to execute his various commissions.

Do write soon and regale me with your inimitable wit.

As always, your affectionate

ARTHUR.

My first reaction was to feel, perhaps unreasonably, angry. I had to admit to myself that my feeling for Arthur had been largely possessive. He was my discovery, my property. I was as hurt as a spinster who has been deserted by her cat. And yet, after all, how silly of me. Arthur was his own master; he wasn't accountable to me for his actions. I began to look round for excuses for his conduct, and, like an indulgent parent, easily found them. Hadn't he, indeed, behaved with considerable nobility? Threatened from every side, he had faced his troubles alone. He had carefully avoided involving me in possible future unpleasantness with the authorities. After all, he had said to himself, I am leaving this country, but William has to stay here and earn his living; I have no right to indulge my personal feelings at his expense. I pictured Arthur taking a last hurried stroll down our street, glancing up with furtive sadness at the window of my room, hesitating, walking sorrowfully away. The end of it was that I sat down and wrote him a chatty, affectionate letter, asking no questions and, indeed, avoiding any remark which might compromise either him or myself. Frl. Schroeder, who was much upset at the news of Arthur's departure, added a long postscript. He was never to forget, she wrote, that there was *one* house in Berlin where he would always be welcome.

My curiosity was far from being satisfied. The obvious thing was to question Otto, but where was I to find him? I decided to try Olga's for a start. Anni, I knew, rented a bedroom there.

I hadn't seen Olga since that party in the small hours of the New Year; but Arthur, who sometimes visited her in the way of business, had told me a good deal about her from time to time. Like most people who still contrived to earn a living in those bankrupt days, she was a woman of numerous occupations. "Not to put too fine a point upon it," as Arthur was fond of saying, she was a procuress, a cocaine-seller, and a receiver of stolen goods; she also let lodgings, took in washing and, when in the mood, did exquisite fancy needlework. Arthur once showed me a tablecentre she had given him for Christmas which was quite a work of art.

I found the house without difficulty and passed under the archway into the court. The courtyard was narrow and deep, like a coffin standing on end. The head of the coffin rested on the earth, for the house-fronts inclined slightly inwards. They were held apart by huge baulks, spanning the gap, high up, against the grey square of sky. Down here, at the bottom, where the rays of the sun could never penetrate, there was a deep twilight, like the light in a mountain gorge. On three sides of the court were windows; on the fourth, an immense blank wall, about eighty feet high, whose plaster surface had swollen into blisters and burst, leaving raw, sooty scars. At the foot of this ghastly precipice stood a queer little hut, probably an outdoor lavatory. Beside it was a broken hand-cart with only one wheel, and a printed notice, now almost illegible, stating the hours at which the inhabitants of the tenement were allowed to beat their carpets.

The staircase, even at this hour of the afternoon, was very dark. I stumbled up it, counting the landings, and knocked at a door which I hoped was the right one. There was a shuffle of slippers, a clink of keys, and the door opened a little way, on the chain.

"Who's there?" a woman's voice asked.

"William," I said.

The name made no impression. The door began, doubtfully, to shut.

"A friend of Arthur's," I added hastily, trying to make my voice sound reassuring. I couldn't see what sort of person I was talking to; inside the flat it was pitch black. It was like speaking to a priest in a confessional.

"Wait a minute," said the voice.

The door shut and the slippers shuffled away. Other footsteps returned. The door reopened and the electric light was switched on in the narrow hall. On the threshold stood Olga herself. Her mighty form was enveloped in a kimono of garish colours which she wore with the majesty of a priestess in her ceremonial robes. I hadn't remembered her as being quite so enormous.

"Well?" she said. "What do you want?"

She hadn't recognized me. For all she knew I might be a detective. Her tone was aggressive and harsh; it showed not the least trace of hesitation or fear. She was ready for all her enemies. Her hard blue eyes, ceaselessly watchful as the eyes of a tigress, moved away over my shoulder into the gloomy well of the staircase. She was wondering whether I had come alone.

"May I speak to Frl. Anni?" I said politely.

"You can't. She's busy."

My English accent had reassured her, however; for she added briefly: "Come inside," and turned, leading the way into the sitting-room. She left me with entire indifference to shut the outer door. I did so meekly and followed.

Standing on the sitting-room table was Otto, in his shirt-sleeves, tinkering with the converted gasolier.

"Why, it's Willi!" he cried, jumping down and dealing me a staggering clap on the shoulder.

We shook hands. Olga lowered herself into a chair facing mine with the deliberation and sinister dignity of a fortune-teller. The bracelets jangled harshly on her swollen wrists. I wondered how old she was; perhaps not more than thirty-five, for there were no wrinkles on her puffy, waxen face. I didn't much like her hearing what I had to say to Otto, but she had plainly no intention of moving as long as I was in the flat. Her blue doll's eyes held mine in a brutal, unwinking regard.

"Haven't I seen you somewhere before?"

"You've seen me in this room," I said, "drunk."

"So." Olga's bosom shook silently. She had laughed.

"Did you see Arthur before he left?" I asked Otto, at the end of a long pause.

Yes, Anni and Otto had both seen him, though quite by chance, as it appeared. Happening to look in on the Sunday afternoon, they had discovered Arthur in the midst of his packing. There had been a great deal of telephoning and running hither and thither. And then Schmidt had appeared. He and Arthur had retired into the bedroom for a conference, and soon Otto and Anni had heard loud, angry voices. Schmidt had come out of the bedroom, with Arthur following him in a state of ineffectual rage. Otto hadn't been able to understand very clearly what it was all about, but the Baron had had something to do with it, and money. Arthur was angry because of something Schmidt had said to the Baron; Schmidt was insulting and contemptuous by turns. Arthur had cried: "You've shown not only the blackest ingratitude, but downright treachery!" Otto was quite positive about this. The phrase seemed to have a special impression on him; perhaps because the word "treachery" had a definitely political flavour in his mind. Indeed, he quite took it for granted that Schmidt had somehow betrayed the Communist Party. "The very first time I saw him, I said to Anni, 'I shouldn't wonder if he's been sent to spy on Arthur. He looks like a Nazi, with that great big swollen head of his.'"

What followed had confirmed Otto in his opinion. Schmidt had been just about to leave the flat when he turned and said to Arthur:

"Well, I'm off. I'll leave you to the tender mercies of your precious communist friends. And when they've swindled you out of your last pfennig ..."

He hadn't got any farther. For Otto, puzzled by all this talk and relieved at last to hear something which he could understand and resent, had taken Schmidt out of the flat by the back of the collar and sent him flying downstairs with a heavy kick on the bottom. Otto, in his narrative, dwelt on the kick with special pride and pleasure. It had been one of the kicks of his life, an inspired kick, beautifully judged and timed. He was anxious that I should understand just how and where it had landed. He made me stand up, and touched me lightly on the buttock with his toe. I was a little uneasy, knowing what an effort of self-control it cost him not to let fly.

"My word, Willi, you should have heard him land! Bing! Bong! Crash! For a minute he didn't seem to know where he was or what had happened to him. And then he began to blubber, just like a baby. I was so weak with laughing at him you could have pushed me downstairs with one finger."

And Otto began to laugh now, as he said it. He laughed heartily, without the least malice or savagery. He bore the discomfited Schmidt no grudge.

I asked whether anything more had been heard of him.

Otto didn't know. Schmidt had picked himself up, slowly and painfully, sobbed out some inarticulate threat, and limped away downstairs. And Arthur, who had been present in the background, had shaken his head doubtfully and protested.

"You shouldn't have done that, you know."

"Arthur's much too kind-hearted," added Otto, coming to the end of his story. "He trusts everybody. And what thanks does he get for it? None. He's always being swindled and betrayed."

No comment on this last remark seemed adequate. I said that I must be going.

Something about me seemed to amuse Olga. Her bosom silently quivered. Without warning, as we reached the door, she gave my cheek a rough, deliberate pinch, as though she were plucking a plum from a tree.

"You're a nice boy," she chuckled harshly. "You must come round here one evening. I'll teach you something you didn't know before."

"You ought to try it once with Olga, Willi," Otto seriously advised. "It's well worth the money."

"I'm sure it is," I said politely, and hurried downstairs.

A few days later, I had a rendezvous with Fritz Wendel at the Troika. Arriving rather too early, I sat down at the bar and found the Baron on the stool next to my own.

"Hullo, Kuno!"

"Good evening."

He inclined his sleek head stiffly. To my surprise, he didn't seem at all pleased to see me. Indeed, quite the reverse. His monocle gleamed polite hostility; his naked eye was evasive and shifty.

"I haven't seen you for ages," I said brightly, trying to appear serenely unconscious of his manner.

His eye travelled round the room; he was positively searching for help, but nobody answered his appeal. The place was still nearly empty. The barman edged over towards us.

"What'll you have to drink?" I asked. His dislike of my society was beginning to intrigue me.

"Er—nothing, thank you. You see, I have to be going."

"What, you're leaving us so soon, Herr Baron?" put in the barman affably; unconsciously adding to his discomfort: "Why, you've hardly been here five minutes, you know."

"Have you heard from Arthur Norris?" With deliberate malice I disregarded his attempts to dismount from his stool. He couldn't do so until I had pushed mine back a little.

The name made Kuno visibly wince.

"No." His tone was icy. "I have not."

"He's in Paris, you know."

"Indeed?"

"Well," I said heartily, "I mustn't keep you any longer." I held out my hand. He barely touched it.

"Goodbye."

Released at last, he made like an arrow for the door. One might have thought that he was escaping from a plague hospital. The barman discreetly smiled, picked up the coins and shovelled them into the till. He had seen spongers snubbed before.

I was left with another mystery to solve.

Like a long train which stops at every dingy little station, the winter dragged slowly past. Each week there were new emergency decrees. Brüning's weary episcopal voice issued commands to the shopkeepers, and was not obeyed. "It's Fascism," complained the Social Democrats. "He's weak," said Helen Pratt. "What these swine need is a man with hair on his chest." The Hessen Document was discovered; but nobody really cared. There had been one scandal too many. The exhausted public had been fed with surprises to the point of indigestion. People said that the Nazis would be in power by Christmas; but Christmas came and they were not. Arthur sent me the compliments of the season on a postcard of the Eiffel Tower.

Chapter Eight

Berlin was in a state of civil war. Hate exploded suddenly, without warning, out of nowhere; at street corners, in restaurants, cinemas, dance halls, swimming-baths; at midnight, after breakfast, in the middle of the afternoon. Knives were whipped out, blows were dealt with spiked rings, beer-mugs, chair-legs, or leaded clubs; bullets slashed the advertisements on the poster-columns, rebounded from the iron roofs of latrines. In the middle of a crowded street a young man would be attacked, stripped, thrashed, and left bleeding on the pavement; in fifteen seconds it was all over and the assailants had disappeared. Otto got a gash over the eye with a razor in a battle on a fair-ground near the Cöpernickerstrasse. The doctor put in three stitches and he was in hospital for a week. The newspapers were full of deathbed photographs of rival martyrs, Nazi, Reichsbanner, and Communist. My pupils looked at them and shook their heads, apologizing to me for the state of Germany. "Dear, dear!" they said, "it's terrible. It can't go on."

The murder reporters and the jazz-writers had inflated the German language beyond recall. The vocabulary of newspaper invective (traitor, Versailles-lackey, murder-swine, Marx-crook, Hitler-swamp, Red-pest) had come to resemble, through excessive use, the formal phraseology of politeness employed by the Chinese. The word *Liebe,* soaring from the Goethe standard, was no longer worth a whore's kiss. *Spring, moonlight, youth, roses, girl, darlings, heart, May:* such was the miserably devaluated currency dealt in by the authors of all those tangoes, waltzes, and fox-trots which advocated the private escape. Find a dear little sweetheart, they advised, and forget the slump, ignore the unemployed. Fly, they urged us, to Hawaii, to Naples, to the Never-Never-Vienna. Hugenberg, behind the Ufa, was serving up nationalism to suit all tastes. He produced battlefield epics, farces of barrack-room life, operettas in which the jinks of a pre-war military aristocracy were reclothed in the fashions of 1932. His brilliant directors and camera-men had to concentrate their talents on cynically beautiful shots of the bubbles in champagne and the sheen of lamplight on silk.

And morning after morning, all over the immense, damp, dreary town and the packing-case colonies of huts in the suburb allotments, young men were waking up to another workless empty day to be spent as they could best contrive; selling boot-laces, begging, playing draughts in the hall of the Labour Exchange, hanging about urinals, opening the doors of cars, helping with crates in the markets, gossiping, lounging, stealing, overhearing racing tips, sharing stumps of cigarette-ends picked up in the gutter, singing folk-songs for groschen in courtyards and between stations in the carriages of the Underground Railway. After the New Year, the snow fell, but did not lie; there was no money to be earned by sweeping it away. The shopkeepers rang all coins on the counter for fear of the forgers. Frl. Schroeder's astrologer foretold the end of the world. "Listen," said Fritz Wendel, between sips of a cocktail in the bar of the Eden Hotel, "I give a damn if this country goes communist. What I mean, we'd have to alter our ideas a bit. Hell, who cares?"

At the beginning of March, the posters for the Presidential Election began to appear. Hindenburg's portrait, with an inscription in gothic lettering beneath it, struck a frankly religious note: "He hath kept faith with you; be ye faithful unto Him." The Nazis managed to evolve a formula which dealt cleverly with this venerable icon and avoided the offence of blasphemy: "Honour Hindenburg; Vote for Hitler." Otto and his comrades set out every night, with paint-pots and brushes, on dangerous expeditions. They climbed high walls, scrambled along roofs, squirmed under hoardings; avoiding the police and the S. A. patrols. And next morning, passers-by would see Thälmann's name boldly inscribed in some prominent and inaccessible position. Otto gave me a bunch of little gum-backed labels: Vote for Thälmann, the Workers' Candidate. I carried these about in my pocket and stuck them on shop windows and doors when nobody was looking.

Brüning spoke in the Sport Palace. We must vote for Hindenburg, he told us, and save Germany. His gestures were sharp and admonitory; his spectacles gleamed emotion in the limelight. His voice quivered with dry academic passion. "Inflation," he threatened, and the audience shuddered. "Tannenberg," he reverently reminded: there was prolonged applause.

Bayer spoke in the Lustgarten, during a snowstorm, from the roof of a van; a tiny hatless figure gesticulating above the vast heaving sea of faces and banners. Behind him was the cold façade of the Schloss; and, lining its stone balustrade, the ranks of armed silent police. "Look at them," cried Bayer. "Poor chaps! It seems a shame to make them stand out of doors in weather like this. Never mind; they've got nice thick coats to keep them warm. Who gave them those coats? We did. Wasn't it kind of us? And who's going to give us coats? Ask me another."

"So the old boy's done the trick again," said Helen Pratt. "I knew he would. Won ten marks off them at the office, the poor fools."

It was the Wednesday after the election, and we were standing on the platform of the Zoo Station. Helen had come to see me off in the train to England.

"By the way," she added, "what became of that queer card you brought along one evening? Morris, wasn't his name?"

"Norris ... I don't know. I haven't heard from him for ages."

It was strange that she should have asked that, because I had been thinking about Arthur myself, only a moment before. In my mind, I always connected him with this station. It would soon be six months since he had gone away; it seemed like last week. The moment I got to London, I decided, I would write him a long letter.

Chapter Nine

NEVERTHELESS, I DIDN'T write. Why, I hardly know. I was lazy and the weather had turned warm. I thought of Arthur often; so often, indeed, that correspondence seemed unnecessary. It was as though we were in some kind of telepathic communication. Finally, I went away into the country for four months, and discovered, too late, that I'd left the post-card with his address in a drawer somewhere in London. Anyhow, it didn't much matter. He had probably left Paris ages ago by this time. If he wasn't in Berlin. The dear old Tauentzienstrasse hadn't changed. Looking out at it through the taxi window on my way from the station, I saw several Nazis in their new S.A. uniforms, now no longer forbidden. They strode along the street very stiff, and were saluted enthusiastically by elderly civilians. Others were posted at street corners, rattling collecting-boxes.

I climbed the familiar staircase. Before I had time to touch the bell, Frl. Schroeder rushed out to greet me with open arms. She must have been watching for my arrival.

"Herr Bradshaw! Herr Bradshaw! Herr Bradshaw! So you've come back to us at last! I declare I must give you a hug! How well you're looking! It hasn't seemed the same since you've been away."

"How have things been going here, Frl. Schroeder?"

"Well ... I suppose I mustn't complain. In the summer they were bad. But now ... Come inside, Herr Bradshaw. I've got a surprise for you."

Gleefully she beckoned me across the hall, flung open the door of the living-room with a dramatic gesture.

"Arthur!"

"My dear William, welcome to Germany!"

"I'd no idea ..."

"Herr Bradshaw, I declare you've grown!"

"Well ... well ... this is indeed a happy reunion. Berlin is herself once more. I propose that we adjourn to my room and drink a glass in celebration of Herr Bradshaw's return. You'll join us, Frl. Schroeder, I hope?"

"Oh ... Most kind of you, Herr Norris, I'm sure."

"After you."

"I couldn't think of it."

There was a good deal more polite deprecation and bowing before the two of them finally got through the doorway. Familiarity didn't seem to have spoilt their manners. Arthur was as gallant, Frl. Schroeder as coquettish as ever.

The big front bedroom was hardly recognizable. Arthur had moved the bed over into the corner by the window and pushed the sofa nearer to the stove. The stuffy-smelling pots of ferns had disappeared, so had the numerous little crochet mats on the dressing-table, and the metal figures of dogs on the bookcase. The three gorgeously tinted photochromes of bathing nymphs were also missing; in their place I recognized three etchings which had hung in Arthur's dining-room. And, concealing the wash-stand, was a handsome Japanese lacquer screen which used to stand in the hall of the Courbierestrasse flat.

"Flotsam," Arthur had followed the direction of my glance, "which I have been able, happily, to save from the wreck."

"Now, Herr Bradshaw," put in Frl. Schroeder, "tell me your candid opinion. Herr Norris will have it that those nymphs were ugly. I always thought them sweetly pretty myself. Of course, I know some people would call them old-fashioned."

"I shouldn't have said they were ugly," I replied, diplomatically. "But it's nice to have a change sometimes, don't you think?"

"Change is the spice of Life," Arthur murmured as he fetched a glass from the cupboard. Inside, I caught sight of an array of bottles: "Which may I offer you, William—kümmel or Benedictine? Frl. Schroeder, I know, prefers cherry brandy."

Now that I could see the two of them by daylight, I was struck by the contrast. Poor Frl. Schroeder seemed to have got much older; indeed, she was quite an old woman. Her face was pouched and wrinkled with worry, and her skin, despite a thick layer of rouge and powder, looked sallow. She hadn't been getting enough to eat. Arthur, on the other hand, looked positively younger. He was fatter in the cheeks and fresh as a rosebud; barbered, manicured, and perfumed. He wore a big turquoise ring I hadn't seen before, and an opulent new brown suit. His wig struck a daring, more luxuriant note. It was composed of glossy, waved locks, which wreathed themselves around his temples in tropical abundance. There was something jaunty, even bohemian, in his whole appearance. He might have been a popular actor or a rich violinist.

"How long have you been back here?" I asked.

"Let me see, it must be nearly two months now ... how time flies! I really must apologize for my shortcomings as a correspondent. I've been so very busy! and Frl. Schroeder seemed uncertain of your London address."

"We're neither of us much good at letter-writing, I'm afraid."

"The spirit was willing, dear boy. I hope you'll believe that. You were ever present in my thoughts. It is indeed a pleasure to have you back again. I feel that a load has been lifted from my mind already."

This sounded rather ominous. Perhaps he was on the rocks

again. I only hoped that poor Frl. Schroeder wouldn't have to suffer for it. There she sat, glass in hand, on the sofa, beaming, drinking in every word; her legs were so short that her black velvet shoes dangled an inch above the carpet.

"Just look, Herr Bradshaw," she extended her wrist, "what Herr Norris gave me for my birthday. I was so delighted, will you believe me, that I started crying."

It was a handsome-looking gold bracelet which must have cost at least fifty marks. I was really touched.

"How nice of you, Arthur!"

He blushed. He was quite confused.

"A trifling mark of esteem. I can't tell you what a comfort Frl. Schroeder has been to me. I should like to engage her permanently as my secretary."

"Oh, Herr Norris, how can you talk such nonsense!"

"I assure you, Frl. Schroeder, I'm quite in earnest."

"You see how he makes fun of a poor old woman, Herr Bradshaw."

She was slightly drunk. When Arthur poured her out a second glass of cherry brandy, she upset some of it over her dress. When the commotion which followed this accident had subsided, he said that he must be going out.

"Sorry as I am to break up this festive gathering ... duty calls. Yes, I shall hope to see you this evening, William. Shall we have dinner together? Would that be nice?"

"Very nice."

"Then I'll say *au revoir,* till eight o'clock."

I got up to go and unpack. Frl. Schroeder followed me into my room. She insisted on helping me. She was still tipsy and kept putting things into the wrong places; shirts into the drawer of the writing-table, books in the cupboard with the socks. She couldn't stop singing Arthur's praises.

"He came as if Heaven had sent him. I'd got into arrears with the rent, as I haven't done since the inflation days. The porter's wife came up to see me about it several times. 'Frl. Schroeder,' she said, 'we know you and we don't want to be hard on you. But we've all got to live.' I declare there were evenings when I was so depressed I'd half a mind to put my head in the oven. And then Herr Norris arrived. I thought he'd just come to pay me a visit as it were. 'How much do you charge for the front bedroom?' he asked. You could have knocked me over with a feather. 'Fifty,' I said. I didn't dare ask more, with the times so bad. I was trembling all over for fear he'd think it was too much. And what do you think he answered? 'Frl. Schroeder,' he said, 'I couldn't possibly dream of letting you have less than sixty. It would be robbery.' I tell you, Herr Bradshaw, I could have kissed his hand."

Tears stood in Frl. Schroeder's eyes. I was afraid she was going to break down.

"And he pays you regularly?"

"On the moment, Herr Bradshaw. He couldn't be more punctual if it was you yourself. I've never known anybody to be so particular. Why, do you know, he won't even let me run up a monthly bill for milk! He settles it by the week. I don't like to feel that I owe anyone a pfennig, he says ... I wish there was more like him."

That evening, when I suggested eating at the usual restaurant, Arthur, to my surprise, objected:

"It's so noisy there, dear boy. My sensitive nerves revolt against the thought of an evening of jazz. As for the cooking, it is remarkable, even in this benighted town, for its vileness. Let's go to the Montmartre."

"But, my dear Arthur, it's so terribly expensive."

"Never mind. Never mind. In this brief life, one cannot always be counting the cost. You're my guest this evening. Let's forget the cares of this harsh world for a few hours and enjoy ourselves."

"It's very kind of you."

At the Montmartre, Arthur ordered champagne.

"This is such a peculiarly auspicious event that I feel we may justifiably relax our rigid revolutionary standards."

I laughed: "Business seems to be flourishing with you, I must say."

Arthur squeezed his chin cautiously between finger and thumb.

"I can't complain, William. At the moment. No. But I fear I see breakers ahead."

"Are you still importing and exporting?"

"Not exactly that … No … Well, in a sense, perhaps."

"Have you been in Paris all this time?"

"More or less. On and off."

"What were you doing there?"

Arthur glanced uneasily round the luxurious little restaurant; smiled with great charm:

"That's a very leading question, my dear William."

"Were you working for Bayer?"

"Er—partly. Yes." A vagueness had come into Arthur's eyes. He was trying to edge away from the subject.

"And you've been seeing him since you got back to Berlin?"

"Of course." He looked at me with sudden suspicion. "Why do you ask?"

"I don't know. When I saw you last, you didn't seem very pleased with him, that's all."

"Bayer and I are on excellent terms." Arthur spoke with emphasis, paused and added:

"You haven't been telling anybody that I've quarrelled with him, have you?"

"No, of course not, Arthur. Who do you suppose I'd tell?"

Arthur was unmistakably relieved.

"I beg your pardon, William. I might have known that I could rely on your admirable discretion. But if, by any chance, the story were to get about that Bayer and I were not friendly, it might be exceedingly awkward for me, you understand?"

I laughed.

"No, Arthur. I don't understand anything."

Smiling, Arthur raised his glass.

"Have patience with me, William. You know, I always like

to have my little secrets. No doubt the time will come when I shall be able to give you an explanation."

"Or to invent one."

"Ha ha. Ha ha. You're as cruel as ever, I see ... which reminds me that I thoughtlessly made an appointment with Anni for ten o'clock ... so that perhaps we ought to be getting on with our dinner."

"Of course. You mustn't keep her waiting."

For the rest of the meal Arthur questioned me about London. The cities of Berlin and Paris were tactfully avoided.

Arthur had certainly transformed the daily routine of life at Frl. Schroeder's. Because he insisted on a hot bath every morning, she had to get up an hour earlier, in order to stoke the little old-fashioned boiler. She didn't complain of this. Indeed, she seemed to admire Arthur for the trouble he caused her.

"He's so particular, Herr Bradshaw. More like a lady than a gentleman. Everything in his room has its place, and I get into trouble if it isn't all just as he wants it. I must say, though, it's a pleasure to wait on anybody who takes such care of his things. You ought to see some of his shirts, and his ties. A perfect dream! And his silk underclothes! 'Herr Norris,' I said to him once, 'you should let *me* wear those; they're too fine for a man.' I was only joking, of course. Herr Norris does enjoy a joke. He takes in four daily papers, you know, not to mention the weekly illustrateds, and I'm not allowed to throw any of them away. They must all be piled up in their proper order, according to the dates, if you please, on top of the cupboard. It makes me wild, sometimes, when I think of the dust they're collecting. And then, every day, before he goes out, Herr Norris gives me a list as long as your arm of messages I've got to give to people who ring up or call. I have to remember all their names, and which ones he wants to see, and which he doesn't. The door-bell's for ever ringing, nowadays, with telegrams for Herr Norris, and express letters and air mail and I don't know what else. This last fortnight it's been specially bad. If you ask me, I think the ladies are his little weakness."

"What makes you think that, Frl. Schroeder?"

"Well, I've noticed that Herr Norris is always getting telegrams from Paris. I used to open them, at first, thinking it might be something important which Herr Norris would like to know at once. But I couldn't make head or tail of them. They were all from a lady named Margot. Very affectionate some of them were, too. 'I am sending you a hug,' and 'last time you forgot to enclose kisses.' I must say I should never have the nerve to write such things myself; fancy the clerks at the post office reading them! These French girls must be a shameless lot. From my experience when a woman makes a parade of her feelings like that, she's not worth much ... And then she wrote such a lot of nonsense besides."

"What sort of nonsense?"

"Oh, I forget half of it. Stuff about teapots and kettles and bread and butter and cake."

"How very queer."

"You're right, Herr Bradshaw. It is queer ... I'll tell you what I think." Frl. Schroeder lowered her voice and glanced towards the door; perhaps she had caught the trick from Arthur. "I believe it's a kind of secret language. You know? Every word has a double meaning."

"A code?"

"Yes, that's it." Frl. Schroeder nodded mysteriously.

"But why should this girl write telegrams to Herr Norris in code, do you suppose? It seems so pointless."

Frl. Schroeder smiled at my innocence.

"Ah, Herr Bradshaw, you don't know everything, although you're so clever and learned. It takes an old woman like me to understand little mysteries of that sort. It's perfectly plain: this Margot, as she calls herself (I don't suppose it's her real name), must be going to have a baby."

"And you think that Herr Norris ..."

Frl. Schroeder nodded her head vigorously.

"It's as clear as the nose on your face."

"Really, I must say, I hardly think …"

"Oh, it's all very well for you to laugh, Herr Bradshaw, but I'm right, you see if I'm not. After all, Herr Norris is still in the prime of life. I've known gentlemen have families who were old enough to be his father. And, besides, what other reason could she have for writing messages like that?"

"I'm sure I don't know."

"You see?" cried Frl. Schroeder triumphantly. "You don't know. Neither do I."

Every morning Frl. Schroeder would come shuffling through the flat at express speed, like a little steam-engine, screaming:

"Herr Norris! Herr Norris! Your bath is ready! If you don't come quick the boiler will explode!"

"Oh dear!" exclaimed Arthur, in English. "Just let me clap on my wig."

He was afraid to go into the bathroom until the water had been turned on and all danger of an explosion was over. Frl. Schroeder would rush in heroically, with face averted and, muffling her hand in a towel, wrench at the hot tap. If the bursting-point was already very near, this would at first emit only clouds of steam, while the water in the boiler boiled with a noise like thunder. Arthur, standing in the doorway, watched Frl. Schroeder's struggles with a nervous snarling grimace, ready at any moment to bolt for his life.

After the bath came the barber's boy, who was sent up daily from the hairdresser's at the corner to shave Arthur and to comb his wig.

"Even in the wilds of Asia," Arthur once told me, "I have never shaved myself when it could possibly be avoided. It's one of those sordid annoying operations which put one in a bad humour for the rest of the day."

When the barber had gone, Arthur would call to me:

"Come in, dear boy, I'm visible now. Come and talk to me while I powder my nose."

Seated before the dressing-table in a delicate mauve wrap,

Arthur would impart to me the various secrets of his toilet. He was astonishingly fastidious. It was a revelation to me to discover, after all this time, the complex preparations which led up to his every appearance in public. I hadn't dreamed, for example, that he spent ten minutes three times a week in thinning his eyebrows with a pair of pincers. ("Thinning, William; *not* plucking. That is a piece of effeminacy which I abhor.") A massage-roller occupied another fifteen minutes daily of his valuable time; and then there was a thorough manipulation of his cheeks with face cream (seven or eight minutes) and a little judicious powdering (three or four). Pedicure, of course, was an extra; but Arthur usually spent a few moments rubbing ointment on his toes to avert blisters and corns. Nor did he ever neglect a gargle and mouthwash. ("Coming into daily contact, as I do, with members of the proletariat, I have to defend myself against positive onslaughts of microbes.") All this is not to mention the days on which he actually made up his face. ("I felt I needed a dash of colour this morning; the weather's so depressing.") Or the great fortnightly ablution of his hands and wrists with depilatory lotion. ("I prefer not to be reminded of our kinship with the larger apes.")

After these tedious exertions, it was no wonder that Arthur had a healthy appetite for his breakfast. He had succeeded in coaching Frl. Schroeder as a toast-maker; nor did she once, after the first few days, bring him an unduly hard-boiled egg. He had home-made marmalade, prepared by an English lady who lived in Wilmersdorf and charged nearly double the market price. He used his own special coffee-pot, which he had brought with him from Paris, and drank a special blend of coffee, which had to be sent direct from Hamburg. "Little things in themselves," as Arthur said, "which I have come, through long and painful experience, to value more than many of the over-advertised and overrated luxuries of life."

At half past ten he went out, and I seldom saw him again until the evening. I was busy with my teaching. After lunch he made a habit of coming home and lying down for an hour on his bed. "Believe me or not, William, I am able to make my mind an absolute blank for whole minutes at a time. It's a matter of practice, of course. Without my siesta, I should quickly become a nervous wreck."

Three nights a week, Frl. Anni came; and Arthur indulged in his singular pleasures. The noise was perfectly audible in the living-room, where Frl. Schroeder sat sewing.

"Dear, dear!" she said to me once, "I do hope Herr Norris won't injure himself. He ought to be more careful at his time of life."

One afternoon, about a week after my arrival, I happened to be in the flat alone. Even Frl. Schroeder had gone out. The door-bell rang. It was a telegram for Arthur, from Paris.

The temptation was simply not to be resisted! and I didn't even struggle against it. To make things easier for me, the envelope had not been properly stuck down; it came open in my hand.

"Am very thirsty," I read, "hope another kettle will boil soon kisses are for good boys.—Margot."

I fetched a bottle of glue from my room and fixed the envelope down carefully. Then I left it on Arthur's table and went out to the cinema.

At dinner, that evening, Arthur was visibly depressed. Indeed, he seemed to have no appetite, and sat staring in front of him with a bilious frown.

"What's the matter?" I asked.

"Things in general, dear boy. The state of this wicked world. A touch of *Weltschmerz*, that's all."

"Cheer up. The course of true love never did run smooth, you know."

But Arthur didn't react. He didn't even ask me what I meant. Towards the end of our meal, I had to go to the back of the restaurant to make a telephone call. As I returned I saw that he was absorbed in reading a piece of paper which he stuffed hastily into his pocket as I approached. He wasn't quick enough. I had recognized the telegram.

Chapter Ten

Arthur looked up at me with eyes which were a little too innocent.

"By the way, William," his tone was carefully casual, "do you happen to be doing anything next Thursday evening?"

"Nothing that I know of."

"Excellent. Then may I invite you to a little dinner party?"

"That sounds very nice. Who else is coming?"

"Oh, it's to be a very small affair. Just ourselves and Baron von Pregnitz."

Arthur had brought out the name in the most offhand manner possible.

"Kuno!" I exclaimed.

"You seem very surprised, William, not to say displeased." He was the picture of innocence. "I always thought you and he were such good friends?"

"So did I, until the last time we met. He practically cut me dead."

"Oh, my dear boy, if you don't mind my saying so I think that must have been partly your imagination. I'm sure he'd never do a thing like that; it doesn't sound like him at all."

"You don't suggest I dreamed it, do you?"

"I'm not doubting your word for an instant, of course. If he was, as you say, a little brusque, I expect he was worried by his many duties. As you probably know, he has a post under the new administration."

"I think I did read about it in the newspapers, yes."

"And anyhow, even if he did behave a little strangely on the occasion you mention, I can assure you that he was acting under a misapprehension which has since been removed."

I smiled.

"You needn't make such a mystery out of it, Arthur. I know half the story already, so you may as well tell me the other half. Your secretary had something to do with it, I think?"

Arthur wrinkled his nose up with a ridiculously fastidious expression.

"Don't call him that, William, please. Just say Schmidt. I don't care to be reminded of the association. Those who are foolish enough to keep snakes as pets usually have cause to regret it, sooner or later."

"All right, then, Schmidt … Go on."

"I see that, as usual, you're better informed than I'd supposed," Arthur sighed. "Well, well, if you want to hear the whole melancholy truth, you must, painful as it is for me to dwell on. As you know, my last weeks at the Courbierestrasse were spent in a state of excruciating financial anxiety."

"I do indeed."

"Well, without going into a lot of sordid details, which are neither here nor there, I was compelled to try and raise money. I cast about in all sorts of likely and unlikely directions. And, as a last desperate resort when the wolf was literally scratching at the door, I put my pride in my pocket …"

"And asked Kuno to lend you some?"

"Thank you, dear boy. With your customary consideration for my feelings, you help me over the most painful part of the story … Yes, I sank so low. I violated one of my most sacred principles—never to borrow from a friend. (For I may say I did regard him as a friend, a dear friend.) Yes …"

"And he refused? The stingy brute!"

"No, William. There you go too fast. You misjudge him. I have no reason to suppose that he would have refused. Quite the contrary. This was the first time I had ever approached him. But Schmidt got to know of my intentions. I can only suppose he had been systematically opening all my letters. At any rate, he went straight to Pregnitz and advised him not to advance me the money; giving all sorts of reasons, most of which were the most monstrous slanders. Despite all my long experience of human nature, I should hardly have believed such treachery and ingratitude possible ..."

"Whatever made him do it?"

"Chiefly, I think, pure spite. As far as one can follow the workings of his foul mind. But, undoubtedly, the creature was afraid that, in this case, he would be deprived of his pound of flesh. He usually arranged these loans himself, you know, and subtracted a percentage before handing over the money at all ... It humbles me to the earth to have to tell you this."

"And I suppose he was right? I mean, you weren't going to give him any, this time, were you?"

"Well, no. After his villainous behaviour over the sitting-room carpet, it was hardly to be expected that I should. You remember the carpet?"

"I should think I did."

"The carpet incident was, so to speak, the declaration of war between us. Although I still endeavoured to meet his demands with the utmost fairness."

"And what did Kuno have to say to all this?"

"He was, naturally, most upset, and indignant. And, I must add, rather unnecessarily unkind. He wrote me a most unpleasant letter. Quite gentlemanly, of course; he is always that. But frigid. Very frigid."

"I'm surprised that he took Schmidt's word against yours."

"No doubt Schmidt had ways and means of convincing him. There are some incidents in my career, as you doubtless know, which are very easily capable of misinterpretation."

"And he brought me into it, as well?"

"I regret to say that he did. That pains me more than anything else in the whole affair; to think that you should have been dragged down into the mud in which I was already wallowing."

"What exactly did he tell Kuno about me?"

"He seems to have suggested, not to put too fine a point upon it, that you were an accomplice in my nefarious crimes."

"Well, I'm damned."

"I need hardly add that he painted us both as Bolsheviks of the deepest crimson."

"He flattered me there, I'm afraid."

"Well—er—yes. That's one way of looking at it, of course. Unfortunately, revolutionary ardour is no recommendation to the Baron's favour. His view of the members of the Left Wing is somewhat primitive. He imagines us with pockets full of bombs."

"And yet, in spite of all this, he's ready to have dinner with us next Thursday?"

"Oh, our relations are very different now, I'm glad to say. I've seen him several times since my return to Berlin. Considerable diplomacy was required, of course; but I think I've more or less convinced him of the absurdity of Schmidt's accusation. By a piece of good luck, I was able to be of service in a little matter. Pregnitz is essentially a reasonable man; he's always open to conviction."

I smiled: "You seem to have put yourself to a good deal of trouble on his account. I hope it'll prove to have been worth while."

"One of my characteristics, William, you may call it a weakness if you like, is that I can never bear to lose a friend, if it can possibly be avoided."

"And you're anxious that I shan't lose a friend either?"

"Well, yes, I must say, if I thought I had been the cause, even indirectly, of a permanent estrangement between Pregnitz and yourself, it would make me very unhappy. If any little doubts or resentments do still exist on either side, I sincerely hope that this meeting will put an end to them."

"There's no ill feeling as far as I'm concerned."

"I'm glad to hear you say that, dear boy. Very glad. It's so stupid to bear grudges. In this life one's apt to lose a great deal through a mistaken sense of pride."

"A great deal of money, certainly."

"Yes ... that too." Arthur pinched his chin and looked thoughtful. "Although I was speaking, just then, more from the spiritual point of view than the material."

His tone implied a gentle rebuke.

"By the way," I asked, "what's Schmidt doing now?"

"My dear William," Arthur looked pained, "how in the world should I know?"

"I thought he might have been bothering you."

"During my first month in Paris, he wrote me a number of letters full of the most preposterous threats and demands for money. I simply disregarded them. Since then, I've heard nothing more."

"He's never turned up at Frl. Schroeder's?"

"Thank God, no. Not up to now. It's one of my nightmares that he'll somehow discover the address."

"I suppose he's more or less bound to, sooner or later?"

"Don't say that, William. Don't say that, please ... I have enough to worry me as it is. The cup of my afflictions would indeed be full."

As we walked to the restaurant on the evening of the dinner-party, Arthur primed me with final instructions. "You will be most careful, won't you, dear boy, not to let drop any reference to Bayer or to our political beliefs?"

"I'm not completely mad."

"Of course not, William. Please don't think I meant anything offensive. But even the most cautious of us betray ourselves at times ... Just one other little point perhaps, at this stage of the proceedings, it would be more politic not to address

Pregnitz by his Christian name. It's as well to preserve one's distance. That sort of thing's so easily misunderstood."

"Don't you worry. I'll be as stiff as a poker."

"Not stiff, dear boy, I do beg. Perfectly easy, perfectly natural. A shade formal, perhaps, just at first. Let him make the advances. A little polite reserve, that's all."

"If you go on much longer you'll get me into such a state that I shan't be able to open my mouth."

We arrived at the restaurant to find Kuno already seated at the table Arthur had reserved. The cigarette between his fingers was burnt down almost to the end; his face wore an expression of well-bred boredom. At the sight of him Arthur positively gasped with horror.

"My dear Baron, do forgive me, please. I wouldn't have had this happen for the world. Did I say half past? I did? And you've been waiting a quarter of an hour? You overwhelm me with shame. Really, I don't know how to apologize enough."

Arthur's fulsomeness seemed to embarrass the Baron as much as it did himself. He made a faint, distasteful gesture with his fin-like hand and murmured something which I couldn't hear.

"... too stupid of me. I simply can't conceive how I can have been so foolish ..."

We all sat down. Arthur prattled on and on; his apologies developed like an air with variations. He blamed his memory and recalled other instances when it had failed him. ("I'm reminded of a most unfortunate occasion in Washington on which I entirely forgot to attend an important diplomatic function at the house of the Spanish Ambassador.") He found fault with his watch; lately, he told us, it had been gaining. ("I usually make a point, about this time of year, of sending it to the makers in Zürich to be overhauled.") And he assured the Baron, at least five times, that I had no responsibility whatever for the mistake. I wished I could sink through the floor. Arthur, I could see, was nervous and unaware of himself; the variations wavered uneasily and threatened, at every moment, to collapse into discords. I had seldom known him to be so verbose and never so boring. Kuno had retired behind his monocle. His face was as discreet as the menu, and as unintelligible.

By the middle of the fish, Arthur had talked himself out. A silence followed which was even more uncomfortable than his chatter. We sat round the elegant little dinner-table like three people absorbed in a difficult chess problem. Arthur manipulated his chin and cast furtive, despairing glances in my direction, signalling for help. I declined to respond. I was sulky and resentful. I'd come here this evening on the understanding that Arthur had already more or less patched things up with Kuno; that the way was paved to a general reconciliation. Nothing of the kind. Kuno was still suspicious of Arthur, and no wonder, considering the way he was behaving now. I felt his eye questioningly upon me from time to time and went on eating, looking neither to right nor to left.

"Mr Bradshaw's just returned from England." It was as though Arthur had given me a violent push into the middle of the stage. His tone implored me to play my part. They were both looking at me now. Kuno was interested but cautious; Arthur frankly abject. They were so funny in their different ways that I had to smile.

"Yes," I said, "at the beginning of the month."

"Excuse me, you were in London?"

"Part of the time, yes."

"Indeed?" Kuno's eyes lit up with a tender gleam. "And how was it there, may I ask?"

"We had lovely weather in September."

"Yes, I see ..." A faint, fishy smile played over his lips; he seemed to savour delicious memories. His monocle shone with a dreamy light. His distinguished, preserved profile became pensive and maudlin and sad.

"I shall always maintain," put in the incorrigible Arthur, "that London in September has a charm all its own. I remember one exceptionally beautiful autumn—in nineteen hundred and five. I used to stroll down to Waterloo Bridge before breakfast and admire St Paul's. At that time I had a suite at the Savoy Hotel ..."

Kuno appeared not to have heard him.

"And, excuse me, how are the Horse Guards?"

"Still sitting there."

"Yes? I am glad to hear this, you see. Very glad ..."

I grinned. Kuno smiled, fishy and subtle. Arthur uttered a surprisingly coarse snigger which he instantly checked with his hand. Then Kuno threw back his head and laughed out loud: "Ho! Ho! Ho!" I had never heard him really laugh before. His laugh was a curiosity, an heirloom; something handed down from the dinner-tables of the last century; aristocratic, manly and sham, scarcely to be heard nowadays except on the legitimate stage. He seemed a little ashamed of it himself, for, recovering, he added, in a tone of apology:

"You see, excuse me, I can remember them very well."

"I'm reminded," Arthur leaned forward across the table; his tone became spicy, "of a story which used to be told about a certain peer of the realm ... let's call him Lord X. I can vouch for it, because I met him once in Cairo, a most eccentric man ..."

There was no doubt about it, the party had been saved. I began to breathe more freely. Kuno relaxed by imperceptible stages, from polite suspicion to positive jollity. Arthur, recovering his nerve, was naughty and funny. We drank a good deal of brandy and three whole bottles of Pommard. I told an extremely stupid story about the two Scotsmen who went into a synagogue. Kuno started to nudge me with his foot. In an absurdly short space of time I looked at the clock and saw it was eleven.

"Good gracious!" exclaimed Arthur. "If you'll forgive me, I must fly. A little engagement ..."

I looked at Arthur questioningly. I had never known him to make appointments at this hour of the night; besides, it wasn't Anni's evening. Kuno didn't seem at all put out, however. He was most gracious.

"Don't mention it, my dear fellow ... We quite understand."

His foot pressed mine under the table.

"You know," I said when Arthur had left us, "I really ought to be getting home, too."

"Oh, surely not."

"I think so," I said firmly, smiling and moving my foot away. He was squeezing a corn.

"You see, I should like so very much to show you my new flat. We can be there in the car in ten minutes,"

"I should love to see it; some other time."

He smiled faintly.

"Then may I perhaps, give you a lift home?"

"Thank you very much."

The remarkably handsome chauffeur saluted pertly, tucked us into the depths of the vast black limousine. As we slid forward along the Kurfürstendamm, Kuno took my hand under the fur rug.

"You're still angry with me," he murmured reproachfully.

"Why should I be?"

"Oh, yes, excuse me, you are."

"Really, I'm not."

Kuno gave my hand a limp squeeze.

"May I ask you something?"

"Ask away."

"You see, I don't wish to be personal. Do you believe in Platonic friendship?"

"I expect so," I said, guardedly.

The answer seemed to satisfy him. His tone became more confidential: "You're sure you won't come up and see my flat? Not for five minutes?"

"Not tonight."

"Quite sure?" He squeezed.

"Quite, quite sure."

"Some other evening?" Another squeeze.

I laughed: "I think I should see it better in the daytime, shouldn't I?"

Kuno sighed gently, but did not pursue the subject. A few moments later the limousine stopped outside my door. Glancing up at Arthur's window, I saw that the light was burning. I didn't remark on this to Kuno, however.

"Well, good night, and thank you for the lift."

"Do not mention it, please."

I nodded towards the chauffeur: "Shall I tell him to take you home?"

"No, thank you." Kuno spoke rather sadly, but with an attempt at a smile. "I'm afraid not. Not just yet."

He sank back upon the cushions, the smile still frozen on his face, his monocle catching a ghostly glassy gleam from the street lamp as he was driven away.

As I entered the flat Arthur appeared, in shirtsleeves, at his bedroom doorway. He seemed rather perturbed.

"Back already, William?"

I grinned: "Aren't you pleased to see me, Arthur?"

"Of course, dear boy. What a question! I didn't expect you quite so soon, that's all."

"I know you didn't. Your appointment doesn't seem to have kept you very long either."

"It—er—fell through." Arthur yawned. He was too sleepy even to tell lies.

I laughed: "You meant well, I know. Don't worry. We parted on the best of terms."

He brightened at once: "You did? Oh, I'm so very glad. For the moment I was afraid some little hitch might have occurred. Now I can go to sleep with a mind relieved. Once again, William, I must thank you for your invaluable support."

"Always glad to oblige," I said. "Good night."

Chapter Eleven

THE FIRST WEEK in November came and the traffic strike was declared. It was ghastly, sopping weather. Everything out of doors was covered with a layer of greasy, fallen dirt. A few trams were running, policemen posted fore and aft. Some of these were attacked, the windows smashed, and the passengers forced to get out. The streets were deserted, wet, raw, and grey. Von Papen's Government was expected to proclaim martial law. Berlin seemed profoundly indifferent. Proclamations, shootings, arrests; they were all nothing new. Helen Pratt was putting her money on Schleicher: "He's the foxiest of the lot," she told me. "Look here, Bill, I'll bet you five marks he's in before Christmas. Like to take me on?" I declined.

Hitler's negotiations with the Right had broken down; the Hakenkreuz was even flirting mildly with the Hammer and Sickle. Telephone conversations, so Arthur told me, had already taken place between the enemy camps. Nazi storm-troopers joined with communists in the crowds which jeered at the blacklegs and pelted them with stones. Meanwhile, on the soaked advertisement pillars, Nazi posters represented the K.P.D. as a bogey skeleton in Red Army uniform. In a few days there would be another election; our fourth this year.

Political meetings were well attended; they were cheaper than going to the movies or getting drunk. Elderly people sat indoors, in the damp, shabby houses, brewing malt coffee or weak tea and talking without animation of the Smash.

On November 7th the election results were out. The Nazis had lost two million votes. The communists had gained eleven seats. They had a majority of over 100,000 in Berlin. "You see," I told Frl. Schroeder, "it's all your doing." We had persuaded her to go down to the beer-shop at the corner and vote, for the first time in her life. And now she was as delighted as if she'd backed a winner: "Herr Norris! Herr Norris! Only think! I did just what you told me; and it's all come out as you said! The porter's wife's ever so cross. She's followed the elections for years, and she would have it that the Nazis were going to win another million this time. I had a good laugh at her, I can tell you. 'Aha, Frau Schneider!' I said to her, 'I understand something about politics, too, you see!'"

During the morning Arthur and I went round to the Wilhelmstrasse to Bayer's office, "for a little taste," as he put it, "of the fruits of victory." Several hundred others seemed to have the same idea. There was such a crowd of people coming and going on the stairs that we had difficulty in getting into the building at all. Everybody was in the best of spirits, shouting to each other, greeting, whistling, singing. As we struggled upwards we met Otto on his way down. He nearly wrung my hand off in his excitement.

"Mensch! Willi! *Jetzt geht's los!* Just let them talk about forbidding the party now! If they do, we'll fight! The old Nazis are done for, that's certain. In six months Hitler won't have any storm-troops left!"

Half a dozen of his friends were with him. They all shook my hand with the warmth of long-lost brothers. Meanwhile, Otto had flung himself upon Arthur like a young bear. "What, Arthur, you old sow, you here too? Isn't it fine? Isn't it grand? Why, I'm so pleased I could knock you into the middle of next week!"

He dealt Arthur an affectionate hook in the ribs which made him squirm. Several of the bystanders laughed sympathetically. "Good old Arthur!" exclaimed one of Otto's friends loudly. The name was overheard, taken up, passed from mouth to mouth. "Arthur ... who's Arthur? Why, man, don't you know who Arthur is?" No, they didn't know. Equally they didn't care. It was a name, a focus-point for the enthusiasm of all these excited young people; it served its purpose. "Arthur! Arthur!" was caught up on all sides. People were shouting it on the floor above us; in the hallway below. "Arthur's here!" "Arthur for ever!" "We want Arthur!" The storm of voices had risen in a moment. A mighty cheer, exuberant, half-humorous, burst spontaneously from a hundred throats. Another followed it, and another. The crazy old staircase shook; a tiny flake of plaster was dislodged from the ceiling. In this confined space, the reverberation was terrific; the crowd was excited to find what a noise it could make. There was a powerful, convulsive, surging movement inwards, towards the unseen object of admiration. A wave of admirers elbowed their way up the stairs, to collide with another wave, cascading down from above. Everybody wanted to touch Arthur. A rain of hand-claps descended on his wincing shoulders. An ill-timed attempt to hoist him into the air nearly resulted in his being pitched headlong over the banisters. His hat had been knocked off. I had managed to save it and was fully expecting to have to rescue his wig as well. Gasping for breath, Arthur tried, in a muddled way, to rise to the occasion: "Thank you ..." he managed to articulate. "Most kind ... really don't deserve ... good gracious! Oh dear!"

He might have been quite seriously injured had not Otto and his friends forced a way for him to the top of the staircase. We scrambled in the wake of their powerful, barging bodies. Arthur clutched my arm, half scared, half shyly pleased. "Fancy their knowing me, William," he panted into my ear.

But the crowd hadn't done with him yet. Now that we had reached the office door, we occupied a position of vantage and could be seen by the mass of struggling people wedged in the staircase below. At the sight of Arthur, another terrific cheer shook the building. "Speech!" yelled somebody. And the cry was echoed: "Speech! Speech! Speech!" Those on the stairs began a rhythmical stamping and shouting; the heavy tread of their boots was as formidable as the stroke of a giant piston. If Arthur didn't do something to stop it, it seemed probable that the entire staircase would collapse.

At this critical moment the door of the office opened. It was Bayer himself, come out to see what all the noise was about. His smiling eyes took in the scene with the amusement of a tolerant schoolmaster. The uproar did not disconcert him in the least; he was used to it. Smiling, he shook hands with the scared and embarrassed Arthur, laying a reassuring hand upon his shoulder. "Ludwig!" roared the onlookers. "Ludwig! Arthur! Speech!" Bayer laughed at them and made a good-humoured gesture of salute and dismissal. Then he turned, escorting Arthur and myself into the office. The noise outside gradually subsided into singing and shouted jokes. In the outer office the typists were doing their best to carry on work amidst groups of eagerly arguing men and women. The walls were plastered with news-sheets displaying the election results. We elbowed our way into Bayer's little room. Arthur sank at once into a chair and began fanning himself with his recovered hat.

"Well, well ... dear me! I feel quite carried away, as it were, in the whirl of history; distinctly battered. This is indeed a red-letter day for the Cause."

Bayer's eyes regarded him with vivid, faintly amused interest. "It surprises you, eh?"

"Well—er—I must admit that hardly, in my most sanguine dreams, had I dared to expect such a very decisive—er—victory."

Bayer nodded encouragingly.

"It is good, yes. But it will be unwise, I think, to exaggerate the importance of this success. Many factors have contributed to it. It is, how do you call, symptomic?"

"Symptomatic," Arthur corrected, with a little cough. His blue eyes shifted uneasily over the litter of papers on Bayer's writing-table. Bayer gave him a brilliant smile.

"Ah, yes. Symptomatic. It is symptomatic of the phase through which we are at present passing. We are not yet ready to cross the Wilhelmstrasse." He made a humorous gesture of his hand, indicating, through the window, the direction of the Foreign Office and Hindenburg's residence. "No. Not quite yet."

"Do you think," I asked, "that this means the Nazis are done for?"

He shook his head with decision. "Unfortunately, no. We may not be so optimistic. The reverse is for them of a temporary character only. You see, Mr Bradshaw, the economic situation is in their favour. We shall hear much more of our friends, I think."

"Oh, please don't say anything so unpleasant," murmured Arthur, fidgeting with his hat. His eyes continued furtively to explore the writing-table. Bayer's glance followed them.

"You do not like the Nazis, eh, Norris?"

His tone was rich with amusement. He appeared to find Arthur extremely funny at this precise moment. I was at a loss to understand why. Moving over to the table, he began, as if abstractedly, to handle the papers which lay there.

"Really!" protested Arthur in shocked tones. "How can you ask? Naturally, I dislike them. Odious creatures ..."

"Ah, but you should not!" With great deliberation, Bayer took a key from his pocket, unlocked a drawer in the writing-table, and drew from it a heavy sealed packet. His red-brown eyes sparkled teasingly. "This outlook is quite false. The Nazi of today can be the communist of tomorrow. When they have seen where their leaders' programme has brought them, they may not be so very difficult to convince. I wish all opposition could be thus overcome. There are others, you see, who will not listen to such arguments."

Smiling, he turned the packet in his hands. Arthur's eyes

were fastened upon it, as if in unwilling fascination; Bayer seemed to be amusing himself by exerting his hypnotic powers. At all events, Arthur was plainly most uncomfortable.

"Er—yes. Well … you may be right …"

There was a curious silence. Bayer was smiling to himself, subtly, with the corners of his lips. I had never seen him in this mood before. Suddenly, he appeared to become aware of what he was holding.

"Why, of course, my dear Norris … These are the documents I had promised to show you. Can you be so kind as to let me have them tomorrow again? We have to forward them, you know, as quickly as possible."

"Certainly. Of course …" Arthur had fairly jumped out of his seat to receive the packet. He was like a dog which has been put on trust for a lump of sugar. "I'll take the greatest care of them, I assure you."

Bayer smiled, but said nothing.

Some minutes later, he escorted us affably out of the premises by the back staircase which led down into the courtyard. Arthur thus avoided another encounter with his admirers.

As we walked away along the street, he seemed thoughtful and vaguely unhappy. Twice he sighed.

"Feeling tired?" I asked.

"Not tired, dear boy. No … I was merely indulging in my favourite vice of philosophizing. When you get to my age you'll see more and more clearly how very strange and complex life is. Take this morning, for instance. The simple enthusiasm of all those young people; it touched me very deeply. On such occasions, one feels oneself so unworthy. I suppose there are individuals who do not suffer from a conscience. But I am not one of them."

The strangest thing about this odd outburst was that Arthur obviously meant what he said. It was a genuine fragment of a confession, but I could make nothing of it.

"Yes," I encouraged experimentally, "I sometimes feel like that myself." Arthur didn't respond. He merely sighed for the third time. A sudden shadow of anxiety passed over his face; hastily he fingered the bulge in his pocket made by the papers which Bayer had given him. They were still there. He breathed relief.

November passed without much event. I had more pupils again, and was busy. Bayer gave me two long manuscripts to translate.

There were rumours that the K.P.D. would be forbidden; soon, in a few weeks. Otto was scornful. The Government would never dare, he said. The Party would fight. All the members of his cell had revolvers. They hung them, he told me, by strings from the bars of a cellar-grating in their *Lokal*, so that the police shouldn't find them. The police were very active these days. Berlin, we heard, was to be cleaned up. Plainclothes men had paid several unexpected calls on Olga, but had failed, so far, to find anything. She was being very careful.

We dined with Kuno several times and had tea at his flat. He was sentimental and preoccupied by turns. The intrigues which were going on within the Cabinet probably caused him a good deal of worry. And he regretted the freedom of his earlier bohemian existence. His public responsibilities debarred him from the society of the young men I had met at his Mecklenburg villa. Only their photographs remained to console him now, bound in a sumptuous album which he kept locked away in an obscure cupboard. Kuno showed it to me one day when we were alone.

"Sometimes, in the evenings, I like to look at them, you see? And then I make up a story to myself that we are all living on a deserted island in the Pacific Ocean. Excuse me, you don't think this very silly, I hope?"

"Not at all," I assured him.

"You see, I knew you'd understand." Encouraged, he proceeded shyly to further confessions. The desert island fantasy was nothing new. He had been cherishing it for months already; it had developed gradually into a private cult. Under its influence he had acquired a small library of stories for boys, most of them in English, which dealt with this particular kind of adventure. He had told his bookseller that he wanted them for a nephew in London. Kuno had found most of the books subtly unsatisfactory. There had been grown-ups in them, or buried treasures, or marvellous scientific inventions. He had no use for any of these. Only one story had really pleased him. It was called *The Seven Who Got Lost.*

"This is the work of genius, I find." Kuno was quite in earnest. His eyes gleamed with enthusiasm. "I should be so very happy, if you would care to read it, you see?"

I took the book home. It was certainly not at all bad of its kind. Seven boys, of ages ranging from sixteen to nineteen, are washed ashore on an uninhabited island, where there is water and plenty of vegetation. They have no food with them and no tools but a broken penknife. The book was a matter-of-fact account, cribbed largely from the *Swiss Family Robinson,* of how they hunted, fished, built a hut, and finally got themselves rescued. I read it at a sitting and brought it back to Kuno next day. He was delighted when I praised it.

"You remember Jack?"

"The one who was so good at fishing? Yes."

"Now tell me, please, is he not like Gunther?"

I had no idea who Gunther was, but rightly guessed him to have been one of the Mecklenburg houseparty.

"Yes, he is, rather."

"Oh, I am so glad you find this, too. And Tony?"

"The one who was such a marvellous climber?"

Kuno nodded eagerly: "Doesn't he remind you of Heinz?"

"I see what you mean."

In this way we worked through the other characters, Teddy, Bob, Rex, Dick: Kuno supplied a counterpart to each. I congratulated myself on having really read the book and being thus able to pass this curious examination with credit. Last of all came Jimmy, the hero, the champion swimmer, the boy who always led the others in an emergency and had a brainwave to solve every difficulty.

"You didn't recognize him, perhaps?"

Kuno's tone was oddly, ludicrously coy. I saw that I must beware of giving the wrong answer. But what on earth was I to say?

"I did have some idea ..." I ventured.

"You did?" He was actually blushing.

I nodded, smiling, trying to look intelligent, waiting for a hint.

"He is myself, you see." Kuno had the simplicity of complete conviction. "When I was a boy. But exactly ... This writer is a genius. He tells things about me which nobody else can know. I am Jimmy. Jimmy is myself. It is marvellous."

"It's certainly very strange," I agreed.

After this, we had several talks about the island. Kuno told me exactly how he pictured it, and dwelt in detail upon the appearance and characteristics of his various imaginary companions. He certainly had a most vivid imagination. I wished that the author of *The Seven Who Got Lost* could have been there to hear him. He would have been startled to behold the exotic fruit of his unambitious labours. I gathered that I was Kuno's only confidant on the subject. I felt as embarrassed as some unfortunate person who has been forcibly made a member of a secret society. If Arthur was with us, Kuno showed only too plainly his desire to get rid of him and be alone with me. Arthur noticed this, of course, and irritated me by putting the obvious construction on our private interviews. All the same, I hadn't the heart to give Kuno's poor little mystery away.

"Look here," I said to him once, "why don't you do it?"

"Please?"

"Why don't you clear out to the Pacific and find an island like the one in the book, and really live there? Other people have done it. There's absolutely no reason why you shouldn't."

Kuno shook his head sadly.

"Excuse me, no. It's impossible."

His tone was so final and so sad that I was silent. Nor did I ever make such a suggestion to him again.

As the month advanced, Arthur became increasingly depressed. I soon noticed that he had less money than formerly. Not that he complained. Indeed, he had become most secretive about his troubles. He made his economies as unobtrusively as possible, giving up taxis on the ground that a bus was just as quick, avoiding the expensive restaurants because, as he said, rich food disagreed with his digestion. Anni's visits were less frequent also. Arthur had taken to going to bed early. During the day, he was out more than ever. He spent a good deal of his time, I discovered, in Bayer's office.

It wasn't long before another telegram arrived from Paris. I had no difficulty in persuading Frl. Schroeder, whose curiosity was as shameless as my own, to steam open the envelope before Arthur's return for his afternoon nap. With heads pressed close together, we read:

> Tea you sent no good at all cannot understand why believe you have another girl no kisses.
>
> Margot

"You see," exclaimed Frl. Schroeder, in delighted horror, "she's been trying to stop it."

"What on earth ..."

"Why, Herr Bradshaw," in her impatience she gave my hand a little slap, "how can you be so dense! The baby, of course. He must have sent her some stuff ... Oh, these men! If he'd only come to me, I could have told him what to do. It never fails."

"For Heaven's sake, Frl. Schroeder, don't say anything about this to Herr Norris."

"Oh, Herr Bradshaw, you can trust me!"

I think, all the same, that her manner must have given Arthur some hint of what we had done. For, after this, the French telegrams ceased to arrive. Arthur, I supposed, had prudently arranged to have them delivered to some other address.

And then one evening early in December, when Arthur was out and Frl. Schroeder was having a bath, the doorbell rang.

I answered it myself. There, on the threshold, stood Schmidt.

"Good evening, Mr Bradshaw."

He looked shabby and unkempt. His great, greasy moon-face was unwholesomely white. At first I thought he must be drunk.

"What do you want?" I asked.

Schmidt grinned unpleasantly. "I want to see Norris." He must have read what was in my mind, for he added: "You needn't bother to tell me any lies, because I know he's living here, now, see?"

"Well, you can't see him now. He's gone out."

"Are you sure he's out?" Schmidt regarded me smiling, through half-closed eyes.

"Perfectly. Otherwise I shouldn't have told you so."

"So ... I see."

We stood looking at each other for some moments, smiling with dislike. I was tempted to slam the door in his face.

"Mr Norris would do better to see me," said Schmidt, after a pause, in an offhand, casual tone, as though this were his first mention of the subject. I put the side of my foot as unostentatiously as possible against the door, in case he should suddenly turn rough.

"I think," I said gently, "that that's a matter for Mr Norris himself to judge."

"Won't you tell him I'm here?" Schmidt glanced down at my foot and impudently grinned. Our voices were so mild and low-pitched that anybody passing up the staircase would have supposed us to be two neighbours, engaged in a friendly chat.

"I've told you once already that Mr Norris isn't at home. Don't you understand German?"

Schmidt's smile was extraordinarily insulting. His half-closed eyes regarded me with a certain amusement, a qualified disapproval, as though I were a picture badly out of drawing. He spoke slowly, with elaborate patience.

"Perhaps it wouldn't be troubling you too much to give Mr Norris a message from me?"

"Yes. I'll do that."

"Will you be so kind as to tell Mr Norris that I'll wait another three days, but no longer? You understand? At the end of this week, if I haven't heard from him, I shall do what I said in my letter. He'll know what I mean. He thinks I daren't, perhaps. Well, he'll soon find out what a mistake he's made. I don't want trouble, unless he asks for it. But I've got to live … I've got to look after myself the same as he has. I mean to have my rights. He needn't think he can keep me down in the gutter …"

He was actually trembling all over. Some violent emotion, rage or extreme weakness, was shaking his body like a leaf. I thought for a moment that he would fall.

"Are you ill?" I asked.

My question had an extraordinary effect on Schmidt. His oily, smiling sneer stiffened into a tense mask of hatred. He had utterly lost control of himself. Coming a step nearer to me, he literally shouted in my face:

"It isn't any business of yours, do you hear? Just you tell Norris what I said. If he doesn't do what I want, I'll make him sorry for the day he was born! And you, too, you swine!"

His hysterical fury infected me suddenly. Stepping back, I flung the door to with a violent slam, hoping to catch his thrust-forward, screaming face on the point of the jaw. But there was no impact. His voice stopped like a gramophone from which the needle is lifted. Nor did he utter another sound. As I stood there behind the closed door, my heart pounding with anger, I heard his light footsteps cross the landing and begin to descend the stairs.

Chapter Twelve

AN HOUR LATER, Arthur returned home. I followed him into his room to break the news.

"Schmidt's been here."

If Arthur's wig had been suddenly jerked from his head by a fisherman, he could hardly have looked more startled.

"William, please tell me the worst at once. Don't keep me in suspense. What time was this? Did you see him yourself? What did he say?"

"He's trying to blackmail you, isn't he?"

Arthur looked at me quickly.

"Did he admit that?"

"He as good as told me. He says he's written to you already, and that if you don't do what he wants by the end of the week there'll be trouble."

"He actually said that? Oh dear …"

"You should have told me he'd written," I said reproachfully.

"I know, dear boy, I know …" Arthur was the picture of distress. "It's been on the tip of my tongue several times this last fortnight. But I didn't want to worry you unnecessarily. I kept hoping that, somehow, it might all blow over."

"Now look here, Arthur; the point is this: does Schmidt

really know anything about you which can do you harm?"

He had been nervously pacing the room, and now sank, a disconsolate shirt-sleeved figure, into a chair, forlornly regarding his button-boots.

"Yes, William." His voice was small and apologetic. "I'm afraid he does."

"What sort of things does he know?"

"Really, I … I don't think, even for you, that I can go into the details of my hideous past."

"I don't want details. What I want to know is, would Schmidt get you involved in any kind of criminal charge?"

Arthur considered this for some moments, thoughtfully rubbing his chin.

"I don't think he dare try it. No."

"I'm not so sure," I said. "He seemed to me to be in a pretty bad way. Desperate enough for anything. He looked as though he wasn't getting much to eat."

Arthur stood up again and began walking about the room, rapidly, with small anxious steps.

"Let's keep quite calm, William. Let's think this out together quietly."

"Do you think, from your experience of Schmidt, that he'd keep quiet if you paid him a lump sum down to leave you alone?"

Arthur did not hesitate:

"I'm quite sure he wouldn't. It would merely whet his appetite for my blood … Oh dear, oh dear!"

"Suppose you left Germany altogether? Would he be able to get at you then?"

Arthur stopped short in the middle of a gesture of extreme agitation.

"No, I suppose … that is, no, quite definitely not." He regarded me with dismay. "You aren't suggesting I should do that, I hope?"

"It seems drastic. But what's the alternative?"

"I see none. Certainly."

"Neither do I."

Arthur moved his shoulders in a shrug of despair. "Yes, yes, my dear boy. It's easy enough to say that. But where's the money coming from?"

"I thought you were pretty well off now?" I pretended mild surprise. Arthur's glance slid away, evasively, from beneath my own.

"Only under certain conditions."

"You mean, you can earn money only here?"

"Well, chiefly ..." He didn't like this catechism, and began to fidget. I could no longer resist trying a shot in the dark.

"But you get paid from Paris?"

I had scored a bull. Arthur's dishonest blue eyes showed a startled flicker, but no more. Perhaps he wasn't altogether unprepared for the question.

"My dear William, I haven't the least idea what you're talking about."

"Never mind, Arthur. It's no business of mine. I only want to help you, if I can."

"It's most kind of you, dear boy, I'm sure." Arthur sighed. "This is all most difficult; most complicated ..."

"Well, we've got one point clear, at any rate ... Now, the best thing you can do is to send Schmidt some money at once, to keep him quiet. How much did he ask for?"

"A hundred down," said Arthur in a subdued voice, "and then fifty a week."

"I must say he's got a nerve. Could you manage a hundred and fifty, do you think?"

"At a pinch, I suppose, yes. It goes against the grain."

"I know. But this'll save you ten times as much in the end. Now what I suggest is, you send him the hundred and fifty, with a letter promising him the balance on the first of January ..."

"Really, William ..."

"Wait a minute. And meanwhile, you'll arrange to be out of Germany before the end of December. That gives you three weeks' grace. If you pay up meekly now, he won't bother you again until then. He'll think he's got you in his pocket."

"Yes. I suppose you're right. I shall have to accustom myself to the idea. All this is so sudden." Arthur had a momentary flare-up of resentment. "That odious serpent! If ever I find an opportunity of dealing with him once for all ..."

"Don't you worry. He'll come to a sticky end sooner or later. The chief problem, at present, is to raise this money for your journey. I suppose there isn't anybody you could borrow it from?"

But Arthur was already following another train of thought.

"I shall find a way out of this somehow." His tone was considerably brighter. "Just let me have time to think."

While Arthur was thinking, a week went by. The weather didn't improve. These dismal short days affected all our spirits. Frl. Schroeder complained of pains in the back. Arthur had a touch of liver. My pupils were unpunctual and stupid. I was depressed and cross. I began to hate our dingy flat, the shabby, staring house-front opposite my window, the damp street, the stuffy, noisy restaurant where we ate an economical supper, the burnt meat, the eternal sauerkraut, the soup.

"My God!" I exclaimed one evening to Arthur, "what wouldn't I give to get out of this hole of a town for a day or two!"

Arthur, who had been picking his teeth in melancholy abstraction, looked at me thoughtfully. Rather to my surprise he seemed prepared to take a sympathetic interest in my grumbling.

"I must say, William, I'd noticed myself that you weren't in your accustomed sprightly vein. You're looking distinctly pale, you know."

"Am I?"

"I fear you've been overworking yourself lately. You don't get out of doors enough. A young man like you needs exercise and fresh air."

I smiled, amused and slightly mystified.

"You know, Arthur, you're getting quite the bedside manner."

"My dear boy"—he pretended to be mildly hurt—"I'm sorry that you mock my genuine concern for your health.

After all, I'm old enough to be your father. I think I may be excused for sometimes feeling myself *in loco parentis.*"

"I beg your pardon, Daddy."

Arthur smiled, but with a certain exasperation. I wasn't giving the right answers. He couldn't find an opening for the topic, whatever it was, which he was thus obscurely trying to broach. After a moment's hesitation, he tried again.

"Tell me, William, have you ever, in the course of your travels, visited Switzerland?"

"For my sins. I once spent three months trying to learn French at a *pension* in Geneva."

"Ah yes, I believe you told me." Arthur coughed uneasily. "But I was thinking more of the winter sports."

"No. I've been spared those."

Arthur appeared positively shocked.

"Really, my dear boy, if you don't mind my saying so, I think you carry your disdain of athleticism too far, I do indeed. Far be it from me to disparage the things of the mind. But, remember, you're still young. I hate to see you depriving yourself of pleasures which you won't, in any case, be able to indulge in later. Be quite frank; isn't it all rather a pose?"

I grinned.

"May I ask, with all due respect, what branch of sport you indulged in yourself at the age of twenty-eight?"

"Well—er—as you know, I have always suffered from delicate health. Our cases are not at all the same. Nevertheless, I may tell you that, during one of my visits to Scotland, I became quite an ardent fisherman. In fact, I frequently succeeded in catching those small fish with pretty red and brown markings. Their name escapes me for the moment."

I laughed and lit a cigarette.

"And now, Arthur, having given such an admirable performance as the fond parent, suppose you tell me what you're driving at?"

He sighed, with resignation, with exasperation; partly, perhaps, with relief. He was excused from further shamming. When he spoke again, it was with a complete change of tone.

"After all, William, I don't know why I should beat about the bush. We've known each other long enough now. How long is it, by the way, since we first met?"

"More than two years."

"Is it? Is it indeed? Let me see. Yes, you're right. As I was saying, we've known each other long enough now for me to be able to appreciate the fact that, although young in years, you're already a man of the world ..."

"You put it charmingly."

"I assure you, I'm quite serious. Now, what I have to say is simply this (and please don't regard it as anything but the very vaguest possibility, because, quite apart from the question of your consent, a very vital question, I know, the whole thing would have to be approved by a third party, who doesn't, at present, know anything about the scheme) ..."

Arthur paused, at the end of this parenthesis, to draw breath, and to overcome his constitutional dislike of laying his cards on the table.

"What I now merely ask you is this: would you, or would you not, be prepared to spend a few days in Switzerland this Christmas, at one or other of the winter sport resorts?"

Having got it out at last, he was covered in confusion, avoided my eye and began fiddling nervously with the cruet-stand. The neural effort required to make this offer appeared to have been considerable. I stared at him for a moment; then burst out laughing in my amazement.

"Well, I'm damned! So that *was* what you were after all this time!"

Arthur joined, rather shyly, in my mirth. He was watching my face, shrewdly and covertly, in its various phases of astonishment. At what he evidently considered to be the psychological moment, he added:

"All expenses would be paid, of course."

"But what on earth ..." I began.

"Never mind, William. Never mind. It's just an idea of mine, that's all. It mayn't, it very likely won't, come to anything. Please don't ask me any more now. All I want to know is: would you be prepared to contemplate such a thing at all, or is it out of the question?"

"Nothing's out of the question, of course. But there are all sorts of things I should want to know. For instance ..."

Arthur held up a delicate white hand.

"Not now, William, I beg."

"Just this: What should I ..."

"I can't discuss anything now," interrupted Arthur firmly. "I simply must not."

And, as if afraid that he would nevertheless be tempted to do so, he called to the waiter for our bill.

The best part of another week passed without Arthur having made any further allusion to the mysterious Swiss project. With considerable self-control, I refrained from reminding him of it; perhaps, like so many of his other brilliant schemes, it was already forgotten. And there were more important things to be thought of. Christmas was upon us, the year would soon be over; yet he hadn't, so far as I knew, the ghost of a prospect of raising the money for his escape. When I asked him about it, he was vague. When I urged him to take steps, evasive. He seemed to be getting into a dangerous state of inertia. Evidently he underrated Schmidt's vindictiveness and power to harm. I did not. I couldn't so easily forget my last unpleasant glimpse of the secretary's face. Arthur's indifference drove me sometimes nearly frantic.

"Don't worry, dear boy," he would murmur vaguely, with abstracted, butterfly fingerings of his superb wig. "Sufficient unto the day, you know ... Yes."

"A day will come," I retorted, "when it'll be sufficient unto two or three years' hard."

Next morning something happened to confirm my fears.

I was sitting in Arthur's room, assisting, as usual, at the ceremonies of the toilet, when the telephone bell rang.

"Will you be kind enough to see who it is, dear boy?" said

Arthur, powder-puff in hand. He never personally answered a call if it could be avoided. I picked up the receiver.

"It's Schmidt," I announced, a moment later, not without a certain gloomy satisfaction, covering the mouthpiece with my hand.

"Oh dear!" Arthur could hardly have been more flustered if his persecutor had actually been standing outside the bedroom door. Indeed, his harassed glance literally swept for an instant under the bed, as though measuring the available space for hiding there:

"Tell him anything. Say I'm not at home ..."

"I think," I said firmly, "that it'd be much better if you were to speak to him yourself. After all, he can't bite you. He may give you some idea of what he means to do."

"Oh, very well, if you must ..." Arthur was quite petulant. "I must say, I should have thought it was very unnecessary."

Gingerly, holding the powder-puff like a defensive weapon, he advanced to the instrument.

"Yes. Yes." The dimple in his chin jerked sideways. He snarled like a nervous Hon. "No ... no, really ... But do please listen one moment ... I can't, I assure you ... I can't ..."

His voice trailed off into a protesting, imploring whisper. He wobbled the hook of the receiver in futile distress.

"William, he's rung off."

Arthur's dismay was so comic that I had to smile. "What did he tell you?"

Arthur crossed the room and sat down heavily on the bed. He seemed quite exhausted. The powder-puff fell to the floor from between his limp fingers.

"I'm reminded of the deaf adder, who heareth not the voice of the charmer ... What a monster, William! May your life never be burdened by such a fiend ..."

"Do tell me what he said."

"He confined himself to threats, dear boy. Mostly incoherent. He wanted merely to remind me of his existence, I think. And that he'll need some more money soon. It was very cruel of you to make me speak to him. Now I shall be upset for the rest of the day. Just feel my hand; it's shaking like a leaf."

"But, Arthur," I picked up the powder-puff and put it on the dressing-table. "It's no good just being upset. This must be a warning to you. You see, he really does mean business. We must do something about it. Haven't you any plan? Are there no steps you can take?"

Arthur roused himself with an effort.

"Yes, yes. You're right, of course. The die is cast. Steps shall be taken. In fact not a moment shall be lost. I wonder if you'd be so good as to get me the *Fernamt* on the telephone and say I wish to put through a call to Paris? I don't think it's too early? No …"

I asked for the number Arthur gave me and tactfully left him alone. I didn't see him again until the evening, when, as usual, we met by appointment at the restaurant for our supper. I noticed at once that he was brighter. He even insisted that we should drink wine, and when I demurred offered to pay my share of the bottle.

"It's so strengthening," he added persuasively.

I grinned. "Still worried about my health?"

"You're very unkind," said Arthur, smiling. But he refused to be drawn. When, a minute or two later, I asked point-blank how things were going, he replied:

"Let's have supper first, dear boy. Be patient with me, please."

But even when supper was over and we both ordered coffee (an additional extravagance), Arthur seemed in no hurry to give me his news. Instead, he appeared anxious to know what I had been doing, which pupils I had had, where I had lunched, and so forth.

"You haven't seen our friend Pregnitz lately, I think?"

"As a matter of fact I'm going to tea with him tomorrow."

"Are you indeed?"

I restrained a smile. I was familiar enough by this time with Arthur's methods of approach. That new intonation in his voice, though suavely concealed, hadn't escaped me. So we were coming to the point at last.

"May I give him any message?"

Arthur's face was a comical study. We regarded each other with the amusement of two people who, night after night, cheat each other at a card game which is not played for money. Simultaneously we began to laugh.

"What, exactly," I asked, "do you want to get out of him?"

"William, please ... you put things so very crudely."

"It saves time."

"Yes, yes. You're right. Time is, alas! important just now. Very well, let's put it that I'm anxious to do a little business with him. Or shall we say to put him in the way of doing it for himself?"

"How very kind of you!"

Arthur tittered, "I am kind, aren't I, William? That's what so few people seem to realize."

"And what is this business? When is it coming off?"

"That remains to be seen. Soon, I hope."

"I suppose you get a percentage?"

"Naturally."

"A big percentage?"

"If it succeeds. Yes."

"Enough for you to be able to leave Germany?"

"Oh, more than enough. Quite a nice little nest-egg, in fact."

"Then that's splendid, isn't it?"

Arthur snarled nervously, regarded his finger-nails with extreme care.

"Unfortunately, there are certain technical difficulties. I need, as so often, your valuable advice."

"Very well, let's hear them."

Arthur considered for some moments. I could see that he was wondering how much he need tell me.

"Chiefly," he said at length, "that this business cannot be transacted in Germany."

"Why not?"

"Because it would involve too much publicity. The other party to the deal is a well-known business man. As you probably know, big-business circles are comparatively small. They all watch each other. News gets round in a moment; the least hint is enough. If this man were to come to Berlin, the business people here would know about it before he'd even arrived. And secrecy is absolutely essential."

"It all sounds very thrilling. But I'd no idea that Kuno was in business at all."

"Strictly speaking, he isn't." Arthur took some trouble to avoid my eye. "This is merely a sideline."

"I see. And where do you propose that this meeting shall take place?"

Arthur carefully selected a toothpick from the little bowl in front of him.

"That, my dear William, is where I hope to have the benefit of your valuable advice. It must be somewhere, of course, within easy reach of the German frontier. Somewhere where people can go, at this time of the year, without attracting attention, on a holiday."

With great deliberation Arthur broke the toothpick into two pieces and laid them side by side on the tablecloth. Without looking up at me, he added:

"Subject to your approval, I'd rather thought of Switzerland."

There was quite a long pause. We were both smiling.

"So that's it?" I said at last.

Arthur re-divided the toothpick into quarters; raised his eyes to mine in a glance of dishonest, smiling innocence.

"That, as you rightly observe, dear boy, is it."

"Well, well. What a foxy old thing you are." I laughed. "I'm beginning to see daylight at last."

"I must confess, William, I was beginning to find you a little slow in the uptake. That isn't like you, you know."

"I'm sorry, Arthur. But all these riddles make me a bit

giddy. Suppose you stop asking them and let's have the whole yam from the beginning?"

"I assure you, my dear boy, I'm more than ready to tell you all I know about this affair, which isn't very much. Well, to cut a long story short, Pregnitz is interested in one of the largest glass-works in Germany. It doesn't matter which. You wouldn't find his name on the list of directors; nevertheless, he has a great deal of unofficial influence. Of course, I don't pretend to understand these matters myself."

"A glass-works? Well, that sounds harmless enough."

"But, my dear boy," Arthur was anxiously reassuring, "of course it's harmless. You mustn't allow your naturally cautious nature to upset your sense of proportion. If this proposition sounds a little odd to you at first, it's only because you aren't accustomed to the ways of high finance. Why, it's the kind of thing which takes place every day. Ask anybody you like. The largest deals are almost always discussed informally."

"All right! All right! Go on."

"Let me see. Where was I? Ah, yes. Now, one of my most intimate friends in Paris is a certain prominent financier—"

"Who signs himself Margot?"

But this time I didn't catch Arthur off his guard. I couldn't even guess whether he was surprised or not. He merely smiled.

"How sharp you are, William! Well, perhaps he does. Anyhow, we'll call him Margot for convenience. Yes ... at all events, Margot is exceedingly anxious to have a chance of meeting Pregnitz. Although he doesn't admit it in so many words, I understand that he wishes to propose some sort of combine between Pregnitz's firm and his own. But that's entirely unofficial; it doesn't concern us. As for Pregnitz, he'll have to hear Margot's propositions for himself and decide whether they're to the advantage of his firm or not. Quite possibly, indeed probably, they will be. If not, there's no harm done. Margot will only have himself to blame. All he's asking me to arrange is that he meets the Baron socially, on neutral ground, where they won't be bothered by a lot of financial reporters and can talk things over quietly."

"And as soon as you've brought them together, you get the cash?"

"When the meeting has taken place," Arthur lowered his voice, "I get half. The other half will be paid only if the deal is successful. But the worst of it is, Margot insists that he must see Pregnitz at once. He's always like that when once he gets an idea into his head. A most impatient man ..."

"And he's really prepared to give you such a lot simply for arranging this meeting?"

"Remember, William, it seems a mere bagatelle to him. If this transaction is successful, he'll probably make millions."

"Well, all I can say is, I congratulate you. It ought to be easy enough to earn."

"I'm glad you think so, my dear boy." Arthur's tone was guarded and doubtful.

"Why, where's the difficulty? All you have to do is to go to Kuno and explain the whole situation."

"William!" Arthur seemed positively horror-stricken. "That would be fatal!"

"I don't see why."

"You don't see why? Really, dear boy, I must own I credited you with more finesse. No, that's entirely out of the question. You don't know Pregnitz as I do. He's extraordinarily sensitive in these matters, as I've discovered to my cost. He'd regard it as an unwarrantable intrusion into his affairs. He'd withdraw at once. He has the true aristocratic outlook, which one so seldom finds in these money-grubbing days. I admit I admire him for it."

I grinned.

"He seems to be a very peculiar sort of business man if he's offended when you offer him a fortune."

But Arthur was quite heated.

"William, please, this is no time to be frivolous. Surely you must see my point. Pregnitz refuses, and I, for one, entirely agree with him, to mix personal with business relationships. Coming from you or from me, any suggestion that he should enter into negotiations with Margot, or with anybody else, would be an impertinence. And he'd resent it as such. Therefore, I do beg of you, don't breathe one word about this to him, on any account."

"No, of course I won't. Don't get excited. But look here, Arthur, do I understand you to mean that Kuno is to go to Switzerland without knowing that he's there to meet Margot?"

"You put it in a nutshell."

"H'm ... That certainly complicates things rather. All the same, I don't see why you should have any special difficulty. Kuno probably goes to the winter sports, anyhow. It's quite in his line. What I don't altogether follow is, where do I come in? Am I to be brought along simply to swell the crowd, or to provide comic relief, or what?"

Arthur chose and divided another toothpick.

"I was just coming to that point, William." His tone was carefully impersonal. "I'm afraid, you see, you'd have to go alone."

"Alone with Kuno?"

"Yes." Arthur began speaking with nervous rapidity. "There are a number of reasons which make it quite impossible for me to come with you, or to deal with this matter myself. In the first place, it would be exceedingly awkward, having once left this country, to return to it, as I should be obliged to do, even if only for a few days. Secondly, this suggestion that we should go together to the winter sports, coming from me, would sound very odd. Pregnitz knows perfectly well that I haven't the constitution or the taste for such things. Coming from you, on the other hand, what could be more natural? He'd probably be only too delighted to travel with such a young and lively companion."

"Yes, I quite see all that ... but how should I get into touch with Margot? I don't even know him by sight."

Arthur dismissed these difficulties with a wave of the hand.

"Leave that to me, dear boy, and to him. Set your mind at rest, forget everything I've told you this evening, and enjoy yourself."

"Nothing but that?"

"Nothing. Once you've got Pregnitz across the frontier your duties are at an end."

"It sounds delightful."

Arthur's face lit up at once.

"Then you'll go?"

"I must think it over."

Disappointed, he squeezed his chin. The tooth-picks were divided into lengths. At the end of a long minute he said hesitantly:

"Quite apart from your expenses, which, as I think I told you, will be paid in advance, I should ask you to accept a little something, you know, for your trouble."

"No, thank you, Arthur."

"I beg your pardon, William." He sounded much relieved. "I might have known you wouldn't."

I grinned.

"I won't deprive you of your honest earnings."

Watching my face carefully, he smiled. He was uncertain how to take me. His manner changed.

"Of course, dear boy, you must do as you think best. I don't want to influence you in any way. If you decide against this scheme, I shan't allude to it again. At the same time, you know what it means to me. It's my only chance. I hate begging favours. Perhaps I'm asking too much of you. I can only say that if you do this for me I shall be eternally grateful. And if it's ever in my power to repay you ..."

"Stop, Arthur. Stop! You'll make me cry." I laughed. "Very well. I'll do my best with Kuno. But, for Heaven's sake, don't build your hopes on it. I don't suppose he'll come. Probably he's engaged already."

On this understanding, the subject was closed for the evening.

Next day, when I returned from the tea-party at Kuno's flat, I found Arthur waiting for me in his bedroom in a state of the most extreme anxiety. He could hardly wait to shut the door before hearing my news.

"Quick, William, please. Tell me the worst. I can bear it. He won't come? No?"

"Yes," I said. "He'll come."

For a moment joy seemed to have made Arthur quite speechless, incapable of motion. Then a spasm passed over all his limbs, he executed a kind of caper in the air.

"My dear boy! I must, I really must embrace you!" And he literally threw his arms round my neck and kissed me, like a French general, on both cheeks. "Tell me all about it. Did you have much difficulty? What did he say?"

"Oh, he more or less suggested the whole thing himself before I had opened my mouth. He wanted to go to the Riesengebirge, but I pointed out that the snow would be much better in the Alps."

"You did? That was brilliant of you, William! Positively inspired ..."

I sat down in a chair. Arthur fluttered round me, admiring and delighted.

"You're quite sure he hasn't the least suspicion?"

"Perfectly sure."

"And how soon shall you be able to start?"

"On Christmas Eve, I think."

Arthur regarded me solicitously.

"You don't sound very enthusiastic, dear boy. I'd hoped this would be a pleasure to you, too. You're not feeling ill by any chance, I trust?"

"Not in the least, thank you." I stood up. "Arthur, I'm going to ask you something."

His eyelids fluttered nervously at my tone.

"Why—er—of course. Ask away, dear boy. Ask away."

"I want you to speak the truth. Are you and Margot going to swindle Kuno? Yes or no?"

"My dear William—er—really ... I think you presume ..."

"I want an answer, please, Arthur. You see, it's important for me to know. I'm mixed up in this now. Are you or aren't you?"

"Well, I must say ... No. Of course not. As I've already explained at some length, I ..."

"Do you swear that?"

"Really, William, this isn't a court of law. Don't look at me like that, please. All right, if it gives you any satisfaction, I swear it."

"Thank you. That's all I wanted. I'm sorry if I sounded rude. You know that, as a rule, I don't meddle in your affairs. Only this is my affair too, you see."

Arthur smiled weakly, rather shaken.

"I quite understand your anxiety, dear boy, of course. But in this case, I do assure you, it's entirely unfounded. I've every reason to believe that Pregnitz will reap great benefits from this transaction, if he's wise enough to accept it."

As a final test, I tried to look Arthur in the eyes. But no, this time-honoured process didn't work. Here were no windows to the soul. They were merely part of his face, light-blue jellies, like naked shell-fish in the crevices of a rock. There was nothing to hold the attention; no sparkle, no inward gleam. Try as I would, my glance wandered away to more interesting features; the soft, snout-like nose, the concertina chin. After three or four attempts, I gave it up. It was no good. There was nothing for it but to take Arthur at his word.

Chapter Thirteen

MY JOURNEY WITH Kuno to Switzerland resembled the honeymoon trip which follows a marriage of convenience. We were polite, mutually considerate, and rather shy. Kuno was a model of discreet attentiveness. With his own hands, he arranged my luggage in the rack, ran out at the last moment to buy me magazines, discovered by roundabout inquiries that I preferred the upper sleeping-car berth to the lower, and retired into the corridor to wait until I was undressed. When I got tired of reading, there he was, affable and informative, waiting to tell me the names of the mountains. We chatted with great animation in five-minute spasms, relapsing into sudden, abstracted silence. Both of us had plenty to think about. Kuno, I suppose, was worrying over the sinister manoeuvres of German politics or dreaming about his island of the seven boys: I had leisure to review the Margot conundrum in all its aspects. Did he really exist? Well, there above my head was a brand-new pigskin suitcase containing a dinner-jacket from the tailor only the day before. Arthur had been positively lordly with our employer's money. "Get whatever you want, dear boy. It would never do for you to be shabby. Besides, what a chance ..." After some hesitation, I had doubtfully followed his advice, though not to the reckless extent which he urged. Arthur even went so far in his interpretation of "travelling expenses" as to press upon me a set of gold cuff-links, a wrist-watch, and a fountain pen. "After all, William, business is business. You don't know these people as I do." His tone, when speaking of Margot, had become remarkably bitter: "If you asked *him* to do anything for you he wouldn't hesitate to squeeze you to the last penny."

On Boxing Day, our first morning, I awoke to the tinny jingle of sleigh-bells from the snowy street below, and a curious clicking noise, also metallic, which proceeded from the bathroom. Through the half-open door Kuno was to be seen, in a pair of gym shorts, doing exercises with a chest-expander. He was straining himself terribly; the veins in his neck bulged and his nostrils arched and stiffened with each desperate effort. He was obviously unaware that he was not alone. His eyes, bare of the monocle, were fixed in a short-sighted visionary stare, which suggested that he was engaged in a private religious rite. To speak to him would have been as intrusive as to disturb a man at his prayers. I turned over in bed and pretended to be asleep. After a few moments, I heard the bathroom door softly close.

Our rooms were on the first floor of the hotel, looking out over the houses of the village scattered along the frozen lake to the sparkling ski-ing slopes, massive and smooth as the contours of an immense body under blankets, crossed by the black spider-line of the funicular which climbed to the start of the toboggan runs. It seemed a curious background for an international business transaction. But, as Arthur had rightly said, I knew nothing of the ways of financiers. I got dressed slowly, thinking about my invisible host. Was Margot here already? The hotel was full up, the manager had told us. To judge from my glimpse of the guests, last night, in the huge dining-room, there must be several hundred of them staying here.

Kuno joined me for breakfast. He was dressed, with scrupulous informality, in grey flannel trousers, a blazer, and the knotted silk scarf of his Oxford college colours.

"You slept well, I hope?"

"Very well, thank you. And you?"

"I, not so well." He smiled, flushed, slightly abashed. "It doesn't matter. In the night-time I had something to read, you see?"

Bashfully he let me see the title of the book he was holding in his hand. It was called *Billy the Castaway*.

"Is it good?" I asked.

"There is one chapter which is very nice, I find ..."

Before I could hear the contents of the nice chapter, however, a waiter appeared with our breakfast on a little wheeled car. We reverted at once to our self-conscious honeymoon manners.

"May I give you some cream?"

"Just a little, please."

"Is this how you like it?"

"Thank you, that's delicious."

Our voices sounded so absurd that I could have laughed out loud. We were like two unimportant characters in the first act of a play, put there to make conversation until it is time for the chief actor to appear.

By the time we had finished breakfast, the immense white slopes were infested already with tiny figures, some skimming and criss-crossing like dragon-flies, some faltering and collapsing like injured ants. The skaters were out in dozens on the lake. Within a roped enclosure, an inhumanly agile creature in black tights performed wonders before an attentive audience. Knapsacked, helmeted, and booted, some of the more active guests were starting out on long, dangerous tours of the upper heights, like soldiers from a luxury barracks. And here and there, amidst the great army, the wounded were to be seen, limping on sticks or with their arms in slings, taking a painful convalescent promenade.

Attentive as ever, Kuno took it for granted that he was to

teach me to ski. I should have much preferred to mess about alone, but my attempts at polite dissuasion were in vain. He regarded it as his duty; there was no more to be said. So we spent two perspiring hours on the beginner's slope; I slithering and stumbling, Kuno admonishing and supporting. "No, excuse me, this is again not quite correct ... you hold yourself in too stiff a manner, you see?" His patience seemed inexhaustible. I longed for lunch.

About the middle of the morning, a young man came circling expertly among the novices in our neighbourhood. He stopped to watch us; perhaps my awkwardness amused him. His presence rather annoyed me; I didn't want an audience. Half by accident, half by design, I made a sudden swerve at him when he least expected it and knocked him clean off his feet. Our mutual apologies were profuse. He helped me to get up and even brushed some of the snow off me with his hand.

"Allow me ... van Hoorn."

His bow, skis and all, was so marvellously stiff that he might have been challenging me to a duel.

"Bradshaw ... very pleased."

I tried to parody it and promptly fell forward on my face, to be raised this time by Kuno himself. Somewhat less formally, I introduced them.

After this, to my relief, Kuno's interest in my instruction considerably decreased. Van Hoorn was a tall, fair boy, handsome in the severe Viking manner, though he had rather spoilt his appearance by shaving off most of his hair. The bald back of his head was sunburnt to an angry scarlet. He had studied for three semesters, he told us, at the University of Hamburg. He was furiously shy and blushed crimson whenever Kuno, with his discreetly flattering smile, addressed him.

Van Hoorn could do a turn which interested Kuno extremely. They went off for some distance to demonstrate and practise it. Presently, it was time for lunch. On our way down to the hotel, the young man introduced us to his uncle, a lively, plump little Dutchman, who was cutting figures on the ice with great skill. The elder Mr van Hoorn was a contrast to his grave nephew. His eyes twinkled merrily, he seemed delighted to make our acquaintance. His face was brown as an old boot and he was quite bald. He wore side-whiskers and a little pointed beard.

"So you've made some friends already?" He addressed his nephew in German. "That's right." His twinkling eyes regarded Kuno and myself. "I tell Piet he should get to know a nice girl, but he won't; he's too shy. I wasn't like that at his age, I can tell you."

Piet van Hoorn blushed, frowned and looked away, refusing to respond to Kuno's discreet glance of sympathy. Mr van Hoorn chattered away to me as he removed his skates.

"So you like it here? My word, so do I! I haven't enjoyed myself so much for years. I bet I've lost a pound or two already. Why, I don't feel a day over twenty-one, this morning."

As we entered the dining-room, Kuno suggested that the van Hoorns should come and sit at our table; he gave a meaningful glance at Piet as he spoke. I felt rather embarrassed. Kuno was certainly a bit crude in his advances. But Mr van Hoorn agreed at once, most heartily. He appeared to find nothing odd in the proposal. Probably he was glad enough to have some extra people to talk to.

During lunch, Kuno devoted himself almost entirely to Piet. He seemed to have succeeded in thawing the ice a little, for, several times, the boy laughed. Van Hoorn, meanwhile, was pouring into my ear a succession of the oldest and most childish smoking-room stories. He related them with extraordinary gusto and enjoyment. I scarcely listened. The warmth of the dining-room made me sleepy, after the sharp air outside; behind the palms, the band played dreamy music. The food was delicious; seldom had I eaten such a lunch. And, all the time, I was vaguely wondering where Margot was, when and how he would appear.

Into my coma intruded, with increasing frequence, a few sentences of French. I could understand only a word here and there: "interesting," "suggestive," "extremely typical." It was the speaker's voice which caught my attention. It proceeded from the table next to our own. Idly I turned my head.

A large, middle-aged man sat facing an exotically pretty blonde girl of the type which Paris alone produces. Both of them were looking in our direction and speaking in carefully restrained tones, obviously about us. The man seemed particularly interested. He had a bald, egg-shaped head; bold, rudely prominent, round, solemn eyes; yellowish-white hair brushed back round the base of the skull like a pair of folded wings. His voice was vibrant and harsh. About his whole appearance there was something indescribably unpleasant and sinister. I felt a curious thrill pass through my nervous system; antagonistic, apprehensive, expectant. I glanced quickly at the others; but no, they seemed entirely unaware of the stranger's cynical, unconcealed inspection. Kuno was bending over to speak to Piet; fishy, caressing, and suave. Mr van Hoorn had stopped talking at last and was making up for lost time on a grilled steak. He had tucked his napkin into his collar and was chewing away with the abandonment of one who need no longer fear gravy-stains on his waistcoat. I fancied I heard our French neighbour pronounced the word "*dégoûtant*."

I had frequently pictured to myself what Margot would look like. I had imagined him fatter, older, more prosaic. My imagination had been altogether too timid; I hadn't dreamed of anything so authentic, so absolutely, immediately convincing. Nobody's intuition could be at fault here. I was as certain of his identity as if I'd known him for years.

It was a thrilling moment. My only regret was that nobody could share its excitement with me. How Arthur would have enjoyed it! I could imagine his ill-concealed, gleeful agitation; his private signals which everybody would observe; his ludicrously forced attempts to cover up the mystery with bright chat. The very thought of them made me want to laugh out loud. I didn't dare risk another glance at our neighbours, lest they should see from my face what I knew. Long ago, I had made up my mind that never, at any stage in the proceedings, would I betray my complicity by so much as the flicker of an eyelid. Margot had kept his part of the bargain; I would show that I, also, could be trustworthy and discreet.

How would he deliver his attack? This was a really fascinating question. I tried to put myself in his position; began to imagine the most extravagant subtleties. Perhaps he, or the girl, would pick Kuno's pocket and introduce themselves later, pretending to have found his note-case on the floor. Perhaps, that night, there would be a sham alarm of fire. Margot would plant smoke-bombs in Kuno's bedroom and then rush in to rescue him from the fumes. It seemed obvious to me that they would do something drastic. Margot didn't look the man to be content with half measures. What were they up to now? I could no longer hear their voices. Dropping my napkin somewhat clumsily on the floor, I bent down to pick it up and get a peep, only to find to my disappointment that the two of them had left the dining-room. I was disappointed, but, on thinking it over, not particularly surprised. This had been merely a reconnoitre. Margot would probably do nothing before the evening.

After, lunch, Kuno earnestly advised me to rest. As a beginner, he explained, it would be most unwise for me to exert myself too much on the first day. I agreed, not without amusement. A few moments later, I heard him arranging with Piet van Hoorn to go out to the toboggan runs. Mr van Hoorn had already retired to his room.

At tea-time, there was dancing in the lounge. Piet and Kuno didn't appear; neither to my relief did Mr van Hoorn. I was quite happy by myself, watching the guests. Presently Margot came in alone. He sat down on the opposite side of the big glass veranda, not more than a couple of yards from my table. Stealing a glance in his direction, I met his eyes. They were cold, prominent, rudely inquisitive as ever. My heart thumped uncomfortably. The situation was getting positively uncanny. Suppose I were to go over and speak to him now? I could save him, after all, a great deal of trouble. I had only to introduce him as an acquaintance of mine, met here by chance. There was no earthly reason why Kuno should suspect anything prearranged. Why should we go on performing this rather sinister charade? I hesitated, half rose to my feet, subsided again. For the second time my eyes met his. And now it seemed to me that I understood him perfectly. "Don't be a little fool," he was saying. "Leave this to me. Don't try to meddle in things you don't understand."

"All right," I mentally told him, with a slight shrug of my shoulders. "Do as you like. It's your own funeral."

And, feeling rather resentful, I got up and walked out of the lounge; I couldn't stand this silent *tête à tête* any longer.

At dinner that night both Kuno and Mr van Hoorn, in their different ways, were in high spirits. Piet looked bored. Perhaps he found his evening clothes as stiff as mine. If so, he had my hearty sympathy. His uncle rallied him from time to time on his silence, and I reflected how much I should dislike to travel with Mr van Hoorn.

We were near the end of our meal when Margot and his companion came into the dining-room. I saw them at once, for I had been subconsciously keeping my eye on the door ever since we had sat down. Margot was wearing a tail-coat, with a flower in his button-hole. The girl was dressed magnificently, in some shimmering material which gleamed like silver armour. They passed down the long lane between the tables with many eyes following them.

"Look, Piet," exclaimed Mr van Hoorn, "there's a pretty girl for you. Ask her for a dance this evening. Her father won't bite you."

To reach their table, Margot had to pass within a few inches of our chairs. As he did so, he briefly inclined his head. Kuno, ever gracious, returned the bow. For a moment I thought Margot would follow up this opening, even if only with a conventional remark about the weather. He did not. The two of them took their places. Almost immediately, we rose to go and drink our coffee in the smoking-room.

Here, Mr van Hoorn's conversation took a surprising turn. It was as if he'd realized that the heartiness and the doubtful stories had been overdone. He began, quite suddenly, to talk about art. He had a house, he told us, in Paris, which was full of old furniture and etchings. Although he spoke modestly, it soon became clear that he was an expert. Kuno was greatly interested. Piet remained indifferent. I saw him cast more than one furtive glance at his wristwatch, presumably to see whether it wasn't time for bed.

"Excuse me, gentlemen."

The harsh voice startled all of us; nobody had seen Margot's approach. He towered above us, an elegant, sardonic figure, holding a cigar in his mottled, yellow hand.

"It is necessary that I ask this young man a question."

His bulging eyes fixed upon Piet with a concentration which suggested that he was observing some minute insect, scarcely visible without the aid of a magnifying glass. The poor boy literally began to sweat with embarrassment. As for myself, I was so amazed at this new turn in Margot's tactics that I could only stare at him, my mouth hanging open. Margot himself evidently enjoyed the effect which his dramatic appearance had created. His lips curved in a smile which was positively diabolic.

"Have you the true Aryan descent?"

And before the astounded Piet could answer, he added:

"I am Marcel Janin."

I don't know whether the others had really heard of him, or whether their polite interest was merely pretended. As it happened, I knew his name quite well. M. Janin was one of Fritz Wendel's favourite authors. Fritz had once lent me a book of his—*The Kiss Under the Midnight Sun*. It was written in the fashionable French manner, half romance, half reportage, and gave a lurid, obviously imaginative account of the erotic life of Hammerfest. And there were half a dozen others, equally sensational and ranging in *milieu* from Santiago to Shanghai. M. Janin's particular brand of pornography, if one was to judge from his clothes, appeared to have hit the public taste. He had just finished his eighth, he told us: it dealt with the amours peculiar to a winter sport hotel. Hence his presence here. After his brusque self-introduction, he proved most affable and treated us, without further request, to a discourse on his career, aims, and methods of work.

"I write very quick," he informed us. "For me, one glance is sufficient. I do not believe in the second impression."

A couple of days ashore from a cruising liner had furnished M. Janin with the material for most of his works. And now Switzerland was disposed of, too. Looking for fresh worlds to conquer, he had fixed on the Nazi movement. He and his secretary were leaving next day for Munich. "Within a week," he concluded ominously, "I shall know all."

I wondered what part M. Janin's secretary (he insisted, several times, on this title) played in his lightning researches. Probably she acted as a kind of rough and ready chemical reagent; in certain combinations she produced certain known results. It was she, it seemed, who had discovered Piet. M. Janin, as excited as a hunter in unfamiliar territory, had rushed, over-precipitately, to the attack. He didn't seem much disappointed, however, to discover that this wasn't his legitimate prey. His generalizations, formulated, to save time, in advance, were not easily disturbed. Dutchman or German, it was all grist to the mill. Piet, I suspected, would nevertheless make his appearance in the new book, dressed up in a borrowed brown shirt. A writer with M. Janin's technique can afford to waste nothing.

One mystery was solved, the other deepened. I puzzled over it for the rest of the evening. If Margot wasn't Janin, who was he? And where? It seemed odd that he should fritter away twenty-four hours like this, after being in such a hurry to get Kuno to come. Tomorrow, I thought, he'll turn up for certain. My meditations were interrupted by Kuno tapping at my door to ask if I had gone to bed. He wanted to talk about Piet van Hoorn, and, sleepy as I felt, I wasn't unkind enough to deny him.

"Tell me, please ... don't you find him a little like Tony?"

"Tony?" I was stupid this evening. "Tony who?"

Kuno regarded me with gentle reproach.

"Why, excuse me ... I mean Tony in the book, you see."

I smiled.

"You think Tony is more like Piet than like Heinz?"

"Oh yes," Kuno was very definite on this point. "Much more like."

So poor Heinz was banished from the island. Having reluctantly agreed to this, we said good night.

Next morning I decided to make some investigations for myself. While Kuno was in the lounge talking to the van Hoorns, I got into conversation with the hall porter. Oh yes, he assured me, a great many business people were here from Paris just now; some of them very important.

"M. Bernstein, for instance, the factory-owner. He's worth millions ... Look, sir, he's over there now, by the desk."

I had just time to catch sight of a fat, dark man with an expression on his face like that of a sulky baby. I had never noticed him anywhere in our neighbourhood. He passed through the doors into the smoking-room, a bundle of letters in his hand.

"Do you know if he owns a glass factory?" I asked.

"I'm sure I couldn't say, sir. I wouldn't be surprised. They say he's got his finger in nearly everything."

The day passed without further developments. In the afternoon Mr van Hoorn at length succeeded in forcing his bashful nephew into the company of some lively Polish girls. They all went off skiing together. Kuno was not best pleased, but he accepted the situation with his usual grace. He seemed to have developed quite a taste for Mr van Hoorn's society. The two of them spent the afternoon indoors.

After tea, as we were leaving the lounge, we came face to face with M. Bernstein. He passed us by without the faintest interest.

As I lay in bed that night I almost reached the conclusion that Margot must be a figment of Arthur's imagination. For what purpose he had been created I couldn't conceive. Nor did I much care. It was very nice here. I was enjoying myself; in a day or two I should have learnt to ski. I would make the most of my holiday, I decided; and, following Arthur's advice, forget the reasons for which I had come. As for Kuno, my fears had been unfounded. He hadn't been cheated out of a farthing. So what was there to worry about?

On the afternoon of the third day of our visit, Piet suggested, of his own accord, that we two should go skating on the lake alone. The poor boy, as I had noticed at lunch, was near the bursting-point. He had had more than enough of his uncle, of Kuno, and of the Polish girls; it had become necessary for him to vent his feelings on somebody, and, of a bad bunch, I seemed the least unlikely to be sympathetic. No sooner were we on the ice than he started: I was astonished to find how much and with what vehemence he could talk.

What did I think of this place? he asked. Wasn't all this luxury sickening? And the people? Weren't they too idiotic and revolting for words? How could they behave as they did, with Europe in its present state? Had they no decency at all? Had they no national pride, to mix with a lot of Jews who were ruining their countries? How did I feel about it, myself?

"What does your uncle say to it all?" I counter-questioned, to avoid an answer.

Piet shrugged his shoulders angrily.

"Oh, my uncle … he doesn't take the least interest in politics. He only cares for his old pictures. He's more of a Frenchman than a Dutchman, my father says."

Piet's studies in Germany had turned him into an ardent Fascist. M. Janin's instinct hadn't been so incorrect after all. The young man was browner than the Browns.

"What my country needs is a man like Hitler. A real leader. A people without ambition is unworthy to exist." He turned his handsome, humourless face and regarded me sternly. "You, with your Empire, you must understand that."

But I refused to be drawn.

"Do you often travel with your uncle?" I asked.

"No. As a matter of fact I was surprised when he asked me to come with him here. At such short notice, too; only a week ago. But I love skiing, and I thought it would all be quite primitive and simple, like the tour I made with some students last Christmas. We went to the Riesengebirge. We used to wash ourselves every morning with snow in a bucket. One must learn to harden the body. Self-discipline is most important in these times ..."

"Which day did you arrive here?" I interrupted.

"Let's see. It must have been the day before you did." A thought suddenly struck Piet. He became more human. He even smiled. "By the way, that's a funny thing I'd quite forgotten ... my uncle was awfully keen to get to know you."

"To know me?"

"Yes ..." Piet laughed and blushed. "As a matter of fact, he told me to try and find out who you were."

"He did?"

"You see, he thought you were the son of a friend of his: an Englishman. But he'd only met the son once, a long time ago, and he wasn't sure. He was afraid that, if you saw him and he didn't recognize you, you'd be offended."

"Well, I certainly helped you to make my acquaintance, didn't I?" We both laughed.

"Yes, you did."

"Ha, ha! How very funny!"

"Yes, isn't it? Very funny indeed."

When we returned to the hotel for tea, we had some trouble in finding Kuno and Mr van Hoorn. They were sitting together in a remote corner of the smoking-room at a distance from the other guests. Mr van Hoorn was no longer laughing; he spoke quietly and seriously, with his eyes on Kuno's face. And Kuno himself was as grave as a judge. I had the impression that he was profoundly disturbed and perplexed by the subject of their conversation. But this was only an impression, and a momentary one. As soon as Mr van Hoom became aware of my approach, he laughed loudly and gave Kuno's elbow a nudge, as if reaching the climax of a funny story. Kuno laughed, too, but with less enthusiasm.

"Well, well!" exclaimed Mr van Hoorn. "Here are the boys! As hungry as hunters, I'll be bound! And we two old fogies have been wasting the whole afternoon yarning away indoors. My goodness, is it as late as that? I say, I want my tea!"

"A telegram for you, sir," said the voice of a pageboy, just behind me. I stepped aside, supposing that he was addressing one of the others, but no; he held the silver tray towards me. There was no mistake. On the envelope I read my name.

"Aha!" cried Mr van Hoorn. "Your sweetheart's getting impatient. She wants you to go back to her."

I tore open the envelope, unfolded the paper. The message was only three words:

Please return immediately.

I read it over several times. I smiled.

"As a matter of fact," I told Mr van Hoorn, "you're quite right. She does."

The telegram was signed "Ludwig."

Chapter Fourteen

SOMETHING HAD HAPPENED to Arthur. That much was obvious. Otherwise, if he'd wanted me, he'd have sent for me himself. And the mess he was in, whatever it was, must have something to do with the Party, since Bayer had signed the telegram. Here my reasoning came to an end. It was bounded by guesses and possibilities as vague and limitless as the darkness which enclosed the train. Lying in my berth, I tried to sleep and couldn't. The swaying of the coach, the clank of the wheels kept time with the excited, anxious throbbing of my heart. Arthur, Bayer, Margot, Schmidt; I tried the puzzle backwards, sideways, all ways up. It kept me awake the whole night.

Years later it seemed, though actually only the next afternoon, I let myself into the flat with the latch-key; quickly pushed open the door of my room. In the middle of it sat Frl. Schroeder, dozing, in the best armchair. She had taken off her slippers and was resting her stockinged feet on the footstool. When one of her lodgers was away, she often did this. She was indulging in the dream of most landladies, that the whole place was hers.

If I had returned from the dead she could hardly have

uttered a more piercing scream on waking and seeing my figure in the doorway.

"Herr Bradshaw! How you startled me!"

"I'm sorry, Frl. Schroeder. No, please don't get up. Where's Herr Norris?"

"Herr Norris?" She was still a bit dazed. "I don't know, I'm sure. He said he'd be back about seven."

"He's still living here, then?"

"Why, of course, Herr Bradshaw. What an idea!" Frl. Schroeder regarded me with astonishment and anxiety. "Is anything the matter? Why didn't you let me know that you were coming home sooner? I was going to have given your room a thorough turn-out tomorrow."

"That's perfectly all right. I'm sure everything looks very nice. Herr Norris hasn't been ill, has he?"

"Why, no." Frl. Schroeder's perplexity was increasing with every moment. "That is, if he has he hasn't said a word about it to me, and he's been up and about from morning to midnight. Did he write and tell you so?"

"Oh, no, he didn't do that ... only ... when I went away I thought he looked rather pale. Has anybody rung up for me or left any messages?"

"Nothing, Herr Bradshaw. You remember, you told all your pupils you would be away until the New Year."

"Yes, of course."

I walked over to the window, looked down into the dank, empty street. No, it wasn't quite empty. Down there, on the corner, stood a small man in a buttoned-up overcoat and a felt hat. He paced quietly up and down, his hands folded behind his back, as if waiting for a girl friend.

"Shall I get you some hot water?" asked Frl. Schroeder tactfully. I caught sight of myself in the mirror. I looked tired, dirty, and unshaved.

"No, thank you," I said, smiling. "There's something I've got to attend to first. I shall be back in about an hour. Perhaps you'll be so kind and heat the bath?"

"Yes, Ludwig's here," the girl in the outer office at the Wilhelmstrasse told me. "Go right in."

Bayer didn't seem in the least surprised to see me. He looked up from his papers with a smile.

"So here you are, Mr Bradshaw! Please sit down. You have enjoyed your holiday, I hope?"

I smiled.

"Well, I was just beginning to ..."

"When you got my telegram? I am sorry, but it was necessary, you see."

Bayer paused; regarded me thoughtfully; continued:

"I'm afraid that what I have to say may be unpleasant for you, Mr Bradshaw. But it is not right that you are kept any longer in ignorance of the truth."

I could hear the clock ticking—somewhere in the room; everything seemed to have become very quiet. My heart was thumping uncomfortably against my ribs. I suppose that I half guessed what was coming.

"You went to Switzerland," Bayer continued, "with a certain Baron Pregnitz?"

"Yes. That's right." I licked my lips with my tongue.

"Now I am going to ask you a question which may seem that I interfere very much in your private affairs. Please do not be offended. If you do not wish it, you will not answer, you understand?"

My throat had gone dry. I tried to clear it and made an absurdly loud, grating sound.

"I'll answer any question you like," I said, rather huskily.

Bayer's eyes brightened approvingly. He leant forward towards me across the writing-table.

"I am glad that you take this attitude, Mr Bradshaw ... You wish to help us. That is good ... Now, will you tell me, please, what was the reason which Norris gave you that you should go with this Baron Pregnitz to Switzerland?"

Again I heard that clock. Bayer, his elbows resting on the table, regarded me benevolently, with encouraging attention.

For the second time I cleared my throat.

"Well," I began, "first of all, you see ..."

It was a long, silly story, which seemed to take hours to tell. I hadn't realized how foolish, how contemptible some of it would sound. I felt horribly ashamed of myself, blushed, tried to be humorous and weakly failed, defended and then accused my motives, avoided certain passages, only to blurt them out a moment later, under the neutral inquisition of his friendly eyes. The story seemed to involve a confession of all my weaknesses to that silent, attentive man. I have never felt so humiliated in all my life.

When at last I had finished, Bayer made a slight movement.

"Thank you, Mr Bradshaw. All this, you see, is very much as we had supposed ... Our workers in Paris know this Mr van Hoorn very well. He is a clever man. He has given us much trouble."

"You mean ... that he's a police agent?"

"Unofficially, yes. He collects information of all kinds and sells it to those who will pay him. There are many who do this; but most of them are quite stupid and not dangerous at all."

"I see ... And van Hoorn's been making use of Norris to collect information?"

"That is so. Yes."

"But how on earth did he get Norris to help him? What story did he tell him? I wonder Norris wasn't suspicious."

In spite of his gravity, Bayer's eyes showed a sparkle of amusement.

"It is possible that Norris was most suspicious indeed. No. You have misunderstood me, Mr Bradshaw. I have not said that van Hoorn deceived him. That was not necessary."

"Not necessary?" I stupidly echoed.

"Not necessary. No ... Norris was quite aware, you see, of what van Hoorn wanted. They understood each other very well. Since Norris returned to Germany he has been receiving regular sums of money through van Hoorn from the French Secret Service."

"I don't believe it!"

"Nevertheless, it is true. I can prove it if you wish. Norris has been paid to keep an eye on us, to give information about our plans and movements." Bayer smiled and raised his hand, as if to anticipate a protest. "Oh, this is not so terrible as it sounds. The information which he had to give was of no importance. In our movement we have not the necessity to make great plots, as are described of us in the capitalist Press and the criminal romances. We act openly. It is easy for all to know what we do. It is possible that Norris can have been able to tell his friends the names of some of our messengers who are going frequently between Berlin and Paris. And, perhaps, also, certain addresses. But this can have been only at the first."

"You've known about him a long time already, then?" I hardly recognized the sound of my own voice.

Bayer smiled brilliantly.

"Quite a long time. Yes." His tone was soothing. "Norris has even been very helpful to us, though he did not wish it. We were able, occasionally, to convey much false impressions to our opponents through this channel."

With bewildering speed the jig-saw puzzle was fitting itself together in my brain. In a flash another piece was added. I remembered the morning after the elections; Bayer in this very room, handing Arthur the sealed packet from his writing-table drawer.

"Yes … I see now …"

"My dear Mr Bradshaw," Bayer's tone was kind, almost paternal, "please do not distress yourself too much. Norris is your friend, I know. Mind, I have not said this against him as a man; the private life is not our concern. We are all convinced that you cannot have known of this. You have acted throughout with good faith towards us. I wish it had been possible to keep you in ignorance over this matter."

"What I still don't understand is, how Pregnitz …"

"Ah, I am coming to that … Norris, you see, found himself unable any longer to satisfy his Paris friends with these reports. They were so often insufficient or false, and so he proposed to van Hoorn the idea of a meeting with Pregnitz."

"And the glass factory?"

"It exists only in the imagination of Norris. Here he made use of your inexperience. It was not for this that van Hoorn paid your expenses to Switzerland. Baron Pregnitz is a politician, not a financier."

"You don't mean …?"

"Yes, this is what I wished to tell you. Pregnitz has access to many secrets of the German Government. It is possible for him to obtain copies of maps, plans, and private documents which van Hoorn's employers will pay very much to see. Perhaps Pregnitz will be tempted. This does not concern us. We wish only to warn you personally, that you may not discover yourself innocently in a prison for the high treason."

"My God … how on earth did you get to know all this?"

Bayer smiled.

"You think that we have also our spies? No, that is not necessary. All information of this sort one can obtain so easily from the police."

"Then the police know?"

"I do not think that they know all for certain, yet. But they are very suspicious. Two of them came here to ask us questions concerning Norris, Pregnitz, and yourself. From these questions one could guess a good deal. I believe we have satisfied them that you are not a dangerous conspirator," Bayer smiled, "nevertheless, it seemed best to telegraph you at once, that you might not be further involved."

"It was very good of you to bother what became of me at all."

"We try always to help those who help us; although, unfortunately, this is sometimes not possible. You have not seen Norris yet?"

"No. He was out when I arrived."

"So? That is excellent. It is better that you should tell him these things yourself. Since a week he has not been here. Tell him, please, that we wish him no harm; but it will be better for himself if he goes away from Germany at once. And warn him also that the police have him under observance. They are opening all letters which he receives or writes; of this I am sure."

"All right," I said, "I'll tell him that."

"You will? That is good." Bayer rose to his feet. "And now, Mr Bradshaw, please do not make yourself reproaches. You have been foolish, perhaps. Never mind; we are all sometimes very, very foolish. You have done nothing to be ashamed. I think that now you will be more careful with whom you make a friend, eh?"

"Yes, I shall."

Bayer smiled. He clapped me encouragingly on the shoulder. "Then now we will forget this unpleasant matter. You would like to do some more work for us soon? Excellent ... You tell Norris what I said, eh? Goodbye."

"Goodbye."

I shook hands with him, I suppose, and got myself off the premises in the usual manner. I must have behaved quite normally, because nobody in the outer office stared. It was only when I was out in the street that I began to run. I was suddenly in a tremendous hurry; I wanted to get this over, quick.

A taxi passed; I was inside it before the driver had had time to slow down. "Drive as fast as you can," I told him. We skidded in and out of the traffic; it had been raining and the roadway was slimy with mud. The lamps were lighted already; it was getting dark. I lit a cigarette and threw it away after a couple of puffs. My hands were trembling, otherwise I was perfectly calm, not angry, not even disgusted; nothing. The puzzle fitted together perfectly. I could see it all, if I wished to look at it, a compact, vivid picture, at a single glance. All I want, I thought, is to get this over. Now.

Arthur was back already. He looked out of his bedroom as I opened the front door of the flat.

"Come in, dear boy! Come in! This is indeed a pleasant

surprise! When Frl. Schroeder told me you'd returned, I could hardly believe it. What was it made you come back so soon? Were you homesick for Berlin? or did you pine for my society? Please say you did! We've all missed you very much here. Our Christmas dinner was tasteless indeed without you. Yes … I must say, you're not looking as well as I'd expected; perhaps you're tired after the journey? Sit down here. Have you had tea? Let me give you a glass of something to refresh you?"

"No, thank you, Arthur."

"You won't? Well, well … perhaps you'll change your mind later. How did you leave our friend Pregnitz? Flourishing, I hope?"

"Yes. He's all right."

"I'm glad to hear that. Very glad. And now, William, I really must congratulate you on the admirable skill and tact with which you fulfilled your little mission. Margot was more than satisfied. And he's very particular, you know; very difficult to please …"

"You've heard from him, then?"

"Oh, yes. I got a long telegram this morning. The money will arrive tomorrow. I'm bound to say this for Margot: he's most punctual and correct in these matters. One can always rely on him."

"Do you mean to say that Kuno's agreed?"

"No, not that, alas! Not yet. These things aren't settled in a day. But Margot's distinctly hopeful. It seems that Pregnitz was a little difficult to persuade at first. He didn't quite see this transaction would be of advantage to his firm. But now he's become definitely interested. He wants time to think it over, of course. Meanwhile, I get half my share as we arranged. I'm thankful to say that it's more than sufficient to cover my travelling expenses; so that's one weight lifted from my mind. As for the rest, I'm convinced, personally, that Pregnitz will agree in the end."

"Yes … I suppose they all do."

"Nearly all, yes …" Arthur agreed absently; became aware,

the next moment, of something strange in my tone.

"I don't think, William, I quite understand what you mean."

"Don't you? I'll put it more plainly: I suppose van Hoorn usually succeeds in getting people to sell him whatever he wants to buy?"

"Well—I don't know that, in this case, one could describe it as a sale. As I think I told you ..."

"Arthur," I interrupted wearily, "you can stop lying now. I know all about it."

"Oh," he began, and was silent. The shock seemed to have taken away his breath. Sinking heavily into a chair, he regarded his finger-nails with unconcealed dismay.

"This is all my own fault really, I suppose. I was a fool ever to have trusted you. To do you justice, you more or less warned me against it, often enough."

Arthur looked up at me quickly, like a spaniel which is going to be whipped. His lips moved, but he didn't speak. The deep-cleft dimple appeared for a moment in his collapsed chin. Furtively, he scratched his jowl, withdrawing his hand again immediately, as though he were afraid this gesture might annoy me.

"I ought to have known that you'd find a use for me, sooner or later; even if it was only a decoy duck. You always find a use for everybody, don't you? If I'd landed up in prison it'd have damn well served me right."

"William, I give you my word of honour, I never ..."

"I won't pretend," I continued, "that I care a damn what happens to Kuno. If he's fool enough to let himself in for this, he does it with his eyes open ... But I must say this, Arthur: if anybody but Bayer had told me you'd ever do the dirty on the Party, I'd have called him a bloody liar. You think that's very sentimental of me, I suppose?"

Arthur started visibly at the name.

"So Bayer knows, does he?"

"Of course."

"Oh dear, oh dear ..."

He seemed to have collapsed into himself, like a scarecrow

in the rain. His loose, stubbly cheeks were blotched and pallid, his lips parted in a vacant snarl of misery.

"I never really told van Hoorn anything of importance, William. I swear to you I didn't."

"I know. You never got the chance. It doesn't seem to me that you're much good, even as a crook."

"Don't be angry with me, dear boy. I can't bear it."

"I'm not angry with you; I'm angry with myself for being such an idiot. I thought you were my friend, you see."

"I don't ask you to forgive me," said Arthur, humbly. "You'll never do that, of course. But don't judge me too harshly. You're young. Your standards are so severe. When you get to my age, you'll see things differently, perhaps. It's very easy to condemn when one isn't tempted. Remember that."

"I don't condemn you. As for my standards, if I ever had any, you've muddled them up completely. I expect you're right. In your place, I'd probably have done just the same."

"You see?" Arthur eagerly followed up his advantage. "I knew you'd come to look at it in that light."

"I don't want to look at it in any light. I'm too utterly sick of the whole filthy business ... My God, I wish you'd go away somewhere where I'll never see you again!"

Arthur sighed.

"How hard you are, William. I should never have expected it. You always seemed to me to have such a sympathetic nature."

"That was what you counted on, I suppose? Well, I think you'll find that the soft ones object to being cheated even more than the others. They mind it more because they feel that they've only themselves to blame."

"You're perfectly justified, of course, I deserve all the unkind things you say. Don't spare me. But I promise you most solemnly, the thought that I was implicating you in any sort of crime never once entered my head. You see, everything has gone off exactly as we planned. After all where was the risk?"

"There was more risk than what you think. The police knew all about our little expedition before we'd even started."

"The police? William, you're not in earnest!"

"You don't think I'm trying to be funny, do you? Bayer told me to warn you. They've been round to see him and make inquiries."

"My God ..."

The last traces of stiffness had gone out of Arthur. He sat there like a crumpled paper bag, his blue eyes vivid with terror.

"But they can't possibly ..."

I went to the window.

"Come and look, if you don't believe me. He's still there."

"Who's still there?"

"The detective who's watching this house."

Without a word, Arthur hurried to my side at the window and took a peep at the man in the buttoned-up overcoat.

Then he slowly went back to his chair. He seemed suddenly to have become much calmer.

"What am I to do?" He appeared to be thinking aloud rather than addressing me.

"You must clear out, of course; the moment you've got this money."

"They'll arrest me, William."

"Oh no, they won't. They'd have done it before this, if they were going to. Bayer says they've been reading all your letters ... Besides, they don't know everything for certain yet, he thinks."

Arthur pondered for some minutes in silence. He looked up at me in nervous appeal.

"Then you're not going to ..." He stopped.

"Not going to what?"

"To tell them, well—er—everything?"

"My God, Arthur!" I literally gasped. "What exactly, do you take me for?"

"No, of course, dear boy ... Forgive me. I might have known ..." Arthur coughed apologetically. "Only, just for the moment, I was afraid. There might be quite a large reward, you see ..."

For several seconds I was absolutely speechless.

Seldom have I been so shocked. Open-mouthed, I regarded him with a mixture of indignation and amusement, curiosity and disgust. Timidly, his eyes met mine. There could be no doubt about it. He was honestly unaware of having said anything to surprise or offend. I found my voice at last.

"Well, of all the …"

But my outburst was cut short by a furious volley of knocks on the bedroom door.

"Herr Bradshaw! Herr Bradshaw!" Frl. Schroeder was in frantic agitation. "The water's boiling and I can't turn on the tap! Come quick this moment, or we shall all be blown to bits!"

"We'll discuss this later," I told Arthur, and hurried out of the room.

Chapter Fifteen

THREE-QUARTERS OF AN hour later, washed and shaved, I returned to Arthur's room. I found him peering cautiously down into the street from behind the shelter of the lace curtain.

"There's a different one there now, William," he told me. "They relieved each other about five minutes ago."

His tone was gleeful; he seemed positively to be enjoying the situation. I joined him at the window. Sure enough, a tall man in a bowler hat had taken the place of his colleague at the thankless task of waiting for the invisible girl friend.

"Poor fellow," Arthur giggled, "he looks terribly cold, doesn't he? Do you think he'd be offended if I sent him down a medicine bottle full of brandy, with my card?"

"He mightn't see the joke."

Strangely enough, it was I who felt embarrassed. With indecent ease, Arthur seemed to have forgotten all the unpleasant things I had said to him less than an hour before. His manner towards me was as natural as if nothing had happened. I felt myself harden towards him again. In my bath, I had softened, regretted some cruel words, condemned others as spiteful or priggish. I had rehearsed a partial reconciliation, on magnanimous terms. But Arthur, of course, was to make the advances. Instead of which, here he was, blandly opening his wine-cupboard with his wonted hospitable air.

"At any rate, William, you won't refuse a glass yourself? It'll give you an appetite for supper."

"No, thank you."

I tried to make my tone stern; it sounded merely sulky. Arthur's face fell at once. His ease of manner, I saw now, had been only experimental. He sighed deeply, resigned to further penitence, assuming an expression which was like a funeral top-hat, lugubrious, hypocritical, discreet. It became him so ill that, in spite of myself, I had to smile.

"It's no good, Arthur. I can't keep it up!"

He was too cautious to reply to this, except with a shy, sly smile. This time, he wasn't going to risk an over-hasty response.

"I suppose," I continued reflectively, "that none of them were ever really angry with you, were they, afterwards?"

Arthur didn't pretend to misunderstand. Demurely he inspected his fingernails.

"Not everybody, alas, has your generous nature, William."

It was no good; we had returned to our verbal card-playing. The moment of frankness, which might have redeemed so much, had been elegantly avoided. Arthur's orientally sensitive spirit shrank from the rough, healthy, modern catch-as-catch-can of home-truths and confessions; he offered me a compliment instead. Here we were, as so often before, at the edge of that delicate, almost visible line which divided our two worlds. We should never cross it now. I wasn't old or subtle enough to find the approach. There was a disappointing pause, during which he rummaged in the cupboard.

"Are you *quite* sure you won't have a drop of brandy?"

I sighed. I gave him up. I smiled.

"All right. Thanks, I will."

We drank ceremoniously, touching glasses. Arthur smacked his lips with unconcealed satisfaction. He appeared to imagine that something had been symbolized: a reconciliation, or, at any rate, a truce. But no, I couldn't feel this. The ugly, dirty fact was still there, right under our noses, and no amount of brandy could wash it away.

Arthur appeared, for the moment, sublimely unconscious of its existence. I was glad. I felt a sudden anxiety to protect him from a realization of what he had done. Remorse is not for the elderly. When it comes to them, it is not purging or uplifting, but merely degrading and wretched, like a bladder disease. Arthur must never repent. And indeed, it didn't seem probable that he ever would.

"Let's go out and eat," I said, feeling that the sooner we got out of this ill-omened room the better. Arthur cast an involuntary glance in the direction of the window.

"Don't you think, William, that Frl. Schroeder would make us some scrambled eggs? I hardly feel like venturing out of doors, just now."

"Of course we must go out, Arthur. Don't be silly. You must behave as normally as possible, or they'll think you're hatching some plot. Besides, think of that unfortunate man down there. How dull it must be for him. Perhaps if we go out, he'll be able to get something to eat, too."

"Well, I must confess," Arthur doubtfully agreed, "I hadn't thought of it in that light. Very well, if you're quite sure it's wise ..."

It is a curious sensation to know that you are being followed by a detective; especially when, as in this case, you are actually anxious not to escape him. Emerging into the street, at Arthur's side, I felt like the Home Secretary leaving the House of Commons with the Prime Minister. The man in the bowler hat was either a novice at his job or exceedingly bored with it. He made no attempt at concealment; stood staring at us from the middle of a pool of lamplight. A sort of perverted sense of courtesy prevented me from looking over my shoulder to see if he was following; as for Arthur, his embarrassment was only too painfully visible. His neck seemed to telescope into his body, so that three-quarters of his face was hidden by his coat collar; his gait was that of a murderer retreating from a corpse. I soon noticed that I was subconsciously regulating my pace; I kept hurrying forward in an instinctive desire to get away from our pursuer, then slowing down, lest we should leave him altogether behind. During the walk to the restaurant, Arthur and I didn't exchange a word.

Barely had we taken our seats when the detective entered. Without a glance in our direction, he strode over to the bar and was soon morosely consuming a boiled sausage and a glass of lemonade.

"I suppose," I said, "that they're not allowed to drink beer when they're on duty."

"Ssh, William!" giggled Arthur, "he'll hear you!"

"I don't care if he does. He can't arrest me for laughing at him."

Nevertheless, such is the latent power of one's upbringing, I lowered my voice almost to a whisper.

"I suppose they pay him his expenses. You know, we really ought to have taken him to the Montmartre, and given him a treat."

"Or to the opera."

"It'd be rather amusing to go to church."

We sniggered together, like two boys poking fun at the schoolmaster. The tall man, if he was aware of our comments, bore himself with considerable dignity. His face, presented to us in profile, was gloomy, thoughtful, even philosophic; he might well have been composing a poem. Having finished the sausage, he ordered an Italian salad.

The joke, such as it was, lasted right through our meal. I prolonged it, consciously, as much as I could. So, I think, did Arthur. Tacitly, we helped each other. We were both afraid of a pause. Silence would be too eloquent. And there was so little left for us to talk about. We left the restaurant as soon as was decently possible, accompanied by our attendant, who followed us home, like a nurse, to see us into bed. Through the window of Arthur's room, we watched him take up his former position, under the lamp-post opposite the house.

"How long will he stay there, do you think?" Arthur asked me anxiously.

"The whole night, probably."

"Oh dear, I do hope not. If he does, I shan't be able to sleep a wink."

"Perhaps if you appear at your window in your pyjamas, he'll go away."

"Really, William, I hardly think I could do anything so immodest." Arthur stifled a yawn.

"Well," I said a bit awkwardly, "I think I'll go to bed now."

"Just what I was going to suggest myself, dear boy." Holding his chin absently between his finger and thumb, Arthur looked vaguely around the room; added, with a simplicity which excluded all hint of irony:

"We've both had a tiring day."

Next morning, at any rate, there was no time to feel embarrassed. We had too much to do. No sooner was Arthur's head free from the barber's hands than I came into his room, in my dressing-gown, to hold a conference. The smaller detective in the overcoat was now on duty. Arthur had to admit that he had no idea if either of them had spent the night outside the house. Compassion hadn't, after all, disturbed his sleep.

The first problem was, of course, to decide on Arthur's destination. Inquiries must be made at the nearest travel bureau as to possible ships and routes. Arthur had already decided finally against Europe.

"I feel I need a complete change of scene, hard as it is to tear oneself away. One's so confined here, so restricted. As you get older, William, you'll feel that the world gets smaller. The frontiers seem to close in, until there's scarcely room to breathe."

"What an unplesant sensation that must be."

"It is," Arthur sighed. "It is indeed. I may be a little overwrought at the present moment, but I must confess that, to me, the countries of Europe are nothing more or less than a collection of mousetraps. In some of them, the cheese is of a superior quality, that is the only difference."

We next discussed which of us should go out and make the inquiries. Arthur was most unwilling to do this.

"But, William, if I go myself, our friend below will most certainly follow me."

"Of course he will. That's just what we want. As soon as you've let the authorities know that you mean to clear out, you'll have set their minds at rest. I'm sure they ask nothing better than to see your back."

But Arthur didn't like it. Such tactics revolted all his secretive instincts. "It seems positively indecent," he added.

"Look here," I said, cunningly. "I'll go if you really want me to. But only on condition that you break the news to Frl. Schroeder yourself while I'm away."

"Really, dear boy … No. I couldn't possibly do that. Very well, have it your own way …"

From my window, half an hour later, I watched him emerge into the street. The detective took, apparently, not the faintest notice of his exit; he was engaged in reading the nameplates within the doorway of the opposite house. Arthur set off briskly, looking neither to left nor right. He reminded me of the man in the poem who fears to catch a glimpse of the demon which is treading in his footsteps. The detective continued to study the nameplates with extreme interest. Then at last, when I had begun to get positively exasperated at his apparent blindness, he straightened himself, pulled out his watch, regarded it with evident surprise, hesitated, appeared to consider, and finally walked away with quick, impatient strides, like a man who has been kept waiting too long. I watched his small figure out of sight in amused admiration. He was an artist.

Meanwhile, I had my own, unpleasant task. I found Frl. Schroeder in the living-room, laying cards, as she did every morning of her life, to discover what would happen during the day. It was no use beating about the bush.

"Frl. Schroeder, Herr Norris has just had some bad news.

He'll have to leave Berlin at once. He asked me to tell you …"

I stopped, feeling horribly uncomfortable, swallowed, blurted out:

"He asked me to tell you that … he'd like to pay for his room for January and the whole of February as well …"

Frl. Schroeder was silent. I concluded, lamely—

"Because of his having to go off at such short notice, you see …"

She didn't look up. There was a muffled sound, and a large tear fell on to the face of the card on a table before her. I felt like crying, too.

"Perhaps …" I was cowardly. "It'll only be for a few months. He may be coming back …"

But Frl. Schroeder either didn't hear or didn't believe this. Her sobs redoubled; she did not attempt to restrain them. Perhaps Arthur's departure was merely the last straw; once started, she had plenty to cry about. The rent and taxes in arrears, the bills she couldn't pay, the rudeness of the coal-man, her pains in the back, her boils, her poverty, her loneliness, her gradually approaching death. It was dreadful to hear her. I began wandering about the room, nervously touching the furniture, in an ecstasy of discomfort.

"Frl. Schroeder … it's all right, really, it is … don't … please …"

She got over it at last. Mopping her eyes on a corner of the table-cloth, she deeply sighed. Sadly, her inflamed glance moved over the array of cards. She exclaimed, with a kind of mournful triumph:

"Well, I never. Just look at that, Herr Bradshaw! The ace of spades … upside down! I might have known something like this would happen. The cards are never wrong."

Arthur arrived back from the travel bureau in a taxi, about an hour later. His hands were full of papers and illustrated brochures. He seemed tired and depressed.

"How did you get on?" I asked.

"Give me time, William. Give me time … I'm a little out of breath …"

Collapsing heavily into a chair, he fanned himself with his hat. I strolled over to the window. The detective wasn't at his usual post. Turning my head to the left, I saw him, however, some way farther down the street, examining the contents of the grocer's shop.

"Is he back already?" Arthur inquired.

I nodded.

"Really? To give the devil his due, that young man will go far in his unsavoury profession … Do you know, William, he had the effrontery to come right into the office and stand beside me at the counter? I even heard him making inquiries about a trip to the Harz."

"Perhaps he really wanted to go there; you never know. He may be having his holidays soon."

"Well, well … at all events, it was most upsetting … I had the greatest difficulty in arriving at the extremely grave decision I had to make."

"And what's the verdict?"

"I much regret to say," Arthur regarded the buttons on his boot despondently, "that it will have to be Mexico."

"Good God!"

"You see, dear boy, the possibilities, at such short notice, are very limited … I should have greatly preferred Rio, of course, or the Argentine. I even toyed with China. But everywhere, nowadays, there are such absurd formalities. All kinds of stupid and impertinent questions are asked. When I was young it was very different … An English gentleman was welcome everywhere, especially with a first-class ticket."

"And when do you leave?"

"There's a boat at midday tomorrow. I think I shall go to Hamburg today, on the evening train. It's more comfortable, and, perhaps, on the whole, wiser; don't you agree?"

"I dare say. Yes … This seems a tremendous step to take, all of a sudden. Have you any friends in Mexico?"

Arthur giggled. "I have friends everywhere, William, or shall I say accomplices?"

"And what shall you do when you arrive?"

"I shall go straight to Mexico City (a most depressing spot; although I expect it's altered a great deal since I was there in nineteen-eleven). I shall then take rooms in the best hotel and await a moment of inspiration ... I don't suppose I shall starve."

"No, Arthur," I laughed, "I certainly don't see you starving!"

We brightened. We had several drinks. We became quite lively.

Frl. Schroeder was called in, for a start had to be made with Arthur's packing. She was melancholy at first, and inclined to be reproachful, but a glass of cognac worked wonders. She had her own explanation of the reasons for Arthur's sudden departure.

"Ah, Herr Norris, Herr Norris! You should have been more careful. A gentleman at your time of life ought to have experience enough of these things ..." She winked tipsily at me, behind his back. "Why didn't you stay faithful to your old Schroeder? She would have helped you, she knew about it all the time!"

Arthur, perplexed and vaguely embarrassed, looked questioningly to me for an explanation. I pretended complete ignorance. And now the trunks arrived, fetched down by the porter and his son from the attics at the top of the house. Frl. Schroeder exclaimed, as she packed, over the magnificence of Arthur's clothes. Arthur himself, generous and gay, began distributing largess. The porter got a suit, the porter's wife a bottle of sherry, their son a pair of snakeskin shoes which were much too small for him, but which he insisted he would squeeze into somehow. The piles of newspapers and periodicals were to be sent to a hospital. Arthur certainly gave things away with an air; he knew how to play the Grand Seigneur. The porter's family went away grateful and deeply impressed. I saw that the beginnings of a legend had been created.

As for Frl. Schroeder herself, she was positively loaded

with gifts. In addition to the etchings and the Japanese screen, Arthur gave her three flasks of perfume, some hair lotion, a powder-puff, the entire contents of his wine-cupboard, two beautiful scarves, and, amidst much blushing, a pair of his coveted silk combinations.

"I do wish, William you'd take something, too. Just some little trifle …"

"All right, Arthur, thank you very much … I tell you what, have you still got *Miss Smith's Torture Chamber?* I always liked it the best of those books of yours."

"You did? Really?" Arthur flushed with pleasure. "How charming of you to say so! You know, William, I really think I must tell you a secret. The last of my secrets … I wrote that book myself!"

"Arthur, you didn't!"

"I did, I assure you!" Arthur giggled, delighted. "Years ago, now … It's a youthful indiscretion of which I've since felt rather ashamed … It was printed privately in Paris. I'm told that some of the best-known collectors in Europe have copies in their libraries. It's exceedingly rare."

"And you never wrote anything else?"

"Never, alas! … I put my genius into my life, not into my art. That remark is not original. Never mind. By the way, since we are on this topic, do you know that I've never said goodbye to my dear Anni? I really think I might ask her to come here this afternoon, don't you? After all, I'm not leaving until after tea."

"Better not, Arthur. You'll need all your strength for the journey."

"Well, ha, ha! You may be right. The *pain* of parting would no doubt be most *severe* …"

After lunch, Arthur lay down to rest. I took his trunks in a taxi to the Lehrter Station and deposited them in the cloakroom. Arthur was anxious to avoid a lengthy ceremony of departure from the house. The tall detective was on duty now. He watched the loading of the taxi with interest, but made no move to follow.

At tea Arthur was nervous and depressed. We sat together in the disordered bedroom, with the doors of the empty cupboards standing open and the mattress rolled up at the foot of the bed. I felt apprehensive, for no reason. Arthur rubbed his chin wearily and sighed:

"I feel like the Old Year, William. I shall soon be gone."

I smiled. "A week from now you'll be sitting on the deck in the sun, while we're still freezing or soaking in this wretched town. I envy you, I can tell you."

"Do you, dear boy? I sometimes wish I didn't have to do so much travelling. Mine is essentially a domestic nature. I ask nothing better than to settle down."

"Well, why don't you, then?"

"That's what I so often ask myself ... Something always seems to prevent it."

At last it was time to go.

With infinite fuss, Arthur put on his coat, lost and found his gloves, gave a last touch to his wig. I picked up his suitcase and went out into the hall. Nothing was left but the worst, the ordeal of saying goodbye to Frl. Schroeder. She emerged from the living-room, moist-eyed.

"Well, Herr Norris ..."

The door-bell rang loudly, and there was a double knock on the door. The interruption made Arthur jump.

"Good gracious! Whoever can that be?"

"It's a postman, I expect," said Frl. Schroeder. "Excuse me, Herr Bradshaw ..."

Barely had she opened the door when the man outside it pushed past her into the hall. It was Schmidt.

That he was drunk was obvious, even before he opened his mouth. He stood swaying uncertainly, hatless, his tie over one shoulder, his collar awry. His huge face was inflamed and swollen so that his eyes were mere slits. The hall was a small place for four people. We were standing so close together that I could smell his breath. It stank vilely.

Arthur, at my side, uttered an incoherent sound of dismay, and I myself could only gape. Strange as it may seem, I was entirely unprepared for this apparition. During the last twenty-four hours I had forgotten Schmidt's existence altogether.

He was the master of the situation, and he knew it. His face fairly beamed with malice. Kicking the front door shut behind him with his foot, he surveyed the two of us; Arthur's coat, the suitcase in my hand.

"Doing a bunk, eh?" He spoke loudly, as if addressing a large audience in the middle distance. "I see ... thought you'd give me the slip, did you?" He advanced a pace; he confronted the trembling and dismayed Arthur. "Lucky I came, wasn't it? Unlucky for you ..."

Arthur emitted another sound, this time a kind of squeak of terror. It seemed to excite Schmidt to a positive frenzy of rage. He clenched his fists, he shouted with astonishing violence:

"You dirty tyke!"

He raised his arm. He may actually have been going to strike Arthur; if so, I shouldn't have had time to prevent it. All I could do, within the instant, was to drop the suitcase to the ground. But Frl. Schroeder's reactions were quicker and more effective. She hadn't the ghost of an idea what the fuss was all about. That didn't worry her. Enough that Herr Norris was being insulted by an unknown, drunken man. With a shrill battle-cry of indignation, she charged. Her outstretched palms caught Schmidt in the small of the back, propelled him forwards, like an engine shunting trucks. Unsteady on his feet and taken completely by surprise, he blundered headlong through the open doorway into the living-room and fell sprawling, face downwards, on the carpet. Frl. Schroeder promptly turned the key in the lock. The whole manoeuvre was the work of about five seconds.

"Such cheek!" exclaimed Frl. Schroeder. Her cheeks were bright red with the exertion. "He comes barging in here as if the place belonged to him. And intoxicated ... *pfui!* ... the disgusting pig!"

She seemed to find nothing particularly mysterious in the incident. Perhaps she connected Schmidt somehow with Margot and the ill-fated baby. If so, she was too tactful to say so. A tremendous rattle of knocks on the living-room door excused me from any attempt at inventing explanations.

"Won't he be able to get out at the back?" Arthur inquired nervously.

"You can set your mind at rest, Herr Norris. The kitchen door's locked." Frl. Schroeder turned menacingly upon the invisible Schmidt. "Be quiet, you scoundrel! I'll attend to you in a minute!"

"All the same ..." Arthur was on pins and needles, "I think we ought to be going ..."

"How are you going to get rid of him?" I asked Frl. Schroeder.

"Oh, don't you worry about that, Herr Bradshaw. As soon as you're gone I'll get the porter's son up. He'll go quietly enough, I promise you. If he doesn't, he'll be sorry..."

We said goodbye hurriedly. Frl. Schroeder was too excited and triumphant to be emotional. Arthur kissed her on both cheeks. She stood waving to us from the top of the stairs. A fresh outburst of muffled knocking was audible behind her.

We were in the taxi, and halfway to the station before Arthur recovered his composure sufficiently to be able to talk.

"Dear me ... I've seldom made such an exceedingly unpleasant exit from any town, I think ..."

"What you might call a rousing send-off." I glanced behind me to make sure that the other taxi, with the tall detective, was still following us.

"What do you think he'll do, William? Perhaps he'll go straight to the police?"

"I'm pretty sure he won't. As long as he's drunk they won't listen to him, and by the time he's sober he'll see himself that it's no good. He hasn't the least idea where we're going either. For all he knows, you'll be out of the country tonight."

"You may be right, dear boy. I hope so, I'm sure. I must say I hate to leave you exposed to his malice. You will be most careful, won't you?"

"Oh, Schmidt won't bother me. I'm not worth it, from his point of view. He'll probably find another victim easily enough. I dare say he's got plenty on his books."

"While he was in my employ he certainly had opportunities," Arthur agreed thoughtfully. "And I've no doubt he made full use of them. The creature had talents—of a perverted kind ... Oh, unquestionably ... yes ..."

At length it was all over. The misunderstanding with the cloak-room official, the fuss about the luggage, the finding of a corner seat, the giving of the tip. Arthur leant out of the carriage window; I stood on the platform. We had five minutes to spare.

"You'll remember me to Otto, won't you?"

"I will."

"And give my love to Anni?"

"Of course."

"I wish they could have been here."

"It's a pity, isn't it?"

"But it would have been unwise, under the circumstances. Don't you agree?"

"Yes."

I longed for the train to start. There was nothing more to say, it seemed, except the things which must never be said now, because it was too late. Arthur seemed aware of the vacuum. He groped about uneasily in his stock of phrases.

"I wish you were coming with me, William ... I shall miss you terribly, you know."

"Shall you?" I smiled awkwardly, feeling exquisitely uncomfortable.

"I shall indeed ... You've always been such a support to me. From the first moment we met ..."

I blushed. It was astonishing what a cad he could make me feel. Hadn't I, after all, misunderstood him? Hadn't I misjudged him? Hadn't I, in some obscure way, behaved very badly? To change the subject, I asked:

"You remember that journey? I simply couldn't understand

why they made such a fuss at the frontier. I suppose they'd got their eye on you already?"

Arthur didn't care much for this reminiscence.

"I suppose they had ... Yes."

Another silence. I glanced at the clock, despairingly. One more minute to go. Fumblingly, he began again.

"Try not to think too hardly of me, William ... I should hate that ..."

"What nonsense, Arthur ..." I did my best to pass it off lightly. "How absurd you are!"

"This life is so very complex. If my behaviour hasn't always been quite consistent, I can truly say that I am and always shall be loyal to the Party, at heart ... Say you believe that, please!"

He was outrageous, grotesque, entirely without shame. But what was I to answer? At that moment, had he demanded it, I'd have sworn that two and two make five.

"Yes, Arthur, I do believe it."

"Thank you, William ... Oh dear, now we really are off. I do hope all my trunks are in the van. God bless you, dear boy. I shall think of you always. Where's my mackintosh? Ah, that's all right. Is my hat on straight? Goodbye. Write often, won't you? Goodbye."

The train, gathering speed, drew his manicured hand from mine. I walked a little way down the platform and stood waving until the last coach was out of sight.

As I turned to leave the station I nearly collided with a man who had been standing just behind me. It was the detective.

"Excuse me, *Herr Kommissar*," I murmured.

But he did not even smile.

Chapter Sixteen

EARLY IN MARCH, after the elections, it turned suddenly mild and warm. "Hitler's weather," said the porter's wife; and her son remarked jokingly that we ought to be grateful to van der Lubbe, because the burning of the Reichstag had melted the snow. "Such a nice-looking boy," observed Frl. Schroeder with a sigh. "However could he go and do a dreadful thing like that?" The porter's wife snorted.

Our street looked quite gay when you turned into it and saw the black-white-red flags hanging motionless from windows against the blue spring sky. On the Nollendorfplatz people were sitting out of doors before the café in their overcoats, reading about the *coup d'état* in Bavaria. Göring spoke from the radio horn at the corner. Germany is awake, he said. An ice-cream shop was open. Uniformed Nazis strode hither and thither, with serious set faces, as though on weighty errands. The newspaper readers by the café turned their heads to watch them pass and smiled and seemed pleased.

They smiled approvingly at these youngsters in their big, swaggering boots who were going to upset the Treaty of Versailles. They were pleased because it would soon be summer, because Hitler had promised to protect the small tradesmen, because their newspapers told them that the good times were coming. They were suddenly proud of being blonde. And they thrilled with a furtive, sensual pleasure, like schoolboys, because the Jews, their business rivals, and the Marxists, a vaguely defined minority of people who didn't concern them, had been satisfactorily found guilty of the defeat and the inflation, and were going to catch it.

The town was full of whispers. They told of illegal midnight arrests, of prisoners tortured in the S.A. barracks, made to spit on Lenin's picture, swallow castor oil, eat old socks. They were drowned by the loud, angry voice of the Government, contradicting through its thousand mouths. But not even Göring could silence Helen Pratt. She had decided to investigate the atrocities on her own account. Morning, noon, and night she nosed round the city, ferreting out the victims or their relations, cross-examining them for details. The unfortunate people were reticent, of course, and deadly scared. They didn't want a second dose. But Helen was as relentless as their torturers. She bribed, cajoled, pestered. Sometimes, losing her patience, she threatened. What would happen to them afterwards frankly didn't interest her. She was out to get facts.

It was Helen who first told me that Bayer was dead. She had absolutely reliable evidence. One of the office staff, since released, had seen his corpse in the Spandau barracks. "It's a funny thing," she added, "his left ear was torn right off ... God knows why. It's my belief that some of this gang are simply looneys. Why, Bill, what's the matter? You're going green round the gills."

"That's how I feel," I said.

An awkward thing had happened to Fritz Wendel. A few days before, he had had a motor accident; he had sprained his wrist and scratched the skin off his cheek. The injuries weren't at all serious, but he had to wear a big piece of sticking-plaster and carry his arm in a sling. And now, in spite of the lovely weather, he wouldn't venture out of doors. Bandages of any kind gave rise to misunderstandings, especially when, like Fritz, you had a dark complexion and coal-black hair. Passers-by made unpleasant and threatening remarks. Fritz wouldn't admit this, of course. "Hell, what I mean, one feels such a darn fool." He had become exceedingly cautious. He wouldn't refer to politics at all, even when we were alone together. "Eventually it had to happen," was his only comment on the new régime. As he said this he avoided my eyes.

The whole city lay under an epidemic of discreet, infectious fear. I could feel it, like influenza, in my bones. When the first news of the house-searchings began to come in, I had consulted with Frl. Schroeder about the papers which Bayer had given me. We hid them and my copy of the *Communist Manifesto* under the wood-pile in the kitchen. Unbuilding and rebuilding the wood-pile took half an hour, and before it was finished our precautions had begun to seem rather childish. I felt a bit ashamed of myself, and consequently exaggerated the importance and danger of my position to Frl. Schroeder, who listened respectfully, with rising indignation. "You mean to say they'd come into *my* flat, Herr Bradshaw? Well, of all the cheek. But just let them try it! Why, I'd box their ears for them; I declare I would!"

A night or two after this I was woken by a tremendous banging on the outside door. I sat up in bed and switched on the light. It was just three o'clock. Now I'm for it, I thought. I wondered if they'd allow me to ring up the Embassy. Smoothing my hair tidy with my hand, I tried, not very successfully, to assume an expression of haughty contempt. But when at last Frl. Schroeder had shuffled out to see what was the matter, it was only a lodger from next door who'd come to the wrong flat because he was drunk.

After this scare, I suffered from sleeplessness. I kept fancying I heard heavy wagons drawing up outside our house. I lay waiting in the dark for the ringing of the door-bell. A minute. Five minutes. Ten. One morning, as I stared, half asleep, at the wall-paper above my head, the pattern suddenly formed itself into a chain of little hooked crosses. What was worse, I noticed that everything in the room was really a kind of brown: either green-brown, black-brown, yellow-brown, or red-brown; but all brown, unmistakably. When I had had breakfast and taken a purgative, I felt better.

One morning I had a visit from Otto.

It must have been about half past six when he rang our bell. Frl. Schroeder wasn't up yet; I let him in myself. He was in a filthy state, his hair tousled and matted, a stain of dirty blood down the side of his face from a scratch on the temples.

"*Servus, Willi,*" he muttered. He put out his hand suddenly and clutched my arm. With difficulty, I saved him from falling. But he wasn't drunk, as I at first imagined; simply exhausted. He flopped down into a chair in my room. When I returned from shutting the outside door, he was already asleep.

It was rather a problem to know what to do with him. I had a pupil coming early. Finally, Frl. Schroeder and I managed, between us, to lug him, still half asleep, into Arthur's old bedroom and lay him on the bed. He was incredibly heavy. No sooner was he laid on his back than he began to snore. His snores were so loud that you could hear them in my room, even when the door was shut; they continued, audibly, throughout the lesson. Meanwhile, my pupil, a very nice young man who hoped soon to become a schoolmaster, was eagerly adjuring me not to believe the stories, "invented by Jewish emigrants," about the political persecution.

"Actually," he assured me, "these so-called communists are merely a handful of criminals, the scum of the streets. And most of them are not Germans at all."

"I thought," I said politely, "that you were telling me just now that they drew up the Weimar Constitution?"

This rather staggered him for the moment; but he made a good recovery.

"No, pardon me, the Weimar Constitution was the work of Marxist Jews."

"Ah, the Jews ... to be sure."

My pupil smiled. My stupidity made him feel a bit superior. I think he even liked me for it. A particularly loud snore came from the next room.

"For a foreigner," he politely conceded, "German politics are very complicated."

"Very," I agreed.

Otto woke about tea-time, ravenously hungry. I went out and bought sausages and eggs and Frl. Schroeder cooked him a meal while he washed. Afterwards we sat together in my room. Otto smoked one cigarette after another; he was very nervy and couldn't sit still. His clothes were getting ragged and the collar of his sweater was frayed. His face was full of hollows. He looked like a grown man now, at least five years older.

Frl. Schroeder made him take off his jacket. She mended it while we talked, interjecting, at intervals: "Is it possible? The idea ... how dare they do such a thing! That's what I'd like to know!"

Otto had been on the run for a fortnight now, he told us. Two nights after the Reichstag fire, his old enemy, Werner Baldow, had come round, with six others of his storm-troop, to "arrest" him. Otto used the word without irony; he seemed to find it quite natural. "There's lots of old scores being paid off nowadays," he added, simply.

Nevertheless, Otto had escaped, through a skylight, after kicking one of the Nazis in the face. They had shot at him twice, but missed. Since then he'd been wandering about Berlin, sleeping only in the daytime, walking the streets at night, for fear of house-raids. The first week hadn't been so bad; comrades had put him up, one passing him on to another. But that was getting too risky now. So many of them were dead or in the concentration camps. He'd been sleeping when he could, taking short naps on benches in parks. But he could never rest properly. He had always to be on the watch. He couldn't stick it any longer. Tomorrow he was going to leave Berlin. He'd try to work his way down to the Saar. Somebody had told him that was the easiest frontier to cross. It was dangerous, of course, but better than being cooped up here.

I asked what had become of Anni. Otto didn't know. He'd heard she was with Werner Baldow again. What else could you expect? He wasn't even bitter; he just didn't care. And Olga? Oh, Olga was doing fine. That remarkable business woman had escaped the clean-up through the influence of one of her customers, an important Nazi official. Others had begun to go there, now. Her future was assured.

Otto had heard about Bayer.

"They say Thälmann's dead, too. And Renn. *Junge, Junge* ..."

We exchanged rumours about other well-known names. Frl. Schroeder shook her head and murmured over each. She was so genuinely upset that nobody would have dreamed she was hearing most of them for the first time in her life.

The talk turned naturally to Arthur. We showed Otto the postcards of Tampico which had arrived, for both of us, only a week ago. He examined them with admiration.

"I suppose he's carrying on the work there?"

"What work?"

"The Party work, of course!"

"Oh, yes," I hastily agreed. "Of course he is."

"It was a bit of luck that he went away when he did, wasn't it?"

"Yes ... it certainly was."

Otto's eyes shone.

"We needed more men like old Arthur in the Party. He was a speaker, if you like!"

His enthusiasm warmed Frl. Schroeder's heart. The tears stood in her eyes.

"I always shall say Herr Norris was one of the best and finest and straightest gentlemen I ever knew."

We were all silent. In the twilit room we dedicated a grateful, reverent moment to Arthur's memory. Then Otto continued in a tone of profound conviction:

"Do you know what I think? He's working for us out there,

making propaganda and raising money; and one day, you'll see, he'll come back. Hitler and the rest of them will have to look out for themselves then ..."

It was getting dark outside. Frl. Schroeder rose to turn on the light. Otto said he must be going. He'd decided to make a start this evening now that he was feeling rested. By daybreak, he'd be clear of Berlin altogether. Frl. Schroeder protested vigorously. She had taken a great fancy to him.

"Nonsense, Herr Otto. You'll sleep here tonight. You need a thorough rest. These Nazis will never find you here. They'd have to cut me into little pieces first."

Otto smiled and thanked her warmly, but he wasn't to be persuaded. We had to let him go. Frl. Schroeder filled his pockets with sandwiches. I gave him three handkerchiefs, an old penknife, and a map of Germany printed on a postcard which had been slipped in through our letter-box to advertise a firm of bicycle manufacturers. Even this would be better than nothing, for Otto's geography was alarmingly weak. Unguided, he would probably have found himself heading for Poland. I wanted to give him some money, too. At first he wouldn't hear of it, and I had to resort to the disingenuous argument that we were brother communists. "Besides," I added craftily, "you can pay me back." We shook hands solemnly on this.

He was astonishingly cheerful at parting. From his manner you would have supposed that it was we who needed encouragement, not he.

"Cheer up, Willi. Don't you worry ... Our time will come."

"Of course it will. Goodbye, Otto. Good luck."

We watched him set off, from my window. Frl. Schroeder had begun to sniff.

"Poor boy ... Do you think he's got a chance, Herr Bradshaw? I declare I shan't sleep the whole night, thinking about him. It's as if he were my own son."

Otto turned once to look back; he waved his hand jauntily and smiled. Then he thrust his hands into his pockets, hunched his shoulders and strode rapidly away, with the heavy agile gait of a boxer, down the long dark street and into the lighted square, to be lost amidst the sauntering crowds of his enemies.

I never saw or heard of him again.

Three weeks later I returned to England.

I had been in London nearly a month, when Helen Pratt came round to see me. She had arrived back from Berlin the day before, having triumphantly succeeded, with a series of scalding articles, in getting the sale of her periodical forbidden throughout Germany. Already she'd been offered a much better job in America. She was sailing within a fortnight to attack New York.

She exuded vitality, success, and news. The Nazi Revolution had positively given her a new lease on life. To hear her talk, you might have thought she had spent the last two months hiding in Dr Goebbels' writing-desk or under Hitler's bed. She had the details of every private conversation and the low-down on every scandal. She knew what Schacht had said to Norman, what von Papen had said to Meissner, what Schleicher might shortly be expected to say to the Crown Prince. She knew the amounts of Thyssen's cheques. She had new stories about Röhm, about Heines, about Göring and his uniforms. "My God, Bill, what a racket!" She talked for hours.

Exhausted at last of all the misdeeds of the great, she started on the lesser fry.

"I suppose you heard all about the Pregnitz affair, didn't you?"

"No. Not a word."

"Gosh, you are behind the times!" Helen brightened at the prospect of yet another story. "Why, that can't have been more than a week after you left. They kept it fairly quiet, of course, in the papers. A pal of mine on the *New York Herald* gave me all the dope."

But, on this occasion, the dope wasn't all on Helen's side. Naturally, she didn't know everything about van Hoorn. The temptation to fill out the gaps in her story, or, at least, to betray my knowledge of them, was considerable. Thank goodness, I didn't yield to it. She was no more to be trusted with news than a cat with a saucer of milk. And, indeed, I was astonished how much her resourceful colleague had found out on his own account.

The police must have been keeping Kuno under observation ever since our Swiss visit. Their patience had certainly been remarkable, because, for three whole months, he had done absolutely nothing to arouse their suspicions. Then, quite suddenly, at the beginning of April, he had got into communication with Paris. He was ready, he said, to reconsider the business they had discussed. His first letter was short and carefully vague; a week later, under pressure from van Hoorn, he wrote a much longer one, giving explicit details of what he proposed to sell. He sent it by special messenger, taking all due precautions and employing a code. Within a few hours, the police had deciphered every word.

They went round to arrest him that afternoon at his flat. Kuno was out, having tea with a friend. His manservant had just time to telephone to him a guarded warning before the detectives took possession. Kuno seems to have lost his head completely. He did the worst thing possible: jumped into a taxi and drove straight to the Zoo Station. The plainclothes men there recognized him at once. They'd been supplied with his description that very morning, and who could mistake Kuno? Cruelly enough, they let him buy a ticket for the next available train; it happened to be going to Frankfurt-on-the-Oder. As he went up the steps to the platform, two detectives came forward to arrest him; but he was ready for that, and bolted down again. The exits were all guarded, of course. Kuno's pursuers lost him in the crowd; caught sight of him again as he ran through the swing doors into the lavatory. By the time they had elbowed their way through the people, he had already locked himself into one of the closets. ("The newspapers," said Helen, scornfully, "called it a telephone-box.") The detectives ordered him to come out. He wouldn't answer. Finally they had to clear the whole place and get ready to break down the door. It was then that Kuno shot himself.

"And he couldn't even make a decent job of that," Helen added. "Fired crooked. Nearly blew his eye out; bled like a pig. They had to take him to hospital to finish him off."

"Poor devil."

Helen looked at me curiously.

"Good riddance to bad rubbish, *I* should have said."

"You see," I apologetically confessed, "I knew him, slightly ..."

"Well, I'm blowed! Did you? Sorry. I must say, Bill, you're a nice little chap, but you do have some queer friends. Well, this ought to interest you, then. You knew Pregnitz was a fairy, of course?"

"I rather guessed something of the kind."

"Well, my pal got on to the inside story of why Pregnitz went in for this treason racket at all. He needed cash quickly, you see, because he was being blackmailed. And who, do you think, was doing the blackmailing? None other than the secretary of another dear old friend of yours, Harris."

"Norris?"

"That's right. Well, it seems that this precious secretary ... what was *his* name, by the way?"

"Schmidt."

"Was it? I dare say. Just suits him ... Schmidt had got hold of a lot of letters Pregnitz had written to some youth. God alone knows how. Pretty hot stuff they must have been, if Pregnitz was prepared to risk his skin to pay for them. Shouldn't have thought it was worth it myself. Rather face the music. But these people never have any guts ..."

"Did your friend find out what happened to Schmidt afterwards?" I asked.

"Don't suppose so, no. Why should he? What *does* happen to these creatures? He's probably abroad somewhere, blowing the cash. He'd got quite a lot out of Pregnitz already, it seems. As far as I'm concerned, he's welcome to it. Who cares?"

"I know one person," I said, "who might be interested."

A few days after this, I got a letter from Arthur. He was in Mexico City now, and hating it.

> Let me advise you, my dear boy, with all the solemnity of which I am capable, *never* to set foot in this odious town. On the material plane, it is true, I manage to provide myself with most of my accustomed comforts. But the complete lack of intelligent society, at least, as *I* understand the term, afflicts me deeply.

Arthur didn't say much about his business affairs; he was more guarded than of old.

"Times are very bad, but, on the whole, I can't complain," was his only admission. On the subject of Germany, he let himself go, however:

> It makes me positively tremble with indignation to think of the workers delivered over to these men, who, whatever you may say, are nothing more or less than *criminals*.

And, a little farther down the page:

> It is indeed tragic to see how, even in these days, a *clever* and *unscrupulous liar* can deceive millions.

In conclusion, he paid a handsome tribute to Bayer:

> A man I always admired and respected. I feel proud to be able to say that I was his friend.

I next heard of Arthur in June, on a postcard from California.

> I am basking here in the sunshine of Santa Monica. After Mexico, this is indeed a Paradise. I have a little venture on foot, not unconnected with the film

industry. I think and hope it may turn out quite profitably. Will write again soon.

He did write, and sooner, no doubt, than he had originally intended. By the next mail, I got another postcard, dated a day later.

The very worst has happened. Am leaving for Costa Rica tonight. All details from there.

This time I got a short letter.

If Mexico was *Purgatory,* this is the *Inferno* itself.

My California idyll was rudely cut short by the appearance of SCHMIDT!!! The creature's ingenuity is positively *superhuman.* Not only had he followed me there, but he had succeeded in finding out the exact nature of the little deal I was hoping to put through. I was entirely at his mercy. I was compelled to give him most of my hard-earned savings and depart at once.

Just imagine, he even had the insolence to suggest that I should *employ* him, as before!!

I don't know yet whether I have succeeded in throwing him off my track. I hardly *dare so* hope.

At least, Arthur wasn't left long in doubt. A postcard soon followed the letter.

The MONSTER has arrived!!! May try Peru.

Other glimpses of this queer journey reached me from time to time. Arthur had no luck in Lima.

Schmidt turned up within the week. From there, the chase proceeded to Chile.

"An attempt to *exterminate* the reptile failed miserably,"

he wrote from Valparaiso. "I succeeded only in arousing its venom."

I suppose this is Arthur's ornate way of saying he had tried to get Schmidt murdered.

In Valparaiso a truce seems, however, to have been at last declared. For the next postcard, announcing a train journey to the Argentine, indicated a new state of affairs.

> We leave this afternoon, *together,* for Buenos Aires.
> Am too depressed to write more now.

At present, they are in Rio. Or were when I last heard. It is impossible to predict their movements. Any day Schmidt may set off for fresh hunting-grounds, dragging Arthur after him, a protesting employer-prisoner. Their new partnership won't be so easy to dissolve as their old one. Henceforward, they are doomed to walk the Earth together. I often think about them and wonder what I should do, if, by any unlucky chance, we were to meet. I am not particularly sorry for Arthur. After all, he no doubt gets his hands on a good deal of money. But he is very sorry for himself.

"Tell me, William," his last letter concluded, "*what* have I done to deserve all this?"

THE END

GOODBYE TO BERLIN

to John & Beatrix Lehmann

A Berlin Diary
Autumn 1930

FROM MY WINDOW, the deep solemn massive street. Cellar-shops where the lamps burn all day, under the shadow of top-heavy balconied façades, dirty plaster frontages embossed with scroll-work and heraldic devices. The whole district is like this: street leading into street of houses like shabby monumental safes crammed with the tarnished valuables and secondhand furniture of a bankrupt middle class.

I am a camera with its shutter open, quite passive, recording, not thinking. Recording the man shaving at the window opposite and the woman in the kimono washing her hair. Some day, all this will have to be developed, carefully printed, fixed.

At eight o'clock in the evening the house-doors will be locked. The children are having supper. The shops are shut. The electric sign is switched on over the night-bell of the little hotel on the corner, where you can hire a room by the hour. And soon the whistling will begin. Young men are calling their girls. Standing down there in the cold, they whistle up at the lighted windows of warm rooms where the beds are already turned down for the night. They want to be let in. Their signals echo down the deep hollow street, lascivious and private and sad. Because of the whistling, I do not care to stay here in the evenings. It reminds me that I am in a foreign city, alone, far from home. Sometimes I determine not to listen to it, pick up a book, try to read. But soon a call is sure to sound, so piercing, so insistent, so despairingly human, that at last I have to get up and peep through the slats of the Venetian blind to make quite sure that it is not—as I know very well it could not possibly be—for me.

The extraordinary smell in this room when the stove is lighted and the window shut; not altogether unpleasant, a mixture of incense and stale buns. The tall tiled stove, gorgeously coloured, like an altar. The washstand like a Gothic shrine. The cupboard also is Gothic, with carved cathedral windows: Bismarck faces the King of Prussia in stained glass. My best chair would do for a bishop's throne. In the corner, three sham medieval halberds (from a theatrical touring company?) are fastened together to form a hatstand. Frl. Schroeder unscrews the heads of the halberds and polishes them from time to time. They are heavy and sharp enough to kill.

Everything in the room is like that: unnecessarily solid, abnormally heavy and dangerously sharp. Here, at the writing-table, I am confronted by a phalanx of metal objects—a pair of candlesticks shaped like entwined serpents, an ashtray from which emerges the head of a crocodile, a paperknife copied from a Florentine dagger, a brass dolphin holding on the end of its tail a small broken clock. What becomes of such things? How could they ever be destroyed? They will probably remain intact for thousands of years: people will treasure them in museums. Or perhaps they will merely be melted down for munitions in a war. Every morning, Frl. Schroeder arranges them very carefully in certain unvarying positions: there they stand, like an uncompromising statement of her views on Capital and Society, Religion and Sex.

All day long she goes padding about the large dingy flat. Shapeless but alert, she waddles from room to room, in carpet slippers and a flowered dressing-gown pinned ingeniously together, so that not an inch of petticoat or bodice is to be seen, flicking with her duster, peeping, spying, poking her short pointed nose into the cupboards and luggage of her lodgers. She has dark, bright, inquisitive eyes and pretty waved brown hair of which she is proud. She must be about fifty-five years old.

Long ago, before the War and the Inflation, she used to be comparatively well off. She went to the Baltic for her summer holidays and kept a maid to do the housework. For the last thirty years she has lived here and taken in lodgers. She started doing it because she liked to have company.

"'Lina,' my friends used to say to me, 'however can you? How can you bear to have strange people living in your rooms and spoiling your furniture, especially when you've got the money to be independent?' And I'd always give them the same answer. '*My* lodgers aren't lodgers,' I used to say. 'They're my guests.'

"You see, Herr Issyvoo, in those days I could afford to be very particular about the sort of people who came to live here. I could pick and choose. I only took them really well connected and well educated—proper gentlefolk (like yourself, Herr Issyvoo). I had a Freiherr once, and a Rittmeister and a Professor. They often gave me presents—a bottle of cognac or a box of chocolates or some flowers. And when one of them went away for his holidays he'd always send me a card—from London, it might be, or Paris, or Baden-Baden. Ever such pretty cards I used to get ..."

And now Frl. Schroeder has not even got a room of her own. She has to sleep in the living-room, behind a screen, on a small sofa with broken springs. As in so many of the older Berlin flats, our living-room connects the front part of the house with the back. The lodgers who live on the front have to pass through the living-room on their way to the bathroom, so that Frl. Schroeder is often disturbed during the night. "But I drop off again at once. It doesn't worry me. I'm much too tired." She has to do all the housework herself and it takes up most of her day. "Twenty years ago, if anybody had told me to scrub my own floors, I'd have slapped his face for him. But you get used to it. You can get used to anything. Why, I remember the time when I'd sooner cut off my right hand than empty this chamber... And now," says Frl. Schroeder, suiting the action to the word, "my goodness! It's no more to me than pouring out a cup of tea!"

She is fond of pointing out to me the various marks and stains left by lodgers who have inhabited this room:

"Yes, Herr Issyvoo, I've got something to remember each of them by ... Look here, on the rug—I've sent it to the cleaners I don't know how often but nothing will get it out—that's where Herr Noeske was sick after his birthday party. What in the world can he have been eating, to make a mess like that? He'd come to Berlin to study, you know. His parents lived in Brandenburg—a first-class family; oh, I assure you! They had pots of money! His Herr Papa was a surgeon, and of course he wanted his boy to follow in his footsteps ... What a charming young man! 'Herr Noeske,' I used to say to him, 'excuse me, but you must really work harder—you with all your brains! Think of your Herr Papa and your Frau Mama; it isn't fair to them to waste their good money like that. Why, if you were to drop it in the Spree it would be better. At least it would make a splash!' I was like a mother to him. And always, when he'd got himself into some scrape—he was terribly thoughtless—he'd come straight to me: 'Schroederschen,' he used to say, 'please don't be angry with me ... We were playing cards last night and I lost the whole of this month's allowance. I daren't tell Father ...' And then he'd look at me with those great big eyes of his. I knew exactly what he was after, the scamp! But I hadn't the heart to refuse. So I'd sit down and write a letter to his Frau Mama and beg her to forgive him just that once and send some more money. And she always would ... Of course, as a woman, I knew how to appeal to a mother's feelings, although I've never had any children of my own ... What are you smiling at, Herr

Issyvoo? Well, well! Mistakes will happen, you know!

"And that's where the Herr Rittmeister always upset his coffee over the wall-paper. He used to sit there on the couch with his fiancée. 'Herr Rittmeister,' I used to say to him, 'do please drink your coffee at the table. If you'll excuse my saying so, there's plenty of time for the other thing afterwards ...' But no, he always would sit on the couch. And then, sure enough, when he began to get a bit excited in his feelings, over went the coffee-cups ... Such a handsome gentleman! His Frau Mama and his sister came to visit us sometimes. They liked coming up to Berlin. 'Fräulein Schroeder,' they used to tell me, 'you don't know how lucky you are to be living here, right in the middle of things. We're only country cousins—we envy you! And now tell us all the latest Court scandals!' Of course, they were only joking. They had the sweetest little house, not far from Halberstadt, in the Harz. They used to show me pictures of it. A perfect dream!

"You see those ink-stains on the carpet? That's where Herr Professor Koch used to shake his fountain-pen. I told him of it a hundred times. In the end, I even laid sheets of blotting-paper on the floor around his chair. He was so absent-minded ... Such a dear old gentleman! And so simple. I was very fond of him. If I mended a shirt for him or darned his socks, he'd thank me with the tears in his eyes. He liked a bit of fun, too. Sometimes, when he heard me coming, he'd turn out the light and hide behind the door; and then he'd roar like a lion to frighten me. Just like a child ..."

Frl. Schroeder can go on like this, without repeating herself, by the hour. When I have been listening to her for some time, I find myself relapsing into a curious trance-like state of depression. I begin to feel profoundly unhappy. Where are all those lodgers now? Where, in another ten years, shall I be, myself? Certainly not here. How many seas and frontiers shall I have to cross to reach that distant day; how far shall I have to travel, on foot, on horseback, by car, push-bike, aeroplane, steamer, train, lift, moving-staircase, and tram? How much money shall

I need for that enormous journey? How much food must I gradually, wearily consume on my way? How many pairs of shoes shall I wear out? How many thousands of cigarettes shall I smoke? How many cups of tea shall I drink and how many glasses of beer? What an awful tasteless prospect! And yet—to have to die ... A sudden vague pang of apprehension grips my bowels and I have to excuse myself in order to go to the lavatory.

Hearing that I was once a medical student, she confides to me that she is very unhappy because of the size of her bosom. She suffers from palpitations and is sure that these must be caused by the strain on her heart. She wonders if she should have an operation. Some of her acquaintances advise her to, others are against it:

"Oh dear, it's such a weight to have to carry about with you! And just think—Herr Issyvoo: I used to be as slim as you are!"

"I suppose you had a great many admirers, Frl. Schroeder?"

Yes, she has had dozens. But only one Friend. He was a married man, living apart from his wife, who would not divorce him.

"We were together eleven years. Then he died of pneumonia. Sometimes I wake up in the night when it's cold and wish he was there. You never seem to get really warm, sleeping alone."

There are four other lodgers in this flat. Next door to me, in the big front-room, is Frl. Kost. In the room opposite, overlooking the courtyard, is Frl. Mayr. At the back, beyond the living-room, is Bobby. And behind Bobby's room, over the bathroom, at the top of a ladder, is a tiny attic which Frl. Schroeder refers to, for some occult reason, as "The Swedish Pavilion." This she lets, at twenty marks a month, to a commercial traveller who is out all day and most of the night. I occasionally come upon him on Sunday mornings, in the kitchen, shuffling about in his vest and trousers, apologetically hunting for a box of matches.

Bobby is a mixer at a west-end bar called the Troika. I don't know his real name. He has adopted this one because English Christian names are fashionable just now in the Berlin demimonde. He is a pale, worried-looking, smartly dressed young man with thin sleek black hair. During the early afternoon, just after he has got out of bed, he walks about the flat in shirt-sleeves, wearing a hair-net.

Frl. Schroeder and Bobby are on intimate terms. He tickles her and slaps her bottom; she hits him over the head with a frying-pan or a mop. The first time I surprised them scuffling like this, they were both rather embarrassed. Now they take my presence as a matter of course.

Frl. Kost is a blonde florid girl with large silly blue eyes. When we meet, coming to and from the bathroom in our dressing-gowns, she modestly avoids my glance. She is plump but has a good figure.

One day I asked Frl. Schroeder straight out: What was Frl. Kost's profession?

"Profession? Ha, ha, that's good! That's just the word for it! Oh, yes, she's got a fine profession. Like this—"

And with the air of doing something extremely comic, she began waddling across the kitchen like a duck, mincingly holding a duster between her finger and thumb. Just by the door, she twirled triumphantly round, flourishing the duster as though it were a silk handkerchief, and kissed her hand to me mockingly:

"Ja, ja, Herr Issyvoo! That's how they do it!"

"I don't quite understand, Frl. Schroeder. Do you mean that she's a tight-rope walker?"

"He, he, he! Very good indeed, Herr Issyvoo! Yes, that's right! That's it! She walks along the line for her living. That just describes her!"

One evening, soon after this, I met Frl. Kost on the stairs, with a Japanese. Frl. Schroeder explained to me later that he is one of Frl. Kost's best customers. She asked Frl. Kost how they spend the time together when not actually in bed, for the Japanese can speak hardly any German.

"Oh, well," said Frl. Kost, "we play the gramophone together, you know, and eat chocolates, and then we laugh a lot. He's very fond of laughing ..."

Frl. Schoeder really quite likes Frl. Kost and certainly hasn't any moral objections to her trade: nevertheless, when she is angry because Frl. Kost has broken the spout of the teapot or omitted to make crosses for her telephone-calls on the slate in the living-room, then invariably she exclaims:

"But after all, what else can you expect from a woman of that sort, a common prostitute! Why, Herr Issyvoo, do you know what she used to be? A servant girl! And then she got to be on intimate terms with her employer and one fine day, of course, she found herself in certain circumstances ... And when that little difficulty was removed, she had to go trot-trot ..."

Frl. Mayr is a music-hall *jodlerin*—one of the best, so Frl. Schroeder reverently assures me, in the whole of Germany. Frl. Schroeder doesn't altogether like Frl. Mayr, but she stands in great awe of her; as well she may. Frl. Mayr has a bull-dog jaw, enormous arms, and coarse string-coloured hair. She speaks a Bavarian dialect with peculiarly aggressive emphasis. When at home, she sits up like a war-horse at the living-room table, helping Frl. Schroeder to lay cards. They are both adept fortune-tellers and neither would dream of beginning the day without consulting the omens. The chief thing they both want to know at present is: when will Frl. Mayr get another engagement? This question interests Frl. Schroeder quite as much as Frl. Mayr, because Frl. Mayr is behind-hand with the rent.

At the corner of the Motzstrasse, when the weather is fine, there stands a shabby pop-eyed man beside a portable canvas booth. On the sides of the booth are pinned astrological diagrams and autographed letters of recommendation from satisfied clients. Frl. Schroeder goes to consult him whenever she can afford the mark for his fee. In fact, he plays a most important part in her life. Her behaviour towards him is a mixture of cajolery and threats. If the good things he promises her come true she will kiss him, she says, invite him to dinner, buy him a gold watch: if they don't, she will throttle him, box his ears, report him to the police. Among other prophecies, the astrologer has told her that she will win some money in the Prussian State Lottery. So far, she has had no luck. But she is always discussing what she will do with her winnings. We are all to have presents, of course. I am to get a hat, because Frl. Schroeder thinks it very improper that a gentleman of my education should go about without one.

When not engaged in laying cards, Frl. Mayr drinks tea and lectures Frl. Schroeder on her past theatrical triumphs:

"And the Manager said to me: 'Fritzi, Heaven must have sent you here! My leading lady's fallen ill. You're to leave for Copenhagen tonight.' And what's more, he wouldn't take no for an answer. 'Fritzi,' he said (he always called me that), 'Fritzi, you aren't going to let an old friend down?' And so I went …" Frl. Mayr sips her tea reminiscently: "A charming man. And so well-bred." She smiles: "Familiar … but he always knew how to behave himself."

Frl. Schroeder nods eagerly, drinking in every word, revelling in it:

"I suppose some of those managers must be cheeky devils? (Have some more sausage, Frl. Mayr?)"

"(Thank you, Frl. Schroeder; just a little morsel.) Yes, some of them … you wouldn't believe! But I could always take care of myself. Even when I was quite a slip of a girl …"

The muscles of Frl. Mayer's nude fleshy arms ripple unappetizingly. She sticks out her chin:

"I'm a Bavarian; and a Bavarian never forgets an injury."

Coming into the living-room yesterday evening, I found Frl. Schroeder and Frl. Mayr lying flat on their stomachs with their ears pressed to the carpet. At intervals, they exchanged grins of delight or joyfully pinched each other, with simultaneous exclamations of *Ssh!*

"Hark!" whispered Frl. Schroeder, "he's smashing all the furniture!"

"He's beating her black and blue!" exclaimed Frl. Mayr, in raptures.

"Bang! Just listen to that!"

"Ssh! Ssh!"

"Ssh!"

Frl. Schroeder was quite beside herself. When I asked what was the matter, she clambered to her feet, waddled forward and, taking me round the waist, danced a little waltz with me: "Herr Issyvoo! Herr Issyvoo! Herr Issyvoo!" until she was breathless.

"But whatever has happened?" I asked.

"Ssh!" commanded Frl. Mayr from the floor. "Ssh! They've started again!"

In the flat directly beneath ours lives a certain Frau Glanterneck. She is a Galician Jewess, in itself a reason why Frl. Mayr should be her enemy: for Frl. Mayr, needless to say, is an ardent Nazi. And, quite apart from this, it seems that Frau Glanterneck and Frl. Mayr once had words on the stairs about Frl. Mayr's yodelling. Frau Glanterneck, perhaps because she is a non-Aryan, said that she preferred the noises made by cats. Thereby, she insulted not merely Frl. Mayr, but all Bavarian, all German women: and it was Frl. Mayr's pleasant duty to avenge them.

About a fortnight ago, it became known among the neighbours that Frau Glanterneck, who is sixty years old and as ugly as a witch, had been advertising in the newspaper for a husband. What was more, an applicant had already appeared: a widowed butcher from Halle. He had seen Frau Glanterneck and was nevertheless prepared to marry her. Here was Frl. Mayr's chance. By roundabout inquiries, she discovered the butcher's name and address and wrote him an anonymous letter. Was he aware that Frau Glanterneck had *(a)* bugs in her flat, *(b)* been arrested for fraud and released on the ground that she was insane, *(c)* leased out her own bedroom for immoral purposes, and *(d)* slept in the beds afterwards without changing the sheets? And now the butcher had arrived to confront Frau Glanterneck with the letter. One could hear both of them quite distinctly: the growling of the enraged Prussian and the shrill screaming of the Jewess. Now and then came the thud of a fist against wood and, occasionally, the crash of glass. The row lasted over an hour.

This morning we hear that the neighbours have complained to the portress of the disturbance and that Frau Glanterneck is to be seen with a black eye. The marriage is off.

The inhabitants of this street know me by sight already. At the grocer's, people no longer turn their heads on hearing my English accent as I order a pound of butter. At the street corner, after dark, the three whores no longer whisper throatily: "Komm, Süsser!" as I pass.

The three whores are all plainly over fifty years old. They do not attempt to conceal their age. They are not noticeably rouged or powdered. They wear baggy old fur coats and longish skirts and matronly hats. I happened to mention them to Bobby and he explained to me that there is a recognized demand for the comfortable type of woman. Many middle-aged men prefer them to girls. They even attract boys in their 'teens. A boy, explained Bobby, feels shy with a girl of his own age but not with a woman old enough to be his mother. Like most barmen, Bobby is a great expert on sexual questions.

The other evening, I went to call on him during business hours.

It was still very early, about nine o'clock, when I arrived at the Troika. The place was much larger and grander than I had expected. A commissionaire braided like an archduke regarded my hatless head with suspicion until I spoke to him in English. A smart cloak-room girl insisted on taking my overcoat, which hides the worst stains on my baggy flannel trousers. A page-boy, seated on the counter, didn't rise to open the inner door. Bobby, to my relief, was at his place behind a blue and silver bar. I made towards him as towards an old friend. He greeted me most amiably:

"Good evening, Mr Isherwood. Very glad to see you here."

I ordered a beer and settled myself on a stool in the comer. With my back to the wall, I could survey the whole room.

"How's business?" I asked.

Bobby's care-worn, powdered, night-dweller's face became grave. He inclined his head towards me, over the bar, with confidential flattering seriousness:

"Not much good, Mr Isherwood. The kind of public we have nowadays ... you wouldn't believe it! Why, a year ago, we'd have turned them away at the door. They order a beer and think they've got the right to sit here the whole evening."

Bobby spoke with extreme bitterness. I began to feel uncomfortable:

"What'll you drink?" I asked, guiltily gulping down my beer; and added, lest there should be any misunderstanding: "I'd like a whisky and soda."

Bobby said he'd have one, too.

The room was nearly empty. I looked the few guests over, trying to see them through Bobby's disillusioned eyes. There were three attractive well-dressed girls sitting at the bar: the one nearest to me was particularly elegant, she had quite a cosmopolitan air. But during a lull in the conversation, I caught fragments of her talk with the other barman. She spoke broad Berlin dialect. She was tired and bored; her mouth dropped. A young man approached her and joined in the discussion; a handsome broad-shouldered boy in a well-cut dinner-jacket, who might well have been an English public-school prefect on holiday.

"*Nee, Nee,*" I heard him say. "*Bei mir nicht!*" He grinned and made a curt, brutal gesture of the streets.

Over in the comer sat a page-boy, talking to the little old lavatory attendant in his white jacket. The boy said something, laughed and broke off suddenly into a huge yawn. The three musicians on their platform were chatting, evidently unwilling to begin until they had an audience worth playing to. At one of the tables, I thought I saw a genuine guest, a stout man with a moustache. After a moment, however, I caught his eye, he made a little bow and I knew that he must be the manager.

The door opened. Two men and two women came in. The women were elderly, had thick legs, cropped hair, and costly evening-gowns. The men were lethargic, pale, probably Dutch. Here, unmistakably, was Money. In an instant, the Troika was transformed. The manager, the cigarette-boy, and the lavatory attendant rose simultaneously to their feet. The lavatory attendant disappeared. The manager said something in a furious undertone to the cigarette-boy, who also disappeared. He then advanced, bowing and smiling, to the guests' table and shook hands with the two men. The cigarette-boy reappeared with his tray, followed by a waiter who hurried forward with the wine-list. Meanwhile, the three-man orchestra struck briskly. The girls at the bar turned on their stools smiling a not-too-direct invitation. The gigolos advanced to them as if to complete strangers, bowed formally, and asked, in cultured tones, for the pleasure of a dance. The page-boy, spruce, discreetly grinning, swaying from the waist like a flower, crossed the room with his tray of cigarettes: "*Zigarren! Zigaretten!*" His voice was mocking, clear-pitched like an actor's. And in the same tone, yet more loudly, mockingly, joyfully so that we could all hear, the waiter ordered from Bobby: "Heidsieck Monopol!"

With absurd, solicitous gravity, the dancers performed their intricate evolutions, showing in their every movement a consciousness of the part they were playing. And the saxophonist, letting his instrument swing loose from the ribbon around his neck, advanced to the edge of the platform with his little megaphone:

Sie werden lachen,
Ich lieb'
Meine eigene Frau ...

He sang with a knowing leer, including us all in the conspiracy, charging his voice with innuendo, rolling his eyes in an epileptic pantomime of extreme joy. Bobby, suave, sleek, five years younger, handled the bottle. And meanwhile the two flaccid gentlemen chatted to each other, probably about business, without a glance at the night-life they had called into being; while their women sat silent, looking neglected, puzzled, uncomfortable, and very bored.

Frl. Hippi Bernstein, my first pupil, lives in the Grünewald, in a house built almost entirely of glass. Most of the richest Berlin families inhabit the Grünewald. It is difficult to understand why. Their villas, in all known styles of expensive ugliness, ranging from the eccentric-rococo folly to the cubist flat-roofed steel-and-glass box, are crowded together in this dank, dreary pinewood. Few of them can afford large gardens, for the ground is fabulously dear: their only view is of their neighbour's backyard, each one protected by a wire fence and a savage dog. Terror of burglary and revolution has reduced these miserable people to a state of siege. They have neither privacy nor sunshine. The district is really a millionaire's slum.

When I rang the bell at the garden gate, a young footman came out with a key from the house, followed by a large growling Alsatian.

"He won't bite you while I'm here," the footman reassured me, grinning.

The hall of the Bernsteins' house has metal-studded doors and a steamer clock fastened to the wall with bolt-heads. There are modernist lamps, designed to look like pressure-guages, thermometers, and switchboard dials. But the furniture doesn't match the house and its fittings. The place is like a power station which the engineers have tried to make comfortable with chairs and tables from an old-fashioned, highly respectable boarding-house. On the austere metal walls hang highly varnished nineteenth-century landscapes in massive gold frames. Herr Bernstein probably ordered the villa from a popular *avant-garde* architect in a moment of recklessness; was horrified at the result and tried to cover it up as much as possible with the family belongings.

Frl. Hippi is a fat pretty girl, about nineteen years old, with glossy chestnut hair, good teeth, and big cow-eyes. She has a lazy, jolly, self-indulgent laugh and a well-formed bust. She speaks schoolgirl English with a slight American accent, quite nicely, to her own complete satisfaction. She has clearly no intention of doing any work. When I tried weakly to suggest a plan for our lessons, she kept interrupting to offer me chocolates, coffee, cigarettes: "Excuse me a minute, there isn't some fruit," she smiled, picking up the receiver of the house-telephone: "Anna, please bring some oranges."

When the maid arrived with the oranges, I was forced, despite my protests, to make a regular meal, with a plate, knife, and fork. This destroyed the last pretence of the teacher-pupil relationship. I felt like a policeman being given a meal in the kitchen by an attractive cook. Frl. Hippi sat watching me eat, with her good-natured, lazy smile:

"Tell me, please, why you come to Germany?"

She is inquisitive about me, but only like a cow idly poking with its head between the bars of a gate. She doesn't particularly want the gate to open. I said that I found Germany very interesting:

"The political and economic situation," I improvised authoritatively, in my schoolmaster voice, "is more interesting in Germany than in any other European country.

"Except Russia, of course," I added experimentally.

But Frl. Hippi didn't react. She just blandly smiled:

"I think it shall be dull for you here? You do not have many friends in Berlin, no?"

This seemed to please and amuse her:

"You don't know some nice girls?"

Here the buzzer of the house-telephone sounded. Lazily smiling, she picked up the receiver, but appeared not to listen to the tiny voice which issued from it. I could hear quite distinctly the real voice of Frau Bernstein, Hippi's mother, speaking from the next room.

"Have you left your *red* book in here?" repeated Frl. Hippi mockingly and smiling at me as though this were a joke which I must share: "No, I don't see it. It must be down in the study. Ring up Daddy. Yes, he's working there." In dumb show, she offered me another orange. I shook my head politely. We both smiled: "Mummy, what have we got for lunch today? Yes? Really? Splendid!"

She hung up the receiver and returned to her cross-examination:

"Do you know no nice girls?"

"*Any* nice girls ..." I corrected evasively. But Frl. Hippi merely smiled, waiting for the answer to her question.

"Yes. One," I had at length to add, thinking of Frl. Kost.

"Only one?" She raised her eyebrows in comic surprise. "And tell me, please, do you find German girls different than English girls?"

I blushed. "Do you find German girls ..." I began to correct her and stopped, realizing just in time that I wasn't absolutely sure whether one says *different from* or *different to.*

"Do you find German girls different than English girls?" she repeated, with smiling persistence.

I blushed deeper than ever. "Yes. Very different," I said boldly.

"How are they different?"

Mercifully the telephone buzzed again. This was somebody from the kitchen, to say that lunch would be an hour earlier than usual. Herr Bernstein was going to the city that afternoon.

"I am so sorry," said Frl. Hippi, rising, "but for today we must finish. And we shall see us again on Friday? Then goodbye, Mr Isherwood. And I thank you very much."

She fished in her bag and handed me an envelope which I stuck awkwardly into my pocket and tore open only when I was out of sight of the Bernsteins' house. It contained a five-mark piece. I threw it into the air, missed it, found it after five minutes' hunt, buried in sand, and ran all the way to the tramstop, singing and kicking stones about the road. I felt extraordinarily guilty and elated, as though I'd successfully committed a small theft.

It is a mere waste of time even pretending to teach Frl. Hippi anything. If she doesn't know a word, she says it in German. If I correct her, she repeats it in German. I am glad, of course, that she's so lazy and only afraid that Frau Bernstein may discover how little progress her daughter is making. But this is very unlikely. Most rich people, once they have decided to trust you at all, can be imposed upon to almost any extent. The only real problem for the private tutor is to get inside the front door.

As for Hippi, she seems to enjoy my visits. From something she said the other day, I gather she boasts to her school friends that she has got a genuine English teacher. We understand each other very well. I am bribed with fruit not to be tiresome about the English language: she, for her part, tells her parents that I am the best teacher she ever had. We gossip in German about the things which interest her. And every three or four minutes, we are interrupted while she plays her part in the family game of exchanging entirely unimportant messages over the house-telephone.

Hippi never worries about the future. Like everyone else in Berlin, she refers continually to the political situation, but only briefly, with a conventional melancholy, as when one speaks of religion. It is quite unreal to her. She means to go to the university, travel about, have a jolly good time and eventually, of course, marry. She already has a great many boy friends. We spend a lot of time talking about them. One has a wonderful car. Another has an aeroplane. Another has fought seven duels. Another has discovered a knack of putting out street-lamps by giving them a smart kick in a certain spot. One night, on the way back from a dance, Hippi and he put out all the street-lamps in the neighbourhood.

Today, lunch was early at the Bernsteins'; so I was invited to it, instead of giving my "lesson." The whole family was present: Frau Bernstein, stout and placid; Herr Bernstein, small and shaky and sly. There was also a younger sister, a schoolgirl of twelve, very fat. She ate and ate, quite unmoved by Hippi's jokes and warnings that she'd burst. They all seem very fond of each other, in their cosy, stuffy way. There was a little domestic argument, because Herr Bernstein didn't want his wife to go shopping in the car that afternoon. During the last few days, there has been a lot of Nazi rioting in the city.

"You can go in the tram," said Herr Bernstein. "I will not have them throwing stones at my beautiful car."

"And suppose they throw stones at me?" asked Frau Bernstein good-humouredly.

"Ach, what does that matter? If they throw stones at you, I will buy you a sticking-plaster for your head. It will cost me only five groschen. But if they throw stones at my car, it will cost me perhaps five hundred marks."

And so the matter was settled. Herr Bernstein then turned his attention to me:

"You can't complain that we treat you badly here, young man, eh? Not only do we give you a nice dinner, but we pay you for eating it!"

I saw from Hippi's expression that this was going a bit far, even for the Bernstein sense of humour; so I laughed and said:

"Will you pay me a mark extra for every helping I eat?"

This amused Herr Bernstein very much: but he was careful to show that he knew I hadn't meant it seriously.

During the last week, our household has been plunged into a terrific row.

It began when Frl. Kost came to Frl. Schroeder and announced that fifty marks had been stolen from her room. She was very much upset; especially, she explained, as this was the money she'd put aside towards the rent and the telephone bill. The fifty-mark note had been lying in the drawer of the cupboard, just inside the door of Frl. Kost's room.

Frl. Schroeder's immediate suggestion was, not unnaturally, that the money had been stolen by one of Frl. Kost's customers. Frl. Kost said that this was quite impossible, as none of them had visted her during the last three days. Moreover, she added, *her* friends were all absolutely above suspicion. They were well-to-do gentlemen, to whom a miserable fifty-mark note was a mere bagatelle. This annoyed Frl. Schroeder very much indeed:

"I suppose she's trying to make out that one of *us* did it! Of all the cheek! Why, Herr Issyvoo, will you believe it, I could have chopped her into little pieces!"

"Yes, Frl. Schroeder. I'm sure you could."

Frl. Schroeder then developed the theory that the money hadn't been stolen at all and that this was just a trick of Frl. Kost's to avoid paying the rent. She hinted so much to Frl. Kost, who was furious. Frl. Kost said that, in any case, she'd raise the money in a few days: which she already has. She also gave notice to leave her room at the end of the month.

Meanwhile, I have discovered, quite by accident, that Frl. Kost has been having an affair with Bobby. As I came in, one evening, I happened to notice that there was no light in Frl. Kost's room. You can always see this, because there is a frosted glass pane in her door to light the hall of the flat. Later, as I lay in bed reading, I heard Frl. Kost's door open and Bobby's voice, laughing and whispering. After much creaking of boards and muffled laughter, Bobby tip-toed out of the flat, shutting the door as quietly as possible behind him. A moment later, he re-entered with a great deal of noise and went straight through into the living-room, where I heard him wishing Frl. Schroeder good night.

If Frl. Schroeder doesn't actually know of this, she at least suspects it. This explains her fury against Frl. Kost: for the truth is, she is terribly jealous. The most grotesque and embarrassing incidents have been taking place. One morning, when I wanted to visit the bathroom, Frl. Kost was using it already. Frl. Schroeder rushed to the door before I could stop her and ordered Frl. Kost to come out at once: and when Frl. Kost naturally didn't obey, Frl. Schroeder began, despite my protests, hammering on the door with her fists. "Come out of my bathroom!" she screamed. "Come out this minute, or I'll call the police to fetch you out!"

After this she burst into tears. The crying brought on palpitations. Bobby had to carry her to the sofa, gasping and sobbing. While we were all standing round, rather helpless, Frl. Mayr appeared in the doorway with a face like a hangman and said, in a terrible voice, to Frl. Kost: “Think yourself lucky, my girl, if you haven’t murdered her!” She then took complete charge of the situation, ordered us all out of the room and sent me down to the grocer’s for a bottle of Baldrian Drops. When I returned, she was seated beside the sofa, stroking Frl. Schroeder’s hand and murmuring, in her most tragic tones: “Lina, my poor little child … what have they done to you?”

Sally Bowles

ONE AFTERNOON, EARLY in October, I was invited to black coffee at Fritz Wendel's flat, Fritz always invited you to "black coffee," with emphasis on the black. He was very proud of his coffee. People used to say that it was the strongest in Berlin.

Fritz himself was dressed in his usual coffee-party costume—a very thick white yachting sweater and very light blue flannel trousers. He greeted me with his full-lipped, luscious smile:

"'lo, Chris!"

"Hullo, Fritz. How are you?"

"Fine." He bent over the coffee-machine, his sleek black hair unplastering itself from his scalp and falling in richly scented locks over his eyes. "This darn thing doesn't go," he added.

"How's business?" I asked.

"Lousy and terrible." Fritz grinned richly. "Or I pull off a new deal in the next month or I go as a gigolo."

"*Either* . . . or . . ." I corrected, from force of professional habit.

"I'm speaking a lousy English just now," drawled Fritz, with great self-satisfaction. "Sally says maybe she'll give me a few lessons."

"Who's Sally?"

"Why, I forgot. You don't know Sally. Too bad of me. Eventually she's coming around here this afternoon."

"Is she nice?"

Fritz rolled his naughty black eyes, handing me a rum-moistened cigarette from his patent tin:

"*Mar*-vellous!" he drawled. "Eventually I believe I'm getting crazy about her."

"And who is she? What does she do?"

"She's an English girl, an actress: sings at the Lady Windermere—hot stuff, believe me!"

"That doesn't sound much like an English girl, I must say."

"Eventually she's got a bit of French in her. Her mother was French."

A few minutes later, Sally herself arrived.

"Am I terribly late, Fritz darling?"

"Only half of an hour, I suppose," Fritz drawled, beaming with proprietary pleasure. "May I introduce Mr Isherwood—Miss Bowles? Mr Isherwood is commonly known as Chris."

"I'm not," I said. "Fritz is about the only person who's ever called me Chris in my life."

Sally laughed. She was dressed in black silk, with a small cape over her shoulders and a little cap like a page-boy's stuck jauntily on one side of her head:

"Do you mind if I use your telephone, sweet?"

"Sure. Go right ahead." Fritz caught my eye. "Come into the other room, Chris. I want to show you something." He was evidently longing to hear my first impressions of Sally, his new acquisition.

"For heaven's sake, don't leave me alone with this man!" she exclaimed. "Or he'll seduce me down the telephone. He's most terribly passionate."

As she dialled the number, I noticed that her fingernails were painted emerald green, a colour unfortunately chosen, for it called attention to her hands, which were much stained by cigarette-smoking and as dirty as a little girl's. She was dark enough to be Fritz's sister. Her face was long and thin, powdered dead white. She had very large brown eyes which should have been darker, to match her hair and the pencil she used for her eyebrows.

"Hilloo," she cooed, pursing her brilliant cherry lips as though she were going to kiss the mouthpiece: "Ist dass Du, mein Liebling?" Her mouth opened in a fatuously sweet smile. Fritz and I sat watching her, like a performance at the theatre. "Was wollen wir machen, Morgen Abend? Oh, wie wunderbar ... Nein, nein, ich werde bleiben Heute Abend zu Hause. Ja, ja, ich werde wirklich bleiben zu Hause ... Auf Wiedersehen, mein Liebling ..."

She hung up the receiver and turned to us triumphantly.

"That's the man I slept with last night," she announced. "He makes love marvellously. He's an absolute genius at business and he's terribly rich—" She came and sat down on the sofa beside Fritz, sinking back into the cushions with a sigh: "Give me some coffee, will you, darling? I'm simply dying of thirst."

And soon we were on to Fritz's favourite topic: he pronounced it Larv.

"On the average," he told us, "I'm having a big affair every two years."

"And how long is it since you had your last?" Sally asked.

"Exactly one year and eleven months!" Fritz gave her his naughtiest glance.

"How marvellous!" Sally puckered up her nose and laughed a silvery little stage-laugh. "*Doo* tell me—what was the last one like?"

This, of course, started Fritz off on a complete autobiography. We had the story of his seduction in Paris, details of a holiday flirtation at Las Palmas, the four chief New York romances, a disappointment in Chicago, and a conquest in Boston; then back to Paris for a little recreation, a very beautiful episode in Vienna, to London to be consoled and, finally, Berlin.

"You know, Fritz darling," said Sally, puckering up her nose at me, "*I* believe the trouble with you is that you've never really found the right woman."

"Maybe that's true—" Fritz took this idea very seriously.

His black eyes became liquid and sentimental: "Maybe I'm still looking for my ideal…"

"But you'll find her one day, I'm absolutely certain you will." Sally included me, with a glance, in the game of laughing at Fritz.

"You think so?" Fritz grinned lusciously, sparkling at her.

"Don't *you* think so?" Sally appealed to me.

"I'm sure I don't know," I said. "Because I've never been able to discover what Fritz's ideal is."

For some reason, this seemed to please Fritz. He took it as a kind of testimonial: "And Chris knows me pretty well," he chimed in. "If Chris doesn't know, well, I guess no one does."

Then it was time for Sally to go.

"I'm supposed to meet a man at the Adlon at five," she explained. "And it's six already! Never mind, it'll do the old swine good to wait. He wants me to be his mistress, but I've told him I'm damned if I will till he's paid all my debts. Why are men always such beasts?" Opening her bag, she rapidly retouched her lips and eyebrows: "Oh, by the way, Fritz darling, could you be a perfect angel and lend me ten marks? I haven't got a bean for a taxi."

"Why, sure!" Fritz put his hand into his pocket and paid up without hesitation, like a hero.

Sally turned to me: "I say, will you come and have tea with me sometime? Give me your telephone number. I'll ring you up."

I suppose, I thought, she imagines I've got cash. Well, this will be a lesson to her, once for all. I wrote my number in her tiny leather book. Fritz saw her out.

"Well!" He came bounding back into the room and gleefully shut the door: "What do you think of her, Chris? Didn't I tell you she was a good-looker?"

"You did indeed!"

"I'm getting crazier about her each time I see her!" With a sigh of pleasure, he helped himself to a cigarette: "More coffee, Chris?"

"No, thank you very much."

"You know, Chris, I think she took a fancy to you, too!"
"Oh, rot!"
"Honestly, I do!" Fritz seemed pleased. "Eventually I guess we'll be seeing a lot of her from now on!"

When I got back to Frl. Schroeder's, I felt so giddy that I had to lie down for half an hour on my bed. Fritz's black coffee was as poisonous as ever.

A few days later, he took me to hear Sally sing.

The Lady Windermere (which now, I hear, no longer exists) was an arty "informal" bar, just off the Tauentzeinstrasse, which the proprietor had evidently tried to make look as much as possible like Montparnasse. The walls were covered with sketches on menu-cards, caricatures and signed theatrical photographs—("To the one and only Lady Windermere." "To Johnny, with all my heart.") The Fan itself, four times life size, was displayed above the bar. There was a big piano on a platform in the middle of the room.

I was curious to see how Sally would behave. I had imagined her, for some reason, rather nervous, but she wasn't, in the least. She had a surprisingly deep husky voice. She sang badly, without any expression, her hands hanging down at her sides—yet her performance was, in its own way, effective because of her startling appearance and her air of not caring a curse what people thought of her. Her arms hanging carelessly limp, and a take-it-or-leave-it grin on her face, she sang:

Now I know why Mother
Told me to be true;
She meant me for Someone
Exactly like you.

There was quite a lot of applause. The pianist, a handsome young man with blond wavy hair, stood up and solemnly kissed Sally's hand. Then she sang two more songs, one in French and the other in German. These weren't so well received.

After the singing, there was a good deal more hand-kissing and a general movement towards the bar. Sally seemed to know everybody in the place. She called them all Thou and Darling. For a would-be-demi-mondaine, she seemed to have surprisingly little business sense or tact. She wasted a lot of time making advances to an elderly gentleman who would obviously have preferred a chat with the barman. Later, we all got rather drunk. Then Sally had to go off to an appointment, and the manager came and sat at our table. He and Fritz talked English Peerage. Fritz was in his element. I decided, as so often before, never to visit a place of this sort again.

Then Sally rang up, as she had promised, to invite me to tea.

She lived a long way down the Kurfürstendamm on the last dreary stretch which rises to Halensee. I was shown into a big gloomy half-furnished room by a fat untidy landlady with a pouchy sagging jowl like a toad. There was a broken-down sofa in one corner—and a faded picture of an eighteenth-century battle, with the wounded reclining on their elbows in graceful attitudes, admiring the prancings of Frederick the Great's horse.

"Oh, hullo, Chris darling!" cried Sally from the doorway. "How sweet of you to come! I was feeling most terribly lonely. I've been crying on Frau Karpf's chest. Nicht wahr, Frau Karpf?" She appealed to the toad landlady, "ich habe geweint auf Dein Brust." Frau Karpf shook her bosom in a toad-like chuckle.

"Would you rather have coffee, Chris, or tea?" Sally continued. "You can have either. Only I don't recommend the tea much. I don't know what Frau Karpf does to it; I think she empties all the kitchen slops together into a jug and boils them up with the tea-leaves."

"I'll have coffee, then."

"Frau Karpf, Liebling, willst Du sein ein Engel und bring zwei Tassen von Kaffee?" Sally's German was not merely incorrect; it was all her own. She pronounced every word in a mincing, specially "foreign" manner. You could tell that she was speaking a foreign language from her expression alone.

"Chris darling, will you be an angel and draw the curtains?"

I did so, although it was still quite light outside. Sally, meanwhile, had switched on the table-lamp. As I turned from the window, she curled herself up delicately on the sofa like a cat, and, opening her bag, felt for a cigarette. But hardly was the pose complete before she'd jumped to her feet again:

"Would you like a Prairie Oyster?" She produced glasses, eggs and a bottle of Worcester sauce from the boot-cupboard under the dismantled washstand: "I practically live on them." Dexterously, she broke the eggs into the glasses, added the sauce and stirred up the mixture with the end of a fountain-pen: "They're about all I can afford." She was back on the sofa again, daintily curled up.

She was wearing the same black dress today, but without the cape. Instead, she had a little white collar and white cuffs. They produced a kind of theatrically chaste effect, like a nun in grand opera. "What are you laughing at, Chris?" she asked.

"I don't know," I said. But still I couldn't stop grinning. There was, at that moment, something so extraordinarily comic in Sally's appearance. She was really beautiful, with her little dark head, big eyes, and finely arched nose—and so absurdly conscious of all these features. There she lay, as complacently feminine as a turtle-dove, with her poised self-conscious head, and daintily arranged hands.

"Chris, you swine, do tell me why you're laughing?"

"I really haven't the faintest idea."

At this, she began to laugh, too: "You are mad, you know!"

"Have you been here long?" I asked, looking round the large gloomy room.

"Ever since I arrived in Berlin. Let's see—that was about two months ago."

I asked what had made her decide to come out to Germany at all. Had she come alone? No, she'd come with a girl friend. An actress. Older than Sally. The girl had been to Berlin before. She'd told Sally that they'd certainly be able to get work with the Ufa. So Sally borrowed ten pounds from a nice old gentleman and joined her.

She hadn't told her parents anything about it until the two of them had actually arrived in Germany: "I wish you'd met Diana. She was the most marvellous gold-digger you can imagine. She'd get hold of men anywhere—it didn't matter whether she could speak their language or not. She made one nearly die of laughing. I absolutely adored her."

But when they'd been together in Berlin three weeks and no job had appeared, Diana had got hold of a banker, who'd taken her off with him to Paris.

"And left you here alone? I must say I think that was pretty rotten of her."

"Oh, I don't know ... Everyone's got to look after themselves. I expect, in her place, I'd have done the same."

"I bet you wouldn't!"

"Anyhow, I'm all right. I can always get along alone."

"How old are you, Sally?"

"Nineteen."

"Good God! And I thought you were about twenty-five!"

"I know. Everyone does."

Frau Karpf came shuffling in with two cups of coffee on a tarnished metal tray.

"Oh, Frau Karpf, Liebling, wie wunderbar von Dich!"

"Whatever makes you stay in this house?" I asked, when the landlady had gone out: "I'm sure you could get a much nicer room than this."

"Yes, I know I could."

"Well then, why don't you?"

"Oh, I don't know. I'm lazy, I suppose."

"What do you have to pay here?"

"Eighty marks a month."

"With breakfast included?"

"No—I don't think so."

"You don't *think* so?" I exclaimed severely. "But surely you must know for certain?"

Sally took this meekly: "Yes, it's stupid of me, I suppose. But, you see, I just give the old girl money when I've got some.

So it's rather difficult to reckon it all up exactly."

"But, good heavens, Sally—I only pay fifty a month for my room, with breakfast, and it's ever so much nicer than this one!"

Sally nodded, but continued apologetically: "And another thing is, you see, Christopher darling, I don't quite know what Frau Karpf would do if I were to leave her. I'm sure she'd never get another lodger. Nobody else would be able to stand her face and her smell and everything. As it is, she owes three months' rent. They'd turn her out at once if they knew she hadn't any lodgers: and if they do that, she says she'll commit suicide."

"All the same, I don't see why you should sacrifice yourself for her."

"I'm not sacrificing myself, really. I quite like being here, you know. Frau Karpf and I understand each other. She's more or less what I'll be in thirty years' time. A respectable sort of landlady would probably turn me out after a week."

"My landlady wouldn't turn you out."

Sally smiled vaguely, screwing up her nose: "How do you like the coffee, Chris darling?"

"I prefer it to Fritz's," I said evasively.

Sally laughed: "Isn't Fritz marvellous? I adore him. I adore the way he says, 'I give a damn.'"

"'Hell, I give a damn.'" I tried to imitate Fritz. We both laughed. Sally lit another cigarette: she smoked the whole time. I noticed how old her hands looked in the lamplight. They were nervous, veined and very thin—the hands of a middle-aged woman. The green finger-nails seemed not to belong to them at all; to have settled on them by chance—like hard, bright, ugly little beetles. "It's a funny thing," she added meditatively, "Fritz and I have never slept together, you know." She paused, asked with interest, "Did you think we had?"

"Well, yes—I suppose I did."

"We haven't. Not once ..." she yawned. "And now I don't suppose we ever shall."

We smoked for some minutes in silence. Then Sally began to tell me about her family. She was the daughter of a Lancashire mill-owner. Her mother was a Miss Bowles, an heiress with an estate, and so, when she and Mr Jackson were married, they joined their names together: "Daddy's a terrible snob, although he pretends not to be. My real name's Jackson-Bowles; but of course, I can't possibly call myself that on the stage. People would think I was crazy."

"I thought Fritz told me your mother was French?"

"No, of course not!" Sally seemed quite annoyed. "Fritz is an idiot. He's always inventing things."

Sally had one sister, named Betty. "She's an absolute angel. I adore her. She's seventeen, but she's still most terribly innocent. Mummy's bringing her up to be very county. Betty would nearly die if she knew what an old whore I am. She knows absolutely nothing whatever about men."

"But why aren't you county, too, Sally?"

"I don't know. I suppose that's Daddy's side of the family coming out. You'd love Daddy. He doesn't care a damn for anyone. He's the most marvellous business man. And about once a month he gets absolutely dead tight and horrifies all Mummy's smart friends. It was he who said I could go to London and learn acting."

"You must have left school very young?"

"Yes. I couldn't bear school. I got myself expelled."

"However did you do that?"

"I told the headmistress I was going to have a baby."

"Oh, rot, Sally, you didn't!"

"I did, honestly! There was the most terrible commotion. They got a doctor to examine me, and sent for my parents. When they found out there was nothing the matter, they were most frightfully disappointed. The head mistress said that a girl who could even think of anything so disgusting couldn't possibly be allowed to stay on and corrupt the other girls. So I got my own way. And then I pestered Daddy till he said I might go to London."

Sally had settled down in London, at a hostel, with other girl students. There, in spite of supervision, she had managed to spend large portions of the night at young men's flats: "The first man who seduced me had no idea I was a virgin until I told him afterwards. He was marvellous. I adored him. He was an absolute genius at comedy parts. He's sure to be terribly famous one day."

After a time, Sally had got crowd-work in films, and finally a small part in a touring company. Then she had met Diana.

"And how much longer shall you stay in Berlin?" I asked.

"Heaven knows. This job at the Lady Windermere only lasts another week. I got it through a man I met at the Eden Bar. But he's gone off to Vienna now. I must ring up the Ufa people again, I suppose. And then there's an awful old Jew who takes me out sometimes. He's always promising to get me a contract; but he only wants to sleep with me, the old swine. I think the men in this country are awful. They've none of them got any money, and they expect you to let them seduce you if they give you a box of chocolates."

"How on earth are you going to manage when this job comes to an end?"

"Oh well, I get a small allowance from home, you know. Not that that'll last much longer. Mummy's already threatened to stop it if I don't come back to England soon ... Of course, they think I'm here with a girl friend. If Mummy knew I was on my own, she'd simply pass right out. Anyhow, I'll get enough to support myself somehow, soon. I loathe taking money from them. Daddy's business is in a frightfully bad way now, from the slump."

"I say, Sally—if you ever really get into a mess I wish you'd let me know."

Sally laughed: "That's terribly sweet of you, Chris. But I don't sponge on my friends."

"Isn't Fritz your friend?" It had jumped out of my mouth. But Sally didn't seem to mind a bit.

"Oh yes, I'm awfully fond of Fritz, of course. But he's got

pots of cash. Somehow, when people have cash, you feel differently about them—I don't know why."

"And how do you know I haven't got pots of cash, too?"

"You?" Sally burst out laughing. "Why, I knew you were hard up the moment I set eyes on you!"

The afternoon Sally came to tea with me, Frl. Schroeder was beside herself with excitement. She put on her best dress for the occasion and waved her hair. When the door-bell rang, she threw open the door with a flourish: "Herr Issyvoo," she announced, winking knowingly at me and speaking very loud, "there's a lady to see you!"

I then formally introduced Sally and Frl. Schroeder to each other. Frl. Schroeder was overflowing with politeness: she addressed Sally repeatedly as "Gnädiges Fräulein." Sally, with her page-boy cap stuck over one ear, laughed her silvery laugh and sat down elegantly on the sofa. Frl. Schroeder hovered about her in unfeigned admiration and amazement. She had evidently never seen anyone like Sally before. When she brought in the tea there was, in place of the usual little chunks of pale unappetizing pastry, a plateful of jam tarts arranged in the shape of a star. I noticed also that Frl. Schroeder had provided us with two tiny paper serviettes, perforated at the edges to resemble lace. (When, later, I complimented her on these preparations, she told me that she had always used the serviettes when the Herr Rittmeister had had his fiancée to tea. "Oh, yes, Herr Issyvoo. You can depend on me! I know what pleases a young lady!")

"Do you mind if I lie down on your sofa, darling?" Sally asked, as soon as we were alone.

"No, of course not."

Sally pulled off her cap, swung her little velvet shoes up on to the sofa, opened her bag and began powdering: "I'm most terribly tired. I didn't sleep a wink last night. I've got a marvellous new lover."

I began to put out the tea. Sally gave me a sidelong glance:

"Do I shock you when I talk like that, Christopher darling?"

"Not in the least."

"But you don't like it?"

"It's no business of mine." I handed her the tea-glass.

"Oh, for God's sake," cried Sally, "don't start being English! Of course it's your business what you think!"

"Well then, if you want to know, it rather bores me."

This annoyed her even more than I had intended. Her tone changed: she said coldly: "I thought you'd understand." She sighed: "But I forgot—you're a man."

"I'm sorry, Sally. I can't help being a man, of course ... But please don't be angry with me. I only meant that when you talk like that it's really just nervousness. You're naturally rather shy with strangers, I think: so you've got into this trick of trying to bounce them into approving or disapproving of you, violently. I know, because I try it myself, sometimes ... Only I wish you wouldn't try it on me, because it just doesn't work and it only makes me feel embarrassed. If you go to bed with every single man in Berlin and come and tell me about it each time, you still won't convince me that you're *La Dame aux Camélias*—because, really and truly, you know, you aren't."

"No ... I suppose I'm not—" Sally's voice was carefully impersonal. She was beginning to enjoy this conversation. I had succeeded in flattering her in some new way: "Then what *am* I, exactly, Christopher darling?"

"You're the daughter of Mr and Mrs Jackson-Bowles."

Sally sipped her tea: "Yes ... I think I see what you mean ... Perhaps you're right... Then you think I ought to give up having lovers altogether?"

"Certainly I don't. As long as you're sure you're really enjoying yourself."

"Of course," said Sally gravely, after a pause, "I'd never let love interfere with my work. Work comes before everything ... But I don't believe that a woman can be a great actress who hasn't had any love-affairs—" she broke off suddenly: "What are you laughing at, Chris?"

"I'm not laughing."

"You're always laughing at me. Do you think I'm the most ghastly idiot?"

"No, Sally. I don't think you're an idiot at all. It's quite true, I *was* laughing. People I like often make me want to laugh at them. I don't know why."

"Then you do like me, Christopher darling?"

"Yes, of course I like you, Sally. What did you think?"

"But you're not in love with me, are you?"

"No. I'm not in love with you."

"I'm awfully glad. I've wanted you to like me ever since we first met. But I'm glad you're not in love with me, because, somehow, I couldn't possibly be in love with you—so, if you had been, everything would have been spoilt."

"Well then, that's very lucky, isn't it?"

"Yes, very ..." Sally hesitated. "There's something I want to confess to you, Chris darling ... I'm not sure if you'll understand or not."

"Remember, I'm only a man, Sally."

Sally laughed: "It's the most idiotic little thing. But somehow, I'd hate it if you found out without my telling you ... You know, the other day, you said Fritz had told you my mother was French?"

"Yes, I remember."

"And I said he must have invented it? Well, he hadn't... You see, I'd told him she was."

"But why on earth did you do that?"

We both began to laugh. "Goodness knows," said Sally. "I suppose I wanted to impress him."

"But what is there impressive in having a French mother?"

"I'm a bit mad like that sometimes, Chris. You must be patient with me."

"All right, Sally, I'll be patient."

"And you'll swear on your honour not to tell Fritz?"

"I swear."

"If you do, you swine," exclaimed Sally, laughing and picking up the paper-knife dagger from my writing-table, "I'll cut your throat!"

Afterwards, I asked Frl. Schroeder what she'd thought of Sally. She was in raptures: "Like a picture, Herr Issyvoo! And so elegant: such beautiful hands and feet! One can see that she belongs to the very best society ... You know, Herr Issyvoo, I should never have expected you to have a lady friend like that! You always seem so quiet..."

"Ah well, Frl. Schroeder, it's often the quiet ones—"

She went off into her little scream of laughter, swaying backwards and forwards on her short legs:

"Quite right, Herr Issyvoo! Quite right!"

On New Year's Eve, Sally came to live at Frl. Schroeder's.

It had all been arranged at the last moment. Sally, her suspicions sharpened by my repeated warnings, had caught out Frau Karpf in a particularly gross and clumsy piece of swindling. So she had hardened her heart and given notice. She was to have Frl. Kost's old room. Frl. Schroeder was, of course, enchanted.

We all had our Sylvester Abend dinner at home: Frl. Schroeder, Frl. Mayr, Sally, Bobby, a mixer colleague from the Troika and myself. It was a great success. Bobby, already restored to favour, flirted daringly with Frl. Schroeder. Frl. Mayr and Sally, talking as one great artiste to another, discussed the possibilities of music-hall work in England. Sally told some really startling lies, which she obviously for the moment half-believed, about how she'd appeared at the Palladium and the London Coliseum. Frl. Mayr capped them with a story of how she'd been drawn through the streets of Munich in a carriage by excited students. From this point it did not take Sally long to perusade Frl. Mayr to sing *Sennerin Abschied von der Alm,* which, after claret cup and a bottle of very inexpensive cognac, so exactly suited my mood that I shed a few tears. We all joined in the repeats and the final, ear-splitting *Juch-he!* Then Sally sang "I've got those Little Boy

Blues" with so much expression that Bobby's mixer colleague, taking it personally, seized her round the waist and had to be restrained by Bobby, who reminded him firmly that it was time to be getting along to business.

Sally and I went with him to the Troika, where we met Fritz. With him was Klaus Linke, the young pianist who used to accompany Sally when she sang at the Lady Windermere. Later, Fritz and I went off alone. Fritz seemed rather depressed: he wouldn't tell me why. Some girls did classical figure-tableaux behind gauze. And then there was a big dancing-hall with telephones on the tables. We had the usual kind of conversations: "Pardon me, Madame, I feel sure from your voice that you're a fascinating little blonde with long black eyelashes—just my type. How did I know? Aha, that's my secret! Yes—quite right: I'm tall, dark, broad-shouldered, military appearance, and the tiniest little moustache ... You don't believe me? Then come and see for yourself!" The couples were dancing with hands on each other's hips, yelling in each other's faces, streaming with sweat. An orchestra in Bavarian costume whooped and drank and perspired beer. The place stank like a zoo. After this, I think I strayed off alone and wandered for hours and hours through a jungle of paper streamers. Next morning, when I woke, the bed was full of them.

I had been up and dressed for some time when Sally returned home. She came straight into my room, looking tired but pleased with herself.

"Hullo, darling! What time is it?"

"Nearly lunch-time."

"I say, is it really? How marvellous! I'm practically starving. I've had nothing for breakfast but a cup of coffee ..." She paused expectantly, waiting for my next question.

"Where have you been?" I asked.

"But darling," Sally opened her eyes very wide in affected surprise: "I thought you knew!"

"I haven't the least idea."

"Nonsense!"

"Really, I haven't, Sally."

"Oh, Christopher darling, how can you be such a liar! Why, it was obvious that you'd planned the whole thing! The way you got rid of Fritz—he looked so cross! Klaus and I nearly died of laughing."

All the same, she wasn't quite at her ease. For the first time, I saw her blush.

"Have you got a cigarette, Chris?"

I gave her one and lit the match. She blew out a long cloud of smoke and walked slowly to the window:

"I'm most terribly in love with him."

She turned, frowning slightly; crossed to the sofa and curled herself up carefully, arranging her hands and feet: "At least, I think I am," she added.

I allowed a respectful pause to elapse before asking: "And is Klaus in love with you?"

"He absolutely adores me." Sally was very serious indeed. She smoked for several minutes: "He says he fell in love with me the first time we met, at the Lady Windermere. But as long as we were working together, he didn't dare to say anything. He was afraid it might put me off my singing ... He says that, before he met me, he'd no idea what a marvellously beautiful thing a woman's body is. He's only had about three women before, in his life ..."

I lit a cigarette.

"Of course, Chris, I don't suppose you really understand ... It's awfully hard to explain ..."

"I'm sure it is."

"I'm seeing him again at four o'clock." Sally's tone was slightly defiant.

"In that case, you'd better get some sleep. I'll ask Frl. Schroeder to scramble you some eggs; or I'll do them myself if she's still too drunk. You get into bed. You can eat them there."

"Thanks, Chris darling. You are an angel." Sally yawned. "What on earth I should do without you, I don't know."

After this, Sally and Klaus saw each other every day. They generally met at our house; and once, Klaus stayed the whole night. Frl. Schroeder didn't say much to me about it, but I could see that she was rather shocked. Not that she disapproved of Klaus: she thought him very attractive. But she regarded Sally as my property, and it shocked her to see me standing so tamely to one side. I am sure, however, that if I hadn't known about the affair, and if Sally had really been deceiving me, Frl. Schroeder would have assisted at the conspiracy with great relish.

Meanwhile, Klaus and I were a little shy of each other. When we happened to meet on the stairs, we bowed coldly, like enemies.

About the middle of January, Klaus left suddenly for England. Quite unexpectedly he had got the offer of a very good job, synchronizing music for the films. The afternoon he came to say goodbye there was a positively surgical atmosphere in the flat, as though Sally were undergoing a dangerous operation. Frl. Schroeder and Frl. Mayr sat in the living-room and laid cards. The results, Frl. Schroeder later assured me, couldn't have been better. The eight of clubs had appeared three times in a favourable conjunction.

Sally spent the whole of the next day curled up on the sofa in her room, with pencil and paper on her lap. She was writing poems. She wouldn't let me see them. She smoked cigarette after cigarette, and mixed Prairie Oysters, but refused to eat more than a few mouthfuls of Frl. Schroeder's omelette.

"Can't I bring you something in, Sally?"

"No thanks, Chris darling. I just don't want to eat anything at all. I feel all marvellous and ethereal, as if I was a kind of most wonderful saint, or something. You've no idea how glorious it feels ... Have a chocolate, darling? Klaus gave me three boxes. If I eat any more, I shall be sick."

"Thank you."

"I don't suppose I shall ever marry him. It would ruin our

careers. You see, Christopher, he adores me so terribly that it wouldn't be good for him to always have me hanging about."

"You might marry after you're both famous."

Sally considered this:

"No ... That would spoil everything. We should be trying all the time to live up to our old selves, if you know what I mean. And we should both be different... He was so marvellously primitive: just like a faun. He made me feel like a most marvellous nymph, or something, miles away from anywhere, in the middle of the forest."

The first letter from Klaus duly arrived. We had all been anxiously awaiting it; and Frl. Schroeder woke me up specially early to tell me that it had come. Perhaps she was afraid that she would never get a chance of reading it herself and relied on me to tell her the contents. If so, her fears were groundless. Sally not only showed the letter to Frl. Schroeder, Frl. Mayr, Bobby and myself, she even read selections from it aloud in the presence of the porter's wife, who had come up to collect the rent.

From the first, the letter left a nasty taste in my mouth. Its whole tone was egotistical and a bit patronizing. Klaus didn't like London, he said. He felt lonely there. The food disagreed with him. And the people at the studio treated him with lack of consideration. He wished Sally were with him: she could have helped him in many ways. However, now that he was in England, he would try to make the best of it. He would work hard and earn money; and Sally was to work hard too. Work would cheer her up and keep her from getting depressed. At the end of the letter came various endearments, rather too slickly applied. Reading them, one felt: he's written this kind of thing several times before.

Sally was delighted, however. Klaus' exhortation made such an impression upon her that she at once rang up several film companies, a theatrical agency and half a dozen of her "business" acquaintances. Nothing definite came of all this, it is true; but she remained very optimistic throughout the next twenty-four hours—even her dreams, she told me, had been full of contracts and four-figure cheques: "It's the most marvellous feeling, Chris. I know I'm going right ahead now and going to become the most wonderful actress in the world."

One morning, about a week after this, I went into Sally's room and found her holding a letter in her hand. I recognized Klaus' handwriting at once.

"Good morning, Chris darling."

"Good morning, Sally."

"How did you sleep?" Her tone was unnaturally bright and chatty.

"All right, thanks. How did you?"

"Fairly all right ... Filthy weather, isn't it?"

"Yes." I walked over to the window to look. It was.

Sally smiled conversationally: "Do you know what this swine's gone and done?"

"What swine?" I wasn't going to be caught out.

"Oh, Chris! For God's sake, don't be so dense!"

"I'm very sorry. I'm afraid I'm a bit slow on the uptake this morning."

"I can't be bothered to explain, darling." Sally held out the letter. "Here, read this, will you? Of all the blasted impudence! Read it aloud. I want to hear how it sounds."

"Mein liebes, armes Kind," the letter began. Klaus called Sally his poor dear child because, as he explained, he was afraid that what he had to tell her would make her terribly unhappy. Nevertheless, he must say it: he must tell her that he had come to a decision. She mustn't imagine that this had been easy for him: it had been very difficult and painful. All the same, he knew he was right. In a word, they must part.

"I see now," wrote Klaus, "that I behaved very selfishly. I thought only of my own pleasure. But now I realize that I must have had a bad influence on you. My dear little girl, you have adored me too much. If we should continue to be together, you would soon have no will and no mind of your own." Klaus went on to advise Sally to live for her work. "Work is the only thing which matters, as I myself have found." He was very much concerned that Sally shouldn't upset herself unduly: "You must be brave, Sally, my poor darling child."

Right at the end of the letter, it all came out:

"I was invited a few nights ago to a party at the house of Lady Klein, a leader of the English aristocracy. I met there a very beautiful and intelligent young English girl named Miss Gore-Eckersley. She is related to an English lord whose name I couldn't quite hear—you will probably know which one I mean. We have met twice since then and had wonderful conversations about many things. I do not think I have ever met a girl who could understand my mind so well as she does—"

"That's a new one on me," broke in Sally bitterly, with a short laugh: "I never suspected the boy of having a mind at all."

At this moment we were interrupted by Frl. Schroeder who had come, sniffing secrets, to ask if Sally would like a bath. I left them together to make the most of the occasion.

"I can't be angry with the fool," said Sally, later in the day, pacing up and down the room and furiously smoking: "I just feel sorry for him in a motherly sort of way. But what on earth'll happen to *his* work, if he chucks himself at these women's heads, I can't imagine."

She made another turn of the room:

"I think if he'd been having a proper affair with another woman, and had only told me about it after it'd been going on for a long time, I'd have minded more. But this girl! Why, I don't suppose she's even his mistress."

"Obviously not," I agreed… "I say, shall we have a Prairie Oyster?"

"How marvellous you are, Chris! You always think of just the right thing. I wish I could fall in love with you. Klaus isn't worth your little finger."

"I know he isn't."

"The blasted cheek," exclaimed Sally, gulping the Worcester sauce and licking her upper lip, "of his saying I adored him! …The worst of it is, I did!"

That evening I went into her room and found her with pen and paper before her:

"I've written about a million letters to him and torn them all up."

"It's no good, Sally. Let's go to the cinema."

"Right you are, Chris darling." Sally wiped her eyes with the corner of her tiny handkerchief: "It's no use bothering, is it?"

"Not a bit of use."

"And now I jolly well *will* be a great actress—just to show him!"

"That's the spirit!"

We went to a little cinema in the Bülowstrasse, where they were showing a film about a girl who sacrificed her stage career for the sake of a Great Love, Home, and Children. We laughed so much that we had to leave before the end.

"I feel ever so much better now," said Sally, as we were coming away.

"I'm glad."

"Perhaps, after all, I can't have been properly in love with him ... What do you think?"

"It's rather difficult for me to say."

"I've often thought I was in love with a man, and then I found I wasn't. But this time," Sally's voice was regretful, "I really did feel *sure* of it... And now, somehow, everything seems to have got a bit confused ..."

"Perhaps you're suffering from shock," I suggested.

Sally was very pleased with this idea: "Do you know, I expect I am! ... You know, Chris, you do understand women most marvellously: better than any man I've ever met... I'm sure that some day you'll write the most marvellous novel which'll sell simply millions of copies."

"Thank you for believing in me, Sally!"

"Do you believe in me, too, Chris?"

"Of course I do."

"No, but honestly?"

"Well... I'm quite certain you'll make a terrific success at something—only I'm not sure what it'll be ... I mean, there's so many things you could do if you tried, aren't there?"

"I suppose there are." Sally became thoughtful. "At least, sometimes I feel like that ... And sometimes I feel I'm no damn' use at anything ... Why I can't even keep a man faithful to me for the inside of a month."

"Oh, Sally, don't let's start all that again!"

"All right, Chris—we won't start all that. Let's go and have a drink."

During the weeks that followed, Sally and I were together most of the day. Curled up on the sofa in the big dingy room, she smoked, drank Prairie Oysters, talked endlessly of the future. When the weather was fine, and I hadn't any lessons to give, we strolled as far as the Wittenbergplatz and sat on a bench in the sunshine, discussing the people who went past. Everybody stared at Sally, in her canary yellow beret and shabby fur coat, like the skin of a mangy old dog.

"I wonder," she was fond of remarking, "what they'd say if they knew that we two old tramps were going to be the most marvellous novelist and the greatest actress in the world."

"They'd probably be very much surprised."

"I expect we shall look back on this time when we're driving about in our Mercedes, and think: After all, it wasn't such bad fun!"

"It wouldn't be such bad fun if we had that Mercedes now."

We talked continually about wealth, fame, huge contracts for Sally, record-breaking sales for the novels I should one day write. "I think," said Sally, "it must be marvellous to be a novelist. You're frightfully dreamy and unpractical and unbusinesslike, and people imagine they can fairly swindle you as much as they want—and then you sit down and write a book about them which fairly shows them what swine they all are, and it's the most terrific success and you make pots of money."

"I expect the trouble with me is that I'm not quite dreamy enough ..."

"... if only I could get a really rich man as my lover. Let's see ... I shouldn't want more than three thousand a year, and a flat, and a decent car. I'd do anything, just now, to get rich. If you're rich you can afford to stand out for a really good contract; you don't have to snap up the first offer you get... Of course, I'd be absolutely faithful to the man who kept me—"

Sally said things like this very seriously and evidently believed she meant them. She was in a curious state of mind, restless and nervy. Often she flew into a temper for no special reason. She talked incessantly about getting work, but made no effort to do so. Her allowance hadn't been stopped, so far, however, and we were living very cheaply, since Sally no longer cared to go out in the evenings or to see other people at all. Once, Fritz came to tea. I left them alone together afterwards to go and write a letter. When I came back Fritz had gone and Sally was in tears.

"That man *bores* me so!" she sobbed. "I hate him! I should like to kill him!"

But in a few minutes she was quite calm again. I started to mix the inevitable Prairie Oyster. Sally, curled up on the sofa, was thoughtfully smoking:

"I wonder," she said suddenly, "if I'm going to have a baby."

"Good God!" I nearly dropped the glass: "Do you really think you are?"

"I don't know. With me it's so difficult to tell: I'm so irregular ... I've felt sick sometimes. It's probably something I've eaten ..."

"But hadn't you better see a doctor?"

"Oh, I suppose so." Sally yawned listlessly. "There's no hurry."

"Of course there's a hurry! You'll go and see a doctor tomorrow!"

"Look here, Chris, who the hell do you think you're ordering about? I wish now I hadn't said anything about it at all!" Sally was on the point of bursting into tears again.

"Oh, all right! All right!" I hastily tried to calm her. "Do just what you like. It's no business of mine."

"Sorry, darling. I didn't mean to be snappy. I'll see how I feel in the morning. Perhaps I will go and see that doctor, after all."

But of course, she didn't. Next day, indeed, she seemed much brighter: "Let's go out this evening, Chris. I'm getting sick of this room. Let's go and see some life!"

"Right you are, Sally. Where would you like to go?"

"Let's go to the Troika and talk to that old idiot Bobby. Perhaps he'll stand us a drink—you never know!"

Bobby didn't stand us any drinks; but Sally's suggestion proved to be a good one, nevertheless. For it was while sitting at the bar of the Troika that we first got into conversation with Clive.

From that moment onwards we were with him almost continuously; either separately or together. I never once saw him sober. Clive told us that he drank half a bottle of whisky before breakfast, and I had no reason to disbelieve him. He often began to explain to us why he drank so much—it was because he was very unhappy. But why he was so unhappy I never found out, because Sally always interrupted to say that it was time to be going out or moving on to the next place or smoking a cigarette or having another glass of whisky. She was drinking nearly as much whisky as Clive himself. It never seemed to make her really drunk, but sometimes her eyes looked awful, as though they had been boiled. Every day the layer of make-up on her face seemed to get thicker.

Clive was a very big man, good-looking in a heavy Roman way, and just beginning to get fat. He had about him that sad, American air of vagueness which is always attractive; doubly attractive in one who possessed so much money. He was vague, wistful, a bit lost: dimly anxious to have a good time and uncertain how to set about getting it. He seemed never to be quite sure whether he was really enjoying himself, whether what we were doing was *really* fun. He had constantly to be reassured. *Was* this the genuine article? *Was* this the real guaranteed height of a Good Time? It was? Yes, yes, of course—it was marvellous! It was great! Ha, ha, ha! His big school-boyish laugh rolled out, re-echoed, became rather forced and died away abruptly on that puzzled note of inquiry. He couldn't venture a step without our support. Yet, even as he appealed to us, I thought I could sometimes detect odd sly flashes of sarcasm. What did he really think of us?

Every morning, Clive sent round a hired car to fetch us to the hotel where he was staying. The chauffeur always brought with him a wonderful bouquet of flowers, ordered from the most expensive flower-shop in the Linden. One morning I had a lesson to give and arranged with Sally to join them later. On arriving at the hotel, I found that Clive and Sally had left early to fly to Dresden. There was a note from Clive, apologizing profusely and inviting me to lunch at the hotel restaurant, by myself, as his guest. But I didn't. I was afraid of that look in the head waiter's eye. In the evening, when Clive and Sally returned, Clive had brought me a present: it was a parcel of six silk shirts. "He wanted to get you a gold cigarette case," Sally whispered in my ear, "but I told him shirts would be better. Yours are in such a state … Besides, we've got to go slow at present. We don't want him to think we're gold-diggers …"

I accepted them gratefully. What else could I do? Clive had corrupted us utterly. It was understood that he was going to put up the money to launch Sally upon a stage career. He often spoke of this, in a thoroughly nice way, as though it were a very trivial matter, to be settled, without fuss, between friends. But no sooner had he touched on the subject than his attention seemed to wander off again—his thoughts were as easily distracted as those of a child. Sometimes Sally was very hard put to it, I could see, to hide her impatience, "Just leave us alone for a bit now, darling," she would whisper to me, "Clive and I are going to talk business." But however tactfully Sally tried to bring him to the point, she never quite succeeded. When I rejoined them, half an hour later, I would find Clive smiling and sipping his whisky; and Sally also smiling, to conceal her extreme irritation.

"I adore him," Sally told me, repeatedly and very solemnly, whenever we were alone together. She was intensely earnest in believing this. It was like a dogma in a newly adopted religious creed: Sally adores Clive. It was a very solemn undertaking to adore a millionaire. Sally's features began to assume, with increasing frequency, the rapt expression of the theatrical nun. And indeed, when Clive, with his charming vagueness, gave a particularly flagrant professional beggar a twenty-mark note, we would exchange glances of genuine awe. The waste of so much good money affected us both like something inspired, a kind of miracle.

There came an afternoon when Clive seemed more nearly sober than usual. He began to make plans. In a few days we were all three of us to leave Berlin, for good. The Orient Express would take us to Athens. Thence, we should fly to Egypt. From Egypt to Marseilles. From Marseilles, by boat to South America. Then Tahiti, Singapore, Japan. Clive pronounced the names as though they had been stations on the Wannsee railway, quite as a matter of course: he had been there already. He knew it all. His matter-of-fact boredom gradually infused reality into the preposterous conversation. After all, he could do it. I began seriously to believe that he meant to do it. With a mere gesture of his wealth, he could alter the whole course of our lives.

What would become of us? Once we started, we should never go back. We could never leave him. Sally, of course, he would marry. I should occupy an ill-defined position: a kind of private secretary without duties. With a flash of vision, I saw myself ten years hence, in flannels and black-and-white shoes, gone heavier round the jowl and a bit glassy, pouring out a drink in the lounge of a Californian hotel.

"Come and cast an eye at the funeral," Clive was saying.

"What funeral, darling?" Sally asked, patiently. This was a new kind of interruption.

"Why, say, haven't you noticed it!" Clive laughed. "It's a most elegant funeral. It's been going past for the last hour."

We all three went out on to the balcony of Clive's room. Sure enough, the street below was full of people. They were burying Hermann Müller. Ranks of pale steadfast clerks, government officials, trade union secretaries—the whole drab weary pageant of Prussian Social Democracy—trudged past under their banners towards the silhouetted arches of the Brandenburger Tor, from which the long black streamers stirred slowly in an evening breeze.

"Say, who was this guy, anyway?" asked Clive, looking down. "I guess he must have been a big swell?"

"God knows," Sally answered, yawning. "Look, Clive darling, isn't it a marvellous sunset?"

She was quite right. We had nothing to do with those Germans down there, marching, or with the dead man in the coffin, or with the words on the banners. In a few days, I thought, we shall have forfeited all kinship with ninety-nine per cent of the population of the world, with the men and women who earn their living, who insure their lives, who are anxious about the future of their children. Perhaps in the Middle Ages people felt like this, when they believed themselves to have sold their souls to the Devil. It was a curious, exhilarating, not unpleasant sensation: but, at the same time, I felt slightly scared. Yes, I said to myself, I've done it, now. I am lost.

Next morning, we arrived at the hotel at the usual time. The porter eyed us, I thought, rather queerly.

"Whom did you wish to see, Madam?"

The question seemed so extraordinary that we both laughed.

"Why, number 365, of course," Sally answered. "Who did you think? Don't you know us by this time?"

"I'm afraid you can't do that, Madam. The gentleman in 365 left early this morning."

"Left? You mean he's gone out for the day? That's funny! What time will he be back?"

"He didn't say anything about coming back, Madam. He was travelling to Budapest."

As we stood there goggling at him, a waiter hurried up with a note.

"Dear Sally and Chris," it said, "I can't stick this darned town any longer, so am off. Hoping to see you sometime, Clive.

"(These are in case I forgot anything.)"

In the envelope were three hundred-mark notes. These, the fading flowers, Sally's four pairs of shoes and two hats (bought in Dresden) and my six shirts were our total assets from Clive's visit. At first, Sally was very angry. Then we both began to laugh:

"Well, Chris, I'm afraid we're not much use as gold-diggers, are we, darling?"

We spent most of the day discussing whether Clive's departure was a premeditated trick. I was inclined to think it wasn't. I imagined him leaving every new town and every new set of acquaintances in much the same sort of way. I sympathized with him, a good deal.

Then came the question of what was to be done with the money. Sally decided to put by two hundred and fifty marks for some new clothes: fifty marks we would blow that evening.

But blowing the fifty marks wasn't as much fun as we'd imagined it would be. Sally felt ill and couldn't eat the wonderful dinner we'd ordered. We were both depressed.

"You know, Chris, I'm beginning to think that men are always going to leave me. The more I think about it, the more men I remember who have. It's ghastly, really."

"I'll never leave you, Sally."

"Won't you, darling? ... But seriously, I believe I'm a sort of Ideal Woman, if you know what I mean. I'm the sort of woman who can take men away from their wives, but I could never keep anybody for long. And that's because I'm the type which every man imagines he wants, until he gets me; and then he finds he doesn't really, after all."

"Well, you'd rather be that than the Ugly Duckling with the Heart of Gold, wouldn't you?"

"... I could kick myself, the way I behaved to Clive. I ought never to have bothered him about money, the way I did. I expect he thought I was just a common little whore, like all the others. And I really did adore him—in a way ... If I'd married him, I'd have made a man out of him. I'd have got him to give up drinking."

"You set him such a good example."

We both laughed.

"The old swine might at least have left me with a decent cheque."

"Never mind, darling. There's more where he came from."

"I don't care," said Sally. "I'm sick of being a whore. I'll never look at a man with money again."

Next morning, Sally felt very ill. We both put it down to the drink. She stayed in bed the whole morning and when she got up she fainted. I wanted her to see a doctor straight away, but she wouldn't. About tea-time, she fainted again and looked so bad afterwards that Frl. Schroeder and I sent for a doctor without consulting her at all.

The doctor, when he arrived, stayed a long time. Frl. Schroeder and I sat waiting in the living-room to hear his diagnosis. But, very much to our surprise, he left the flat suddenly, in a great hurry, without even looking in to wish us good afternoon. I went at once to Sally's room. Sally was sitting up in bed, with a rather fixed grin on her face:

"Well, Christopher darling, I've been made an April Fool of."

"What do you mean?"

Sally tried to laugh:

"He says I'm going to have a baby."

"Oh my God!"

"Don't look so scared, darling! I've been more or less expecting it, you know."

"It's Klaus', I suppose?"

"Yes."

"And what are you going to do about it?"

"Not have it, of course." Sally reached for a cigarette. I sat stupidly staring at my shoes.

"Will the doctor ..."

"No, he won't. I asked him straight out. He was terribly shocked. I said, 'My dear man, what do you imagine would happen to the unfortunate child if it was born? Do I look as if I'd make a good mother?'"

"And what did he say to that?"

"He seemed to think it was quite beside the point. The only thing which matters to him is his professional reputation."

"Well then, we've got to find someone without a professional reputation, that's all."

"I should think," said Sally, "we'd better ask Frl. Schroeder."

So Frl. Schroeder was consulted. She took it very well: she was alarmed but extremely practical. Yes, she knew of somebody. A friend of a friend's friend had once had difficulties. And the doctor was a fully qualified man, very clever indeed. The only trouble was, he might be very expensive.

"Thank goodness," Sally interjected, "we haven't spent all that swine Clive's money!"

"I must say, I think Klaus ought—"

"Look here, Chris. Let me tell you this once for all: if I catch you writing to Klaus about this business, I'll never forgive you and I'll never speak to you again!"

"Oh, very well... Of course I won't. It was just a suggestion, that's all."

I didn't like the doctor. He kept stroking and pinching Sally's arm and pawing her hand. However, he seemed the right man for the job. Sally was to go into his private nursing home as soon as there was a vacancy for her. Everything was perfectly official and above-board. In a few polished sentences the dapper little doctor dispelled the least whiff of sinister illegality. Sally's state of health, he explained, made it quite impossible for her to undergo the risks of childbirth: there would be a certificate to that effect. Needless to say, the certificate would cost a lot of money. So would the nursing-home and so would the operation itself. The doctor wanted two hundred and fifty marks down before he would make any arrangements at all. In the end, we beat him down to two hundred. Sally wanted the extra fifty, she explained to me later, to get some new nightdresses.

At last it was spring. The cafés were putting up wooden platforms on the pavement and the ice-cream shops were opening, with their rainbow-wheels. We drove to the nursing-home in an open taxi. Because of the lovely weather, Sally was in better spirits than I had seen her in for weeks. But Frl. Schroeder, though she bravely tried to smile, was on the verge of tears. "The doctor isn't a Jew, I hope?" Frl. Mayr asked me sternly. "Don't you let one of those filthy Jews touch her. They always try to get a job of that kind, the beasts!"

Sally had a nice room, clean and cheerful, with a balcony. I called there again in the evening. Lying there in bed without her make-up, she looked years younger, like a little girl.

"Hullo, darling ... They haven't killed me yet, you see. But they've been doing their best to ... Isn't this a funny place? ... I wish that pig Klaus could see me ... This is what comes of not understanding his *mind* ..."

She was a bit feverish and laughed a great deal. One of the nurses came in for a moment, as if looking for something, and went out again almost immediately.

"She was dying to get a peep at you," Sally explained. "You see, I told her you were the father. You don't mind, do you, darling ..."

"Not at all. It's a compliment."

"It makes everything so much simpler. Otherwise, if there's no one, they think it so odd. And I don't care for being sort of looked down on and pitied as the poor betrayed girl who gets abandoned by her lover. It isn't particularly flattering for me, is it? So I told her we were most terribly in love but fearfully hard up, so that we couldn't afford to marry, and how we dreamed of the time when we'd both be rich and famous and then we'd have a family of ten, just to make up for this one. The nurse was awfully touched, poor girl. In fact, she wept. Tonight, when she's on duty, she's going to show me pictures of *her* young man. Isn't it sweet?"

Next day, Frl. Schroeder and I went round to the nursing-home together. We found Sally lying flat, with the bedclothes up to her chin:

"Oh, hullo, you two! Won't you sit down? What time is it?" She turned uneasily in bed and rubbed her eyes: "Where did all these flowers come from?"

"We brought them."

"How marvellous of you!" Sally smiled vacantly. "Sorry to be such a fool today … It's this bloody chloroform … My head's full of it."

We only stayed a few minutes. On the way home, Frl. Schroeder was terribly upset: "Will you believe it, Herr Issyvoo, I couldn't take it more to heart if it was my own daughter? Why, when I see the poor child suffering like that, I'd rather it was myself lying there in her place—I would indeed!"

Next day Sally was much better. We all went to visit her: Frl. Schroeder, Frl. Mayr, Bobby and Fritz. Fritz, of course, hadn't the faintest idea what had really happened. Sally, he had been told, was being operated upon for a small internal ulcer. As always is the way with people when they aren't in the know, he made all kinds of unintentional and startlingly apt references to storks, gooseberry-bushes, perambulators and babies generally; and even recounted a special new item of scandal about a well-known Berlin society lady who was said to have undergone a recent illegal operation. Sally and I avoided each other's eyes.

On the evening of the next day, I visited her at the nursing-home for the last time. She was to leave in the morning. She was alone and we sat together on the balcony. She seemed more or less all right now and could walk about the room.

"I told the Sister I didn't want to see anybody today except you." Sally yawned languidly. "People make me feel so tired."

"Would you rather I went away too?"

"Oh no," said Sally, without much enthusiasm. "If you go, one of the nurses will only come in and begin to chatter; and if I'm not lively and bright with her, they'll say I have to stay in this hellish place a couple of extra days, and I couldn't stand that."

She stared out moodily over the quiet street:

"You know, Chris, in some ways I wish I'd had that kid ... It would have been rather marvellous to have had it. The last day or two, I've been sort of feeling what it would be like to be a mother. Do you know, last night, I sat here for a long time by myself and held this cushion in my arms and imagined it was my baby. And I felt a most marvellous sort of shut-off feeling from all the rest of the world. I imagined how it'd grow up and how I'd work for it, and how, after I'd put it to bed at nights, I'd go out and make love to filthy old men to get money to pay for its food and clothes ... It's all very well for you to grin like that, Chris ... I did really!"

"Well, why don't you marry and have one?"

"I don't know ... I feel as if I'd lost faith in men. I just haven't any use for them at all ... Even you, Christopher, if you were to go out into the street now and be run over by a taxi... I should be sorry in a way, of course, but I shouldn't really *care* a damn."

"Thank you, Sally."

We both laughed.

"I didn't mean that, of course, darling—at least, not personally. You mustn't mind what I say while I'm like this. I get all sorts of crazy ideas into my head. Having babies makes you feel awfully primitive, like a sort of wild animal or something, defending its young. Only the trouble is, I haven't any young to defend... I expect that's what makes me so frightfully bad-tempered to everybody just now."

It was partly as the result of this conversation that I suddenly decided, that evening, to cancel all my lessons, leave Berlin as soon as possible, go to some place on the Baltic and try to start working. Since Christmas, I had hardly written a word.

Sally, when I told her my idea, was rather relieved, I think. We both needed a change. We talked vaguely of her joining me later; but even then, I felt that she wouldn't. Her plans were very uncertain. Later, she might go to Paris, or to the Alps, or to the South of France, she said—if she could get the cash. "But probably," she added, "I shall just stay on here. I should be quite happy. I seem to have got sort of used to this place."

I returned to Berlin towards the middle of July.

All this time I had heard nothing of Sally, beyond half a dozen postcards, exchanged during the first month of my absence. I wasn't much surprised to find she'd left her room in our flat.

"Of course, I quite understand her going. I couldn't make her as comfortable as she'd the right to expect; especially as we haven't any running water in the bedrooms." Poor Frl. Schroeder's eyes had filled with tears. "But it was a terrible disappointment to me, all the same ... Frl. Bowles behaved very handsomely, I can't complain about that. She insisted on paying for her room until the end of July. I was entitled to the money, of course, because she didn't give notice until the twenty-first—but I'd never have mentioned it... She was such a charming young lady—"

"Have you got her address?"

"Oh yes, and the telephone number. You'll be ringing her up, of course. She'll be delighted to see you ... The other gentlemen came and went, but you were her real friend, Herr Issyvoo. You know, I always used to hope that you two would get married. You'd have made an ideal couple. You always had such a good steady influence on her, and she used to brighten you up a bit when you got too deep in your books and studies ... Oh yes, Herr Issyvoo, you may laugh—but you never can tell! Perhaps it isn't too late yet!"

•

Next morning, Frl. Schroeder woke me in great excitement:

"Herr Issyvoo, what do you think! They've shut the Darmstädter und National! There'll be thousands ruined, I shouldn't wonder! The milkman says we'll have civil war in a fortnight! Whatever do you say to that!"

As soon as I'd got dressed, I went down into the street. Sure enough, there was a crowd outside the branch bank on the Nollendorfplatz corner, a lot of men with leather satchels and women with string-bags—women like Frl. Schroeder herself. The iron lattices were drawn down over the bank windows. Most of the people were staring intently and rather stupidly at the locked door. In the middle of the door was fixed a small notice, beautifully printed in Gothic type, like a page from a classic author. The notice said that the Reichs-president had guaranteed the deposits. Everything was quite all right. Only the bank wasn't going to open.

A little boy was playing with a hoop amongst the crowd. The hoop ran against a woman's legs. She flew out at him at once: "Du, sei bloss nicht so frech! Cheeky little brat! What do you want here!" Another woman joined in, attacking the scared boy: "Get out! You can't understand it, can you?" And another asked, in furious sarcasm: "Have you got your money in the bank too, perhaps?" The boy fled before their pent-up, exploding rage.

In the afternoon it was very hot. The details of the new emergency decrees were in the early evening papers—terse, governmentally inspired. One alarmist headline stood out boldly, barred with blood-red ink: "Everything Collapses!" A Nazi journalist reminded his readers that tomorrow, the fourteenth of July, was a day of national rejoicing in France; and doubtless, he added, the French would rejoice with especial fervour this year, at the prospect of Germany's downfall. Going into an outfitters, I bought myself a pair of ready-made flannel trousers for twelve marks fifty—a gesture of confidence by England. Then I got into the Underground to go and visit Sally.

She was living in a block of three-room flats, designed as an Artists' Colony, not far from the Breitenbachplatz. When I rang the bell, she opened the door to me herself:

"Hillooo, Chris, you old swine!"

"Hullo, Sally darling!"

"How are you? … Be careful, darling, you'll make me untidy. I've got to go out in a few minutes."

I had never seen her all in white before. It suited her. But her face looked thinner and older. Her hair was cut in a new way and beautifully waved.

"You're very smart," I said.

"Am I?" Sally smiled her pleased, dreamy, self-conscious smile. I followed her into the sitting-room of the flat. One wall was entirely window. There was some cherry-coloured wooden furniture and a very low divan with gaudy fringed cushions. A fluffy white miniature dog jumped to its feet and yapped. Sally picked it up and went through the gestures of kissing it, just not touching it with her lips:

"Freddi, mein Liebling, Du bist *soo* süss!"

"Yours?" I asked, noticing the improvement in her German accent.

"No. He belongs to Gerda, the girl I share this flat with."

"Have you known her long?"

"Only a week or two."

"What's she like?"

"Not bad. As stingy as hell. I have to pay for practically everything."

"It's nice here."

"Do you think so? Yes, I suppose it's all right. Better than that hole in the Nollendorfstrasse, anyhow."

"What made you leave? Did you and Frl. Schroeder have a row?"

"No, not exactly. Only I got so sick of hearing her talk. She nearly talked my head off. She's an awful bore, really."

"She's very fond of you."

Sally shrugged her shoulders with a slight impatient listless movement. Throughout this conversation, I noticed that she avoided my eyes. There was a long pause. I felt puzzled and vaguely embarrassed. I began to wonder how soon I could make an excuse to go.

Then the telephone bell rang. Sally yawned, pulled the instrument across on to her lap:

"Hilloo, who's there? Yes, it's me ... No ... No ... I've really no idea ... *Really* I haven't! I'm to guess?" Her nose wrinkled: "Is it Erwin? No? Paul? No? Wait a minute ... Let me see ...

"And now, darling, I must fly!" cried Sally, when, at last, the conversation was over: "I'm about two hours late already!"

"Got a new boyfriend?"

But Sally ignored my grin. She lit a cigarette with a faint expression of distaste.

"I've got to see a man on business," she said briefly.

"And when shall we meet again?"

"I'll have to see, darling ... I've got such a lot on, just at present... I shall be out in the country all day tomorrow, and probably the day after ... I'll let you know ... I may be going to Frankfurt quite soon."

"Have you got a job there?"

"No. Not exactly." Sally's voice was brief, dismissing this subject. "I've decided not to try for any film work until the autumn, anyhow. I shall take a thorough rest."

"You seem to have made a lot of new friends."

Again, Sally's manner became vague, carefully casual:

"Yes, I suppose I have ... It's probably a reaction from all those months at Frl. Schroeder's, when I never saw a soul."

"Well," I couldn't resist a malicious grin, "I hope for your sake that none of your new friends have got their money in the Darmstädter und National."

"Why?" She was interested at once. "What's the matter with it?"

"Do you really mean to say you haven't heard?"

"Of course not. I never read the papers, and I haven't been out today, yet."

I told her the news of the crisis. At the end of it, she was looking quite scared.

"But why on earth," she exclaimed impatiently, "didn't you tell me all this before? It may be serious."

"I'm sorry, Sally. I took it for granted that you'd know already … especially as you seem to be moving in financial circles, nowadays—"

But she ignored this little dig. She was frowning, deep in her own thoughts:

"If it was *very* serious, Leo would have rung up and told me …" she murmured at length. And this reflection appeared to ease her mind considerably.

We walked out together to the corner of the street, where Sally picked up a taxi.

"It's an awful nuisance living so far off," she said. "I'm probably going to get a car soon.

"By the way," she added just as we were parting, "what was it like on Ruegen?"

"I bathed a lot."

"Well, goodbye darling. I'll see you sometime."

"Goodbye, Sally. Enjoy yourself."

About a week after this, Sally rang me up:

"Can you come round at once, Chris? It's very important. I want you to do me a favour."

This time, also, I found Sally alone in the flat.

"Do you want to earn some money, darling?" she greeted me.

"Of course."

"Splendid! You see, it's like this …" She was in a fluffy pink dressing-wrap and inclined to be breathless: "There's a man I know who's starting a magazine. It's going to be most terribly highbrow and artistic, with lots of marvellous modern photographs, ink-pots and girls' heads upside down—you know the sort of thing … The point is, each number is going to take a special country and kind of review it, with articles about the manners and customs, and all that ... Well, the first country they're going to do is England and they want me to write an article on the English Girl ... Of course, I haven't the foggiest idea what to say, so what I thought was: you could write the article in my name and get the money—I only want not to disoblige this man who's editing the paper, because he may be terribly useful to me in other ways, later on ..."

"All right, I'll try."

"Oh, marvellous!"

"How soon do you want it done?"

"You see, darling, that's the whole point. I must have it at once ... Otherwise it's no earthly use, because I promised it four days ago and I simply must give it him this evening ... It needn't be very long. About five hundred words."

"Well, I'll do my best ..."

"Good. That's wonderful ... Sit down wherever you like. Here's some paper. You've got a pen? Oh, and here's a dictionary, in case there's a word you can't spell ... I'll just be having my bath."

When, three-quarters of an hour later, Sally came in dressed for the day, I had finished. Frankly, I was rather pleased with my effort.

She read it through carefully, a slow frown gathering between her beautifully pencilled eyebrows. When she had finished, she laid down the manuscript with a sigh:

"I'm sorry, Chris. It won't do at all."

"Won't do?" I was genuinely taken aback.

"Of course, I dare say it's very good from a literary point of view, and all that ..."

"Well then, what's wrong with it?"

"It's not nearly snappy enough." Sally was quite final. "It's not the kind of thing this man wants, at all."

I shrugged my shoulders: "I'm sorry, Sally. I did my best. But journalism isn't really in my line, you know."

There was a resentful pause. My vanity was piqued.

"My goodness, I know who'll do it for me if I ask him!" cried Sally, suddenly jumping up. "Why on earth didn't I think of him before?" She grabbed the telephone and dialled a number: "Oh, hilloo, Kurt darling ..."

In three minutes, she had explained all about the article. Replacing the receiver on its stand, she announced triumphantly: "That's marvellous! He's going to do it at once ..." She paused impressively and added: "That was Kurt Rosenthal."

"Who's he?"

"You've never heard of him?" This annoyed Sally; she pretended to be immensely surprised: "I thought you took an interest in the cinema? He's miles the best young scenario writer. He earns pots of money. He's only doing this as a favour to me, of course ... He says he'll dictate it to his secretary while he's shaving and then send it straight round to the editor's flat ... He's marvellous!"

"Are you sure it'll be what the editor wants, this time?"

"Of course it will! Kurt's an absolute genius. He can do anything. Just now, he's writing a novel in his spare time. He's fearfully busy, he can only dictate it while he's having breakfast. He showed me the first few chapters, the other day. Honestly, I think it's easily the best novel I've ever read."

"Indeed?"

"That's the sort of writer I admire," Sally continued. She was careful to avoid my eye. "He's terribly ambitious and he works the whole time; and he can write anything—anything you like: scenarios, novels, plays, poetry, advertisements ... He's not a bit stuck-up about it either. Not like these young men who, because they've written one book, start talking about Arts and imagining they're the most wonderful authors in the world ... They make me sick ..."

Irritated as I was with her, I couldn't help laughing:

"Since when have you disapproved so violently, Sally?"

"I don't disapprove of you"—but she couldn't look me in the face—"not exactly."

"I merely make you sick?"

"I don't know what it is ... You seem to have changed, somehow ..."

"How have I changed?"

"It's difficult to explain ... You don't seem to have any energy or want to get anywhere. You're so dilettante. It annoys me."

"I'm sorry." But my would-be facetious tone sounded rather forced. Sally frowned down at her tiny black shoes.

"You must remember I'm a woman, Christopher. All women like men to be strong and decided and following out their careers. A woman wants to be motherly to a man and protect his weak side, but he must have a strong side too, which she can respect ... If you ever care for a woman, I don't advise you to let her see that you've got no ambition. Otherwise she'll get to despise you."

"Yes, I see ... And that's the principle on which you choose your friends—your *new* friends?"

She flared up at this:

"It's very easy for you to sneer at my friends for having good business heads. If they've got money, it's because they've worked for it ... I suppose you consider yourself better than they are?"

"Yes, Sally, since you ask me—if they're at all as I imagine them—I do."

"There you go, Christopher! That's typical of you. That's what annoys me about you: you're conceited and lazy. If you say things like that, you ought to be able to prove them."

"How does one prove that one's better than somebody else? Besides, that's not what I said. I said I considered myself better—it's simply a matter of taste."

Sally made no reply. She lit a cigarette, slightly frowning.

"You say I seem to have changed," I continued. "To be quite frank, I've been thinking the same thing about *you.*"

Sally didn't seem surprised: "Have you, Christopher? Perhaps you're right. I don't know ... Or perhaps we've neither of us changed. Perhaps we're just seeing each other as we really are. We're awfully different in lots of ways, you know."

"Yes, I've noticed that."

"I think," said Sally, smoking meditatively, her eyes on her shoes, "that we may have sort of outgrown each other, a bit."

"Perhaps we have ..." I smiled: Sally's real meaning was so obvious: "At any rate, we needn't quarrel about it, need we?"

"Of course not, darling."

There was a pause. Then I said that I must be going. We were both rather embarrassed, now, and extra polite.

"Are you certain you won't have a cup of coffee?"

"No, thanks awfully."

"Have some tea? It's specially good. I got it as a present."

"No, thanks very much indeed, Sally. I really must be getting along."

"Must you?" She sounded, after all, rather relieved. "Be sure and ring me up some time soon, won't you?"

"Yes, rather."

It wasn't until I had actually left the house and was walking quickly away up the street that I realized how angry and ashamed I felt. What an utter little bitch she is, I thought. After all, I told myself, it's only what I've always known she was like—right from the start. No, that wasn't true: I hadn't known it. I'd flattered myself—why not be frank about it?—that she was fond of me. Well, I'd been wrong, it seemed; but could I blame her for that? Yet I did blame her, I was furious with her; nothing would have pleased me more, at that moment, than to see her soundly whipped. Indeed, I was so absurdly upset that I began to wonder whether I hadn't all this time, in my own peculiar way, been in love with Sally myself.

But no, it wasn't love either—it was worse. It was the cheapest, most childish kind of wounded vanity. Not that I cared a curse what she thought of my article—well, just a little, perhaps, but only a very little; my literary self-conceit was proof against anything *she* could say—it was her criticism of myself. The awful sexual flair women have for taking the stuffing out of a man! It was no use telling myself that Sally had the vocabulary and mentality of a twelve-year-old schoolgirl, that she was altogether preposterous; it was no use—I only knew that I'd been somehow made to feel a sham. Wasn't I a bit of a sham anyway—though not for her ridiculous reasons—with my arty talk to lady pupils and my newly acquired parlour-socialism? Yes, I was. But she knew nothing about that. I could quite easily have impressed her. That was the most humiliating part of the whole business; I had mismanaged our interview from the very beginning. I had blushed and squabbled, instead of being wonderful, convincing, superior, fatherly, mature. I had tried to compete with her beastly little Kurt on his own ground; just the very thing, of course, which Sally had wanted and expected me to do! After all these months, I had made the one really fatal mistake—I had let her see that I was not only incompetent but jealous. Yes, vulgarly jealous. I could have kicked myself. The mere thought made me prickly with shame from head to foot.

Well, the mischief was done, now. There was only one thing for it, and that was to forget the whole affair. And of course it would be quite impossible for me ever to see Sally again.

It must have been about ten days after this that I was visited, one morning, by a small pale dark-haired young man who spoke American fluently with a slight foreign accent. His name, he told me, was George P. Sandars. He had seen my English-teaching advertisement in the B.Z. am Mittag.

"When would you like to begin?" I asked him.

But the young man shook his head hastily. Oh no, he hadn't come to take lessons, at all. Rather disappointed, I waited politely for him to explain the reason of his visit. He seemed in no hurry to do this. Instead, he accepted a cigarette, sat down and began to talk chattily about the States. Had I ever been to Chicago? No? Well, had I heard of James L. Schraube? I hadn't? The young man uttered a faint sigh. He had the air of being very patient with me, and with the world in general. He had evidently been over the same ground with a good many other people already. James L. Schraube, he explained, was a very big man in Chicago: he owned a whole chain of restaurants and several cinemas. He had two large country houses and a yacht on Lake Michigan. And he possessed no less than four cars. By this time, I was beginning to drum with my fingers on the table. A pained expression passed over the young man's face. He excused himself for taking up my valuable time; he had only told me about Mr Schraube, he said, because he thought I might be interested—his tone implied a gentle rebuke—and because Mr Schraube, had I known him, would certainly have vouched for his friend Sandars' respectability. However ... it couldn't be helped ... well, would I lend him two hundred marks? He needed the money in order to start a business; it was a unique opportunity, which he would miss altogether if he didn't find the money before tomorrow morning. He would pay me back within three days. If I gave him the money now he would return that same evening with papers to prove that the whole thing was perfectly genuine.

No? Ah well ... He didn't seem unduly surprised. He rose to go at once, like a business man who has wasted a valuable twenty minutes on a prospective customer: the loss, he contrived politely to imply, was mine, not his. Already at the door, he paused for a moment: Did I happen, by any chance, to know some film actresses? He was travelling, as a sideline, in a new kind of face-cream specially invented to keep the skin from getting dried up by the studio lights. It was being used by all the Hollywood stars already, but in Europe it was still quite unknown. If he could find half a dozen actresses to use and recommend it, they should have free sample jars and permanent supplies at half-price.

After a moment's hesitation, I gave him Sally's address. I don't know quite why I did it. Partly, of course, to get rid of the young man, who showed signs of wishing to sit down again and continue our conversation. Partly, perhaps, out of malice. It would do Sally no harm to have to put up with his chatter for an hour or two: she had told me that she liked men with ambition. Perhaps she would even get a jar of the face-cream—if it existed at all. And if he touched her for the two hundred marks—well, that wouldn't matter so very much either. He couldn't deceive a baby.

"But whatever you do," I warned him, "don't say that I sent you."

He agreed to this at once, with a slight smile. He must have had his own explanation of my request, for he didn't appear to find it in the least strange. He raised his hat politely as he went downstairs. By the next morning, I had forgotten about his visit altogether.

A few days later, Sally herself rang me up. I had been called away in the middle of a lesson to answer the telephone and was very ungracious.

"Oh, is that you, Christopher darling?"

"Yes. It's me."

"I say, can you come round and see me at once?"

"No."

"Oh ..." My refusal evidently gave Sally a shock. There was a little pause, then she continued, in a tone of unwonted humility: "I suppose you're most terribly busy?"

"Yes. I am."

"Well ... would you mind frightfully if I came round to see you?"

"What about?"

"Darling"—Sally sounded positively desperate—"I can't possibly explain to you over the telephone ... It's something really serious."

"Oh, I see"—I tried to make this as nasty as possible—"another magazine article, I suppose?"

Nevertheless, as soon as I'd said it, we both had to laugh.

"Chris, you are a brute!" Sally tinkled gaily along the wire; then checked herself abruptly: "No, darling—this time I promise you: it's most terribly serious, really and truly it is." She paused; then impressively added: "And you're the only person who can possibly help."

"Oh, all right ..." I was more than half melted already. "Come in an hour."

"Well, darling, I'll begin at the very beginning, shall I? ... Yesterday morning, a man rang me up and asked if he could come round and see me. He said it was on very important business; and as he seemed to know my name and everything of course I said: Yes, certainly, come at once ... So he came. He told me his name was Rakowski—Paul Rakowski—and that he was a European agent of Metro-Goldwyn-Mayer and that he'd come to make me an offer. He said they were looking out for an English actress who spoke German to act in a comedy film they were going to shoot on the Italian Riviera. He was most frightfully convincing about it all; he told me who the director was and the camera-man and the art-director and who'd written the script. Naturally, I hadn't heard of any of them before. But that didn't seem so surprising: in fact, it really made it sound much more real, because most people would have chosen the names you see in the newspapers ... Anyhow, he said that, now he'd seen me, he was sure I'd be just the person for the part, and could practically promise it to me, as long as the test was all right ... so of course I was simply thrilled and I asked when the test would be and he said not for a day or two, as he had to make arrangements with the Ufa people ... So then we began to talk about Hollywood and he told me all kinds of stories—I suppose they *could* have been things he'd read in fan magazines, but somehow I'm pretty sure they weren't—and then he told me how they make sound-effects and how they do the trick-work; he was really most awfully interesting and he certainly must have been inside a great many studios ... Anyhow, when we'd finished talking about Hollywood, he started to tell me about the rest of America and the people he knew, and about the gangsters and about New York. He said he'd only just arrived from there and all his luggage was still in the customs at Hamburg. As a matter of fact, I *had* been thinking to myself that it seemed rather queer he was so shabbily dressed; but after he said that, of course, I thought it was quite natural ... Well—now you must promise not to laugh at this part of the story, Chris, or I simply shan't be able to tell you—presently he started making the most passionate love to me. At first I was rather angry with him, for sort of mixing business with pleasure; but then, after a bit, I didn't mind so much: he was quite attractive, in a Russian kind of way ... And the end of it was, he invited me to have dinner with him, so we went to Horcher's and had one of the most marvellous dinners I've ever had in my life (that's one consolation); only, when the bill came, he said, 'Oh, by the way, darling, could you lend me three hundred marks until tomorrow? I've only got dollar bills on me, and I'll have to get them changed at the Bank.' So, of course, I gave them to him: as bad luck would have it, I had quite a lot of money on me, that evening ... And then he said: 'Let's have a bottle of champagne to celebrate your film contract.' So I agreed, and I suppose by that time I must have been pretty tight because when he asked me to spend the night with him, I said Yes. We went to one of those little hotels in the Augsburgerstrasse—I forget its name, but I can find it again, easily ... It was the most ghastly hole ... Anyhow, I don't remember much more about what happened that evening. It was early this morning that I started to think about things properly, while he was still asleep; and I began to wonder if everything was really quite all right ... I hadn't noticed his underclothes before: they gave me a bit of a shock. You'd expect an important film man to wear silk next to his skin, wouldn't you? Well, his were the most extraordinary kind of stuff like camel-hair or something; they looked as if they might have belonged to John the Baptist. And then he had a regular Woolworth's tin clip for his tie. It wasn't so much that his things were shabby; but you could see they'd never been any good, even when they were new ... I was just making up my mind to get out of bed and take a look inside his pockets, when he woke up and it was too late. So we ordered breakfast ... I don't know if he thought I was madly in love with him by this time and wouldn't notice, or whether he just couldn't be bothered to go on pretending, but this morning he was like a completely different person—just a common little guttersnipe. He ate his jam off the blade of his knife, and of course most of it went on the sheets. And he sucked the insides out of the eggs with a most terrible squelching noise. I couldn't help laughing at him, and that made him quite cross ... Then he said: 'I must have a beer!' Well, I said all right; ring down to the office and ask for some. To tell you the truth, I was beginning to be a bit frightened of him. He'd started to scowl in the most cavemannish way; I felt sure he must be mad. So I thought I'd humour him as much as I could ... Anyhow, he seemed to think I'd made quite a good suggestion, and he picked up the telephone and had a long conversation and got awfully angry, because he said they refused to send beer up to the rooms. I realize now that he must have been holding the hook all the time and just acting; but he did it most awfully well, and anyhow I was much too scared to notice things much. I thought he'd probably start murdering me because he couldn't get his beer ... However, he took it quietly. He said he must get dressed and go downstairs and fetch it himself. All right, I said ... Well, I waited and waited and he didn't come back. So at last I rang the bell and asked the maid if she'd seen him go out. And she said: 'Oh yes, the gentleman paid the bill and went away about an hour ago ... He said you weren't to be disturbed.' I was so surprised, I just said: 'Oh, right, thanks ...' The funny thing was, I'd so absolutely made up my mind by this time that he was looney that I'd stopped suspecting him of being a swindler. Perhaps that was what he wanted ... Anyhow, he wasn't such a looney, after all, because, when I looked in my bag, I found he'd helped himself to all the rest of my money, as well as the change from the three hundred marks I'd lent him the night before ... What really annoys me about the whole business is that I bet he thinks I'll be ashamed to go to the police. Well, I'll just show him he's wrong—"

"I say, Sally, what exactly did this young man look like?"

"He was about your height. Pale. Dark. You could tell he wasn't a born American; he spoke with a foreign accent—"

"Can you remember if he mentioned a man named Schraube, who lives in Chicago?"

"Let's see ... Yes, of course he did! He talked about him a lot ... But, Chris, how on earth did you know?"

"Well, it's like this ... Look here, Sally, I've got a most awful confession to make to you ... I don't know if you'll ever forgive me ..."

We went to the Alexanderplatz that same afternoon.

The interview was even more embarrassing than I had expected. For myself at any rate. Sally, if she felt uncomfortable, did not show it by so much as the movement of an eyelid. She detailed the facts of the case to the two bespectacled police officials with such brisk matter-of-factness that one might have supposed she had come to complain about a strayed lapdog or an umbrella lost in a bus. The two officials—both obviously fathers of families—were at first inclined to be shocked. They dipped their pens excessively in the violet ink, made nervous inhibited circular movements with their elbows, before beginning to write, and were very curt and gruff.

"Now about this hotel," said the elder of them sternly: "I suppose you knew, before going there, that it was an hotel of a certain kind?"

"Well, you didn't expect us to go to the Bristol, did you?" Sally's tone was very mild and reasonable: "They wouldn't have let us in there without luggage anyway."

"Ah, so you had no luggage?" The younger one pounced upon this fact triumphantly, as of supreme importance. His violet copperplate police-hand began to travel steadily across a ruled sheet of foolscap paper. Deeply inspired by this theme, he paid not the slightest attention to Sally's retort:

"I don't usually pack a suitcase when a man asks me out to dinner."

The elder one caught the point, however, at once:

"So it wasn't till you were at the restaurant that this young man invited you to—er—accompany him to the hotel?"

"It wasn't till after dinner."

"My dear young lady," the elder one sat back in his chair, very much the sarcastic father, "may I inquire whether it is your usual custom to accept invitations of this kind from perfect strangers?"

Sally smiled sweetly. She was innocence and candour itself:

"But you see, Herr Kommissar, he wasn't a perfect stranger. He was my fiancé."

That made both of them sit up with a jerk. The younger one even made a small blot in the middle of his virgin page—the only blot, perhaps, to be found in all the spotless dossiers of the Polizeipräsidium.

"You mean to tell me, Frl. Bowles"—but in spite of his gruffness, there was already a gleam in the elder one's eye—"you mean to tell me that you became engaged to this man when you'd only known him a single afternoon?"

"Certainly."

"Isn't that, well—rather unusual?"

"I suppose it is," Sally seriously agreed. "But nowadays, you know, a girl can't afford to keep a man waiting. If he asks her once and she refuses him, he may try somebody else. It's all these surplus women—"

At this, the elder official frankly exploded. Pushing back his chair, he laughed himself quite purple in the face. It was nearly a minute before he could speak at all. The young one was much more decorous; he produced a large handkerchief and pretended to blow his nose. But the nose-blowing developed into a kind of sneeze which became a guffaw; and soon he too had abandoned all attempt to take Sally seriously. The rest of the interview was conducted with comic-opera informality, accompanied by ponderous essays in gallantry. The elder official, particularly, became quite daring; I think they were both sorry that I was present. They wanted her to themselves.

"Now don't you worry, Frl. Bowles," they told her, patting her hand at parting, "we'll find him for you, if we have to turn Berlin inside out to do it!"

"Well!" I exclaimed admiringly, as soon as we were out of earshot, "you do know how to handle them, I must say!"

Sally smiled dreamily: she was feeling very pleased with herself: "How do you mean, exactly, darling?"

"You know as well as I do—getting them to laugh like that: telling them he was your fiancé! It was really inspired!"

But Sally didn't laugh. Instead, she coloured a little, looking down at her feet. A comically guilty, childish expression came over her face:

"You see, Chris, it happened to be quite true—"

"True!"

"Yes, darling." Now, for the first time, Sally was really embarrassed: she began speaking very fast: "I simply couldn't tell you this morning: after everything that's happened, it would have sounded too idiotic for words ... He asked me to marry him while we were at the restaurant, and I said Yes ... You see, I thought that, being in films, he was probably quite used to quick engagements, like that: after all, in Hollywood, it's quite the usual thing ... And, as he was an American, I thought we could get divorced again easily, any time we wanted to ... And it would have been a good thing for my career—I mean, if he'd been genuine—wouldn't it? ... We were to have got married today, if it could have been managed ... It seems funny to think of, now—"

"But Sally!" I stood still. I gaped at her. I had to laugh: "Well, really ... You know, you're the most extraordinary creature I ever met in my life!"

Sally giggled a little, like a naughty child which has unintentionally succeeded in amusing the grown-ups:

"I always told you I was a bit mad, didn't I? Now perhaps you'll believe it—"

It was more than a week before the police could give us any news. Then, one morning, two detectives called to see me. A young man answering to our description had been traced and was under observation. The police knew his address, but wanted me to identify him before making the arrest. Would I come round with them at once to a snack-bar in the Kleiststrasse? He was to be seen there, about this time, almost every day. I should be able to point him out to them in the crowd and leave again at once, without any fuss or unpleasantness.

I didn't like the idea much, but there was no getting out of it now. The snack-bar, when we arrived, was crowded, for this was the lunch-hour. I caught sight of the young man almost immediately: he was standing at the counter, by the tea-urn, cup in hand. Seen thus, alone and off his guard, he seemed rather pathetic: he looked shabbier and far younger—a mere boy. I very nearly said: "He isn't here." But what would have been the use? They'd have got him, anyway. "Yes, that's him," I told the detectives. "Over there." They nodded. I turned and hurried away down the street, feeling guilty and telling myself: I'll never help the police again.

A few days later, Sally came round to tell me the rest of the story: "I had to see him, of course ... I felt an awful brute; he looked so wretched. All he said was: 'I thought you were my friend.' I'd have told him he could keep the money, but he'd spent it all, anyway ... The police said he really had been to the States, but he isn't American; he's a Pole ... He won't be prosecuted, that's one comfort. The doctor's seen him and he's going to be sent to a home. I hope they treat him decently there ..."

"So he was looney, after all?"

"I suppose so. A sort of mild one ..." Sally smiled. "Not very flattering to me, is it? Oh, and Chris, do you know how old he was? You'd never guess!"

"Round about twenty, I should think."

"Sixteen!"

"Oh, rot!"

"Yes, honestly ... The case would have to have been tried in the Children's Court!"

We both laughed. "You know, Sally," I said, "what I really

like about you is that you're awfully easy to take in. People who never get taken in are so dreary."

"So you still like me, Chris darling?"

"Yes, Sally. I still like you."

"I was afraid you'd be angry with me—about the other day."

"I was. Very."

"But you're not, now?"

"No ... I don't think so."

"It's no good my trying to apologize, or explain, or anything ... I get like that, sometimes ... I expect you understand, don't you, Chris?"

"Yes," I said. "I expect I do."

I have never seen her since. About a fortnight later, just when I was thinking I ought really to ring her up, I got a postcard from Paris: "Arrived here last night. Will write properly tomorrow. Heaps of love." No letter followed. A month after this, another postcard arrived from Rome, giving no address: "Am writing in a day or two," it said. That was six years ago.

So now I am writing to her.

When you read this, Sally—if you ever do—please accept it as a tribute, the sincerest I can pay, to yourself and to our friendship.

And send me another postcard.

On Ruegen Island
Summer 1931

I WAKE EARLY AND go out to sit on the veranda in my pyjamas. The wood casts long shadows over the fields. Birds call with sudden uncanny violence, like alarm-clocks going off. The birch-trees hang down laden over the rutted, sandy earth of the country road. A soft bar of cloud is moving up from the line of trees along the lake. A man with a bicycle is watching his horse graze on a patch of grass by the path; he wants to disentangle the horse's hoof from its tether-rope. He pushes the horse with both hands, but it won't budge. And now an old woman in a shawl comes walking with a little boy. The boy wears a dark sailor suit; he is very pale and his neck is bandaged. They soon turn back. A man passes on a bicycle and shouts something to the man with the horse. His voice rings out, quite clear yet unintelligible, in the morning stillness. A cock crows. The creak of the bicycle going past. The dew on the white table and chairs in the garden arbour, and dripping from the heavy lilac. Another cock crows, much louder and nearer. And I think I can hear the sea, or very distant bells.

The village is hidden in the wood, away up to the left. It consists almost entirely of boarding-houses, in various styles of seaside architecture—sham Moorish, old Bavarian, Taj Mahal, and the rococo doll's house, with white fretwork balconies. Behind the woods is the sea. You can reach it without going through the village, by a zig-zag path, which brings you out abruptly to the edge of some sandy cliffs, with the beach below you, and the tepid shallow Baltic lying almost at your feet. This end of the bay is quite deserted; the official bathing-beach is round the corner of the headland. The white onion-domes of the Strand Restaurant at Baabe wobble in the distance, behind fluid waves of heat, a kilometre away.

In the wood are rabbits and adders and deer. Yesterday morning I saw a roe being chased by a Borzoi dog, right across the fields and in amongst the trees. The dog couldn't catch the roe, although it seemed to be going much the faster of the two, moving in long graceful bounds, while the roe went bucketing over the earth with wild rigid jerks, like a grand piano bewitched.

There are two people staying in this house, besides myself. One of them is an Englishman, named Peter Wilkinson, about my own age. The other is a German working-class boy from Berlin, named Otto Nowak. He is sixteen or seventeen years old.

Peter—as I already call him; we got rather tight the first evening, and quickly made friends—is thin and dark and nervous. He wears horn-rimmed glasses. When he gets excited, he digs his hands down between his knees and clenches them together. Thick veins stand out at the sides of his temples. He trembles all over with suppressed, nervous laughter, until Otto, rather irritated, exclaims: *"Mensch, reg' Dich bloss nicht so auf!"*

Otto has a face like a very ripe peach. His hair is fair and thick, growing low on his forehead. He has small sparkling eyes, full of naughtiness, and a wide, disarming grin, which is much too innocent to be true. When he grins, two large dimples appear in his peach-bloom cheeks. At present, he makes up to me assiduously, flattering me, laughing at my jokes, never missing an opportunity of giving me a crafty, understanding wink. I think he looks upon me as a potential ally in his dealings with Peter.

This morning we all bathed together. Peter and Otto are busy building a large sand fort. I lay and watched Peter as he worked furiously, enjoying the glare, digging away savagely with his child's spade, like a chain-gang convict under the eyes of an armed warder. Throughout the long, hot morning, he never sat still for a moment. He and Otto swam, dug, wrestled, ran races or played with a rubber football, up and down the sands. Peter is skinny but wiry. In his games with Otto, he holds his own, it seems, only by an immense, furious effort of will. It is Peter's will against Otto's body. Otto is his whole body; Peter is only his head. Otto moves fluidly, effortlessly; his gestures have the savage, unconscious grace of a cruel, elegant animal. Peter drives himself about, lashing his stiff, ungraceful body with the whip of his merciless will.

Otto is outrageously conceited. Peter has bought him a chest-expander, and, with this, he exercises solemnly at all hours of the day. Coming into their bedroom, after lunch, to look for Peter, I found Otto wrestling with the expander like Laocoön, in front of the looking-glass, all alone: "Look, Christoph!" he gasped. "You see, I can do it! All five strands!" Otto certainly has a superb pair of shoulders and chest for a boy of his age—but his body is nevertheless somehow slightly ridiculous. The beautiful ripe lines of the torso taper away too suddenly to his rather absurd little buttocks and spindly, immature legs. And these struggles with the chest-expander are daily making him more and more top-heavy.

This evening Otto had a touch of sunstroke, and went to bed early, with a headache. Peter and I walked up to the village, alone. In the Bavarian café, where the band makes a noise like Hell unchained, Peter bawled into my ear the story of his life.

Peter is the youngest of a family of four. He has two sisters, both married. One of the sisters lives in the country and hunts. The other is what the newspapers call "a popular society hostess." Peter's elder brother is a scientist and explorer. He has been on expeditions to the Congo, the New Hebrides, and the Great Barrier Reef. He plays chess, speaks with the voice of a man of sixty, and has never, to the best of Peter's belief, performed the sexual act. The only member of the family with whom Peter is at present on speaking terms is his hunting sister, but they seldom meet, because Peter hates his brother-in-law.

Peter was delicate, as a boy. He did not go to a preparatory school but, when he was thirteen, his father sent him to a public school. His father and mother had a row about this which lasted until Peter, with his mother's encouragement, developed heart trouble and had to be removed at the end of his second term. Once escaped, Peter began to hate his mother for having petted and coddled him into a funk. She saw that he could not forgive her and so, as Peter was the only one of her children whom she cared for, she got ill herself and soon afterwards died.

It was too late to send Peter back to school again, so Mr Wilkinson engaged a tutor. The tutor was a very high-church young man who intended to become a priest. He took cold baths in winter and had crimpy hair and a Grecian jaw. Mr Wilkinson disliked him from the first, and the elder brother made satirical remarks, so Peter threw himself passionately on to the tutor's side. The two of them went for walking-tours in the Lake District and discussed the meaning of the Sacrament amidst austere moorland scenery. This kind of talk got them, inevitably, into a complicated emotional tangle which was abruptly unravelled, one evening, during a fearful row in a barn. Next morning, the tutor left, leaving a ten-page letter behind him. Peter meditated suicide. He heard later indirectly that the tutor had grown a moustache and gone out to Australia. So Peter got another tutor, and finally went up to Oxford.

Hating his father's business and his brother's science, he made music and literature into a religious cult. For the first year, he liked Oxford very much indeed. He went out to tea-parties and ventured to talk. To his pleasure and surprise people appeared to be listening to what he said. It wasn't until he had done this often that he began to notice their air of slight embarrassment. "Somehow or other," said Peter, "I always struck the wrong note."

Meanwhile, at home, in the big Mayfair house, with its four bath-rooms and garage for three cars, where there was always too much to eat, the Wilkinson family was slowly falling to pieces, like something gone rotten. Mr Wilkinson with his diseased kidneys, his whisky, and his knowledge of "handling men," was angry and confused and a bit pathetic. He snapped and growled at his children when they passed near him, like a surly old dog. At meals nobody ever spoke. They avoided each other's eyes, and hurried upstairs afterwards to write letters, full of hatred and satire, to their intimate friends. Only Peter had no friend to write to. He shut himself up in his tasteless, expensive bedroom and read and read.

And now it was the same at Oxford. Peter no longer went to tea-parties. He worked all day, and, just before the examinations, he had a nervous breakdown. The doctor advised a complete change of scene, other interests. Peter's father let him play at farming for six months in Devonshire, then he began to talk of the business. Mr Wilkinson had been unable to persuade any of his other children to take even a polite interest in the source of their incomes. They were all unassailable in their different worlds. One of his daughters was about to marry into the peerage, the other frequently hunted with the Prince of Wales. His elder son read papers to the Royal Geographical Society. Only Peter hadn't any justification for his existence. The other children behaved selfishly, but knew what they wanted. Peter also behaved selfishly, and didn't know.

However, at the critical moment, Peter's uncle, his mother's brother, died. This uncle lived in Canada. He had seen Peter once as a child and had taken a fancy to him, so he left him all his money, not very much, but enough to live on, comfortably.

Peter went to Paris and began studying music. His teacher told him that he would never be more than a good second-rate amateur, but he only worked all the harder. He worked merely to avoid thinking, and had another nervous breakdown, less serious than at first. At this time, he was convinced that he would soon go mad. He paid a visit to London and found only his father at home. They had a furious quarrel on the first evening; thereafter, they hardly exchanged a word. After a week of silence and huge meals, Peter had a mild attack of homicidal mania. All through breakfast, he couldn't take his eyes off a pimple on his father's throat. He was fingering the bread-knife. Suddenly the left side of his face began to twitch. It twitched and twitched, so that he had to cover his cheek with his hand. He felt certain that his father had noticed this, and was intentionally refusing to remark on it—was, in fact, deliberately torturing him. At last, Peter could stand it no longer. He jumped up and rushed out of the room, out of the house, into the garden, where he flung himself face downwards on the wet lawn. There he lay, too frightened to move. After a quarter of an hour, the twitching stopped.

That evening Peter walked along Regent Street and picked up a whore. They went back together to the girl's room, and talked for hours. He told her the whole story of his life at home, gave her ten pounds and left her without even kissing her. Next morning a mysterious rash appeared on his left thigh. The doctor seemed at a loss to explain its origin, but prescribed some ointment. The rash became fainter, but did not altogether disappear until last month. Soon after the Regent Street episode, Peter also began to have trouble with his left eye.

For some time already, he had played with the idea of consulting a psycho-analyst. His final choice was an orthodox Freudian with a sleepy, ill-tempered voice and very large feet. Peter took an immediate dislike to him, and told him so. The Freudian made notes on a piece of paper, but did not seem offended. Peter later discovered that he was quite uninterested in anything except Chinese art. They met three times a week and each visit cost two guineas.

After six months Peter abandoned the Freudian, and started going to a new analyst, a Finnish lady with white hair and a bright conversational manner. Peter found her easy to talk to. He told her, to the best of his ability, everything he had ever done, ever said, ever thought, or ever dreamed. Sometimes, in moments of discouragement, he told her stories which were absolutely untrue, or anecdotes collected from case-books. Afterwards, he would confess to these lies, and they would discuss his motives for telling them, and agree that they were very interesting. On red-letter nights Peter would have a dream, and this gave them a topic of conversation for the next few weeks. The analysis lasted nearly two years, and was never completed.

This year Peter got bored with the Finnish lady. He heard of a good man in Berlin. Well, why not? At any rate, it would be a change. It was also an economy. The Berlin man only cost fifteen marks a visit.

"And you're still going to him?" I asked.

"No ..." Peter smiled. "I can't afford to, you see."

Last month, a day or two after his arrival, Peter went out to Wannsee, to bathe. The water was still chilly, and there were not many people about. Peter had noticed a boy who was turning somersaults by himself, on the sand. Later the boy came up and asked for a match. They got into conversation. It was Otto Nowak.

"Otto was quite horrified when I told him about the analyst. 'What!' he said, 'you give that man fifteen marks a day just for letting you talk to him! You give me ten marks and I'll talk to you all day, and all night as well!'" Peter began to shake all over with laughter, flushing scarlet and wringing his hands.

Curiously enough, Otto wasn't being altogether preposterous when he offered to take the analyst's place. Like many very animal people, he has considerable instinctive powers of healing—when he chooses to use them. At such times, his treatment of Peter is unerringly correct. Peter will be sitting at the table, hunched up, his downward-curving mouth lined with childhood fears: a perfect case-picture of his twisted, expensive upbringing. Then in comes Otto, grins, dimples, knocks over a chair, slaps Peter on the back, rubs his hands and exclaims fatuously: "*Ja, ja ... so ist die Sache!*" And, in a moment, Peter is transformed. He relaxes, begins to hold himself naturally; the tightness disappears from his mouth, his eyes lose their hunted look. As long as the spell lasts, he is just like an ordinary person.

Peter tells me that, before he met Otto, he was so terrified of infection that he would wash his hands with carbolic after picking up a cat. Nowadays, he often drinks out of the same glass as Otto, uses his sponge, and will share the same plate.

Dancing has begun at the Kurhaus and the café on the lake. We saw the announcements of the first dance two days ago, while we were taking our evening walk up the main street of the village. I noticed that Otto glanced at the poster wistfully, and that Peter had seen him do this. Neither of them, however, made any comment.

Yesterday was chilly and wet. Otto suggested that we should hire a boat and go fishing on the lake: Peter was pleased with this plan, and agreed at once. But when we had waited three quarters of an hour in the drizzle for a catch, he began to get irritable. On the way back to the shore, Otto kept splashing with his oars—at first because he couldn't row properly, later merely to annoy Peter. Peter got very angry indeed, and swore at Otto, who sulked.

After supper, Otto announced that he was going to dance at the Kurhaus. Peter took this without a word, in ominous silence, the comers of his mouth beginning to drop; and Otto, either genuinely unconscious of his disapproval or deliberately overlooking it, assumed that the matter was settled.

After he had gone out, Peter and I sat upstairs in my cold room, listening to the pattering of the rain on the window.

"I thought it couldn't last," said Peter gloomily. "This is the beginning. You'll see."

"Nonsense, Peter. The beginning of what? It's quite natural that Otto should want to dance sometimes. You musn't be so possessive."

"Oh, I know, I know. As usual, I'm being utterly unreasonable ... All the same, this is the beginning ..."

Rather to my own surprise the event proved me right. Otto arrived back from the Kurhaus before ten o'clock. He had been disappointed. There had been very few people there, and the band was poor.

"I'll never go again," he added, with a languishing smile at me. "From now on I'll stay every evening with you and Christoph. It's much more fun when we're all three together isn't it?"

Yesterday morning, while we were lying in our fort on the beach, a little fair-haired man with ferrety blue eyes and a small moustache came up to us and asked us to join in a game with him. Otto, always over-enthusiastic about strangers, accepted at once, so that Peter and I had either to be rude or follow his example.

The little man, after introducing himself as a surgeon from a Berlin hospital, at once took command, assigning to us the places where we were to stand. He was very firm about this—instantly ordering me back when I attempted to edge a little nearer, so as not to have such a long distance to throw. Then it appeared that Peter was throwing in quite the wrong way: the little doctor stopped the game in order to demonstrate this. Peter was amused at first, and then rather annoyed. He retorted with considerable rudeness, but the doctor's skin wasn't pierced. "You hold yourself so stiff," he explained, smiling. "That is an error. You try again, and I will keep my hand on your shoulder-blade to see whether you really relax ... No. Again you do not!"

He seemed delighted, as if this failure of Peter's were a

special triumph for his own methods of teaching. His eye met Otto's. Otto grinned understandingly.

Our meeting with the doctor put Peter in a bad temper for the rest of the day. In order to tease him, Otto pretended to like the doctor very much: "That's the sort of chap I'd like to have for a friend," he said with a spiteful smile. "A real sportsman! You ought to take up sport, Peter! Then you'd have a figure like he has!"

Had Peter been in another mood, this remark would probably have made him smile. As it was, he got very angry: "You'd better go off with your doctor now, if you like him so much!"

Otto grinned teasingly. "He hasn't asked me to—yet!"

Yesterday evening, Otto went out to dance at the Kurhaus and didn't return till late.

There are now a good many summer visitors to the village. The bathing-beach by the pier, with its array of banners, begins to look like a medieval camp. Each family has its own enormous hooded wicker beach-chair, and each chair flies a little flag. There are the German city-flags—Hamburg, Hanover, Dresden, Rostock and Berlin, as well as the National, Republican and Nazi colours. Each chair is encircled by a low sand bulwark upon which the occupants have set inscriptions in fir-cones: *Waldesruh. Familie Walter. Stahlhelm. Heil Hitler!* Many of the forts are also decorated with the Nazi swastika. The other morning I saw a child of about five years old, stark naked, marching along all by himself with a swastika flag over his shoulder and singing *"Deutschland über alles."*

The little doctor fairly revels in this atmosphere. Nearly every morning he arrives, on a missionary visit, to our fort. "You really ought to come round to the other beach," he tells us. "It's much more amusing there. I'd introduce you to some nice girls. The young people here are a magnificent lot! I, as a doctor, know how to appreciate them. The other day I was over at Hiddensee. Nothing but Jews! It's a pleasure to get back here and see real Nordic types!"

"Let's go to the other beach," urged Otto. "It's so dull here. There's hardly anyone about."

"You can go if you like," Peter retorted with angry sarcasm: "I'm afraid I should be rather out of place. I had a grandmother who was partly Spanish."

But the little doctor won't let us alone. Our opposition and more or less openly expressed dislike seem actually to fascinate him. Otto is always betraying us into his hands. One day, when the doctor was speaking enthusiastically about Hitler, Otto said, "It's no good your talking like that to Christoph, Herr Doktor. He's a communist!"

This seemed positively to delight the doctor. His ferrety blue eyes gleamed with triumph. He laid his hands affectionately on my shoulder.

"But you *can't* be a communist! You *can't!*"

"Why can't I?" I asked coldly, moving away. I hate him to touch me.

"Because there isn't any such thing as communism. It's just an hallucination. A mental disease. People only imagine that they're communists. They aren't really."

"What are they, then?"

But he wasn't listening. He fixed me with his triumphant, ferrety smile.

"Five years ago I used to think as you do. But my work at the clinic has convinced me that communism is a mere hallucination. What people need is discipline, self-control. I can tell you this as a doctor. I know it from my own experience."

This morning we were all together in my room, ready to start out to bathe. The atmosphere was electric, because Peter and Otto were still carrying on an obscure quarrel which they had begun before breakfast, in their own bedroom. I was turning over the pages of a book, not paying much attention to them. Suddenly Peter slapped Otto hard on both cheeks. They closed immediately and staggered grappling about the room, knocking over the chairs. I looked on, getting out of their way as well as I could. It was funny, and, at the same time, unpleasant, because rage made their faces strange and ugly. Presently Otto got Peter down on the ground and began twisting his arm: "Have you had enough?" he kept asking. He grinned: at that moment he was really hideous, positively deformed with malice. I knew that Otto was glad to have me there, because my presence was an extra humiliation for Peter. So I laughed, as though the whole thing were a joke, and went out of the room. I walked through the woods to Baabe, and bathed from the beach beyond. I felt I didn't want to see either of them again for several hours.

If Otto wishes to humiliate Peter, Peter in his different way also wishes to humiliate Otto. He wants to force Otto into making a certain kind of submission to his will, and this submission Otto refuses instinctively to make. Otto is naturally and healthily selfish, like an animal. If there are two chairs in a room, he will take the more comfortable one without hesitation, because it never even occurs to him to consider Peter's comfort. Peter's selfishness is much less honest, more civilized, more perverse. Appealed to in the right way, he will make any sacrifice, however unreasonable and unnecessary. But when Otto takes the better chair as if by right, then Peter immediately sees a challenge which he dare not refuse to accept. I suppose that—given their two natures—there is no possible escape from this situation. Peter is bound to go on fighting to win Otto's submission. When, at last, he ceases to do so, it will merely mean that he has lost interest in Otto altogether.

The really destructive feature of their relationship is its inherent quality of boredom. It is quite natural for Peter often to feel bored with Otto—they have scarcely a single interest in common—but Peter, for sentimental reasons, will never admit that this is so. When Otto, who has no such motives for pretending, says, "It's so dull here!" I invariably see Peter wince and look pained. Yet Otto is actually far less often bored than Peter himself; he finds Peter's company genuinely amusing, and is quite glad to be with him most of the day. Often, when Otto has been chattering rubbish for an hour without stopping, I can see that Peter really longs for him to be quiet and go away. But to admit this would be, in Peter's eyes, a total defeat, so he only laughs and rubs his hands, tacitly appealing to me to support him in his pretence of finding Otto inexhaustibly delightful and funny.

On my way back through the woods, after my bathe, I saw the ferrety little blond doctor advancing to meet me. It was too late to turn back. I said "Good morning" as politely and coldly as possible. The doctor was dressed in running-shorts and a sweater; he explained that he had been taking a "*Waldlauf.*" "But I think I shall turn back now," he added. "Wouldn't you like to run with me a little?"

"I'm afraid I can't," I said rashly. "You see, I twisted my ankle a bit yesterday."

I could have bitten my tongue out as I saw the gleam of triumph in his eyes. "Ah, you've sprained your ankle? Please let me look at it!" Squirming with dislike, I had to submit to his prodding fingers. "But it is nothing, I assure you. You have no cause for alarm."

As we walked the doctor began to question me about Peter and Otto, twisting his head to look up at me, as he delivered each sharp, inquisitive little thrust. He was fairly consumed with curiosity.

"My work in the clinic has taught me that it is no use trying to help this type of boy. Your friend is very generous and very well meaning, but he makes a great mistake. This type of boy always reverts. From a scientific point of view, I find him exceedingly interesting."

As though he were about to say something specially momentous, the doctor suddenly stood still in the middle of the path, paused a moment to engage my attention, and smilingly announced:

"He has a criminal head!"

"And you think that people with criminal heads should be left to become criminals?"

"Certainly not. I believe in discipline. These boys ought to be put into labour-camps."

"And what are you going to do with them when you've got them there? You say that they can't be altered, anyhow, so I suppose you'd keep them locked up for the rest of their lives?"

The doctor laughed delightedly, as though this were a joke against himself which he could, nevertheless, appreciate. He laid a caressing hand on my arm:

"You are an idealist! Do not imagine that I don't understand your point of view. But it is unscientific, quite unscientific. You and your friend do not understand such boys as Otto. I understand them. Every week, one or two such boys come to my clinic, and I must operate on them for adenoids, or mastoid, or poisoned tonsils. So, you see, I know them through and through!"

"I should have thought it would be more accurate to say you knew their throats and ears."

Perhaps my German wasn't quite equal to rendering the sense of this last remark. At all events, the doctor ignored it completely. "I know this type of boy very well," he repeated. "It is a bad degenerate type. You cannot make anything out of these boys. Their tonsils are almost invariably diseased."

There are perpetual little rows going on between Peter and Otto, yet I cannot say that I find living with them actually unpleasant. Just now, I am very much taken up with my new novel. Thinking about it, I often go out for long walks, alone. Indeed, I find myself making more and more frequent excuses to leave them to themselves; and this is selfish, because, when I am with them, I can often choke off the beginnings of a quarrel by changing the subject or making a joke. Peter, I know, resents my desertions. "You're quite an ascetic," he said maliciously the other day, "always withdrawing for your contemplations." Once, when I was sitting in a cafe near the pier, listening to the band, Peter and Otto came past. "So this is where you've been hiding!" Peter exclaimed. I saw that, for the moment, he really disliked me.

One evening, we were all walking up the main street, which was crowded with summer visitors. Otto said to Peter, with his most spiteful grin: "Why must you always look in the same direction as I do?" This was surprisingly acute, for, whenever Otto turned his head to stare at a girl, Peter's eyes mechanically followed his glance with instinctive jealousy. We passed the photographer's window, in which, every day, the latest groups snapped by the beach camera-men are displayed. Otto paused to examine one of the new pictures with great attention, as though its subject were particularly attractive. I saw Peter's lips contract. He was struggling with himself, but he couldn't resist his own jealous curiosity—he stopped too. The photograph was of a fat old man with a long beard, waving a Berlin flag. Otto, seeing that his trap had been successful, laughed maliciously.

Invariably, after supper, Otto goes dancing at the Kurhaus or the café by the lake. He no longer bothers to ask Peter's permission to do this; he has established the right to have his evenings to himself. Peter and I generally go out too, into the village. We lean over the rail of the pier for a long time without speaking, staring down at the cheap jewellery of the Kurhaus lights reflected in the black water, each busy with his own thoughts. Sometimes we go into the Bavarian café and Peter gets steadily drunk — his stern, Puritan mouth contracting slightly with distaste as he raises the glass to his lips. I say nothing. There is too much to say. Peter, I know, wants me to make some provocative remark about Otto which will give him the exquisite relief of losing his temper. I don't, and drink—keeping up a desultory conversation about books and concerts and plays. Later, when we are returning home, Peter's footsteps will gradually quicken until, as we enter the house, he leaves me and runs upstairs to his bedroom. Often we don't get back till half past twelve or a quarter to one, but it is very seldom that we find Otto already there.

Down by the railway station, there is a holiday home for children from the Hamburg slums. Otto has got to know one of the teachers from this home, and they go out dancing together nearly every evening. Sometimes the girl, with her little troop of children, comes marching past the house. The children glance up at the windows and, if Otto happens to be looking out, indulge in precocious jokes. They nudge and pluck at their young teacher's arm to persuade her to look up, too.

On these occasions, the girl smiles coyly and shoots one glance at Otto from under her eyelashes, while Peter, watching behind the curtains, mutters through clenched teeth: "Bitch … bitch … bitch …" This persecution annoys him more than the actual friendship itself. We always seem to be running across the children when we are out walking in the woods. The children sing as they march—patriotic songs about the Homeland—in voices as shrill as birds. From far off, we hear them approaching, and have to turn hastily in the opposite direction. It is, as Peter says, like Captain Hook and the Crocodile.

Peter has made a scene, and Otto has told his friend that she musn't bring her troop past the house any more. But now they have begun bathing on our beach, not very far from the fort. The first morning this happened, Otto's glance kept turning in their direction. Peter was aware of this, of course, and remained plunged in gloomy silence.

"What's the matter with you today, Peter?" said Otto. "Why are you so horrid to me?"

"Horrid to *you?*" Peter laughed savagely.

"Oh, very well then." Otto jumped up. "I see you don't want me here." And, bounding over the rampart of our fort, he began to run along the beach towards the teacher and her children, very gracefully, displaying his figure to the best possible advantage.

Yesterday evening there was a gala dance at the Kurhaus. In a mood of unusual generosity, Otto had promised Peter not to be later than a quarter to one, so Peter sat up with a book to wait for him. I didn't feel tired, and wanted to finish a chapter, so suggested that he should come into my room and wait there.

I worked. Peter read. The hours went slowly by. Suddenly I looked at my watch and saw that it was a quarter past two. Peter had dozed off in his chair. Just as I was wondering whether I should wake him, I heard Otto coming up the stairs. His footsteps sounded drunk. Finding no one in his room, he banged my door open. Peter sat up with a start.

Otto lolled grinning against the doorpost. He made me a half-tipsy salute. "Have you been reading all this time?" he asked Peter.

"Yes," said Peter, very self-controlled.

"Why?" Otto smiled fatuously.

"Because I couldn't sleep."

"Why couldn't you sleep?"

"You know quite well," said Peter between his teeth.

Otto yawned in his most offensive manner. "I don't know and I don't care ... Don't make such a fuss."

Peter rose to his feet. "God, you little swine!" he said, smacking Otto's face hard with the flat of his hand. Otto didn't attempt to defend himself. He gave Peter an extraordinarily vindictive look out of his bright little eyes. "Good!" He spoke rather thickly. "Tomorrow I shall go back to Berlin." He turned unsteadily on his heel.

"Otto, come here," said Peter. I saw that, in another moment, he would burst into tears of rage. He followed Otto out on to the landing. "Come here," he said again, in a sharp tone of command.

"Oh, leave me alone," said Otto, "I'm sick of you. I want to sleep now. Tomorrow I'm going back to Berlin."

This morning, however, peace has been restored—at a price. Otto's repentance has taken the form of a sentimental outburst over his family: "Here I've been enjoying myself and never thinking of them ... Poor mother has to work like a dog, and her lungs are so bad ... Let's send her some money, shall we, Peter? Let's send her fifty marks ..." Otto's generosity reminded him of his own needs. In addition to the money for Frau Nowak, Peter has been talked into ordering Otto a new suit, which will cost a hundred and eighty, as well as a pair of shoes, a dressing-gown, and a hat.

In return for this outlay, Otto has volunteered to break off his relations with the teacher. (We now discover that, in any case, she is leaving the island tomorrow.) After supper, she appeared, walking up and down outside the house.

"Just let her wait till she's tired," said Otto. "I'm not going down to her."

Presently the girl, made bold by impatience, began to whistle. This sent Otto into a frenzy of glee. Throwing open the window, he danced up and down, waving his arms and making hideous faces at the teacher who, for her part, seemed struck dumb with amazement at this extraordinary exhibition.

"Get away from here!" Otto yelled. "Get out!"

The girl turned, and walked slowly away, a rather pathetic figure, into the gathering darkness.

"I think you might have said goodbye to her," said Peter, who could afford to be magnanimous, now that he saw his enemy routed.

But Otto wouldn't hear of it.

"What's the use of all those rotten girls, anyhow? Every night they came pestering me to dance with them ... And you know how I am, Peter—I'm so easily persuaded ... Of course, it was horrid of me to leave you alone, but what could I do? It was all their fault, really ..."

Our life has now entered upon a new phase. Otto's resolutions were short-lived. Peter and I are alone together most of the day. The teacher has left, and with her, Otto's last inducement to bathe with us from the fort. He now goes off, every morning, to the bathing-beach by the pier, to flirt and play ball with his dancing-partners of the evening. The little doctor has also disappeared, and Peter and I are free to bathe and loll in the sun as unathletically as we wish.

After supper, the ritual of Otto's preparations for the dance begins. Sitting in my bedroom, I hear Peter's footsteps cross the landing, light and springy with relief—for now comes the only time of the day when Peter feels himself altogether excused from taking any interest in Otto's activities. When he taps on my door, I shut my book at once. I have been out already to the village to buy half-a-pound of peppermint creams. Peter says goodbye to Otto, with a vain lingering hope that, perhaps tonight, he will, after all, be punctual: "Till half past twelve, then ..."

"Till one," Otto bargains.

"All right," Peter concedes. "Till one. But don't be late."

"No, Peter, I won't be late."

As we open the garden gate and cross the road into the wood, Otto waves to us from the balcony. I have to be careful to hide the peppermint creams under my coat, in case he should see them. Laughing guiltily, munching the peppermints, we take the woodland path to Baabe. We always spend our evenings in Baabe, nowadays. We like it better than our own village. Its single sandy street of low-roofed houses among the pine-trees has a romantic, colonial air; it is like a ramshackle, lost settlement somewhere in the backwoods, where people come to look for a nonexistent gold mine and remain, stranded, for the rest of their lives.

In the little restaurant, we eat strawberries and cream, and talk to the young waiter. The waiter hates Germany and longs to go to America. *"Hier ist nichts los."* During the season, he is allowed no free time at all, and in the winter he earns nothing. Most of the Baabe boys are Nazis. Two of them come into the restaurant sometimes and engage us in good-humoured political arguments. They tell us about their field-exercises and military games.

"You're preparing for war," says Peter indignantly. On these occasions—although he has really not the slightest interest in politics—he gets quite heated.

"Excuse me," one of the boys contradicts, "that's quite

wrong. The Führer does not want war. Our programme stands for peace, with honour. All the same …" he adds wistfully, his face lighting up, "war can be fine, you know! Think of the ancient Greeks!"

"The ancient Greeks," I object, "didn't use poison gas."

The boys are rather scornful at this quibble. One of them answers loftily, "That's a purely technical question."

At half past ten we go down, with most of the other inhabitants, to the railway station, to watch the arrival of the last train. It is generally empty. It goes clanging away through the dark woods, sounding its harsh bell. At last it is late enough to start home; this time, we take the road. Across the meadows, you can see the illuminated entrance of the café by the lake, where Otto goes to dance.

"The lights of Hell are shining brightly this evening," Peter is fond of remarking.

Peter's jealousy has turned into insomnia. He has begun taking sleeping-tablets, but admits that they seldom have any effect. They merely make him feel drowsy next morning, after breakfast. He often goes to sleep for an hour or two in our fort, on the shore.

This morning the weather was cool and dull, the sea oyster-grey. Peter and I hired a boat, rowed out beyond the pier, then let ourselves drift, gently, away from the land. Peter lit a cigarette. He said abruptly:

"I wonder how much longer this will go on …"

"As long as you let it, I suppose."

"Yes … We seem to have got into a pretty static condition, don't we? I suppose there's no particular reason why Otto and I should ever stop behaving to each other as we do at present …" He paused, added: "Unless, of course, I stop giving him money."

"What do you think would happen then?"

Peter paddled idly in the water with his fingers. "He'd leave me."

The boat drifted on for several minutes. I asked: "You don't think he cares for you, at all?"

"At the beginning he did, perhaps ... Not now. There's nothing between us now but my cash."

"Do you still care for him?"

"No ... I don't know. Perhaps ... I still hate him, sometimes—if that's a sign of caring."

"It might be."

There was a long pause. Peter dried his fingers on his handkerchief. His mouth twitched nervously.

"Well," he said at last, "what do you advise me to do?"

"What do you want to do?"

Peter's mouth gave another twitch.

"I suppose, really, I want to leave him."

"Then you'd better leave him."

"At once?"

"The sooner the better. Give him a nice present and send him back to Berlin this afternoon." Peter shook his head, smiled sadly:

"I can't."

There was another long pause. Then Peter said: "I'm sorry, Christopher ... You're absolutely right, I know. If I were in your place, I'd say the same thing ... But I can't. Things have got to go on as they are—until something happens. They can't last much longer, anyhow ... Oh, I know I'm very weak ..."

"You needn't apologize to me," I smiled, to conceal a slight feeling of irritation: "I'm not one of your analysts!"

I picked up the oars and began to row back towards the shore. As we reached the pier, Peter said:

"It seems funny to think of now—when I first met Otto, I thought we should live together for the rest of our lives."

"Oh, my God!" The vision of a life with Otto opened before me, like a comic inferno. I laughed out loud. Peter laughed, too, wedging his locked hands between his knees. His face turned from pink to red, from red to purple. His veins bulged. We were still laughing when we got out of the boat.

•

In the garden the landlord was waiting for us. "What a pity!" he exclaimed. "The gentlemen are too late!" He pointed over the meadows, in the direction of the lake. We could see the smoke rising above the line of poplars, as the little train drew out of the station: "Your friend was obliged to leave for Berlin, suddenly, on urgent business. I hoped the gentlemen might have been in time to see him off. What a pity!"

This time, both Peter and I ran upstairs. Peter's bedroom was in a terrible mess—all the drawers and cupboards were open. Propped up on the middle of the table was a note, in Otto's cramped, scrawling hand:

> Dear Peter. Please forgive me I couldn't stand it any longer here so I am going home.
>
> Love from Otto.
> Don't be angry.

(Otto had written it, I noticed, on a fly-leaf torn out of one of Peter's psychology books: *Beyond the Pleasure-Principle.)*

"Well …!" Peter's mouth began to twitch. I glanced at him nervously, expecting a violent outburst, but he seemed fairly calm. After a moment, he walked over to the cupboards and began looking through the drawers. "He hasn't taken much," he announced, at the end of his search. "Only a couple of my ties, three shirts—lucky my shoes don't fit him!—and, let's see … about two hundred marks …" Peter started to laugh, rather hysterically: "Very moderate, on the whole!"

"Do you think he decided to leave quite suddenly?" I asked, for the sake of saying something.

"Probably he did. That would be just like him … Now I come to think of it, I told him we were going out in that boat, this morning—and he asked me if we should be away for long …"

"I see …"

I sat down on Peter's bed—thinking, oddly enough, that Otto has at last done something which I rather respect.

Peter's hysterical high spirits kept him going for the rest of the morning; at lunch he turned gloomy, and wouldn't say a word.

"Now I must go and pack," he told me when we had finished.

"You're off, too?"

"Of course."

"To Berlin?"

Peter smiled. "No, Christopher. Don't be alarmed! Only to England ..."

"Oh ..."

"There's a train which'll get me to Hamburg late tonight. I shall probably go straight on ... I feel I've got to keep travelling until I'm clear of this bloody country ..."

There was nothing to say. I helped him pack, in silence. As Peter put his shaving-mirror into the bag, he asked: "Do you remember how Otto broke this, standing on his head?"

"Yes, I remember."

When we had finished, Peter went out on to the balcony of his room: "There'll be plenty of whistling outside here, tonight," he said.

I smiled: "I shall have to go down and console them."

Peter laughed: "Yes. You will!"

I went with him to the station. Luckily, the engine-driver was in a hurry. The train only waited a couple of minutes.

"What shall you do when you get to London?" I asked.

Peter's mouth curved down at the corners; he gave me a kind of inverted grin: "Look round for another analyst, I suppose."

"Well, mind you beat down his prices a bit!"

"I will."

As the train moved out, he waved his hand: "Well, goodbye, Christopher. Thank you for all your moral support!"

Peter never suggested that I should write to him, or visit him at home. I suppose he wants to forget this place, and everybody concerned with it. I can hardly blame him.

•

It was only this evening, turning over the pages of a book I have been reading, that I found another note from Otto, slipped between the leaves.

> Please dear Christoph don't you be angry with me too because you aren't an idiot like Peter. When you are back in Berlin I shall come and see you because I know where you live; I saw the address on one of your letters and we can have a nice talk.
>
> Your loving friend,
>
> Otto.

I thought, somehow, that he wouldn't be got rid of quite so easily.

Actually, I am leaving for Berlin in a day or two, now. I thought I should stay on till the end of August, and perhaps finish my novel, but suddenly, the place seems so lonely. I miss Peter and Otto, and their daily quarrels, far more than I should have expected. And now Otto's dancing-partners have stopped lingering sadly in the twilight, under my window.

The Nowaks

THE ENTRANCE TO the Wassertorstrasse was a big stone archway, a bit of old Berlin, daubed with hammers and sickles and Nazi crosses and plastered with tattered bills which advertised auctions or crimes. It was a deep, shabby cobbled street, littered with sprawling children in tears. Youths in woollen sweaters circled waveringly across it on racing bikes and whooped at girls passing with milk-jugs. The pavement was chalk-marked for the hopping game called Heaven and Earth. At the end of it, like a tall, dangerously sharp, red instrument, stood a church.

Frau Nowak herself opened the door to me. She looked far iller than when I had seen her last, with big blue rings under her eyes. She was wearing the same hat and mangy old black coat. At first, she didn't recognize me.

"Good afternoon, Frau Nowak."

Her face changed slowly from poking suspicion to a brilliant, timid, almost girlish smile of welcome:

"Why, if it isn't Herr Christoph! Come in, Herr Christoph! Come in and sit down."

"I'm afraid you were just going out, weren't you?"

"No, no, Herr Christoph—I've just come in; just this minute." She was wiping her hands hastily on her coat before shaking mine: "This is one of my charring days. I don't get finished till half past two, and it makes the dinner so late."

She stood aside for me to enter. I pushed open the door and, in doing so, jarred the handle of the frying-pan on the stove which stood just behind it. In the tiny kitchen there was barely room for the two of us together. A stifling smell of potatoes fried in cheap margarine filled the flat.

"Come and sit down, Herr Christoph," she repeated, hastily doing the honours. "I'm afraid it's terribly untidy. You must excuse that. I have to go out so early and my Grete's such a lazy great lump, though she's turned twelve. There's no getting her to do anything, if you don't stand over her all the time."

The living-room had a sloping ceiling stained with old patches of damp. It contained a big table, six chairs, a sideboard and two large double beds. The place was so full of furniture that you had to squeeze your way into it sideways.

"Grete!" cried Frau Nowak. "Where are you? Come here this minute!"

"She's gone out," came Otto's voice from the inner room.

"Otto! Come and see who's here!"

"Can't be bothered. I'm busy mending the gramophone."

"Busy, indeed! You! You good-for-nothing! That's a nice way to speak to your mother! Come out of that room, do you hear me?"

She had flown into a rage instantly, automatically, with astonishing violence. Her face became all nose: thin, bitter and inflamed. Her whole body trembled.

"It doesn't really matter, Frau Nowak," I said. "Let him come out when he wants to. He'll get all the bigger surprise."

"A nice son I've got! Speaking to me like that."

She had pulled off her hat and was unpacking greasy parcels from a string bag: "Dear me," she fussed. "I wonder where that child's got to? Always down in the street, she is. If I've told her once, I've told her a hundred times. Children have no consideration."

"How has your lung been keeping, Frau Nowak?"

She sighed: "Sometimes it seems to me it's worse than ever. I get such a burning, just here. And when I finish work it's as if I was too tired to eat. I come over so bilious . . . I don't think the doctor's satisfied either. He talks about sending me to a sanatorium later in the winter. I was there before, you know. But there's always so many waiting to go . . . Then, the flat's so damp at this time of year. You see those marks on the ceiling? There's days we have to put a foot-bath under them to catch the drips. Of course, they've no right to let these attics as dwellings at all, really. The inspector's condemned them time and time again. But what are you to do? One must live somewhere. We applied for a transfer over a year ago and they keep promising they'll see about it. But there's a lot of others are worse off still, I dare say . . . My husband was reading out of the newspapers the other day about the English and their Pound. It keeps on falling, they say. I don't understand such things, myself. I hope you haven't lost any money, Herr Christoph?"

"As a matter of fact, Frau Nowak, that's partly why I came down to see you today. I've decided to go into a cheaper room and I was wondering if there was anywhere round here you could recommend me?"

"Oh dear, Herr Christoph, I *am* sorry!"

She was quite genuinely shocked: "But you can't live in this part of the town—a gentleman like you! Oh, no. I'm afraid it wouldn't suit you at all."

"I'm not so particular as you think, perhaps. I just want a quiet, clean room for about twenty marks a month. It doesn't matter how small it is. I'm out most of the day."

She shook her head doubtfully: "Well, Herr Christoph, I shall have to see if I can't think of something . . ."

"Isn't dinner ready yet, mother?" asked Otto, appearing in shirt-sleeves at the doorway of the inner room: "I'm nearly starving!"

"How do you expect it to be ready when I have to spend the whole morning slaving for you, you great lump of laziness!" cried Frau Nowak, shrilly, at the top of her voice. Then, transposing without the least pause into her ingratiating social tone, she added: "Don't you see who's here?"

"Why ... it's Christoph!" Otto, as usual, had begun acting at once. His face was slowly illuminated by a sunrise of extreme joy. His cheeks dimpled with smiles. He sprang forward, throwing one arm around my neck, wringing my hand: "Christoph, you old soul, where have you been hiding all this time?" His voice became languishing, reproachful: "We've missed you so much! Why have you never come to see us?"

"Herr Christoph is a very busy gentleman," put in Frau Nowak reprovingly: "He's got no time to waste running after a do-nothing like you."

Otto grinned, winked at me: then he turned reproachfully upon Frau Nowak:

"Mother, what are you thinking of? Are you going to let Christoph sit there without so much as a cup of coffee? He must be thirsty, after climbing all these stairs!"

"What you mean is, Otto, that *you're* thirsty, don't you? No, thank you, Frau Nowak, I won't have anything—really. And I won't keep you from your cooking any longer ... Look here, Otto, will you come out with me now and help me find a room? I've just been telling your mother that I'm coming to live in this neighbourhood ... You shall have your cup of coffee with me outside."

"What, Christoph—you're going to live here, in Hallesches Tor!" Otto began dancing with excitement: "Oh, mother, won't that be grand! Oh, I am so pleased!"

"You may just as well go out and have a look around with Herr Christoph, now," said Frau Nowak. "Dinner won't be ready for at least an hour, yet. You're only in my way here. Not *you,* Herr Christoph, of course. You'll come back and have something to eat with us, won't you?"

"Well, Frau Nowak, it's very kind of you indeed, but I'm afraid I can't today. I shall have to be getting back home."

"Just give me a crust of bread before I go, mother," begged Otto piteously. "I'm so empty that my head's spinning round like a top."

"All right," said Frau Nowak, cutting a slice of bread and half throwing it at him in her vexation, "but don't blame me if there's nothing in the house this evening when you want to make one of your sandwiches … Goodbye, Herr Christoph. It was very kind of you to come and see us. If you really decide to live near here, I hope you'll look in often … though I doubt if you'll find anything to your liking. It won't be what you've been accustomed to …"

As Otto was about to follow me out of the flat she called him back. I heard them arguing; then the door shut. I descended slowly the five flights of stairs to the courtyard. The bottom of the court was clammy and dark, although the sun was shining on a cloud, in the sky overhead. Broken buckets, wheels off prams and bits of bicycle tyre lay scattered about like things which have fallen down a well.

It was a minute or two before Otto came clattering down the stairs to join me:

"Mother didn't like to ask you," he told me, breathless. "She was afraid you'd be annoyed … But I said that I was sure you'd far rather be with us, where you can do just what you like and you know everything's clean, than in a strange house full of bugs … Do say yes, Christoph, please! It'll be such fun! You and I can sleep in the back room. You can have Lothar's bed—he won't mind. He can share the double-bed with Grete … And in the mornings you can stay in bed as long as ever you like. If you want, I'll bring your breakfast … You will come, won't you?"

And so it was settled.

My first evening as a lodger at the Nowaks' was something of a ceremony. I arrived with my two suitcases soon after five o'clock, to find Frau Nowak already cooking the evening meal. Otto whispered to me that we were to have lung hash, as a special treat.

"I'm afraid you won't think very much of our food," said Frau Nowak, "after what you've been used to. But we'll do our best." She was all smiles, bubbling over with excitement. I smiled and smiled, feeling awkward and in the way. At length, I clambered over the living-room furniture and sat down on my bed. There was no space to unpack in, and nowhere, apparently, to put my clothes. At the living-room table, Grete was playing with her cigarette-cards and transfers. She was a lumpish child of twelve years old, pretty in a sugary way, but round-shouldered and too fat. My presence made her very self-conscious. She wriggled, smirked and kept calling out, in an affected, sing-song, "grown-up" voice:

"Mummy! Come and look at the pretty flowers!"

"I've got no time for your pretty flowers," exclaimed Frau Nowak at length, in great exasperation: "Here am I with a daughter the size of an elephant, having to slave all by myself, cooking the supper!"

"Quite right, mother!" cried Otto, gleefully joining in. He turned upon Grete, righteously indignant: "Why don't you help her, I should like to know? You're fat enough. You sit around all day doing nothing. Get off that chair this instant, do you hear! And put those filthy cards away, or I'll burn them!"

He grabbed at the cards with one hand and gave Grete a slap across the face with the other. Grete, who obviously wasn't hurt, at once set up a loud theatrical wail: "Oh, Otto, you've *hurt* me!" She covered her face with her hands and peeped at me between the fingers.

"*Will* you leave that child alone!" cried Frau Nowak shrilly from the kitchen. "I should like to know who *you* are, to talk about laziness! And you, Grete, just you stop that howling—or I'll tell Otto to hit you properly, so that you'll have something to cry for. You two between you, you drive me distracted."

"But, mother!" Otto ran into the kitchen, took her round the waist and began kissing her: "Poor little Mummy, little Mutti, little Muttchen," he crooned, in tones of the most mawkish solicitude. "You have to work so hard and Otto's so horrid to you. But he doesn't mean to be, you know—he's just stupid ... Shall I fetch the coal up for you tomorrow, Mummy? Would you like that?"

"Let go of me, you great humbug!" cried Frau Nowak, laughing and struggling. "I don't want any of your soft soap! Much *you* care for your poor old mother! Leave me to get on with my work in peace."

"Otto's not a bad boy," she continued to me, when he had let go of her at last, "but he's such a scatterbrain. Quite the opposite of my Lothar—there's a model son for you! He's not too proud to do any job, whatever it is, and when he's scraped a few groschen together, instead of spending them on himself he comes straight to me and says: 'Here you are, mother. Just buy yourself a pair of warm house-shoes for the winter.'" Frau Nowak held out her hand to me with the gesture of giving money. Like Otto, she had the trick of acting every scene she described.

"Oh, Lothar this, Lothar that," Otto interrupted crossly: "it's always Lothar. But tell me this, mother, which of us was it that gave you a twenty-mark note the other day? Lothar couldn't earn twenty marks in a month of Sundays. Well, if that's how you talk, you needn't expect to get any more; not if you come to me on your knees."

"You wicked boy," she was up in arms again in an instant, "have you no more shame than to speak of such things in front of Herr Christoph! Why, if he knew where that twenty marks came from—and plenty more besides—he'd disdain to stay in the same house with you another minute; and quite right, too! And the cheek of you—saying you *gave* me that money! You know very well that if your father hadn't seen the envelope ..."

"That's right!" shouted Otto, screwing up his face at her like a monkey and beginning to dance with excitement. "That's just what I wanted! Admit to Christoph that you stole it! You're a thief! You're a thief!"

"Otto, how dare you!" Quick as fury, Frau Nowak's hand grabbed up the lid of the saucepan. I jumped back a pace to be out of range, tripped over a chair and sat down hard. Grete uttered an affected little shriek of joy and alarm. The door opened. It was Herr Nowak, come back from his work.

He was a powerful, dumpy little man, with pointed moustache, cropped hair and bushy eyebrows. He took in the scene with a long grunt which was half a belch. He did not appear to understand what had been happening; or perhaps he merely did not care. Frau Nowak said nothing to enlighten him. She hung the saucepan-lid quietly on a hook. Grete jumped up from her chair and ran to him with outstretched arms: "Pappi! Pappi!"

Herr Nowak smiled down at her, showing two or three nicotine-stained stumps of teeth. Bending, he picked her up, carefully and expertly, with a certain admiring curiosity, like a large valuable vase. By profession he was a furniture remover. Then he held out his hand—taking his time about it, gracious, not fussily eager to please:

"Servus, Herr!"

"Aren't you glad that Herr Christoph's come to live with us, Pappi?" chanted Grete, perched on her father's shoulder, in her sugary sing-song tones. At this Herr Nowak, as if suddenly acquiring new energy, began shaking my hand again, much more warmly, and thumping me on the back:

"Glad? Yes, of course I'm glad!" He nodded his head in vigorous approval. "Englisch man? Anglais, eh? Ha, ha. That's right? Oh, yes, I talk French, you see. Forgotten most of it now. Learnt in the war. I was *Feldwebel*—on the West Front. Talked to lots of prisoners. Good lads. All the same as us ..."

"You're drunk again, father!" exclaimed Frau Nowak in disgust. "Whatever will Herr Christoph think of you!"

"Christoph doesn't mind; do you, Christoph?" Herr Nowak patted my shoulder.

"Christoph, indeed! He's *Herr* Christoph to you! Can't you tell a gentleman when you see one?"

"I'd much rather you called me Christoph," I said.

"That's right! Christoph's right! We're all the same flesh and blood ... *Argent,* money—all the same! Ha, ha!"

Otto took my other arm: "Christoph's quite one of the family, already!"

Presently we sat down to an immense meal of lung hash,

black bread, malt coffee and boiled potatoes. In the first recklessness of having so much money to spend (I had given her ten marks in advance for the week's board) Frau Nowak had prepared enough potatoes for a dozen people. She kept shovelling them on to my plate from a big saucepan, until I thought I should suffocate: "Have some more, Herr Christoph. You're eating nothing."

"I've never eaten so much in my whole life, Frau Nowak."

"Christoph doesn't like our food," said Herr Nowak. "Never mind, Christoph, you'll get used to it. Otto was just the same when he came back from the seaside. He'd got used to all sorts of fine ways, with his Englishman ..."

"Hold your tongue, father!" said Frau Nowak warningly. "Can't you leave the boy alone? He's old enough to be able to decide for himself what's right and wrong—more shame to him!"

We were still eating when Lothar came in. He threw his cap on the bed, shook hands with me politely but silently, with a little bow, and took his place at the table. My presence did not appear to surprise or interest him in the least: his glance barely met mine. He was, I knew, only twenty; but he might well have been years older. He was a man already. Otto seemed almost childish beside him. He had a lean, bony, peasant's face, soured by racial memory of barren fields.

"Lothar's going to night-school," Frau Nowak told me with pride. "He had a job in a garage, you know; and now he wants to study engineering. They won't take you in anywhere nowadays, unless you've got a diploma of some sort. He must show you his drawings, Herr Christoph, when you've got time to look at them. The teacher said they were very good indeed."

"I should like to see them."

Lothar didn't respond. I sympathized with him and felt rather foolish. But Frau Nowak was determined to show him off:

"Which nights are your classes, Lothar?"

"Mondays and Thursdays." He went on eating, deliberately, obstinately, without looking at his mother. Then perhaps to show that he bore me no ill-will, he added: "From eight to ten-thirty." As soon as we had finished, he got up without a word, shook hands with me, making the same small bow, took his cap and went out.

Frau Nowak looked after him and sighed: "He's going round to his Nazis, I suppose. I often wish he'd never taken up with them at all. They put all kinds of silly ideas into his head. It makes him so restless. Since he joined them he's been a different boy altogether ... Not that I understand these politics myself. What I always say is—why can't we have the Kaiser back? Those were the good times, say what you like."

"Ach, to hell with your old Kaiser," said Otto. "What we want is a communist revolution."

"A communist revolution!" Frau Nowak snorted. "The idea! The communists are all good-for-nothing lazybones like you, who've never done an honest day's work in their lives."

"Christoph's a communist," said Otto. "Aren't you, Christoph?"

"Not a proper one, I'm afraid."

Frau Nowak smiled: "What nonsense will you be telling us next! How could Herr Christoph be a communist? He's a gentleman."

"What I say is—" Herr Nowak put down his knife and fork and wiped his moustache carefully on the back of his hand: "we're all equal as God made us. You're as good as me; I'm as good as you. A Frenchman's as good as an Englishman; an Englishman's as good as a German. You understand what I mean?"

I nodded.

"Take the war, now—" Herr Nowak pushed back his chair from the table: "One day I was in a wood. All alone, you understand. Just walking through the wood by myself, as I might be walking down the street ... And suddenly—there before me, stood a Frenchman. Just as if he'd sprung out of the earth. He was no further away from me than you are now." Herr Nowak sprang to his feet as he spoke. Snatching up the bread-knife from the table he held it before him, in a posture of defence, like a bayonet. He glared at me from beneath his bushy eyebrows, re-living the scene: "There we stand. We look at each other. That Frenchman was as pale as death. Suddenly he cries: 'Don't shoot me!' Just like that." Herr Nowak clasped his hands in a piteous gesture of entreaty. The bread-knife was in the way now: he put it down on the table. "'Don't shoot me! I have five children.' (He spoke French, of course: but I could understand him. I could speak French perfectly in those days; but I've forgotten some of it now.) Well, I look at him and he looks at me. Then I say: 'Ami.' (That means Friend.) And then we shake hands." Herr Nowak took my hand in both of his and pressed it with great emotion. "And then we begin to walk away from each other—backwards; I didn't want him to shoot me in the back." Still glaring in front of him Herr Nowak began cautiously retreating backwards, step by step, until he collided violently with the sideboard. A framed photograph fell off it. The glass smashed.

"Pappi! Pappi!" cried Grete in delight. "Just look what you've done!"

"Perhaps that'll teach you to stop your fooling, you old clown!" exclaimed Frau Nowak angrily. Grete began loudly and affectedly laughing, until Otto slapped her face and she set up her stagey whine. Meanwhile Herr Nowak had restored his wife's good temper by kissing her and pinching her cheek.

"Get away from me, you great lout!" She protested, laughing, coyly pleased that I was present: "Let me alone, you stink of beer!"

At that time, I had a great many lessons to give. I was out most of the day. My pupils were scattered about the fashionable suburbs of the west—rich, well-preserved women of Frau Nowak's age, but looking ten years younger; they liked to make a hobby of a little English conversation on dull afternoons when their husbands were away at the office. Sitting on silk cushions in front of open fireplaces, we discussed

Point Counter Point and *Lady Chatterley's Lover.* A manservant brought in tea with buttered toast. Sometimes, when they got tired of literature, I amused them by descriptions of the Nowak household. I was careful, however, not to say that I lived there: it would have been bad for my business to admit that I was really poor. The ladies paid me three marks an hour; a little reluctantly, having done their best to beat me down to two marks fifty. Most of them also tried, deliberately or subconsciously, to cheat me into staying longer than my time. I always had to keep an eye on the clock.

Fewer people wanted lessons in the morning; and so it happened that I usually got up much later than the rest of the Nowak family. Frau Nowak had her charring, Herr Nowak went off to his job at the furniture-removers', Lothar, who was out of work, was helping a friend with a paper-round, Grete went to school. Only Otto kept me company; except on the mornings when, with endless nagging, he was driven out to the labour-bureau by his mother, to get his card stamped.

After fetching our breakfast, a cup of coffee and a slice of bread and dripping, Otto would strip off his pyjamas and do exercises, shadow-box or stand on his head. He flexed his muscles for my admiration. Squatting on my bed, he told me stories:

"Did I ever tell you, Christoph, how I saw the Hand?"

"No, I don't think so."

"Well, listen ... Once, when I was very small, I was lying in bed at night. It was very dark and very late. And suddenly I woke up and saw a great big black hand stretching over the bed. I was so frightened I couldn't even scream. I just drew my legs up under my chin and stared at it. Then, after a minute or two, it disappeared and I yelled out. Mother came running in and I said: 'Mother, I've seen the Hand.' But she only laughed. She wouldn't believe it."

Otto's innocent face, with its two dimples, like a bun, had become very solemn. He held me with his absurdly small bright eyes, concentrating all his narrative powers:

"And then, Christoph, several years later, I had a job as apprentice to an upholsterer. Well, one day—it was in the middle of the morning, in broad daylight—I was sitting working on my stool. And suddenly it seemed to go all dark in the room and I looked up and there was the Hand, as near to me as you are now, just closing over me. I felt my arms and legs turn cold and I couldn't breathe and I couldn't cry out. The master saw how pale I was and he said: 'Why, Otto, what's the matter with you? Aren't you well?' And as he spoke to me it seemed as if the Hand drew right away from me again, getting smaller and smaller, until it was just a little black speck. And when I looked up again the room was quite light, just as it always was, and where I'd seen the black speck there was a big fly crawling across the ceiling. But I was so ill the whole day that the master had to send me home."

Otto's face had gone quite pale during this recital and, for a moment, a really frightening expression of fear had passed over his features. He was tragic now; his little eyes bright with tears:

"One day I shall see the Hand again. And then I shall die."

"Nonsense," I said, laughing. "We'll protect you."

Otto shook his head very sadly:

"Let's hope so, Christoph. But I'm afraid not. The Hand will get me in the end."

"How long did you stay with the upholsterer?" I asked.

"Oh, not long. Only a few weeks. The master was so unkind to me. He always gave me the hardest jobs to do—and I was such a little chap then. One day I got there five minutes late. He made a terrible row; called me a *verfluchter Hund.* And do you think I put up with that?" Otto leant forward, thrust his face, contracted into a dry monkey-like leer of malice, towards me. *"Nee, nee! Bei mir nicht!"* His little eyes focused upon me for a moment with an extraordinary intensity of simian hatred; his puckered-up features became startlingly ugly. Then they relaxed. I was no longer the upholsterer. He laughed gaily and innocently, throwing back his hair, showing his teeth: "I pretended I was going to hit him. I frightened him, all right!"

He imitated the gesture of a scared middle-aged man avoiding a blow. He laughed.

"And then you had to leave?" I asked.

Otto nodded. His face slowly changed. He was turning melancholy again.

"What did your father and mother say to that?"

"Oh, they've always been against me. Ever since I was small. If there were two crusts of bread, mother would always give the bigger one to Lothar. Whenever I complained they used to say: 'Go and work. You're old enough. Get your own food. Why should we support you?'" Otto's eyes moistened with the most sincere self-pity: "Nobody understands me here. Nobody's good to me. They all hate me really. They wish I was dead."

"How can you talk such rubbish, Otto! Your mother certainly doesn't hate you."

"Poor mother!" agreed Otto. He had changed his tone at once, seeming utterly unaware of what he had just said: "It's terrible. I can't bear to think of her working like that, every day. You know, Christoph, she's very, very ill. Often, at night she coughs for hours and hours. And sometimes she spits out blood. I lie awake wondering if she's going to die."

I nodded. In spite of myself I began to smile. Not that I disbelieved what he had said about Frau Nowak. But Otto himself, squatting there on the bed, was so animally alive, his naked brown body, so sleek with health, that his talk of death seemed ludicrous, like the description of a funeral by a painted clown. He must have understood this, for he grinned back, not in the least shocked at my apparent callousness. Straightening his legs he bent forward without effort and grasped his feet with his hands: "Can you do that, Christoph?"

A sudden notion pleased him: "Christoph, if I show you something, will you swear not to tell a single soul?"

"All right."

He got up and rummaged under his bed. One of the floorboards was loose in the corner by the window: lifting it, he fished out a tin box which had once contained biscuits. The tin was full of letters and photographs. Otto spread them out on the bed:

"Mother would burn these if she found them ... Look, Christoph, how do you like her? Her name's Hilde. I met her at the place where I go dancing ... And this is Marie. Hasn't she got beautiful eyes? She's wild about me—all the other boys are jealous. But she's not really my type." Otto shook his head seriously: "You know, it's a funny thing, but as soon as I know that a girl's keen on me, I lose interest in her. I wanted to break with her altogether; but she came round here and made such a to-do in front of mother. So I have to see her sometimes to keep her quiet ... And here's Trude—honestly, Christoph, would you believe she was twenty-seven? It's a fact! Hasn't she a marvellous figure? She lives in the West End, in a flat of her own! She's been divorced twice. I can go there whenever I like. Here's a photo her brother took of her. He wanted to take some of us two together, but I wouldn't let him. I was afraid he'd sell them, afterwards—you can be arrested for it, you know ..." Otto smirked, handed me a packet of letters: "Here, read these; they'll make you laugh. This one's from a Dutchman. He's got the biggest car I ever saw in my life. I was with him in the spring. He writes to me sometimes. Father got wind of it, and now he watches out to see if there's any money in the envelopes—the dirty dog! But I know a trick worth two of that! I've told all my friends to address their letters to the bakery on the corner. The baker's son is a pal of mine ..."

"Do you ever hear from Peter?" I asked.

Otto regarded me very solemnly for a moment: "Christoph?"

"Yes?"

"Will you do me a favour?"

"What is it?" I asked cautiously: Otto always chose the least expected moments to ask for a small loan.

"Please ..." he was gently reproachful, "please, never mention Peter's name to me again ..."

"Oh, all right," I said, very much taken aback: "If you'd rather not."

"You see, Christoph ... Peter hurt me very much. I thought he was my friend. And then, suddenly, he left me—all alone ..."

Down in the murky pit of the courtyard where the fog, in this clammy autumn weather, never lifted, the street singers and musicians succeeded each other in a performance which was nearly continuous. There were parties of boys with mandolins, an old man who played the concertina and a father who sang with his little girls. Easily the favourite tune was: *Aus der Jugendzeit.* I often heard it a dozen times in one morning. The father of the girls was paralysed and could only make desperate throttled noises like a donkey; but the daughters sang with the energy of fiends: "Sie *kommt,* sie *kommt* nicht mehr!" they screamed in unison, like demons of the air, rejoicing in the frustration of mankind. Occasionally a groschen, screwed in a corner of newspaper, was tossed down from a window high above. It hit the pavement and ricocheted like a bullet, but the little girls never flinched.

Now and then the visiting nurse called to see Frau Nowak, shook her head over the sleeping arrangements and went away again. The inspector of housing, a pale young man with an open collar (which he obviously wore on principle), came also and took copious notes. The attic, he told Frau Nowak, was absolutely insanitary and uninhabitable. He had a slightly reproachful air as he said this, as though we ourselves were partly to blame. Frau Nowak bitterly resented these visits. They were, she thought, simply attempts to spy on her. She was haunted by the fear that the nurse or the inspector would look in at a moment when the flat was untidy. So deep were her suspicions that she even told lies—pretending that the leak in the roof wasn't serious—to get them out of the house as quickly as possible.

Another regular visitor was the Jewish tailor and outfitter, who sold clothes of all kinds on the instalment plan. He was small and gentle and very persuasive. All day long he made his rounds of the tenements in the district, collecting fifty pfennigs here, a mark there, scratching up his precarious livelihood, like a hen, from this apparently barren soil. He never pressed hard for money; preferring to urge his debtors to take more of his goods and embark upon a fresh series of payments. Two years ago Frau Nowak had bought a little suit and an overcoat for Otto for three hundred marks. The suit and the overcoat had been worn out long ago, but the money was not nearly repaid. Shortly after my arrival Frau Nowak invested in clothes for Grete to the value of seventy-five marks. The tailor made no objection at all.

The whole neighbourhood owed him money. Yet he was not unpopular: he enjoyed the status of a public character, whom people curse without real malice. "Perhaps Lothar's right," Frau Nowak would sometimes say: "When Hitler comes, he'll show these Jews a thing or two. They won't be so cheeky then." But when I suggested that Hitler, if he got his own way, would remove the tailor altogether, then Frau Nowak would immediately change her tone: "Oh, I shouldn't like that to happen. After all, he makes very good clothes. Besides, a Jew will always let you have time if you're in difficulties. You wouldn't catch a Christian giving credit like he does ... You ask the people round here, Herr Christoph: they'd never turn out the Jews."

Towards evening Otto, who had spent the day in gloomy lounging—either lolling about the flat or chatting with his friends downstairs at the courtyard entrance—would begin to brighten up. When I got back from work I generally found him changing already from his sweater and knicker-bockers into his best suit, with its shoulders padded out to points, small, tight, double-breasted waistcoat and bell-bottomed trousers. He had quite a large selection of ties and it took him half an hour at least to choose one of them and to knot it to his satisfaction. He stood smirking in front of the cracked triangle of looking-glass in the kitchen, his pink plum-face dimpled with conceit, getting in Frau Nowak's way and disregarding her protests. As soon as supper was over he was going out dancing.

I generally went out in the evenings, too. However tired I was, I couldn't go to sleep immediately after my evening meal: Grete and her parents were often in bed by nine o'clock. So I went to the cinema or sat in a café and read the newspapers and yawned. There was nothing else to do.

At the end of the street there was a cellar *lokal* called the Alexander Casino. Otto showed it to me one evening, when we happened to leave the house together. You went down four steps from the street level, opened the door, pushed aside the heavy leather curtain which kept out the draught and found yourself in a long, low, dingy room. It was lit by red chinese lanterns and festooned with dusty paper streamers. Round the walls stood wicker tables and big shabby settees which looked like the seats of English third-class railway-carriages. At the far end were trellis-work alcoves, arboured over with imitation cherry-blossom twined on wires. The whole place smelt damply of beer.

I had been here before: a year ago, in the days when Fritz Wendel used to take me on Saturday evening excursions round "the dives" of the city. It was all just as we had left it; only less sinister, less picturesque, symbolic no longer of a tremendous truth about the meaning of existence—because, this time, I wasn't in the least drunk. The same proprietor, an ex-boxer, rested his immense stomach on the bar, the same hangdog waiter shuffled forward in his soiled white coat: two girls, the very same, perhaps, were dancing together to the wailing of the loud-speaker. A group of youths in sweaters and leather jackets were playing Sheep's Head; the spectators leaning over to see the cards. A boy with tattooed arms sat by the stove, deep in a crime shocker. His shirt was open at the neck, with the sleeves rolled up to his armpits; he wore shorts and socks, as if about to take part in a race. Over in the far alcove, a man and a boy were sitting together. The boy had a round childish face and heavy reddened eyelids which looked swollen as if from lack of sleep. He was relating something to the elderly, shaven-headed, respectable-looking man, who sat rather unwillingly listening and smoking a short cigar. The boy told his story carefully and with great patience. At intervals, to emphasize a point, he laid his hand on the elderly man's knee and looked up into his face, watching its every movement shrewdly and intently, like a doctor with a nervous patient.

Later on, I got to know this boy quite well. He was called Pieps. He was a great traveller. He ran away from home at the age of fourteen because his father, a woodcutter in the Thuringian Forest, used to beat him. Pieps set out to walk to Hamburg. At Hamburg he stowed away on a ship bound for Antwerp and from Antwerp he walked back into Germany and along the Rhine. He had been in Austria, too, and Czechoslovakia. He was full of songs and stories and jokes: he had an extraordinarily cheerful and happy nature, sharing what he had with his friends and never worrying where his next meal was coming from. He was a clever pickpocket and worked chiefly in an amusement-hall in the Friedrichstrasse, not far from the Passage, which was full of detectives and getting too dangerous nowadays. In this amusement-hall there were punch-balls and peep-shows and try-your-grip machines. Most of the boys from the Alexander Casino spent their afternoons there, while their girls were out working the Friedrichstrasse and the Linden for possible pick-ups.

Pieps lived together with his two friends, Gerhardt and Kurt, in a cellar on the canal-bank, near the station of the overhead railway. The cellar belonged to Gerhardt's aunt, an elderly Friedrichstrasse whore, whose legs and arms were tattooed with snakes, birds and flowers. Gerhardt was a tall boy with a vague, silly, unhappy smile. He did not pick pockets, but stole from the big department-stores. He had never yet been caught, perhaps because of the lunatic brazenness of his thefts. Stupidly grinning, he would stuff things into his pockets right under the noses of the shop-assistants. He gave everything he stole to his aunt, who cursed him for his laziness and kept him very short of money. One day, when we were together, he took from his pocket a brightly coloured lady's leather belt: "Look, Christoph, isn't it pretty?"

"Where did you get it from?"

"From Landauers'," Gerhardt told me. "Why ... what are you smiling at?"

"You see, the Landauers are friends of mine. It seems funny—that's all."

At once, Gerhardt's face was the picture of dismay: "You won't tell them, Christoph, will you?"

"No," I promised. "I won't."

Kurt came to the Alexander Casino less often than the others. I could understand him better than I could understand Pieps or Gerhardt, because he was consciously unhappy. He had a reckless, fatal streak in his character, a capacity for pure sudden flashes of rage against the hopelessness of his life. The Germans call it *Wut.* He would sit silent in his corner, drinking rapidly, drumming with his fists on the table, imperious and sullen. Then, suddenly, he would jump to his feet, exclaim: *"Ach, Scheiss!"* and go striding out. In this mood, he picked quarrels deliberately with the other boys, fighting them three or four at a time, until he was flung out into the street, half stunned and covered with blood. On these occasions even Pieps and Gerhardt joined against him as against a public danger: they hit him as hard as anyone else and dragged him home between them afterwards without the least malice for the black eyes he often managed to give them. His behaviour did not appear to surprise them in the least. They were all good friends again next day.

By the time I arrived back Herr and Frau Nowak had probably been asleep for two or three hours. Otto generally arrived later still. Yet Herr Nowak, who resented so much else in his son's behaviour, never seemed to mind getting up and opening the door to him, whatever the time of night. For some strange reason, nothing would induce the Nowaks to let either of us have a latchkey. They couldn't sleep unless the door was bolted as well as locked.

In these tenements each lavatory served for four flats. Ours was on the floor below. If, before retiring, I wished to relieve nature, there was a second journey to be made through the living-room in the dark to the kitchen, skirting the table, avoiding the chairs, trying not to collide with the head of the Nowaks' bed or jolt the bed in which Lothar and Grete were sleeping. However cautiously I moved, Frau Nowak would wake up: she seemed to be able to see me in the dark, and embarrassed me with polite directions: "No, Herr Christoph—not there, if you please. In the bucket on the left, by the stove."

Lying in bed, in the darkness, in my tiny corner of the enormous human warren of the tenements, I could hear, with uncanny precision, every sound which came up from the courtyard below. The shape of the court must have acted as a gramophone-horn. There was someone going downstairs: our neighbour, Herr Müller, probably: he had a night-shift on the railway. I listened to his steps getting fainter, flight by flight; then they crossed the court, clear and sticky on the wet stone. Straining my ears, I heard, or fancied I heard, the grating of the key in the lock of the big street door. A moment later, the door closed with a deep, hollow boom. And now, from the next room, Frau Nowak had an outburst of coughing. In the silence which followed it, Lothar's bed creaked as he turned over muttering something indistinct and threatening in his sleep. Somewhere on the other side of the court a baby began to scream, a window was slammed to, something very heavy, deep in the innermost recesses of the building, thudded dully against a wall. It was alien and mysterious and uncanny, like sleeping out in the jungle alone.

Sunday was a long day at the Nowaks. There was nowhere to go in this wretched weather. We were all of us at home. Grete and Herr Nowak were making a trap for sparrows which Herr Nowak had made and fixed up in the window. They sat there, hour by hour, intent upon it. The string which worked the trap was in Grete's hand. Occasionally, they giggled at each other and looked at me. I was sitting on the opposite side of the table, frowning at a piece of paper on which I had written:

"But, Edward, can't you *see?*" I was trying to get on with my novel. It was about a family who lived in a large country house on unearned incomes and were very unhappy. They spent their time explaining to each other why they couldn't enjoy their lives; and some of the reasons—though I say it myself—were most ingenious. Unfortunately I found myself taking less and less interest in my unhappy family: the atmosphere of the Nowak household was not very inspiring. Otto, in the inner room with the door open, was amusing himself by balancing ornaments on the turntable of an old gramophone, which was now minus sound-box and tone-arm, to see how long it would be before they flew off and smashed. Lothar was filing keys and mending locks for the neighbours, his pale sullen face bent over his work in obstinate concentration. Frau Nowak, who was cooking, began a sermon about the Good and the Worthless Brother: "Look at Lothar. Even when he's out of a job he keeps himself occupied. But all you're good for is to smash things. You're no son of mine."

Otto lolled sneering on his bed, occasionally spitting out an obscene word or making a farting noise with his lips. Certain tones of his voice were maddening: they made one want to hurt him—and he knew it. Frau Nowak's shrill scolding rose to a scream:

"I've a good mind to turn you out of the house! What have you ever done for us? When there's any work going you're too tired to do it; but you're not too tired to go gallivanting about half the night—you wicked unnatural good-for-nothing ..."

Otto sprang to his feet, and began dancing about the room with cries of animal triumph. Frau Nowak picked up a piece of soap and flung it at him. He dodged, and it smashed the window. After this Frau Nowak sat down and began to cry. Otto ran to her at once and began to soothe her with noisy kisses. Neither Lothar nor Herr Nowak took much notice of the row. Herr Nowak seemed even rather to have enjoyed it: he winked at me slyly. Later, the hole in the window was stopped with a piece of cardboard. It remained unmended; adding one more to the many draughts in the attic.

During supper, we were all jolly. Herr Nowak got up from the table to give imitations of the different ways in which Jews and Catholics pray. He fell down on his knees and bumped his head several times vigorously on the ground, gabbling nonsense which was supposed to represent Hebrew and Latin prayers: "Koolyvotchka, koolyvotchka, koolyvotchka. Amen." Then he told stories of executions, to the horror and delight of Grete and Frau Nowak: "William the First—the old William—never signed a death-warrant; and do you know why? Because once, quite soon after he'd come to the throne, there was a celebrated murder-case and for a long time the judges couldn't agree whether the prisoner was guilty or innocent, but at last they condemned him to be executed. They put him on the scaffold and the executioner took his axe—so; and swung it—like this; and brought it down: *Kernack!* (They're all trained men of course: you or I couldn't cut a man's head off with one stroke, if they gave us a thousand marks.) And the head fell into the basket—flop!" Herr Nowak rolled up his eyes again, let his tongue hang out from the corner of his mouth and gave a really most vivid and disgusting imitation of the decapitated head: "And then the head spoke, all by itself, and said: 'I am innocent!' (Of course, it was only the nerves; but it spoke, just as plainly as I'm speaking now.) 'I am innocent!' it said ... And a few months later, another man confessed on his death-bed that he'd been the real murderer. So, after that, William never signed a death-warrant again!"

In the Wassertorstrasse one week was much like another. Our leaky stuffy little attic smelt of cooking and bad drains. When the living-room stove was alight, we could hardly breathe; when it wasn't we froze. The weather had turned very cold. Frau Nowak tramped the streets, when she wasn't at work, from the clinic to the board of health offices and back again: for hours she waited on benches in draughty corridors or puzzled over complicated application-forms. The doctors couldn't agree about her case. One was in favour of sending her to a sanatorium at once. Another thought she was too far gone to be worth sending at all—and told her so. Another assured her that there was nothing serious the matter: she merely needed a fortnight in the Alps. Frau Nowak listened to all three of them with the greatest respect and never failed to impress upon me, describing these interviews, that each was the kindest and cleverest professor to be found in the whole of Europe.

She returned home, coughing and shivering, with sodden shoes, exhausted and semi-hysterical. No sooner was she inside the flat than she began scolding at Grete or at Otto, quite automatically, like a clockwork doll unwinding its spring:

"You mark my words—you'll end in prison! I wish I'd packed you off to a reformatory when you were fourteen. It might have done you some good ... And to think that, in my whole family, we've never had anybody before who wasn't respectable and decent!"

"*You* respectable!" Otto sneered. "When you were a girl you went around with every pair of trousers you could find."

"I forbid you to speak to me like that! Do you hear? I forbid you! Oh, I wish I'd died before I bore you, you wicked, unnatural child!"

Otto skipped around her, dodging her blows, wild with glee at the row he had started. In his excitement he pulled hideous grimaces.

"He's mad!" exclaimed Frau Nowak. "Just look at him now, Herr Christoph. I ask you, isn't he a raving madman? I must take him to the hospital to be examined."

This idea appealed to Otto's romantic imagination. Often, when we were alone together, he would tell me with tears in his eyes:

"I shan't be here much longer, Christoph. My nerves are breaking down. Very soon they'll come and take me away. They'll put me in a strait-waistcoat and feed me through a rubber tube. And when you come to visit me, I shan't know who you are."

Frau Nowak and Otto were not the only ones with "nerves." Slowly but surely the Nowaks were breaking my powers of resistance. Every day I found the smell from the kitchen sink a little nastier: every day Otto's voice when quarrelling seemed harsher and his mother's a little shriller. Grete's whine made me set my teeth. When Otto slammed a door I winced irritably. At nights I couldn't get to sleep unless I was half drunk. Also, I was secretly worrying about an unpleasant and mysterious rash: it might be due to Frau Nowak's cooking, or worse.

I now spent most of my evenings at the Alexander Casino. At a table in the corner by the stove I wrote letters, talked to Pieps and Gerhardt or simply amused myself watching the other guests. The place was usually very quiet. We all sat round or lounged at the bar, waiting for something to happen. No sooner came the sound of the outer door than a dozen pairs of eyes were turned to see what new visitor would emerge from behind the leather curtain. Generally, it was only a biscuit-seller with his basket, or a Salvation Army girl with her collecting-box and tracts. If the biscuit-seller had been doing good business or was drunk he would throw dice with us for packets of sugar-wafers. As for the Salvation Army girl, she rattled her way drably round the room, got nothing and departed, without making us feel in the least uncomfortable. Indeed, she had become such a part of the evening's routine that Gerhardt and Pieps did not even make jokes about her when she was gone. Then an old man would shuffle in, whisper something to the barman and retire with him into the room behind the bar. He was a cocaine-addict. A moment later he reappeared, raised his hat to all of us with a vague courteous gesture, and shuffled out. The old man had a nervous tic and kept shaking his head all the time, as if saying to Life: No. No. No.

Sometimes the police came, looking for wanted criminals or escaped reformatory boys. Their visits were usually expected and prepared for. At any rate you could always, as Pieps explained to me, make a last-minute exit through the lavatory window into the courtyard at the back of the house: "But you must be careful Christoph," he added. "Take a good big jump. Or you'll fall down the coal-shoot and into the cellar. I did, once. And Hamburg Werner, who was coming after me, laughed so much that the bulls caught him."

On Saturday and Sunday evenings the Alexander Casino was full. Visitors from the West End arrived, like ambassadors from another country. There were a good number of foreigners—Dutchmen mostly, and Englishmen. The Englishmen talked in loud, high, excited voices. They discussed communism and Van Gogh and the best restaurants. Some of them seemed a little scared: perhaps they expected to be knifed in this den of thieves. Pieps and Gerhardt sat at their tables and mimicked their accents, cadging drinks and cigarettes. A stout man in horn spectacles asked: "Were you at that delicious party Bill gave for the Negro singers?" And a young man with a monocle murmured: "All the poetry in the world is in that face." I knew what he was feeling at that moment: I could sympathize with, even envy him. But it was saddening to know that, two weeks hence, he would boast about his exploits here, to a select party of clubmen or dons—warmed discreet smilers around a table furnished with historic silver and legendary port. It made me feel older.

At last the doctors made up their minds: Frau Nowak was to be sent to the sanatorium after all: and quite soon—shortly before Christmas. As soon as she heard this she ordered a new dress from the tailor. She was as excited and pleased as if she had been invited to a party: "The matrons are always very particular, you know, Herr Christoph. They see to it that we keep ourselves neat and tidy. If we don't we get punished—and quite right, too … I'm sure I shall enjoy being there," Frau Nowak sighed, "if only I can stop myself worrying about the family. What they'll do when I'm gone, goodness only knows. They're as helpless as a lot of sheep …" In the evenings she spent hours stitching warm flannel underclothes, smiling to herself, like a woman who is expecting a child.

On the afternoon of my departure Otto was very depressed.

"Now you're going, Christoph, I don't know what'll happen to me. Perhaps, six months from now, I shan't be alive at all."

"You got on all right before I came, didn't you?"

"Yes … but now mother's going, too. I don't suppose father'll give me anything to eat."

"What rubbish!"

"Take me with you, Christoph. Let me be your servant. I could be very useful, you know. I could cook for you and mend your clothes and open the door for your pupils …" Otto's eyes brightened as he admired himself in this new role. "I'd wear a little white jacket—or perhaps blue would be better, with silver buttons."

"I'm afraid you're a luxury I can't afford."

"Oh, but, Christoph, I shouldn't want any wages, of course." Otto paused feeling that this offer had been a bit too generous. "That is," he added cautiously, "only a mark or two to go dancing, now and then."

"I'm very sorry."

We were interrupted by the return of Frau Nowak. She had come home early to cook me a farewell meal. Her string-bag was full of things she had bought; she had tired herself out carrying it. She shut the kitchen-door behind her with a sigh and began to bustle about at once, her nerves on edge, ready for a row.

"Why, Otto, you've let the stove go out! After I specially told you to keep an eye on it! Oh, dear, can't I rely on anybody in this house to help me with a single thing?"

"Sorry, mother," said Otto. "I forgot."

"Of course you forgot! Do you ever remember anything? You *forgot!*" Frau Nowak screamed at him, her features puckered into a sharp little stabbing point of fury: "I've worked myself into my grave for you, and that's my thanks. When I'm gone I hope your father'll turn you out into the streets. We'll see how you like that! You great, lazy, hulking lump! Get out of my sight, do you hear? Get out of my sight!"

"All right. Christoph, you hear what she says?" Otto turned to me, his face convulsed with rage; at that moment the resemblance between them was quite startling; they were like creatures demoniacally possessed. "I'll make her sorry for it as long as she lives!"

He turned and plunged into the inner bedroom, slamming the rickety door behind him. Frau Nowak turned at once to the stove and began shovelling out the cinders. She was trembling all over and coughing violently. I helped her, putting firewood and pieces of coal into her hands; she took them from me, blindly, without a glance or a word. Feeling, as usual, that I was only in the way, I went into the living-room and stood stupidly by the window, wishing that I could simply disappear. I had had enough. On the window-sill lay a stump of pencil. I picked it up and drew a small circle on the wood, thinking: I have left my mark. Then I remembered how I had done exactly the same thing, years ago, before leaving a boarding-house in North Wales. In the inner room all was quiet. I decided to confront Otto's sulks. I had still got my suitcases to pack.

When I opened the door Otto was sitting on his bed. He was staring as if hypnotized at a gash on his left wrist, from which the blood was trickling down over his open palm and spilling in big drops on the floor. In his right hand between finger and thumb, he held a safety-razor blade. He didn't resist when I snatched it from him. The wound itself was nothing much; I bandaged it with his handerchief. Otto seemed to turn faint for a moment and lolled against my shoulder.

"How on earth did you manage to do it?"

"I wanted to show her," said Otto. He was very pale. He had evidently given himself a nasty scare: "You shouldn't have stopped me, Christoph."

"You little idiot," I said angrily, for he had frightened me, too: "One of these days you'll really hurt yourself—by mistake."

Otto gave me a long, reproachful look. Slowly his eyes filled with tears.

"What does it matter, Christoph? I'm no good ... What'll become of me, do you suppose, when I'm older?"

"You'll get work."

"Work ..." The very thought made Otto burst into tears.

Sobbing violently, he smeared the back of his hand across his nose.

I pulled out the handkerchief from my pocket. "Here. Take this."

"Thanks, Christoph ..." He wiped his eyes mournfully and blew his nose. Then something about the handkerchief itself caught his attention. He began to examine it, listlessly at first, then with extreme interest.

"Why, Christoph," he exclaimed indignantly, "this is one of mine!"

One afternoon, a few days after Christmas, I visited the Wassertorstrasse again. The lamps were alight already, as I turned in under the archway and entered the long, damp street, patched here and there with dirty snow. Weak yellow gleams shone out from the cellar shops. At a hand-cart under a gas-flare, a cripple was selling vegetables and fruit. A crowd of youths, with raw, sullen faces, stood watching two boys fighting at a doorway: a girl's voice screamed excitedly as one of them tripped and fell. Crossing the muddy courtyard, inhaling the moist, familiar rottenness of the tenement buildings, I thought: Did I really ever live here? Already, with my comfortable bed-sitting-room in the West End and my excellent new job, I had become a stranger to the slums.

The lights on the Nowaks' staircase were out of order: it was pitch-dark. I groped my way upstairs without much difficulty and banged on their door. I made as much noise as I could because, to judge from the shouting and singing and shrieks of laughter within, a party was in progress.

"Who's there?" bawled Herr Nowak's voice.

"Christoph."

"Aha! Christoph! Anglais! Englisch man! Come in! Come in!"

The door was flung open. Herr Nowak swayed unsteadily on the threshold, with arms open to embrace me. Behind him stood Grete, shaking like a jelly, with tears of laughter pouring down her cheeks. There was nobody else to be seen.

"Good old Christoph!" cried Herr Nowak, thumping me on the back. "I said to Grete: I know he'll come. Christoph won't desert us!" With a large burlesque gesture of welcome he pushed me violently into the living-room. The whole place was fearfully untidy. Clothing of various kinds lay in a confused heap on one of the beds; on the other were scattered cups, saucers, shoes, knives and forks. On the sideboard was a frying-pan full of dried fat. The room was lighted by three candles stuck into empty beer-bottles.

"All light's been cut off," explained Herr Nowak, with a negligent sweep of his arm: "the bill isn't paid ... Must pay it sometime, of course. Never mind—it's nicer like this, isn't it? Come on, Grete, let's light up the Christmas tree."

The Christmas tree was the smallest I had ever seen. It was so tiny and feeble that it could only carry one candle, at the very top. A single thin strand of tinsel was draped around it. Herr Nowak dropped several lighted matches on the floor before he could get the candle to bum. If I hadn't stamped them out the table-cloth might easily have caught fire.

"Where's Lothar and Otto?" I asked.

"Don't know. Somewhere about ... They don't show themselves much nowadays—it doesn't suit them, here ... Never mind, we're quite happy by ourselves, aren't we, Grete?" Herr Nowak executed a few elaphantine dance-steps and began to sing:

"*O Tannenbaum! O Tannenbaum!...* Come on, Christoph, all together now! *Wie treu sind Deine Blätter!*"

After all this was over I produced my presents: cigars for Herr Nowak, for Grete chocolates and a clockwork mouse. Herr Nowak then brought a bottle of beer from under the bed. After a long search for his spectacles, which were finally discovered hanging on the water-tap in the kitchen, he read me a letter which Frau Nowak had written from the sanatorium. He repeated every sentence three or four times, got lost in the middle, swore, blew his nose, and picked his ears.

I could hardly understand a word. Then he and Grete began playing with the clockwork mouse, letting it run about the table, shrieking and roaring whenever it neared the edge. The mouse was such a success that my departure was managed briefly, without any fuss. "Goodbye, Christoph. Come again soon," said Herr Nowak and turned back to the table at once. He and Grete were bending over it with the eagerness of gamblers as I made my way out of the attic.

Not long after this I got a call from Otto himself. He had come to ask me if I would go with him the next Sunday to see Frau Nowak. The sanatorium had its monthly visiting-day: there would be a special bus running from Hallesches Tor.

"You needn't pay for me, you know," Otto added grandly. He was fairly shining with self-satisfaction.

"That's very handsome of you, Otto ... A new suit?"

"Do you like it?"

"It must have cost a good bit."

"Two hundred and fifty marks."

"My word! Has your ship come home?"

Otto smirked: "I'm seeing a lot of Trade now. Her uncle's left her some money. Perhaps, in the spring, we'll get married."

"Congratulations ... I suppose you're still living at home?"

"Oh, I look in there occasionally," Otto drew down the corners of his mouth in a grimace of languid distaste, "but father's always drunk."

"Disgusting, isn't it?" I mimicked his tone. We both laughed.

"My goodness, Christoph, is it as late as that? I must be getting along ... Till Sunday. Be good."

We arrived at the sanatorium about midday.

There was a bumpy cart-track winding for several kilometres through snowy pine-woods and then, suddenly, a Gothic brick gateway like the entrance to a churchyard, with big red buildings rising behind. The bus stopped. Otto and I were the last passengers to get out. We stood stretching ourselves and blinking at the bright snow: out here in the country everything was dazzling white. We were all very stiff, for the bus was only a covered van, with packing-cases and school-benches for seats. The seats had not shifted much during the journey, for we had been packed together as tightly as books on a shelf.

And now the patients came running out to meet us—awkward padded figures muffled in shawls and blankets, stumbling and slithering on the trampled ice of the path. They were in such a hurry that their blundering charge ended in a slide. They shot skidding into the arms of their friends and relations, who staggered under the violence of the collision. One couple, amid shrieks of laughter, had tumbled over.

"Otto!"

"Mother!"

"So you've really come! How well you're looking!"

"Of course we've come, mother! What did you expect?" Frau Nowak disengaged herself from Otto to shake hands with me. "How do you do, Herr Christoph?"

She looked years younger. Her plump, oval, innocent face, lively and a trifle crafty, with its small peasant eyes, was like the face of a young girl. Her cheeks were brightly dabbed with colour. She smiled as though she could never stop.

"Ah, Herr Christoph, how nice of you to come! How nice of you to bring Otto to visit me!"

She uttered a brief, queer, hysterical little laugh. We mounted some steps into the house. The smell of the warm, clean, antiseptic building entered my nostrils like a breath of fear.

"They've put me in one of the smaller wards," Frau Nowak told us. "There's only four of us altogether. We get up to all sorts of games." Proudly throwing open the door, she made the introductions: "This is Muttchen—she keeps us in order! And this is Erna. And this is Erika—our baby!"

Erika was a weedy blonde girl of eighteen, who giggled: "So here's the famous Otto! We've been looking forward to seeing him for weeks!"

Otto smiled subtly, discreetly, very much at his ease. His brand-new brown suit was vulgar beyond words; so were his lilac spats and his pointed yellow shoes. On his finger was an enormous signet-ring with a square, chocolate-coloured stone. Otto was extremely conscious of it and kept posing his hand in graceful attitudes, glancing down furtively to admire the effect. Frau Nowak simply couldn't leave him alone. She must keep hugging him and pinching his cheeks.

"Doesn't he look well!" she exclaimed. "Doesn't he look splendid! Why, Otto, you're so big and strong, I believe you could pick me up with one hand!"

Old Muttchen had a cold, they said. She wore a bandage round her throat, tight under the collar of her old-fashioned black dress. She seemed a nice old lady, but somehow slightly obscene, like an old dog with sores. She sat on the edge of her bed with the photographs of her children and grandchildren on the table beside her, like prizes she had won. She looked slyly pleased, as though she were glad to be so ill. Frau Nowak told us that Muttchen had been three times in this sanatorium already. Each time she had been discharged as cured, but within nine months or a year she would have a relapse and have to be sent back again.

"Some of the cleverest professors in Germany have come here to examine her," Frau Nowak added, with pride, "but you always fool them, don't you, Muttchen dear?"

The old lady nodded, smiling, like a clever child which is being praised by its elders.

"And Erna is here for the second time," Frau Nowak continued. "The doctors said she'd be all right; but she didn't get enough to eat. So now she's come back to us, haven't you, Erna?"

"Yes, I've come back," Erna agreed.

She was a skinny, bobbed-haired woman of about thirty-five, who must once have been very feminine, appealing, wistful and soft. Now in her extreme emaciation, she seemed possessed by a kind of desperate resolution, a certain defiance.

She had immense, dark, hungry eyes. The wedding-ring was loose on her bony finger. When she talked and became excited her hands flitted tirelessly about in sequences of aimless gestures, like two shrivelled moths.

"My husband beat me and then ran away. The night he went he gave me such a thrashing that I had the marks afterwards for months. He was such a great strong man. He nearly killed me." She spoke calmly, deliberately, yet with a certain suppressed excitement, never taking her eyes from my face. Her hungry glance bored into my brain, reading eagerly what I was thinking. "I dream about him now, sometimes," she added, as if faintly amused.

Otto and I sat down at the table while Frau Nowak fussed around us with coffee and cakes which one of the sisters had brought. Everything which happened to me today was curiously without impact: my senses were muffled, insulated, functioning as if in a vivid dream. In this calm, white room, with its great windows looking out over the silent snowy pine-woods—the Christmas tree on the table, the paper festoons above the beds, the nailed-up photographs, the plate of heart-shaped chocolate biscuits—these four women lived and moved. My eyes could explore every corner of their world: the temperature charts, the fire extinguisher, the leather screen by the door. Dressed daily in their best clothes, their clean hands no longer pricked by the needle or roughened from scrubbing, they lay out on the terrace, listening to the wireless, forbidden to talk. Women being shut up together in this room had bred an atmosphere which was faintly nauseating, like soiled linen locked in a cupboard without air. They were playful with each other and shrill, like overgrown schoolgirls. Frau Nowak and Erika indulged in sudden furtive bouts of ragging. They plucked at each other's clothes, scuffled silently, exploded into shrilly strained laughter. They were showing off in front of us.

"You don't know how we've looked forward to today," Erna told me. "To see a real live man!"

Frau Nowak giggled.

"Erika was such an innocent girl until she came here . . . You didn't know anything, did you, Erika?"

Erika sniggered.

"I've learnt enough since then . . ."

"Yes, I should think you have! Would you believe it, Herr Christoph—her aunt sent her this little mannikin for Christmas, and now she takes it to bed with her every night, because she says she must have a man in her bed!"

Erika laughed boldly. "Well, it's better than nothing, isn't it?"

She winked at Otto, who rolled his eyes, pretending to be shocked.

After lunch Frau Nowak had to put in an hour's rest. So Erna and Erika took possession of us for a walk in the grounds.

"We'll show them the cemetery first," Erna said.

The cemetery was for pet animals belonging to the sanatorium staff which had died. There were about a dozen little crosses and tombstones, pencilled with mock-heroic inscriptions in verse. Dead birds were buried there and white mice and rabbits, and a bat which had been found frozen after a storm.

"It makes you fed sad to think of them lying there, doesn't it?" said Erna. She scooped away the snow from one of the graves. There were tears in her eyes.

But, as we walked away down the path, both she and Erika were very gay. We laughed and threw snowballs at each other. Otto picked up Erika and pretended he was going to throw her into a snow-drift. A little further on we passed close to a summer-house, standing back from the path on a mound among the trees. A man and a woman were just coming out of it.

"That's Frau Klemke," Erna told me. "She's got her husband here today. Just think, that old hut's the only place in the whole grounds where two people can be alone together . . ."

"It must be pretty cold in this weather."

"Of course it is! Tomorrow her temperature will be up again and she'll have to stay in bed for a fortnight... But who cares! If I were in her place I'd do the same myself." Erna squeezed my arm: "We've got to live while we're young, haven't we?"

"Of course we have!"

Erna looked up quickly into my face; her big dark eyes fastened on to mine like hooks; I could imagine I felt them pulling me down.

"I'm not really a consumptive, you know, Christoph ... You didn't think I was, did you, just because I'm here?"

"No Erna, of course I didn't."

"Lots of the girls here aren't. They just need looking after for a bit, like me ... The doctor says that if I take care of myself I shall be as strong as ever I was ... And what do you think the first thing is I shall do when they let me out of here?"

"What?"

"First I shall get my divorce, and then I shall find a husband," Erna laughed, with a kind of bitter triumph. "That won't take me long—I can promise you!"

After tea we sat upstairs in the ward. Frau Nowak had borrowed a gramophone so that we could dance. I danced with Erna. Erika danced with Otto. She was tomboyish and clumsy, laughing loudly whenever she slipped or trod on his toes. Otto, sleekly smiling, steered her backwards and forwards with skill, his shoulders bunched in the fashionable chimpanzee stoop of Hallesches Tor. Old Muttchen sat looking on from her bed. When I held Erna in my arms I felt her shivering all over. It was almost dark now, but nobody suggested turning on the light.

After a while we stopped dancing and sat round in a circle on the beds. Frau Nowak had begun to talk about her childhood days, when she had lived with her parents on a farm in East Prussia. "We had a sawmill of our own," she told us, "and thirty horses. My father's horses were the best in the district; he won prizes with them, many a time, at the show ..." The ward was quite dark now. The windows were big pale rectangles in the darkness. Erna, sitting beside me on the bed, felt down for my hand and squeezed it; then she reached behind me and drew my arm round her body. She was trembling violently. "Christoph …" she whispered in my ear.

"… and in the summer time," Frau Nowak was saying, "we used to go dancing in the big barn down by the river …"

My mouth pressed against Erna's hot, dry lips. I had no particular sensation of contact: all this was part of the long, rather sinister symbolic dream which I seemed to have been dreaming throughout the day. "I'm so happy, this evening …" Erna whispered.

"The postmaster's son used to play the fiddle," said Frau Nowak. "He played beautifully … it made you want to cry …"

From the bed on which Erika and Otto were sitting came sounds of scuffling and a loud snigger. "Otto, you naughty boy … I'm surprised at you! I shall tell your mother!"

Five minutes later a sister came to tell us that the bus was ready to start.

"My word, Christoph," Otto whispered to me, as we were putting on our overcoats. "I could have done anything I liked with that girl! I felt her all over … Did you have a good time with yours? A bit skinny, wasn't she—but I bet she's hot stuff!"

Then we were clambering into the bus with the other passengers. The patients crowded round to say goodbye. Wrapped and hooded in their blankets, they might have been members of an aboriginal forest tribe.

Frau Nowak had begun crying, though she tried hard to smile.

"Tell your father I'll be back soon …"

"Of course you will, mother! You'll soon be well now. You'll soon be home."

"It's only a short time …" sobbed Frau Nowak; the tears running down over her hideous frog-like smile. And suddenly she started coughing—her body seemed to break in half like a hinged doll. Clasping her hands over her breast, she uttered short yelping coughs like a desperate injured animal. The blanket slipped back from her head and shoulders: a wisp of hair, working loose from the knot, was getting into her eyes—she shook her head blindly to avoid it. Two sisters gently tried to lead her away, but at once she began to struggle furiously. She wouldn't go with them.

"Go in, mother," begged Otto. He was almost in tears himself. "Please go in! You'll catch your death of cold!"

"Write to me sometimes, won't you, Christoph?" Erna was clutching my hand as though she were drowning. Her eyes looked up at me with a terrifying intensity of unashamed despair. "It doesn't matter if it's only a postcard ... just sign your name."

"Of course I will ..."

They all thronged round us for a moment in the little circle of light from the panting bus, their lit faces ghastly like ghosts against the black stems of the pines. This was the climax of my dream: the instant of nightmare in which it would end. I had an absurd pang of fear that they were going to attack us—a gang of terrifying soft muffled shapes—clawing us from our seats, dragging us hungrily down, in dead silence. But the moment passed. They drew back—harmless, after all, as mere ghosts—into the darkness, while our bus, with a great churning of its wheels, lurched forward towards the city, through the deep unseen snow.

The Landauers

ONE NIGHT IN October 1930, about a month after the Elections, there was a big row on the Leipzigerstrasse. Gangs of Nazi roughs turned out to demonstrate against the Jews. They manhandled some dark-haired, large-nosed pedestrians, and smashed the windows of all the Jewish shops. The incident was not, in itself, very remarkable; there were no deaths, very little shooting, not more than a couple of dozen arrests. I remember it only because it was my first introduction to Berlin politics.

Frl. Mayr, of course, was delighted: "Serves them right!" she exclaimed. "This town is sick with Jews. Turn over any stone, and a couple of them will crawl out. They're poisoning the very water we drink! They're strangling us, they're robbing us, they're sucking our life-blood. Look at all the big department stores: Wertheim, K.D.W., Landauers'. Who owns them? Filthy thieving Jews!"

"The Landauers are personal friends of mine," I retorted icily, and left the room before Frl. Mayr had time to think of a suitable reply.

This wasn't strictly true. As a matter of fact, I had never met any member of the Landauer family in my life. But, before leaving England, I had been given a letter of introduction to them by a mutual friend. I mistrust letters of introduction, and should probably never have used this one, if it hadn't been for Frl. Mayr's remark. Now, perversely, I decided to write to Frau Landauer at once.

Natalia Landauer, as I saw her, for the first time, three days later, was a schoolgirl of eighteen. She had dark fluffy hair; far too much of it—it made her face, with its sparkling eyes, appear too long and too narrow. She reminded me of a young fox. She shook hands straight from the shoulder in the modern student manner. "In here, please." Her tone was peremptory and brisk.

The sitting-room was large and cheerful, pre-War in taste, a little over-furnished. Natalia had begun talking at once, with terrific animation, in eager stumbling English, showing me gramophone records, pictures, books. I wasn't allowed to look at anything for more than a moment:

"You like Mozart? Yes? Oh, I also! Vairy much! ... These picture is in the Kronprinz Palast. You have not seen it? I shall show you one day, yes? ... You are fond of Heine? Say quite truthfully, please." She looked up from the bookcase, smiling, but with a certain school-marm severity: "Read. It's beautiful, I find."

I hadn't been in the house for more than a quarter of an hour before Natalia had put aside four books for me to take with me when I left—*Tonio Kröger,* Jacobsen's stories, a volume of Stefan George, Goethe's letters. "You are to tell me your truthful opinions," she warned me.

Suddenly, a maid parted the sliding glass doors at the end of the room, and we found ourselves in the presence of Frau Landauer, a large, pale woman with a mole on her left cheek and her hair brushed back smooth into a knot, seated placidly at the dining-room table, filling glasses from a samovar with tea. There were plates of ham and cold cut wurst and a bowl of those thin wet slippery sausages which squirt you with hot water when their skins are punctured by a fork; as well as cheese, radishes, pumpernickel and bottled beer. "You will drink beer," Natalia ordered, returning one of the glasses of tea to her mother.

Looking round me, I noticed that the few available wall-spaces between pictures and cupboards were decorated with eccentric life-size figures, maidens with flying hair or oblique-eyed gazelles, cut out of painted paper and fastened down with drawing-pins. They made a comically ineffectual protest against the bourgeois solidity of the mahogany furniture. I knew, without being told, that Natalia must have designed them. Yes, she'd made them and fixed them up there for a party; now she wanted to take them down, but her mother wouldn't let her. They had a little argument about this—evidently part of the domestic routine. "Oh, but they're *tairrible,* I find!" cried Natalia, in English. "I think they're very pretty," replied Frau Landauer placidly, in German, without raising her eyes from the plate, her mouth full of pumpernickel and radish.

As soon as we had finished supper, Natalia made it clear that I was to say a formal good night to Frau Landauer. We then returned to the sitting-room. She began to cross-examine me. Where was my room? How much was I paying for it? When I told her, she said immediately that I'd chosen quite the wrong district (Wilmersdorf was far better), and that I'd been swindled. I could have got exactly the same thing, with running water and central heating thrown in, for the same price. "You should have asked me," she added, apparently quite forgetting that we'd met that evening for the first time: "I should have found it for you myself."

"Your friend tells us you are a writer?" Natalia challenged suddenly.

"Not a real writer," I protested.

"But you have written a book? Yes?"

Yes, I had written a book.

Natalia was triumphant: "You have written a book and you say you are not a writer. You are mad, I think."

Then I had to tell her the whole history of *All The Conspirators,* why it had that title, what it was about, when it was published, and so forth.

"You will bring me a copy, please."

"I haven't got one," I told her, with satisfaction, "and it's out of print."

This rather dashed Natalia for the moment, then she sniffed eagerly at a new scent: "And this what you will write in Berlin? Tell me, please."

To satisfy her, I began to tell the story of a story I had written years before, for a college magazine at Cambridge. I improved it as much as possible extempore, as I went along. Telling this story again quite excited me—so much so that I began to feel that the idea in it hadn't been so bad after all, and that I might really be able to rewrite it. At the end of every sentence, Natalia pressed her lips tight together and nodded her head so violently that the hair flopped up and down over her face.

"Yes, yes," she kept saying. "Yes, yes."

It was only after some minutes that I realized she wasn't taking in anything I said. She evidently couldn't understand my English, for I was talking much faster now, and not choosing my words. In spite of her tremendous devotional effort of concentration, I could see that she was noticing the way I parted my hair, and that my tie was worn shiny at the knot. She even flashed a furtive glance at my shoes. I pretended, however, not to be aware of all this. It would have been rude of me to stop short and most unkind to spoil Natalia's pleasure in the mere fact that I was talking so intimately to her about something which really interested me, although we were practically strangers.

When I had finished, she asked at once: "And it will be ready—how soon?" For she had taken possession of the story, together with all my other affairs. I answered that I didn't know. I was lazy.

"You are lazy?" Natalia opened her eyes mockingly. "So? Then I am sorry. I can't help you."

Presently, I said that I must go. She came with me to the door: "And you will bring me this story soon," she persisted.

"Yes."

"How soon?"

"Next week," I feebly promised.

It was a fortnight before I called on the Landauers again. After dinner, when Frau Landauer had left the room, Natalia informed me that we were to go together to the cinema. "We are the guests of my mother." As we stood up to go, she suddenly grabbed two apples and an orange from the sideboard and stuffed them into my pockets. She had evidently made up her mind that I was suffering from undernourishment. I protested weakly.

"When you say another word, I am angry," she warned me.

"And you have brought it?" she asked, as we were leaving the house.

Knowing perfectly well that she meant the story, I made my voice as innocent as I could: "Brought what?"

"You know. What you promise."

"I don't remember promising anything."

"Don't remember?" Natalia laughed scornfully. "Then I'm sorry. I can't help you."

By the time we got to the cinema, she had forgiven me, however. The big film was a Pat and Patachon. Natalia remarked severely: "You do not like this kind of film, I think? It isn't something clever enough for you?"

I denied that I only liked "clever" films, but she was sceptical: "Good. We shall see."

All through the film, she kept glancing at me to see if I was laughing. At first, I laughed exaggeratedly. Then, getting tired of this, I stopped laughing altogether. Natalia got more and more impatient with me. Towards the end of the film, she even began to nudge me at moments when I should laugh. No sooner were the lights turned up, than she pounced:

"You see? I was right. You did not like it, no?"

"I liked it very much indeed."

"Oh, yes, I believe! And now say truthfully."

"I have told you. I liked it."

"But you did not laugh. You are sitting always with your face so ..." Natalia tried to imitate me, "and not once laughing."

"I never laugh when I am amused," I said.

"Oh, yes, perhaps! That shall be one of your English customs, not to laugh?"

"No Englishman ever laughs when he's amused."

"You wish I believe that? Then I will tell you: your Englishmen are mad."

"That remark is not very original."

"And must always my remarks be so original, my dear sir?"

"When you are with me, yes."

"Imbecile!"

We sat for a little in a café near the Zoo Station and ate ices. The ices were lumpy and tasted slightly of potato. Suddenly, Natalia began to talk about her parents:

"I do not understand what this modern books mean when they say: the mother and father always must have quarrel with the children. You know, it would be impossible that I can have quarrel with my parents. Impossible."

Natalia looked hard at me to see whether I believed this. I nodded.

"Absolutely impossible," she repeated solemnly. "Because I know that my father and my mother love me. And so they are thinking always not of themselves but of what is for me the best. My mother, you know, she is not strong. She is having sometimes the most tairrible headaches. And then, of course, I cannot leave her alone. Vairy often, I would like to go out to a cinema or theatre or concert, and my mother, she say nothing, but I look at her and see that she is not well, and so I say No, I have change my mind, I will not go. But never it happens that she say one word about the pain she is suffered. Never."

(When next I called on the Landauers, I spent two marks fifty on roses for Natalia's mother. It was worth it. Never once did Frau Landauer have a headache on an evening when I proposed going out with Natalia.)

"My father will always that I have the best of everything," Natalia continued. "My father will always that I say: My parents are rich, I do not need to think for money." Natalia sighed: "But I am different than this. I await always that the worst will come. I know how things are in Germany today, and suddenly it can be that my father lose all. You know, that is happened once already? Before the War, my father has had a big factory in Posen. The War comes, and my father has to go. Tomorrow, it can be here the same. But my father, he is such a man that to him it is equal. He can start with one pfennig and work and work until he gets all back.

"And that is why," Natalia went on, "I wish to leave school and begin to learn something useful, that I can win my bread. I cannot know how long my parents have money. My father will that I make my Abitur and go to the university. But now I will speak with him and ask if I cannot go to Paris and study art. If I can draw and paint I can perhaps make my life; and also I will learn cookery. Do you know that I cannot cook, not the simplest thing?"

"Neither can I."

"For a man, that is not so important, I find. But a girl must be prepared for all.

"If I want," added Natalia earnestly, "I shall go away with the man I love and I shall live with him; even if we cannot become married it will not matter. Then I must be able to do all for myself, you understand? It is not enough to say: I have made my Abitur, I have my degree at the university. He will answer: 'Please, where is my dinner?'"

There was a pause.

"You are not shocked at what I say just now," asked Natalia suddenly. "That I would live with a man without that we were married?"

"No, of course not."

"Do not misunderstand me, please. I do not admirate the women who is going always from one man to another—that is all so," Natalia made a gesture of distaste, "so degenerated, I find."

"You don't think that women should be allowed to change their minds?"

"I do not know. I do not understand such questions ... But it is degenerated."

I saw her home. Natalia had a trick of leading you right up on to the doorstep, and then, with extraordinary rapidity, shaking hands, whisking into the house and slamming the door in your face.

"You ring me up? Next week? Yes?" I can hear her voice now. And then the door slammed and she was gone without waiting for an answer.

Natalia avoided all contacts, direct and indirect. Just as she wouldn't stand chatting with me on her own doorstep, she preferred always, I noticed, to have a table between us if we sat down. She hated me to help her into her coat: "I am not yet sixty years, my dear sir!" If we stood up to leave a cafe or a restaurant and she saw my eye moving towards the peg from which her coat hung, she would pounce instantly upon it and carry it off with her into a corner, like an animal guarding its food.

One evening, we went into a cafe and ordered two cups of chocolate. When the chocolate came, we found that the waitress had forgotten to bring Natalia a spoon. I'd already sipped my cup and had stirred it with my spoon after sipping it. It seemed quite natural to offer my spoon to Natalia, and I was surprised and a little impatient when she refused it with an expression of slight distaste. She declined even this indirect contact with my mouth.

Natalia got tickets for a concert of Mozart concertos. The evening was not a success. The severe Corinthian hall was chilly, and my eyes were uncomfortably dazzled by the classic brilliance of the electric lights. The shiny wooden chairs were austerely hard. The audience plainly regarded the concert as a religious ceremony. Their taut, devotional enthusiasm oppressed me like a headache; I couldn't, for a moment, lose consciousness of all those blind, half-frowning, listening heads. And despite Mozart, I couldn't help feeling: What an extraordinary way this is of spending an evening!

On the way home, I was tired and sulky, and this resulted in a little tiff with Natalia. She began it by talking about Hippi Bernstein. It was Natalia who had got me my job with the Bernsteins: she and Hippi went to the same school. A couple of days before, I had given Hippi her first English lesson.

"And how do you like her?" Natalia asked.

"Very much. Don't you?"

"Yes, I also … But she's got two bad faults. I think you will not have notice them yet?"

As I didn't rise to this, she added solemnly: "You know I wish you would tell me truthfully what are *my* faults?"

In another mood, I would have found this amusing, and even rather touching. As it was, I only thought: "She's fishing," and I snapped:

"I don't know what you mean by 'faults.' I don't judge people on a half-term-report basis. You'd better ask one of your teachers."

This shut Natalia up for the moment. But presently, she started again. Had I read any of the books she'd lent me?

I hadn't, but said: Yes, I'd read Jacobsen's *Frau Marie Grubbe.*

And what did I think of it?

"It's very good," I said, peevish because guilty.

Natalia looked at me sharply: "I'm afraid you are vairy insincere. You do not give your real meaning."

I was suddenly, childishly cross:

"Of course I don't. Why should I? Arguments bore me. I don't intend to say anything which you're likely to disagree with."

"But if that is so," she was really dismayed, "then it is no use for us to speak of anything seriously."

"Of course it isn't."

"Then shall we not talk at all?" asked poor Natalia.

"The best of all," I said, "would be for us to make noises like farmyard animals. I like hearing the sound of your voice, but I don't care a bit what you're saying. So it'd be far better if we just said *Bow-wow* and *Baa* and *Meaow.*"

Natalia flushed. She was bewildered and deeply hurt. Presently, after a long silence, she said: "Yes. I see."

As we approached her house, I tried to patch things up and turn the whole business into a joke, but she didn't respond. I went home feeling very much ashamed of myself.

Some days after this, however, Natalia rang up of her own accord and asked me to lunch. She opened the door herself—she had evidently been waiting to do so—and greeted me by exclaiming: "Bow-wow! Baa! Meaow!"

For a moment, I really thought she must have gone mad. Then I remembered our quarrel. But Natalia, having made her joke, was quite ready to be friends again.

We went into the sitting-room, and she began putting aspirin tablets into the bowls of flowers—to revive them, she said. I asked what she'd been doing during the last few days.

"All this week," said Natalia, "I am not going in the school. I have been unwell. Three days ago, I stand there by the piano, and suddenly I fall down—so. How do you say—*ohnmächtig*?"

"You mean, you fainted?"

Natalia nodded vigorously: "Yes, that's right. I am *ohnmächtig.*"

"But in that case you ought to be in bed now." I felt suddenly very masculine and protective: "How are you feeling?"

Natalia laughed gaily, and, certainly, I had never seen her looking better:

"Oh, it's not so important!

"There is one thing I must tell you," she added. "It shall be a nice surprise for you, I think—today is coming my father, and my cousin Bernhard."

"How very nice."

"Yes! Is it not? My father makes us great joy when he comes, for now he is often on travel. He has much business everywhere, in Paris, in Vienna, in Prague. Always he must be going in the train. You shall like him, I think."

"I'm certain I shall."

And sure enough, when the glass doors parted, there was Herr Landauer, waiting to receive me. Beside him stood Bernhard Landauer, Natalia's cousin, a tall pale young man in a dark suit, only a few years older than myself. "I am very pleased to make your acquaintance," Bernhard said, as we shook hands. He spoke English without the faintest trace of a foreign accent.

Herr Landauer was a small lively man, with dark leathery wrinkled skin, like an old well-polished boot. He had shiny brown boot-button eyes and low-comedian's eyebrows—so thick and black that they looked as if they had been touched up with burnt cork. It was evident that he adored his family. He opened the door for Frau Landauer in a way which suggested that she was a very beautiful young girl. His benevolent, delighted smile embraced the whole party—Natalia sparkling with joy at her father's return, Frau Landauer faintly flushed, Bernhard smooth and pale and politely enigmatic: even I myself was included. Indeed, Herr Landauer addressed almost the whole of his conversation to me, carefully avoiding any reference to family affairs which might have reminded me that I was a stranger at his table.

"Thirty-five years ago I was in England," he told me, speaking with a strong accent, "I came to your capital to write a thesis for my doctorate, on the condition of Jewish workers in the East End of London. I saw a great deal that your English officials did not desire me to see. I was quite a young fellow then: younger, I suspect, than you are today. I had some exceedingly interesting conversations with dock-hands and prostituted women and the keepers of your so-called Public Houses. Very interesting ..." Herr Landauer smiled reminiscently: "And this insignificant little thesis of mine caused a great deal of discussion. It has been translated into no less than five languages."

"Five languages!" repeated Natalia, in German, to me. "You see, my father is a writer, too!"

"Ah, that was thirty-five years ago! Long before you were

born, my dear." Herr Landauer shook his head deprecatingly, his boot-button eyes twinkling with benevolence: "Now I have not the time for such studies." He turned to me again: "I have just been reading a book in the French language about your great English poet, Lord Byron. A most interesting book. Now I should be very glad to have your opinion, as a writer, on this most important question—was Lord Byron guilty of the crime of incest? What do you think, Mr Isherwood?"

I felt myself beginning to blush. For some odd reason, it was the presence of Frau Landauer, placidly chewing her lunch, not of Natalia, which chiefly embarrassed me at this moment. Bernhard kept his eyes on his plate, subtly smiling. "Well," I began, "it's rather difficult ..."

"This is a very interesting problem," interrupted Herr Landauer, looking benevolently round upon us all and masticating with the greatest satisfaction. "Shall we allow that the man of genius is an exceptional person who may do exceptional things? Or shall we say: No—you may write a beautiful poem or paint a beautiful picture, but in your daily life, you must behave like an ordinary person, and you must obey these laws which we have made for ordinary persons? We will not allow you to be *extra*-ordinary." Herr Landauer fixed each of us in turn, triumphantly, his mouth full of food. Suddenly his eyes focused beamingly upon me: "Your dramatist Oscar Wilde ... this is another case. I put this case to you Mr Isherwood. I should like very much to hear your opinion. Was your English Law justified in punishing Oscar Wilde, or was it not justified? Please tell me what you think?"

Herr Landauer regarded me delightedly, a forkful of meat poised half-way up to his mouth. In the background, I was aware of Bernhard, discreetly smiling.

"Well ..." I began, feeling my ears burning red. This time, however, Frau Landauer unexpectedly saved me, by making a remark to Natalia in German, about the vegetables. There was a little discussion, during which Herr Landauer seemed to forget all about his question. He went on eating contentedly. But now Natalia must needs chip in:

"Please tell my father the name of your book. I could not remember it. It's such a funny name."

I tried to direct a private frown of disapproval at her which the others would not notice. "*All the Conspirators*," I said, coldly.

"*All the Conspirators* ... oh, yes, of course!"

"Ah, you write criminal romances, Mr Isherwood?" Herr Landauer beamed approvingly.

"I'm afraid this book has nothing to do with criminals," I said, politely. Herr Landauer looked puzzled and disappointed: "Not to do with criminals?"

"You will explain to him, please," Natalia ordered.

I drew a long breath: "The title was meant to be symbolic ... It's taken from Shakespeare's *Julius Caesar* ..."

Herr Landauer brightened at once: "Ah, Shakespeare! Splendid! This is most interesting ..."

"In German," I smiled slightly at my own cunning: I was luring him down a side-track, "you have wonderful translations of Shakespeare, I believe?"

"Indeed, yes! These translations are among the finest works in our language. Thanks to them, your Shakespeare has become, as it were, almost a German poet ..."

"But you do not tell," Natalia persisted, with what seemed really devilish malice, "what was your book about?"

I set my teeth: "It's about two young men. One of them is an artist and the other a student of medicine."

"Are these the only two persons in your book, then?" Natalia asked.

"Of course not ... But I'm surprised at your bad memory. I told you the whole story only a short time ago."

"Imbecile! It is not for myself I ask. Naturally, I remember all what you have told me. But my father has not yet heard. So you will please tell ... And what is then?"

"The artist has a mother and a sister. They are all very unhappy."

"But why are they unhappy? My father and my mother and I, we are not unhappy."

I wished the earth would swallow her: "Not all people are alike," I said carefully, avoiding Herr Landauer's eye.

"Good," said Natalia. "They are unhappy ... And what is then?"

"The artist runs away from home and his sister gets married to a very unpleasant young man."

Natalia evidently saw that I wouldn't stand much more of this. She delivered one final pin-prick: "And how many copies did you sell?"

"Five."

"Five! But that is very few, isn't it?"

"Very few indeed."

At the end of lunch, it seemed tacitly understood that Bernhard and his uncle and aunt were to discuss family affairs together. "Do you like," Natalia asked me, "that we shall walk together a little?"

Herr Landauer took a ceremonial farewell of me: "At all times, Mr Isherwood, you are welcome under my roof." We both bowed profoundly. "Perhaps," said Bernhard, giving me his card, "you would come one evening and enliven my solitude for a little?" I thanked him and said that I should be delighted.

"And what do you think of my father?" Natalia asked, as soon as we were out of the house.

"I think he's the nicest father I've ever met."

"You do truthfully?" Natalia was delighted.

"Yes, truthfully."

"And now confess to me, my father shocked you when he was speaking of Lord Byron—no? You were quite red as a lobster in your cheeks."

I laughed: "Your father makes me feel old-fashioned. His conversation's so modern."

Natalia laughed triumphantly: "You see, I was right! You were shocked. Oh, I am so glad! You see, I say to my father: A vairy intelligent young man is coming here to see us—and so he wish to show you that he also can be modern and speak of all this subjects. You thought my father would be a stupid old man? Tell the truth, please."

"No," I protested. "I never thought that!"

"Well, he is not stupid, you see … He is vairy clever. Only he does not have so much time for reading, because he must work always. Sometimes he must work eighteen and nineteen hours in the day; it is tairrible … And he is the best father in the whole world!"

"Your cousin Bernhard is your father's partner, isn't he?"

Natalia nodded: "It is he who manages the store, here in Berlin. He also is vairy clever."

"I suppose you see a good deal of him?"

"No … It is not often that he comes to our house … He is a strange man, you know? I think he like to be vairy much alone. I am surprise when he ask you to make him a visit … You must be careful."

"Careful? Why on earth should I be careful?"

"He is vairy sarcastical, you see. I think perhaps he laugh at you."

"Well that wouldn't be very terrible, would it? Plenty of people laugh at me … You do, yourself, sometimes."

"Oh, I! That is different." Natalia shook her head solemnly: she evidently spoke from unpleasant experience. "When I laugh, it is to make fun, you know? But when Bernhard laugh at you, it is not nice …"

Bernhard had a flat in a quiet street not far from the Tiergarten. When I rang at the outer entrance, a gnome-like caretaker peeped up at me through a tiny basement window, asked whom I wished to visit, and finally, after regarding me for a few moments with profound mistrust, pressed a button releasing the lock of the outer door. This door was so heavy that I had to push it open with both hands; it closed behind me with a hollow boom, like the firing of a cannon. Then came a pair of doors opening into the courtyard, then the door of the Gartenhaus, then five flights of stairs, then the door of the flat.

Four doors to protect Bernhard from the outer world.

This evening he was wearing a beautifully embroidered kimono over his town clothes. He was not quite as I remembered him from our first meeting: I hadn't seen him, then, as being in the least oriental—the kimono, I suppose, brought this out. His over-civilized, prim, finely drawn, beaky profile gave him something of the air of a bird in a piece of Chinese embroidery. He was soft, negative, I thought, yet curiously potent, with the static potency of a carved ivory figure in a shrine. I noticed again his beautiful English, and the deprecatory gestures of his hands, as he showed me a twelfth-century sandstone head of Buddha from Khmer which stood at the foot of his bed—"keeping watch over my slumbers." On the low white bookcase were little Greek and Siamese and Indo-Chinese statuettes and stone heads, most of which Bernhard had brought home with him from his travels. Amongst volumes of Kunst-Geschichte, photographic reproductions and monographs on sculpture and antiquities, I saw Vachell's *The Hill* and Lenin's *What is to be done?* The flat might well have been in the depths of the country: you couldn't hear the faintest outside sound. A staid housekeeper in an apron served supper. I had soup, fish, a chop and savoury; Bernhard drank milk, ate only tomatoes and rusks.

We talked of London, which Bernhard had never visited, and of Paris, where he had studied for a time in a sculptor's atelier. In his youth, he had wanted to be a sculptor, "but," Bernhard sighed, smiled gently, "Providence has ordained otherwise."

I wanted to talk to him about the Landauer business, but didn't—fearing it might not be tactful. Bernhard himself referred to it, however, in passing: "You must pay us a visit, one day, it would interest you—for I suppose that it is interesting, if only as a contemporary economic phenomenon." He smiled, and his face was masked with exhaustion: the thought crossed my mind that he was perhaps suffering from a fatal disease.

After supper, he seemed brighter, however: he began telling me about his travels. A few years before, he had been right round the world—gently inquisitive, mildly satiric, poking his delicate beak-like nose into everything: Jewish village communities in Palestine, Jewish settlements on the Black Sea, revolutionary committees in India, rebel armies in Mexico. Hesitating, delicately choosing his words, he described a conversation with a Chinese ferryman about demons, and a barely credible instance of the brutality of the police in New York.

Four or five times during the evening, the telephone bell rang, and, on each occasion, it seemed that Bernhard was being asked for help and advice. "Come and see me tomorrow," he said, in his tired, soothing voice. "Yes ... I'm sure it can all be arranged ... And now, please don't worry any more. Go to bed and sleep. I prescribe two or three tablets of aspirin ..." He smiled softly, ironically. Evidently he was about to lend each of his applicants some money.

"And please tell me," he asked, just before I left, "if I am not being impertinent—what has made you come to live in Berlin?"

"To learn German," I said. After Natalia's warning, I wasn't going to trust Bernhard with the history of my life.

"And are you happy here?"

"Very happy."

"That is wondeful, I think ... Most wonderful ..." Bernhard laughed his gentle ironical laugh: "A spirit possessed of such vitality that it can be happy, even in Berlin. You must teach me your secret. May I sit at your feet and learn wisdom?"

His smile contracted, vanished. Once again, the impassivity of mortal weariness fell like a shadow across his strangely youthful face. "I hope," he said, "that you will ring me up whenever you have nothing better to do."

Soon after this, I went to call on Bernhard at the business.

Landauers' was an enormous steel and glass building, not far from the Potsdamer Platz. It took me nearly a quarter of an hour to find my way through departments of underwear, outfitting, electrical appliances, sport and cutlery to the private world behind the scenes—the wholesale, travellers' and buying rooms, and Bernhard's own little suite of offices. A porter showed me into a small waiting-room, panelled in some highly polished streaky wood, with a rich blue carpet and one picture, an engraving of Berlin in the year 1803. After a few moments, Bernhard himself came in. This morning, he looked younger, sprucer, in a bow-tie and a light grey suit. "I hope that you give your approval to this room," he said. "I think that, as I keep so many people waiting here, they ought at least to have a more or less sympathetic atmosphere to allay their impatience."

"It's very nice," I said, and added, to make conversation—for I was feeling a little embarrassed: "What kind of wood is this?"

"Caucasian Nut." Bernhard pronounced the words with his characteristic primness, very precisely. He grinned suddenly. He seemed, I thought, in much better spirits: "Come and see the shop."

In the hardware department, an overalled woman demonstrator was exhibiting the merits of a patent coffee-strainer. Bernhard stopped to ask her how the sales were going, and she offered us cups of coffee. While I sipped mine, he explained that I was a well-known coffee-merchant from London, and that my opinion would therefore be worth having. The woman half believed this, at first, but we both laughed so much that she became suspicious. Then Bernhard dropped his coffee-cup and broke it. He was quite distressed and apologized profusely. "It doesn't matter," the demonstrator reassured him—as though he were a minor employee who might get sacked for his clumsiness: "I've got two more."

Presently we came to the toys. Bernhard told me that he and his uncle wouldn't allow toy soldiers or guns to be sold at Landauers'. Lately, at a directors' meeting, there had been a heated argument about toy tanks, and Bernhard had succeeded in getting his own way. "But this is really the thin end of the wedge," he added, sadly, picking up a toy tractor with caterpillar wheels.

Then he showed me a room in which children could play while their mothers were shopping. A uniformed nurse was helping two little boys to build a castle of bricks. "You observe," said Bernhard, "that philanthropy is here combined with advertisement. Opposite this room, we display specially cheap and attractive hats. The mothers who bring their children here fall immediately into temptation ... I'm afraid you will think us sadly materialistic ..."

I asked why there was no book department.

"Because we dare not have one. My uncle knows that I should remain there all day."

All over the stores, there were brackets of coloured lamps, red, green, blue and yellow. I asked what they were for, and Bernhard explained that each of these lights was the signal for one of the heads of the firm: "I am the blue light. That is, perhaps, to some degree, symbolic." Before I had time to ask what he meant, the blue lamp we were looking at began to flicker. Bernhard went to the nearest telephone and was told that somebody wished to speak to him in his office. So we said goodbye. On the way out, I bought a pair of socks.

During the early part of that winter, I saw a good deal of Bernhard. I cannot say that I got to know him much better through these evenings spent together. He remained curiously remote from me—his face impassive with exhaustion under the shaded lamplight, his gentle voice moving on through sequences of mildly humorous anecdotes. He would describe, for instance, a lunch with some friends who were very strict Jews. "Ah," Bernhard had said, conversationally, "so we're having lunch out of doors today? How delightful! The weather's still so warm for the time of year, isn't it? And your garden's looking lovely." Then, suddenly, it had occurred to him that his hosts were regarding him rather sourly, and he remembered, with horror, that this was the Feast of Tabernacles.

I laughed. I was amused. Bernhard told stories very well. But, all the time, I was aware of feeling a certain impatience. Why does he treat me like a child? I thought. He treats us all as children—his uncle and aunt, Natalia and myself. He tells us stories. He is sympathetic, charming. But his gestures, offering me a glass of wine or a cigarette, are clothed in arrogance, in the arrogant humility of the East. He is not going to tell me what he is really thinking or feeling, and he despises me because I do not know. He will never tell me anything about himself, or about the things which are most important to him. And because I am not as he is, because I am the opposite of this, and would gladly share my thoughts and sensations with forty million people if they cared to read them, I half admire Bernhard but also half dislike him.

We seldom talked about the political condition of Germany, but, one evening, Bernhard told me a story of the days of the civil war. He had been visited by a student friend who was taking part in the fighting. The student was very nervous and refused to sit down. Presently he confessed to Bernhard that he had been ordered to take a message through to one of the newspaper office-buildings which the police were besieging; to reach this office, it would be necessary to climb and crawl over roofs which were exposed to machine-gun fire. Naturally, he wasn't anxious to start. The student was wearing a remarkably thick overcoat, which Bernhard pressed him to take off, for the room was well heated and his face was literally streaming with sweat. At length, after much hesitation, the student did so, revealing, to Bernhard's intense alarm, that the lining of the coat was fitted with inside pockets stuffed full of hand-grenades. "And the worst of it was," said Bernhard, "that he'd made up his mind not to take any more risks, but to leave the overcoat with me. He wanted to put it into the bath and turn on the cold-water tap. At last I persuaded him that it would be much better to take it out after dark and to drop it into the canal—and this he ultimately succeeded in doing ... He is now one of the most distinguished professors in a certain provincial university. I am sure that he has long since forgotten this somewhat embarrassing escapade ..."

"Were *you* ever a communist, Bernhard?" I asked.

At once—I saw it in his face—he was on the defensive. After a moment, he said slowly:

"No, Christopher. I'm afraid I was always constitutionally incapable of bringing myself to the required pitch of enthusiasm."

I felt suddenly impatient with him; angry, even: "—ever to believe in anything?"

Bernhard smiled faintly at my violence. It may have amused him to have roused me like this.

"Perhaps ..." Then he added, as if to himself: "No ... that is not quite true ..."

"What *do* you believe in, then?" I challenged.

Bernhard was silent for some moments, considering this—his beaky delicate profile impassive, his eyes half-closed. At last he said: "Possibly I believe in discipline."

"In discipline?"

"You don't understand that, Christopher? Let me try to explain ... I believe in discipline for myself, not necessarily for others. For others, I cannot judge. I know only that I myself must have certain standards which I obey and without which I am quite lost ... Does that sound very dreadful?"

"No," I said—thinking: He is like Natalia.

"You must not condemn me too harshly, Christopher." The mocking smile was spreading over Bernhard's face. "Remember that I am a cross-breed. Perhaps, after all, there is one drop of pure Prussian blood in my polluted veins. Perhaps this little finger," he held it up to the light, "is the finger of a Prussian drill-sergeant ... You, Christopher, with your centuries of Anglo-Saxon freedom behind you, with your Magna Carta engraved upon your heart, cannot understand that we poor barbarians need the stiffness of a uniform to keep us standing upright."

"Why do you always make fun of me, Bernhard?"

"Make fun of you, my dear Christopher! I shouldn't dare!"

Yet, perhaps, on this occasion, he told me a little more than he had intended.

I had long meditated the experiment of introducing Natalia to Sally Bowles. I think I knew beforehand what the result of their meeting would be. At any rate, I had the sense not to invite Fritz Wendel.

We were to meet at a smart café in the Kurfürstendamm. Natalia was the first to arrive. She was a quarter of an hour late—probably because she'd wanted to have the advantage of coming last. But she had reckoned without Sally: she hadn't the nerve to be late in the grand manner. Poor Natalia! She had tried to make herself look more grown-up—with the result that she appeared merely rather dowdy. The long townified dress she'd put on didn't suit her at all. On the side of her head, she had planted a little hat—an unconscious parody of Sally's page-boy cap. But Natalia's hair was much too fuzzy for it: it rode the waves like a half-swamped boat on a rough sea.

"How do I look?" she immediately asked, sitting down opposite to me, rather flurried.

"You look very nice."

"Tell me, please, truthfully, what will she think of me?"

"She'll like you very much."

"How can you say that?" Natalia was indignant. "You do not know!"

"First you want my opinion, and then you say I don't know!"

"Imbecile! I do not ask for compliments!"

"I'm afraid I don't understand what you *do* ask for."

"Oh no?" cried Natalia scornfully. "You do not understand? Then I am sorry. I can't help you!"

At this moment, Sally arrived.

"Hilloo, darling," she exclaimed, in her most cooing accents, "I'm *terribly* sorry I'm late—can you forgive me?" She sat down daintily, enveloping us in wafts of perfume, and began, with languid miniature gestures, to take off her gloves:

"I've been making love to a dirty old Jew producer. I'm hoping he'll give me a contract—but no go, so far ..."

I kicked Sally hastily, under the table, and she stopped short, with an expression of absurd dismay—but now, of course, it was too late. Natalia froze before our eyes. All I'd said and hinted beforehand, in hypothetic pre-excuse of Sally's conduct, was instantly made void. After a moment's glacial pause, Natalia asked me if I'd seen *Sous les Toits de Paris.* She spoke German. She wasn't going to give Sally a chance of laughing at her English.

Sally immediately chipped in, however, quite unabashed. *She'd* seen the film, and thought it was marvellous, and wasn't Prejean marvellous, and did we remember the scene where a train goes past in the background while they're starting to fight? Sally's German was so much more than usually awful that I wondered whether she wasn't deliberately exaggerating it in order, somehow, to make fun of Natalia.

During the rest of the interview I suffered mental pins and needles. Natalia hardly spoke at all. Sally prattled on in her murderous German, making what she imagined to be light general conversation, chiefly about the English film industry. But as every anecdote involved explaining that somebody was someone else's mistress, that this one drank and that one took drugs, this didn't make the atmosphere any more agreeable. I found myself getting increasingly annoyed with both of them—with Sally for her endless silly pornographic talk; with Natalia for being such a prude. At length, after what seemed an eternity but was, in fact, barely twenty minutes, Natalia said that she must be going.

"My God, so must I!" cried Sally, in English. "Chris, darling, you'll take me as far as the Eden, won't you?"

In my cowardly way, I glanced at Natalia, trying to convey my helplessness. This, I knew only too well, was going to be regarded as a test of my loyalty—and, already, I had failed it. Natalia's expression showed no mercy. Her face was set. She was very angry indeed.

"When shall I see you?" I ventured to ask.

"I don't know," said Natalia—and she marched off down the Kurfürstendamm as if she never wished to set eyes on either of us again.

Although we had only a few hundred yards to go, Sally insisted that we must take a taxi. It would never do, she explained, to arrive at the Eden on foot.

"That girl didn't like me much, did she?" she remarked, as we were driving off.

"No, Sally. Not much."

"I'm sure I don't know why ... I went out of my way to be nice to her."

"If that's what you call being nice ...!" I laughed, in spite of my vexation.

"Well, what ought I to have done?"

"It's more a question of what you ought *not* to have done ... Haven't you *any* small-talk except adultery?"

"People have got to take me as I am," retorted Sally, grandly.

"Finger-nails and all?" I'd noticed Natalia's eyes returning to them again and again, in fascinated horror.

Sally laughed: "Today, I specially didn't paint my toe-nails."

"Oh, rot, Sally! Do you really?"

"Yes, of course I do."

"But what on earth's the point? I mean, nobody—" I corrected myself, "very few people can see them ..."

Sally gave me her most fatuous grin: "I know, darling ... But it makes me feel so marvellously sensual ..."

From this meeting, I date the decline of my relations with Natalia. Not that there was ever any open quarrel between us, or definite break. Indeed, we met again only a few days later; but at once I was aware of a change in the temperature of our friendship. We talked, as usual, of art, music, books—carefully avoiding the personal note. We had been walking about the Tiergarten for the best part of an hour, when Natalia abruptly asked:

"You like Miss Bowles vairy much?" Her eyes, fixed on the leaf-strewn path, were smiling maliciously.

"Of course I do ... We're going to be married, soon."

"Imbecile!"

We marched on for several minutes in silence.

"You know," said Natalia suddenly, with the air of one who makes a surprising discovery: "I do not like your Miss Bowles?"

"I know you don't."

My tone vexed her—as I intended that it should: "What I think, it is not of importance?"

"Not in the least," I grinned teasingly.

"Only your Miss Bowles, she is of importance?"

"She is of great importance."

Natalia reddened and bit her lip. She was getting angry: "Some day, you will see that I am right."

"I've no doubt I shall."

We walked all the way back to Natalia's home without exchanging a single word. On the doorstep, however, she asked, as usual: "Perhaps you will ring me up, one day ..." then paused, delivered her parting shot: "if your Miss Bowles permits?"

I laughed: "Whether she permits or not, I shall ring you up very soon." Almost before I had finished speaking, Natalia had shut the door in my face.

Nevertheless, I didn't keep my word. It was a month before I finally dialled Natalia's number. I had half intended to do so, many times, but, always, my disinclination had been stronger than my desire to see her again. And when, at length, we did meet, the temperature had dropped several degrees lower still; we seemed mere acquaintances. Natalia was convinced, I suppose, that Sally had become my mistress, and I didn't see why I should correct her mistake—doing so would only have involved a long heart-to-heart talk for which I simply wasn't in the mood. And, at the end of all the explanations, Natalia would probably have found herself quite as much shocked as she was at present, and a good deal more jealous. I didn't flatter myself that Natalia had ever wanted me as a lover, but she had certainly begun to behave towards me as a kind of bossy elder sister, and it was just this rôle—absurdly enough—which Sally had stolen from her. No, it was a pity, but on the whole, I decided, things were better as they were. So I played up to Natalia's indirect questions and insinuations, and even let drop a few hints of domestic bliss: "When Sally and I were having breakfast together, this morning ..." or "How do you like this tie? Sally chose it ..." Poor Natalia received them in glum silence; and, as so often before, I felt guilty and unkind. Then, towards the end of February, I rang up her home, and was told that she'd gone abroad.

Bernhard, too, I hadn't seen for some time. Indeed, I was quite surprised to hear his voice on the telephone one morning. He wanted to know if I would go with him that evening "into the country" and spend the night. This sounded very mysterious, and Bernhard only laughed when I tried to get out of him where we were going and why.

He called for me about eight o'clock, in a big closed car with a chauffeur. The car, Bernhard explained, belonged to the business. Both he and his uncle used it. It was typical, I thought, of the patriarchal simplicity in which the Landauers lived that Natalia's parents had no private car of their own, and that Bernhard even seemed inclined to apologize to me for the existence of this one. It was a complicated simplicity, the negation of a negation. Its roots were entangled deep in the awful guilt of possession. Oh dear, I sighed to myself, shall I ever get to the bottom of these people, shall I ever understand them? The mere act of thinking about the Landauers' psychic make-up overcame me, as always, with a sense of absolute, defeated exhaustion.

"You are tired?" Bernhard asked, solicitous, at my elbow.

"Oh no ..." I roused myself. "Not a bit."

"You will not mind if we call first at the house of a friend of mine? There is somebody else coming with us, you see ... I hope you don't object."

"No, of course not," I said politely.

"He is very quiet. An old friend of the family." Bernhard, for some reason, seemed amused. He chuckled faintly to himself.

The car stopped outside a villa in the Fasanenstrasse. Bernhard rang the bell and was let in: a few moments later, he reappeared, carrying in his arms a Skye terrier. I laughed.

"You were exceedingly polite," said Bernhard, smiling. "All the same, I think I detected a certain uneasiness on your part ... Am I right?"

"Perhaps ..."

"I wonder whom you were expecting? Some terribly boring old gentleman, perhaps?" Bernhard patted the terrier. "But I fear, Christopher, that you are far too well bred ever to confess that to me now."

The car slowed down and stopped before the toll-gate of the Avus motor-road.

"Where are we going?" I asked. "I wish you'd tell me!"

Bernhard smiled his soft expansive Oriental smile: "I'm very mysterious, am I not?"

"Very."

"Surely it must be a wonderful experience for you to be driving away into the night, not knowing whither you are bound? If I tell you that we are going to Paris, or to Madrid, or to Moscow, then there will no longer be any mystery and you will have lost half your pleasure ... Do you know, Christopher, I quite envy you because you do not know where we are going?"

"That's one way of looking at it, certainly ... But, at any rate, I know already we aren't going to Moscow. We're driving in the opposite direction."

Bernhard laughed: "You are very English sometimes, Christopher. Do you realize that, I wonder?"

"You bring out the English side of me, I think," I answered and immediately felt a little uncomfortable, as though this remark were somehow insulting. Bernhard seemed aware of my thought.

"Am I to understand that as a compliment, or as a reproof?"

"As a compliment, of course."

The car whirled along the black Avus, into the immense darkness of the winter countryside. Giant reflector signs glittered for a moment in the headlight beams, expired like burnt-out matches. Already Berlin was a reddish glow in the sky behind us, dwindling rapidly beyond a converging forest of pines. The searchlight on the Funkturm swung its little ray through the night. The straight black road roared headlong to meet us, as if to its destruction. In the upholstered darkness of the car, Bernhard was patting the restless dog upon his knees.

"Very well, I will tell you ... We are going to a place on the shores of the Wannsee which used to belong to my father. What you call in England a country cottage."

"A cottage? Very nice ..."

My tone amused Bernhard. I could hear from his voice that he was smiling:

"I hope you won't find it uncomfortable?"

"I'm sure I shall love it."

"It may seem a little primitive, at first ..." Bernhard laughed quietly to himself: "Nevertheless, it is amusing ..."

"It must be ..."

I suppose I had been vaguely expecting a hotel, lights, music, very good food. I reflected bitterly that only a rich, decadently over-civilized town-dweller would describe camping out for the night in a poky, damp country cottage in the middle of the winter as "amusing." And how typical that he should drive me to that cottage in a luxurious car! Where would the chauffeur sleep? Probably in the best hotel in Potsdam ... As we passed the lamps of the toll-house at the far end of the Avus, I saw that Bernhard was still smiling to himself.

The car swung to the right, downhill, along a road through silhouetted trees. There was a feeling of nearness to the big lake lying invisibly behind the woodland on our left. I had hardly realized that the road had ended in a gateway and a private drive: we pulled up at the door of a large villa.

"Where's this?" I asked Bernhard, supposing confusedly that he must have something else to call for—another terrier, perhaps. Bernhard laughed gaily:

"We have arrived at our destination, my dear Christopher! Out you get!"

A manservant in a striped jacket opened the door. The dog jumped out, and Bernhard and I followed. Resting his hand upon my shoulder, he steered me across the hall and up the stairs. I was aware of a rich carpet and framed engravings. He opened the door of a luxurious pink-and-white bedroom, with a luscious quilted silk eiderdown on the bed. Beyond was a bathroom, gleaming with polished silver, and hung with fleecy white towels.

Bernhard grinned:

"Poor Christopher! I fear you are disappointed in our cottage? It is too large for you, too ostentatious? You were looking forward to the pleasure of sleeping on the floor—amidst the black-beetles?"

The atmosphere of this joke surrounded us through dinner. As the manservant brought in each new course on its silver dish, Bernhard would catch my eye and smile a deprecatory smile. The dining-room was tame baroque, elegant, and rather colourless. I asked him when the villa had been built.

"My father built this house in 1904. He wanted to make it as much as possible like an English home—for my mother's sake ..."

After dinner, we walked down the windy garden, in the darkness. A strong wind was blowing up through the trees, from over the water. I followed Bernhard, stumbling against the body of the terrier which kept running between my legs, down flights of stone steps to a landing-stage. The dark lake was full of waves, and beyond, in the direction of Potsdam, a sprinkle of bobbing lights were comet-tailed in the black water. On the parapet, a dismantled gas-bracket rattled in the wind, and, below us, the waves splashed uncannily soft and wet, against unseen stone.

"When I was a boy, I used to come down these steps in the winter evenings and stand for hours here ..." Bernhard had begun to speak. His voice was pitched so low that I could hardly hear it; his face was turned away from me, in the darkness, looking out over the lake. When a stronger puff of wind blew, his words came more distinctly—as though the wind itself were talking: "That was during the War-time. My elder brother had been killed, right at the beginning of the War ... Later, certain business rivals of my father began to make propaganda against him, because his wife was an English woman, so that nobody would come to visit us, and it was rumoured that we were spies. At last, even the local tradespeople did not wish to call at the house ... It was all rather ridiculous, and at the same time rather terrible, that human beings could be possessed by such malice ..."

I shivered a little, peering out over the water. It was cold. Bernhard's soft, careful voice continued in my ear:

"I used to stand here on those winter evenings and pretend to myself that I was the last human being left alive in the world ... I was a queer sort of boy, I suppose ... I never got on well with other boys, although I wished very much to be popular and to have friends. Perhaps that was my mistake—I was too eager to be friendly. The boys saw this and it made them cruel to me. Objectively, I can understand that ... possibly I might even have been capable of cruelty myself, had circumstances been otherwise. It is difficult to say ... But, being what I was, school was a kind of Chinese torture ... So you can understand that I liked to come down here at night to the lake, and be alone. And then there was the War ... At this time, I believed that the War would go on for ten, or fifteen, or even twenty years. I knew that I myself should soon be called up. Curiously enough, I don't remember that I felt at all afraid. I accepted it. It seemed quite natural that we should all have to die. I suppose that this was the general wartime mentality. But I think that, in my case, there was also something characteristically Semitic in my attitude ... It is very difficult to speak quite impartially of these things. Sometimes one is unwilling to make certain admissions to oneself, because they are displeasing to one's self-esteem ..."

We turned slowly and began to climb the slope of the garden from the lake. Now and then, I heard the panting of the terrier, out hunting in the dark. Bernhard's voice went on, hesitating, choosing its words:

"After my brother had been killed, my mother scarcely ever left this house and its grounds. I think she tried to forget that such a land as Germany existed. She began to study Hebrew and to concentrate her whole mind upon ancient Jewish history and literature. I suppose that this is really symptomatic of a modern phase of Jewish development—this turning away from European culture and European traditions. I am aware of it, sometimes, in myself ... I remember my mother going about the house like a person walking in sleep. She grudged every moment which she did not spend at her studies, and this was rather terrible because, all the while, she was dying of cancer ... As soon as she knew what was the matter with her, she refused to see a doctor. She feared an operation ... At last, when the pain became very bad, she killed herself ..."

We had reached the house, Bernhard opened a glass door, and we passed through a little conservatory into a big drawing-room full of jumping shadows from the fire burning in an open English fireplace. Bernhard switched on a number of lamps, making the room quite dazzlingly bright.

"Need we have so much illumination?" I asked. "I think the firelight is much nicer."

"Do you?" Bernhard smiled subtly. "So do I ... But I thought, somehow, you would prefer the lamps."

"Why on earth should I?" I mistrusted his tone at once.

"I don't know. It's merely part of my conception of your character. How very foolish I am!"

Bernhard's voice was mocking. I made no reply. He got up

and turned out all but one small lamp on a table at my side. There was a long silence.

"Would you care to listen to the wireless?"

This time his tone made me smile: "You don't have to entertain me, you know! I'm perfectly happy just sitting here by the fire."

"If you are happy, then I am glad ... It was foolish of me—I had formed the opposite impression."

"What do you mean?"

"I was afraid, perhaps, that you were feeling bored."

"Of course not! What nonsense!"

"You are very polite, Christopher. You are always very polite. But I can read quite clearly what you are thinking ..." I had never heard Bernhard's voice sound like this, before; it was really hostile: "You are wondering why I brought you to this house. Above all, you are wondering why I told you what I told you just now."

"I'm glad you told me ..."

"No, Christopher. That is not true. You are a little shocked. One does not speak of such things, you think. It disgusts your English public-school training, a little—this Jewish emotionalism. You like to flatter yourself that you are a man of the world and that no form of weakness disgusts you, but your training is too strong for you. People ought not to talk to each other like this, you feel. It is not good form."

"Bernhard, you're being fantastic!"

"Am I? Perhaps ... But I do not think so. Never mind ... Since you wish to know, I will try to explain to you why I brought you here ... I wished to make an experiment."

"An experiment? Upon me, you mean?"

"No. An experiment upon myself. That is to say ... For ten years, I have never spoken intimately, as I have spoken to you tonight, to any human soul ... I wonder if you can put yourself in my place, imagine what that means? And this evening ... Perhaps, after all, it is impossible to explain ... Let me put it another way. I bring you down here, to this house, which has no associations for you. You have no reason to feel oppressed by the past. Then I tell you my story ... It is possible that, in this way, one can lay ghosts ... I express myself very badly. Does it sound very absurd as I say it?"

"No. Not in the least ... But why did you choose me for your experiment?"

"Your voice was very hard as you said that, Christopher. You are thinking that you despise me."

"No, Bernhard. I'm thinking that you must despise *me* ... I often wonder why you have anything to do with me at all. I feel sometimes that you actually dislike me, and that you say and do things to show it—and yet, in a way, I suppose you don't, or you wouldn't keep asking me to come and see you ... All the same, I'm getting rather tired of what you call your experiments. Tonight wasn't the first of them by any means. The experiments fail, and then you're angry with me. I must say, I think that's very unjust ... But what I can't stand is that you show your resentment by adopting this mock-humble attitude ... Actually, you're the least humble person I've ever met."

Bernhard was silent. He had lit a cigarette, and now expelled the smoke slowly through his nostrils. At last he said:

"I wonder if you are right ... I think not altogether. But partly ... Yes, there is some quality in you which attracts me and which I very much envy, and yet this very quality of yours also arouses my antagonism ... Perhaps that is merely because I also am partly English, and you represent to me an aspect of my own character ... No, that is not true, either ... It is not so simple as I would wish ... I'm afraid," Bernhard passed his hand, with a wearily humorous gesture, over his forehead and eyes, "that I am a quite unnecessarily complicated piece of mechanism."

There was a moment's silence. Then he added:

"But this is all stupid egotistical talk. You must forgive me. I have no right to speak to you in this way."

He rose to his feet, went softly across the room, and switched on the wireless. In rising, he had rested his hand for an instant on my shoulder. Followed by the first strains of the music, he came back to his chair before the fire, smiling. His smile was soft, and yet curiously hostile. It had the hostility of something ancient. I thought of one of the Oriental statuettes in his flat.

"This evening," he smiled softly, "they are relaying the last act of *Die Meistersinger*."

"Very interesting," I said.

Half an hour later, Bernhard took me up to my bedroom door, his hand upon my shoulder, still smiling. Next morning, at breakfast, he looked tired, but was gay and amusing. He did not in any way refer to our conversation of the evening before.

We drove back to Berlin, and he dropped me on the corner of the Nollendorfplatz.

"Ring me up soon," I said.

"Of course. Early next week."

"And thank you very much."

"Thank you for coming, my dear Christopher."

I didn't see him again for nearly six months.

One Sunday, early in August, a referendum was held to decide the fate of the Brüning government. I was back at Frl. Schroeder's; lying in bed through the beautiful hot weather, cursing my toe: I had cut it on a piece of tin, bathing for the last time at Ruegen, and now it had suddenly festered and was full of poison. I was quite delighted when Bernhard unexpectedly rang me up.

"You remember a certain little country cottage on the shores of the Wannsee? You do? I was wondering if you would care to spend a few hours there, this afternoon ... Yes, your landlady has told me already about your misfortune. I am so sorry ... I can send the car for you. I think it will be good to escape for a little from this city? You can do whatever you like there—just lie quiet and rest. Nobody will interfere with your liberty."

Soon after lunch, the car duly arrived to pick me up. It was a glorious afternoon, and, during the drive, I blessed Bernhard for his kindness. But, when we arrived at the villa, I got a nasty shock: the lawn was crowded with people.

I was really annoyed. It was a dirty trick, I thought. Here was I, in my oldest clothes, with a bandaged foot and a stick, lured into the middle of a slap-up garden-party! And here was Bernhard in flannel trousers and a boyish jumper. It was astonishing how young he looked. Bounding to meet me, he vaulted over the low railing:

"Christopher! Here you are at last! Make yourself comfortable!"

In spite of my protests, he forcibly removed my coat and hat. As ill-luck would have it, I was wearing braces. Most of the other guests were in smart Riviera flannels. Smiling sourly, adopting instinctively the armour of sulky eccentricity which protects me on such occasions, I advanced hobbling into their midst. Several couples were dancing to a portable gramophone; two young men were pillow-fighting with cushions, cheered on by their respective women; most of the party were lying chatting on rugs on the grass. It was all so very informal, and the footmen and the chauffeurs stood discreetly aside, watching their antics, like the nurse-maids of titled children.

What were they doing here? Why had Bernhard asked them? Was this another and more elaborate attempt to exorcize his ghosts? No, I decided; it was more probably only a duty-party, given once a year, to all the relatives, friends and dependants of the family. And mine was just another name to be ticked off, far down the list. Well, it was silly to be ungracious. I was here. I would enjoy myself.

Then, to my great surprise, I saw Natalia. She was dressed in some light yellow material, with small puffed sleeves, and carried a big straw hat in her hand. She looked so pretty that I should hardly have recognized her. She advanced gaily to welcome me:

"Ah, Christopher! You know, I am so pleased!"

"Where have you been, all this time?"

"In Paris ... You did not know? Truthfully? I await always a letter from you—and there is nothing!"

"But, Natalia, you never sent me your address."

"Oh, I did!"

"Well, in that case, I never got the letter ... I've been away too, you know."

"So? You have been away? Then I'm sorry ... I can't help you!"

We both laughed. Natalia's laugh had changed, like everything else about her. It was no longer the laugh of the severe schoolgirl who had ordered me to read Jacobsen and Goethe. And there was a dreamy, delighted smile upon her face—as though, I thought, she were listening, all the time, to lively, pleasant music. Despite her obvious pleasure at seeing me again, she seemed hardly to be attending to our conversation.

"And what are you doing in Paris? Are you studying art, as you wanted to?"

"But of course!"

"Do you like it?"

"Wonderful!" Natalia nodded vigorously. Her eyes were sparkling. But the word seemed intended to describe something else.

"Is your mother with you?"

"Yes. Yes ..."

"Have you got a flat together?"

"Yes ..." Again she nodded. "A flat ... Oh, it's wonderful!"

"And you go back there, soon?"

"Why, yes ... Of course! Tomorrow!" She seemed quite surprised that I should ask the question—surprised that the whole world didn't know ... How well I knew that feeling! I was certain, now: Natalia was in love.

We talked for several minutes more—Natalia always smiling, always dreamily listening, but not to me. Then, all at once, she was in a hurry. She was late, she said. She'd got to pack. She must go at once. She squeezed my hand, and I watched her run gaily across the lawn to a waiting car. She had forgotten, even, to ask me to write, or to give me her address. As I waved goodbye to her, my poisoned toe gave a sharp twinge of envy.

Later, the younger members of the party bathed, splashing about in the dirty lake-water at the foot of the stone stairs. Bernhard bathed, too. He had a white, strangely innocent body, like a baby's, with a baby's round, slightly protruding stomach. He laughed and splashed and shouted louder than anybody. When he caught my eye, he made more noise than ever—was it, I imagined, with a certain defiance? Was he thinking, as I was, of what he had told me, standing in this very place, six months ago? "Come in, too, Christopher!" he shouted. "It'll do your foot good!" When, at last, they had all come out of the water and were drying themselves, he and a few other young men chased each other, laughing, among the garden trees.

Yet, in spite of all Bernhard's frisking, the party didn't really "go." It split up into groups and cliques; and, even when the fun was at its height, at least a quarter of the guests were talking politics in low, serious voices. Indeed, some of them had so obviously come to Bernhard's house merely to meet each other and to discuss their own private affairs that they scarcely troubled to pretend to take part in the sociabilities. They might as well have been sitting in their own offices, or at home.

When it got dark, a girl began to sing. She sang in Russian, and, as always, it sounded sad. The footmen brought out glasses and a huge bowl of claret-cup. It was getting chilly on the lawn. There were millions of stars. Out on the great calm brimming lake, the last ghost-like sails were tacking hither and thither with the faint uncertain night-breeze. The gramophone played. I lay back on the cushions, listening to a Jewish surgeon who argued that France cannot understand Germany because the French have experienced nothing comparable to the neurotic post-War life of the German people. A girl laughed suddenly, shrilly, from the middle of a group of young men. Over there, in the city, the votes were being counted. I thought of Natalia: she has escaped—none too soon, perhaps. However often the decision may be delayed, all these people are ultimately doomed. This evening is the dress-rehearsal of a disaster. It is like the last night of an epoch.

At half past ten, the party began to break up. We all stood about in the hall or around the front door while someone telephoned through to Berlin to get the news. A few moments' hushed waiting, and the dark listening face at the telephone relaxed into a smile. The Government was safe, he told us. Several of the guests cheered, semi-ironical but relieved. I turned to find Bernhard at my elbow: "Once again, Capitalism is saved." He was subtly smiling.

He had arranged that I should be taken home in the dicky of a Berlin-bound car. As we came to the Tauentzienstrasse, they were selling papers with the news of the shooting on the Bülowplatz. I thought of our party lying out there on the lawn by the lake, drinking our claret-cup while the gramophone played; and of that police-officer, revolver in hand, stumbling mortally wounded up the cinema steps to fall dead at the feet of a cardboard figure advertising a comic film.

Another pause—eight months, this time. And here I was, ringing the bell of Bernhard's flat. Yes, he was in.

"This is a great honour, Christopher. And, unfortunately, a very rare one."

"Yes, I'm sorry. I've so often meant to come and see you … I don't know why I haven't …"

"You've been in Berlin all this time? You know, I rang up twice at Frl. Schroeder's, and a strange voice answered and said that you'd gone away to England."

"I told Frl. Schroeder that. I didn't want her to know that I was still here."

"Oh, indeed? You had a quarrel?"

"On the contrary. I told her that I was going to England, because, otherwise, she'd have insisted on supporting me. I got a bit hard up ... Everything's perfectly all right again, now," I added hastily, seeing a look of concern on Bernhard's face.

"Quite certain? I am very glad ... But what have you been doing with yourself, all this time?"

"Living with a family of five in a two-room attic in Hallesches Tor."

Bernhard smiled: "By Jove, Christopher—what a romantic life you lead!"

"I'm glad you call that kind of thing romantic. I don't!"

We both laughed.

"At any rate," Bernhard said, "it seems to have agreed with you. You're looking the picture of health."

I couldn't return the compliment. I thought I had never seen Bernhard looking so ill. His face was pale and drawn; the weariness did not lift from it even when he smiled. There were deep, sallow half-moons under his eyes. His hair seemed thinner. He might have added ten years to his age.

"And how have you been getting on?" I asked.

"My existence, in comparison with yours, is sadly humdrum, I fear ... Nevertheless, there are certain tragi-comic diversions."

"What sort of diversions?"

"This, for example—" Bernhard went over to his writing-desk, picked up a sheet of paper and handed it to me: "It arrived by post this morning."

I read the typed words:

> "Bernhard Landauer, beware. We are going to settle the score with you and your uncle and all other filthy Jews. We give you twenty-four hours to leave Germany. If not, you are dead men."

Bernhard laughed: "Bloodthirsty, isn't it?"

"It's incredible ... Who do you suppose sent it?"

"An employee who has been dismissed, perhaps. Or a practical joker. Or a madman. Or a hot-headed Nazi schoolboy."

"What shall you do?"

"Nothing."

"Surely you'll tell the police?"

"My dear Christopher, the police would very soon get tired of hearing such nonsense. We receive three or four such letters every week."

"All the same, this one may quite well be in earnest … The Nazis may write like schoolboys, but they're capable of anything. That's just why they're so dangerous. People laugh at them, right up to the last moment …"

Bernhard smiled his tired smile: "I appreciate very much this anxiety of yours on my behalf. Nevertheless, I am quite unworthy of it … My existence is not of such vital importance to myself or to others that the forces of the Law should be called upon to protect me … As for my uncle he is at present in Warsaw …"

I saw that he wished to change the subject:

"Have you any news of Natalia and Frau Landauer?"

"Oh yes, indeed! Natalia is married. Didn't you know? To a young French doctor … I hear that they are very happy."

"I'm so glad!"

"Yes … It's pleasant to think of one's friends being happy, isn't it?" Bernhard crossed to the waste-paper basket and dropped the letter into it: "Especially in another country …" He smiled, gently, and sadly.

"And what do you think will happen in Germany, now?" I asked. "Is there going to be a Nazi putsch or a communist revolution?"

Bernhard laughed: "You have lost none of your enthusiasm, I see! I only wish that this question seemed as momentous to me as it does to you …"

"It'll seem momentous enough, one of these fine mornings"—the retort rose to my lips: I am glad now that I didn't utter it. Instead, I asked: "Why do you wish that?"

"Because it would be a sign of something healthier in my own character … It is right, nowadays, that one should be interested in such things; I recognize that. It is sane. It is healthy … And because all this seems to me a little unreal, a little—please don't be offended, Christopher—trivial, I know that I am getting out of touch with existence. That is bad, of course … One must preserve a sense of proportion … Do you know, there are times when I sit here alone in the evenings, amongst these books and stone figures, and there comes to me such a strange sensation of unreality, as if this were my whole life? Yes, actually, sometimes, I have felt a doubt as to whether our firm—that great building packed from floor to roof with all our accumulation of property—really exists at all, except in my imagination … And then I have had an unpleasant feeling, such as one has in a dream, that I myself do not exist. It is very morbid, very unbalanced, no doubt … I will make a confession to you, Christopher … One evening, I was so much troubled by this hallucination of the non-existence of Landauers' that I picked up my telephone and had a long conversation with one of the night-watchmen, making some stupid excuse for having troubled him. Just to reassure myself, you understand? Don't you think I must be becoming insane?"

"I don't think anything of the kind … It could have happened to anyone who has overworked."

"You recommend a holiday? A month in Italy, just as the spring is beginning? Yes … I remember the days when a month of Italian sunshine would have solved all my troubles. But now, alas, that drug has lost its power. Here is a paradox for you! Landauers' is no longer real to me, yet I am more than ever its slave! You see the penalty of a life of sordid materialism. Take my nose away from the grindstone, and I become positively unhappy … Ah, Christopher, be warned by my fate!"

He smiled, spoke lightly, half banteringly. I didn't like to pursue the subject further.

"You know," I said, "I really *am* going to England, now. I'm leaving in three or four days."

"I am sorry to hear it. How long do you expect to stay there?"

"Probably the whole summer."

"You are tired of Berlin, at last?"

"Oh no ... I feel more as if Berlin had got tired of me."

"Then you will come back?"

"Yes, I expect so."

"I believe that you will always come back to Berlin, Christopher. You seem to belong here."

"Perhaps I do, in a way."

"It is strange how people seem to belong to places—especially to places where they were not born ... When I first went to China, it seemed to me that I was at home there, for the first time in my life ... Perhaps, when I die, my spirit will be wafted to Peking."

"It'd be better if you let a train waft your body there, as soon as possible!"

Bernhard laughed: "Very well ... I will follow your advice! But on two conditions—first, that you come with me; second, that we leave Berlin this evening."

"You mean it?"

"Certainly I do."

"What a pity! I should like to have come ... Unfortunately, I've only a hundred and fifty marks in the world."

"Naturally, you would be my guest."

"Oh, Bernhard, how marvellous! We'd stop a few days in Warsaw, to get the visas. Then on to Moscow, and take the trans-Siberian ..."

"So you'll come?"

"Of course!"

"This evening?"

I pretended to consider: "I'm afraid I can't, this evening ... I'd have to get my washing back from the laundry, first ... What about tomorrow?"

"Tomorrow is too late."

"What a pity!"

"Yes, isn't it?"

We both laughed. Bernhard seemed to be specially tickled by his joke. There was even something a little exaggerated in his laughter, as though the situation had some further dimension of humour to which I hadn't penetrated. We were still laughing when I said goodbye.

Perhaps I am slow at jokes. At any rate, it took me nearly eighteen months to see the point of this one—to recognize it as Bernhard's last, most daring and most cynical experiment upon us both. For now I am certain—absolutely convinced—that his offer was perfectly serious.

When I returned to Berlin, in the autumn of 1932, I duly rang Bernhard up, only to be told that he was away, on business, in Hamburg. I blame myself now—one always does blame oneself afterwards—for not having been more persistent. But there was so much for me to do, so many pupils, so many other people to see; the weeks turned into months; Christmas came—I sent Bernhard a card but got no answer: he was away again, most likely; and then the New Year began.

Hitler came, and the Reichstag fire, and the mock-elections. I wondered what was happening to Bernhard. Three times I rang him up—from call-boxes, lest I should get Frl. Schroeder into trouble: there was never any reply. Then, one evening early in April, I went round to his house. The caretaker put his head out of the tiny window, more suspicious than ever: at first, he seemed even inclined to deny that he knew Bernhard at all. Then he snapped: "Herr Landauer has gone away … gone right away."

"Do you mean he's moved from here?" I asked. "Can you give me his address?"

"He's gone away," the caretaker repeated, and slammed the window shut.

I left it at that—concluding, not unnaturally, that Bernhard was somewhere safe abroad.

On the morning of the Jewish boycott, I walked round to take a look at Landauers'. Things seemed very much as usual, superficially. Two or three uniformed S.A. boys were posted at each of the big entrances. Whenever a shopper approached, one of them would say: "Remember this is a Jewish business!" The boys were quite polite, grinning, making jokes among themselves. Little knots of passers-by collected to watch the performance—interested, amused or merely apathetic; still uncertain whether or not to approve. There was nothing of the atmosphere one read of later in the small provincial towns, where purchasers were forcibly disgraced with a rubber ink-stamp on the forehead and cheek. Quite a lot of people went into the building. I went in myself, bought the first thing I saw—it happened to be a nutmeg-grater—and strolled out again, twirling my small parcel. One of the boys at the door winked and said something to his companion. I remembered having seen him once or twice at the Alexander Casino, in the days when I was living with the Nowaks.

In May, I left Berlin for the last time. My first stop was at Prague—and it was there, sitting one evening alone, in a cellar restaurant, that I heard, indirectly, my last news of the Landauer family.

Two men. were at the next table, talking German. One of them was certainly an Austrian; the other I couldn't place—he was fat and sleek, about forty-five, and might well have owned a small business in any European capital, from Belgrade to Stockholm. Both of them were undoubtedly prosperous, technically Aryan, and politically neuter. The fat man startled me into attention by saying:

"You know Landauers'? Landauers' of Berlin?"

The Austrian nodded: "Sure I do ... Did a lot of business with them, one time ... Nice place they've got there. Must have cost a bit ..."

"Seen the papers, this morning?"

"No. Didn't have time ... Moving into our new flat, you know. The wife's coming back."

"She's coming back? You don't say! Been in Vienna, hasn't she?"

"That's right."

"Had a good time?"

"Trust her! It cost enough, anyway."

"Vienna's pretty dear, these days."

"It is that."

"Food's dear."

"It's dear everywhere."

"I guess you're right." The fat man began to pick his teeth: "What was I saying?"

"You were saying about Landauers'."

"So I was ... You didn't read the papers, this morning?"

"No, I didn't read them."

"There was a bit in about Bernhard Landauer."

"Bernhard?" said the Austrian. "Let's see—he's the son, isn't he?"

"I wouldn't know ..." The fat man dislodged a tiny fragment of meat with the point of his toothpick. Holding it up to the light, he regarded it thoughtfully.

"I think he's the son," said the Austrian. "Or maybe the nephew ... No, I think he's the son."

"Whoever he is," the fat man flicked the scrap of meat on to his plate with a gesture of distaste: "He's dead."

"You don't say!"

"Heart failure." The fat man frowned, and raised his hand to cover a belch. He was wearing three gold rings: "That's what the newspapers said."

"Heart failure!" The Austrian shifted uneasily in his chair: "You don't say!"

"There's a lot of heart failure," said the fat man, "in Germany these days."

The Austrian nodded: "You can't believe all you hear. That's a fact."

"If you ask me," said the fat man, "anyone's heart's liable to fail, if it gets a bullet inside it."

The Austrian looked very uncomfortable: "Those Nazis ..." he began.

"They mean business." The fat man seemed rather to enjoy making his friend's flesh creep. "You mark my words: they're going to clear the Jews right out of Germany. Right out."

The Austrian shook his head: "I don't like it."

"Concentration camps," said the fat man, lighting a cigar. "They get them in there, make them sign things ... Then their hearts fail."

"I don't like it," said the Austrian. "It's bad for trade."

"Yes," the fat man agreed. "It's bad for trade."

"Makes everything so uncertain."

"That's right. Never know who you're doing business with." The fat man laughed. In his own way, he was rather macabre: "It might be a corpse."

The Austrian shivered a little: "What about the old man, old Landauer? Did they get him, too?"

"No, he's all right. Too smart for them. He's in Paris."

"You don't say!"

"I reckon the Nazis'll take over the business. They're doing that, now."

"Then old Landauer'll be ruined, I guess?"

"Not him!" The fat man flicked the ash from his cigar, contemptuously. "He'll have a bit put by, somewhere. You'll see. He'll start something else. They're smart, those Jews ..."

"That's right," the Austrian agreed. "You can't keep a Jew down."

The thought seemed to cheer him, a little. He brightened: "That reminds me! I knew there was something I wanted to tell you ... Did you ever hear the story about the Jew and the Goy girl, with the wooden leg?"

"No." The fat man puffed at his cigar. His digestion was working well, now. He was in the right after-dinner mood: "Go ahead ..."

A Berlin Diary

Winter 1932–3

TONIGHT, FOR THE first time this winter, it is very cold. The dead cold grips the town in utter silence, like the silence of intense midday summer heat. In the cold the town seems actually to contract, to dwindle to a small black dot, scarcely larger than hundreds of other dots, isolated and hard to find, on the enormous European map. Outside, in the night, beyond the last new-built blocks of concrete flats, where the streets end in frozen allotment gardens, are the Prussian plains. You can feel them all round you, tonight, creeping in upon the city, like an immense waste of unhomely ocean—sprinkled with leafless copses and ice-lakes and tiny villages which are remembered only as the outlandish names of battlefields in half-forgotten wars. Berlin is a skeleton which aches in the cold: it is my own skeleton aching. I feel in my bones the sharp ache of the frost in the girders of the overhead railway, in the iron-work of balconies, in bridges, tramlines, lamp-standards, latrines. The iron throbs and shrinks, the stone and the bricks ache dully, the plaster is numb.

Berlin is a city with two centres—the cluster of expensive hotels, bars, cinemas, shops round the Memorial Church, a sparkling nucleus of light, like a sham diamond, in the shabby twilight of the town; and the self-conscious civic centre of buildings round the Unter den Linden, carefully arranged. In grand international styles, copies of copies, they assert our dignity as a capital city—a parliament, a couple of museums, a State bank, a cathedral, an opera, a dozen embassies, a triumphal arch; nothing has been forgotten. And they are all so pompous, so very correct—all except the cathedral, which betrays in its architecture, a flash of that hysteria which flickers always behind every grave, grey Prussian façade. Extinguished by its absurd dome, it is, at first sight, so startlingly funny that one searches for a name suitably preposterous—the Church of the Immaculate Consumption.

But the real heart of Berlin is a small damp black wood—the Tiergarten. At this time of the year, the cold begins to drive the peasant boys out of their tiny unprotected villages into the city, to look for food, and work. But the city, which glowed so brightly and invitingly in the night sky above the plains, is cold and cruel and dead. Its warmth is an illusion, a mirage of the winter desert. It will not receive these boys. It has nothing to give. The cold drives them out of its streets, into the wood which is its cruel heart. And there they cower on benches, to starve and freeze, and dream of their far-away cottage stoves.

Frl. Schroeder hates the cold. Huddled in her furlined velvet jacket, she sits in the corner with her stockinged feet on the stove. Sometimes she smokes a cigarette, sometimes she sips a glass of tea, but mostly she just sits, staring dully at the stove tiles in a kind of hibernation-doze. She is lonely, nowadays. Frl. Mayr is away in Holland, on a cabaret-tour. So Frl. Schroeder has nobody to talk to, except Bobby and myself.

Bobby, anyhow, is in deep disgrace. Not only is he out of work and three months behind with the rent, but Frl. Schroeder has reason to suspect him of stealing money from her bag. "You know, Herr Issyvoo," she tells me, "I shouldn't wonder at all if he didn't pinch those fifty marks from Frl. Kost ... He's quite capable of it, the pig! To think I could ever have been so mistaken in him! Will you believe it, Herr Issyvoo, I treated him as if he were my own son—and this is the thanks I get! He says he'll pay me every pfennig if he gets this job as barman at the Lady Windermere ... if, *if* ..." Frl. Schroeder sniffs with intense scorn: "I dare say! If my grandmother had wheels, she'd be an omnibus!"

Bobby has been turned out of his old room and banished to the "Swedish Pavilion." It must be terribly draughty, up there. Sometimes poor Bobby looks quite blue with cold. He has changed very much during the last year—his hair is thinner, his clothes are shabbier, his cheekiness has become defiant and rather pathetic. People like Bobby *are* their jobs—take the job away and they partially cease to exist. Sometimes, he sneaks into the living-room, unshaven, his hands in his pockets, and lounges about uneasily defiant, whistling to himself—the dance tunes he whistles are no longer quite new. Frl. Schroeder throws him a word, now and then, like a grudging scrap of bread, but she won't look at him or make any room for him by the stove. Perhaps she has never really forgiven him for his affair with Frl. Kost. The tickling and bottom-slapping days are over.

Yesterday we had a visit from Frl. Kost herself. I was out at the time: when I got back I found Frl. Schroeder quite excited. "Only think, Herr Issyvoo—I wouldn't have known her! She's quite the lady now! Her Japanese friend has bought her a fur coat—real fur, I shouldn't like to think what he must have paid for it! And her shoes—genuine snakeskin! Well, well, I bet she earned them! That's the one kind of business that still goes well, nowadays ... I think I shall have to take to the line myself!" But however much Frl. Schroeder might effect sarcasm at Frl. Kost's expense, I could see that she'd been greatly and not unfavourably impressed. And it wasn't so much the fur coat or the shoes which had impressed her:

Frl. Kost had achieved something higher—the hall-mark of respectability in Frl. Schroeder's world—she had had an operation in a private nursing home. "Oh, not what you think, Herr Issyvoo! It was something to do with her throat. Her friend paid for that, too, of course ... Only imagine—the doctors cut something out of the back of her nose; and now she can fill her mouth with water and squirt it out through her nostrils, just like a syringe! I wouldn't believe it at first—but she did it to show me! My word of honour, Herr Issyvoo, she could squirt it right across the kitchen! There's no denying, she's very much improved, since the time when she used to live here ... I shouldn't be surprised if she married a bank director one of these days. Oh, yes, you mark my words, that girl will go far ..."

Herr Krampf, a young engineer, one of my pupils, describes his childhood during the days of the War and the Inflation. During the last years of the War, the straps disappeared from the windows of railway carriages: people had cut them off in order to sell the leather. You even saw men and women going about in clothes made from carriage upholstery. A party of Krampf's school friends broke into a factory one night and stole all the leather driving-belts. Everybody stole. Everybody sold what they had to sell—themselves included. A boy of fourteen, from Krampf's class, peddled cocaine between school hours, in the streets.

Farmers and butchers were omnipotent. Their slightest whim had to be gratified, if you wanted vegetables or meat. The Krampf family knew of a butcher in a little village outside Berlin who always had meat to sell. But the butcher had a peculiar sexual perversion. His greatest erotic pleasure was to pinch and slap the cheeks of a sensitive, well-bred girl or woman. The possibility of thus humiliating a lady like Frau Krampf excited him enormously: unless he was allowed to realize his fantasy, he refused, absolutely, to do business. So, every Sunday, Krampf's mother would travel out to the village with her children, and patiently offer her cheeks to be slapped and pinched, in exchange for some cutlets or a steak.

At the far end of the Potsdamerstrasse, there is a fair-ground, with merry-go-rounds, swings, and peep-shows. One of the chief attractions of the fair-grounds is a tent where boxing and wrestling matches are held. You pay your money and go in, the wrestlers fight three or four rounds, and the referee then announces that, if you want to see any more, you must pay an extra ten pfennigs. One of the wrestlers is a bald man with a very large stomach: he wears a pair of canvas trousers rolled up at the bottoms, as though he were going paddling. His opponent wears black tights, and leather kneelets which look as if they had come off an old cab-horse. The wrestlers throw each other about as much as possible, turning somersaults in the air to amuse the audience. The fat man who plays the part of loser pretends to get very angry when he is beaten, and threatens to fight the referee.

One of the boxers is a Negro. He invariably wins. The boxers hit each other with the open glove, making a tremendous amount of noise. The other boxer, a tall, well-built young man, about twenty years younger and obviously much stronger than the Negro, is "knocked out" with absurd ease. He writhes in great agony on the floor, nearly manages to struggle to his feet at the count of ten, then collapses again, groaning. After this fight, the referee collects ten more pfennigs and calls for a challenger from the audience. Before any bona fide challenger can reply, another young man, who has been quite openly chatting and joking with the wrestlers, jumps hastily into the ring and strips off his clothes, revealing himself already dressed in shorts and boxer's boots. The referee announces a purse of five marks; and, this time, the Negro is "knocked out."

The audience took the fights dead seriously, shouting encouragement to the fighters, and even quarrelling and betting amongst themselves on the results. Yet nearly all of them had been in the tent as long as I had, and stayed on after I had left.

The political moral is certainly depressing: these people could be made to believe in anybody or anything.

Walking this evening along the Kleiststrasse, I saw a little crowd gathered round a private car. In the car were two girls: on the pavement stood two young Jews, engaged in a violent argument with a large blond man who was obviously rather drunk. The Jews, it seemed, had been driving slowly along the street, on the look-out for a pick-up, and had offered these girls a ride. The two girls had accepted and got into the car. At this moment, however, the blond man had intervened. He was a Nazi, he told us, and as such felt it his mission to defend the honour of all German women against the obscene anti-Nordic menace. The two Jews didn't seem in the least intimidated; they told the Nazi energetically to mind his own business. Meanwhile, the girls, taking advantage of the row, slipped out of the car and ran off down the street. The Nazi then tried to drag one of the Jews with him to find a policeman, and the Jew whose arm he had seized gave him an uppercut which laid him sprawling on his back. Before the Nazi could get to his feet, both young men had jumped into their car and driven away. The crowd dispersed slowly, arguing. Very few of them sided openly with the Nazi: several supported the Jews; but the majority confined themselves to shaking their heads dubiously and murmuring: "*Allerhand!*"

When, three hours later, I passed the same spot, the Nazi was still patrolling up and down, looking hungrily for more German womanhood to rescue.

We have just got a letter from Frl. Mayr: Frl. Schroeder called me in to listen to it. Frl. Mayr doesn't like Holland. She has been obliged to sing in a lot of second-rate cafés in third-rate towns, and her bedroom is often badly heated. The Dutch, she writes, have no culture; she has only met one truly refined and superior gentleman, a widower. The widower tells her that she is a really womanly woman—he has no use for young chits of girls. He has shown his admiration for her art by presenting her with a complete new set of underclothes.

Frl. Mayr has also had trouble with her colleagues. At one town, a rival actress, jealous of Frl. Mayr's vocal powers, tried to stab her in the eye with a hatpin. I can't help admiring that actress's courage. When Frl. Mayr had finished with her, she was so badly injured that she couldn't appear on the stage again for a week.

Last night, Fritz Wendel proposed a tour of the "dives." It was to be in the nature of a farewell visit, for the Police have begun to take a great interest in these places. They are frequently raided, and the names of their clients are written down. There is even talk of a general Berlin clean-up.

I rather upset him by insisting on visiting the Salomé, which I had never seen. Fritz, as a connoisseur of night-life, was most contemptuous. It wasn't even genuine, he told me. The management run it entirely for the benefit of provincial sightseers.

The Salomé turned out to be very expensive and even more depressing than I had imagined. A few stage lesbians and some young men with plucked eyebrows lounged at the bar, uttering occasional raucous guffaws or treble hoots—supposed, apparently, to represent the laughter of the damned. The whole premises are painted gold and inferno-red—crimson plush inches thick, and vast gilded mirrors. It was pretty full. The audience consisted chiefly of respectable middle-aged tradesmen and their families, exclaiming in good-humoured amazement: "Do they really?" and "Well, I never!" We went out half-way through the cabaret performance, after a young man in a spangled crinoline and jewelled breast-caps had painfully but successfully executed three splits.

At the entrance we met a party of American youths, very drunk, wondering whether to go in. Their leader was a small stocky young man in pince-nez, with an annoyingly prominent jaw.

"Say," he asked Fritz, "what's on here?"

"Men dressed as women," Fritz grinned.

The little American simply couldn't believe it. "Men dressed as *women*? As *women,* hey? Do you mean they're *queer*?"

"Eventually we're all queer," drawled Fritz solemnly, in lugubrious tones. The young man looked us over slowly. He had been running and was still out of breath. The others grouped themselves awkwardly behind him, ready for anything—though their callow, open-mouthed faces in the greenish lamp-light looked a bit scared.

"You *queer,* too, hey?" demanded the little American, turning suddenly on me.

"Yes," I said, "very queer indeed."

He stood there before me a moment, panting, thrusting out his jaw, uncertain, it seemed, whether he ought not to hit me in the face. Then he turned, uttered some kind of wild college battle-cry, and, followed by the others, rushed headlong into the building.

"Ever been to that communist dive near the Zoo?" Fritz asked me, as we were walking away from the Salomé. "Eventually we should cast an eye in there ... In six months, maybe, we'll all be wearing red shirts ..."

I agreed. I was curious to know what Fritz's idea of a "communist dive" would be like.

It was, in fact, a small whitewashed cellar. You sat on long wooden benches at big bare tables; a dozen people together—like a school dining-hall. On the walls were scribbled expressionist drawings involving actual newspaper clippings, real playing-cards, nailed-on-beer-mats, match-boxes, cigarette cartons, and heads cut out of photographs. The café was full of students, dressed mostly with aggressive political untidiness—the men in sailor's sweaters and stained baggy trousers, the girls in ill-fitting jumpers, skirts held visibly together with safety-pins and carelessly knotted gaudy gipsy scarves. The proprietress was smoking a cigar. The boy who acted as a waiter lounged about with a cigarette between his lips and slapped customers on the back when taking their orders.

It was all thoroughly sham and gay and jolly: you couldn't help feeling at home, immediately. Fritz, as usual, recognized plenty of friends. He introduced me to three of them—a man called Martin, an art student named Werner, and Inge, his girl. Inge was broad and lively—she wore a little hat with a feather in it which gave her a kind of farcical resemblance to Henry the Eighth. While Werner and Inge chattered, Martin sat silent: he was thin and dark and hatchet-faced with the sardonically superior smile of the conscious conspirator. Later in the evening, when Fritz and Werner and Inge had moved down the table to join another party, Martin began to talk about the coming civil war. When the war breaks out, Martin explained, the communists, who have very few machine-guns, will get command of the roof-tops. They will then keep the Police at bay with hand-grenades. It will only be necessary to hold out for three days, because the Soviet fleet will make an immediate dash for Swinemünde and begin to land troops. "I spend most of my time now making bombs," Martin added. I nodded and grinned, very much embarrassed—uncertain whether he was making fun of me, or deliberately committing some appalling indiscretion. He certainly wasn't drunk, and he didn't strike me as merely insane.

Presently, a strikingly handsome boy of sixteen or seventeen came into the café. His name was Rudi. He was dressed in a Russian blouse, leather shorts and despatch-rider's boots, and he strode up to our table with all the heroic mannerisms of a messenger who returns successful from a desperate mission. He had, however, no message of any kind to deliver. After his whirlwind entry, and a succession of curt, martial handshakes, he sat down quite quietly beside us and ordered a glass of tea.

This evening, I visited the "communist" café again. It is really a fascinating little world of intrigue and counter-intrigue. Its Napoleon is the sinister bomb-making Martin; Werner is its Danton; Rudi its Joan of Arc. Everybody suspects everybody else. Already Martin has warned me against Werner: he is "politically unreliable"—last summer he stole the entire funds of a communist youth organization. And Werner has warned me against Martin: he is either a Nazi agent, or a police spy, or in the pay of the French Government. In addition to this, both Martin and Werner earnestly advise me to have nothing to do with Rudi—they absolutely refuse to say why.

But there was no question of having nothing to do with Rudi. He planted himself down beside me and began talking at once—a hurricane of enthusiasm. His favourite word is "knorke": "Oh, *ripping*!" He is a pathfinder. He wanted to know what the boy scouts were like in England. Had they got the spirit of adventure? "All German boys are adventurous. Adventure is ripping. Our Scoutmaster is a ripping man. Last year he went to Lapland and lived in a hut, all through the summer, alone ... Are you a communist?"

"No. Are you?"

Rudi was pained.

"Of course! We all are, here ... I'll lend you some books, if you like ... You ought to come and see our clubhouse. It's ripping ... We sing the Red Flag, and all the forbidden songs ... Will you teach me English? I want to learn all languages."

I asked if there were any girls in his pathfinder group. Rudi was as shocked as if I'd said something really indecent.

"Women are no good," he told me bitterly. "They spoil everything. They haven't got the spirit of adventure. Men understand each other much better when they're alone together. Uncle Peter (that's our Scoutmaster) says women should stay at home and mend socks. That's all they're fit for!"

"Is Uncle Peter a communist, too?"

"Of course!" Rudi looked at me suspiciously. "Why do you ask that?"

"Oh, no special reason," I replied hastily. "I think perhaps I was mixing him up with somebody else ..."

This afternoon I travelled out to the reformatory to visit one of my pupils, Herr Brink, who is a master there. He is a small, broad-shouldered man, with the chin, dead-looking fair hair, mild eyes, and bulging, over-heavy forehead of the German vegetarian intellectual. He wears sandals and an open-necked shirt. I found him in the gymnasium, giving physical instruction to a class of mentally deficient children—for the reformatory houses mental deficients as well as juvenile delinquents. With a certain melancholy pride, he pointed out the various cases: one little boy was suffering from hereditary syphilis—he had a fearful squint; another, the child of elderly drunkards, couldn't stop laughing. They clambered about the wall-bars like monkeys, laughing and chattering, seemingly quite happy.

Then we went up to the workshop, where older boys in blue overalls—all convicted criminals—were making boots. Most of the boys looked up and grinned when Brink came in, only a few were sullen. But I couldn't look them in the eyes. I felt horribly guilty and ashamed: I seemed, at that moment, to have become the sole representative of their gaolers, of Capitalist Society. I wondered if any of them had actually been arrested in the Alexander Casino, and, if so, whether they recognized me.

We had lunch in the matron's room. Herr Brink apologized for giving me the same food as the boys themselves ate—potato soup with two sausages, and a dish of apples and stewed prunes. I protested—as, no doubt, I was intended to protest—that it was very good. And yet the thought of the boys having to eat it, or any other kind of meal, in that building made each spoonful stick in my throat. Institution food has an indescribable, perhaps purely imaginary, taste. (One of the most vivid and sickening memories of my own school life is the smell of ordinary white bread.)

"You don't have any bars or locked gates here," I said. "I thought all reformatories had them ... Don't your boys often run away?"

"Hardly ever," said Brink, and the admission seemed to make him positively unhappy; he sank his head wearily in his hands. "Where shall they run to? Here it is bad. At home it is worse. The majority of them know that."

"But isn't there a kind of natural instinct for freedom?"

"Yes, you are right. But the boys soon lose it. The system helps them to lose it. I think perhaps that, in Germans, this instinct is never very strong."

"You don't have much trouble here, then?"

"Oh, yes. Sometimes ... Three months ago, a terrible thing happened. One boy stole another boy's overcoat. He asked for permission to go into the town—that is allowed—and possibly he meant to sell it. But the owner of the overcoat followed him, and they had a fight. The boy to whom the overcoat belonged took up a big stone and flung it at the other boy; and this boy, feeling himself hurt, deliberately smeared dirt into the wound, hoping to make it worse and so escape punishment. The wound did get worse. In three days the boy died of blood-poisoning. And when the other boy heard of this he killed himself with a kitchen knife ..." Brink sighed deeply: "Sometimes I almost despair," he added. "It seems as if there were a kind of badness, a disease, infecting the world today."

"But what can you really do for these boys?" I asked.

"Very little. We teach them a trade. Later, we try to find them work—which is almost impossible. If they have work in the neighbourhood, they can still sleep here at nights ... The Principal believes that their lives can be changed through the teachings of the Christian religion. I'm afraid I cannot feel this. The problem is not so simple. I'm afraid that most of them, if they cannot get work, will take to crime. After all, people cannot be ordered to starve."

"Isn't there any alternative?"

Brink rose and led me to the window.

"You see those two buildings? One is the engineering-works, the other is the prison. For the boys of this district there used to be two alternatives ... But now the works are bankrupt. Next week they will close down."

This morning I went to see Rudi's clubhouse, which is also the office of a pathfinder's magazine. The editor and scoutmaster,

Uncle Peter, is a haggard, youngish man, with a parchment-coloured face and deeply sunken eyes, dressed in corduroy jacket and shorts. He is evidently Rudi's idol. The only time Rudi will stop talking is when Uncle Peter has something to say. They showed me dozens of photographs of boys, all taken with the camera tilted upwards, from beneath, so that they look like epic giants, in profile against enormous clouds. The magazine itself has articles on hunting, tracking, and preparing food—all written in super-enthusiastic style, with a curious underlying note of hysteria, as though the actions described were part of a religious or erotic ritual. There were half-a-dozen boys in the room with us: all of them in a state of heroic semi-nudity, wearing the shortest of shorts and the thinnest of shirts or singlets, although the weather is so cold.

When I had finished looking at the photographs, Rudi took me into the club-meeting room. Long coloured banners hung down the walls, embroidered with initials and mysterious totem devices. At one end of the room was a low table covered with a crimson embroidered cloth—a kind of altar. On the table were candles in brass candlesticks.

"We light them on Thursdays," Rudi explained, "when we have our camp-fire palaver. Then we sit round in a ring on the floor, and sing songs and tell stories."

Above the table with the candlesticks was a sort of icon—the framed drawing of a young pathfinder of unearthly beauty, gazing sternly into the far distance, a banner in his hand. The whole place made me fed profoundly uncomfortable. I excused myself and got away as soon as I could.

Overheard in a café: a young Nazi is sitting with his girl; they are discussing the future of the Party. The Nazi is drunk.

"Oh, I know we shall win, all right," he exclaims impatiently, "but that's not enough!" He thumps the table with his fist: "Blood must flow!"

The girl strokes his arm reassuringly. She is trying to get him to come home. "But, *of course,* it's going to flow, darling," she coos soothingly, "the Leader's promised that in our programme."

Today is "Silver Sunday." The streets are crowded with shoppers. All along the Tauentzienstrasse, men, women, and boys are hawking postcards, flowers, song-books, hair-oil, bracelets. Christmas-trees are stacked for sale along the central path between the tram-lines. Uniformed S.A. men rattle their collecting-boxes. In the side-streets, lorry-loads of police are waiting; for any large crowd, nowadays, is capable of turning into a political riot. The Salvation Army have a big illuminated tree on the Wittenbergplatz, with a blue electric star. A group of students were standing round it, making sarcastic remarks. Among them I recognized Werner, from the "communist" café.

"This time next year," said Werner, "that star will have changed its colour!" He laughed violently—he was in an excited, slightly hysterical mood. Yesterday, he told me, he'd had a great adventure: "You see, three other comrades and myself decided to make a demonstration at the Labour Exchange in Neukölln. I had to speak, and the others were to see I wasn't interrupted. We went round there at about half past ten, when the bureau's most crowded. Of course, we'd planned it all beforehand—each of the comrades had to hold one of the doors, so that none of the clerks in the office could get out. There they were, cooped up like rabbits ... Of course, we couldn't prevent their telephoning for the Police, we knew that. We reckoned we'd got about six or seven minutes ... Well, as soon as the doors were fixed, I jumped onto a table. I just yelled out whatever came into my head—I don't know what I said. They liked it, anyhow ... In half a minute I had them so excited I got quite scared. I was afraid they'd break into the office and lynch somebody. There was a fine old shindy, I can tell you! But just when things were beginning to look properly lively, a comrade came up from below to tell us the Police were there already—just getting out of their car. So we had to make a dash for it ... I think they'd have got us, only the crowd was on our side, and wouldn't let them through until we were out by the other door, into the street ..." Werner finished breathlessly. "I tell you, Christopher," he added, "the capitalist system can't possibly last much longer now. The workers are on the move."

Early this evening I was in the Bülowstrasse. There had been a big Nazi meeting at the Sportpalast, and groups of men and boys were just coming away from it, in their brown or black uniforms. Walking along the pavement ahead of me were three S.A. men. They all carried Nazi banners on their shoulders, like rifles, rolled tight around the staves—the banner-staves had sharp metal points, shaped into arrow-heads.

All at once, the three S.A. men came face to face with a youth of seventeen or eighteen, dressed in civilian clothes, who was hurrying along in the opposite direction. I heard one of the Nazis shout: "That's him!" and immediately all three of them flung themselves upon the young man. He uttered a scream, and tried to dodge, but they were too quick for him. In a moment they had jostled him into the shadow of a house entrance, and were standing over him, kicking him and stabbing at him with the sharp metal points of their banners. All this happened with such incredible speed that I could hardly believe my eyes—already, the three S.A. men had left their victim, and were barging their way through the crowd; they made for the stairs which led up to the station of the Overhead Railway.

Another passer-by and myself were the first to reach the doorway where the young man was lying. He lay huddled crookedly in the corner, like an abandoned sack. As they picked him up, I got a sickening glimpse of his face—his left eye was poked half out, and blood poured from the wound. He wasn't dead. Somebody volunteered to take him to the hospital in a taxi.

By this time, dozens of people were looking on. They

seemed surprised, but not particularly shocked—this sort of thing happened too often, nowadays. "*Allerhand...*" they murmured. Twenty yards away, at the Potsdamerstrasse corner, stood a group of heavily armed policemen. With their chests out, and their hands on their revolver belts, they magnificently disregarded the whole affair.

Werner has become a hero. His photograph was in the *Rote Fahne* a few days ago, captioned: "Another victim of the Police blood-bath." Yesterday, which was New Year's Day, I went to visit him in hospital.

Just after Christmas, it seems, there was a street-fight near the Stettiner Bahnhof. Werner was on the edge of the crowd, not knowing what the fight was about. On the off-chance that it might be something political, he began yelling: "Red Front!" A policeman tried to arrest him. Werner kicked the policeman in the stomach. The policeman drew his revolver and shot Werner three times through the leg. When he had finished shooting, he called another policeman, and together they carried Werner into a taxi. On the way to the police-station, the policemen hit him on the head with their truncheons, until he fainted. When he has sufficiently recovered, he will, most probably, be prosecuted.

He told me all this with the greatest satisfaction, sitting up in bed surrounded by his admiring friends, including Rudi and Inge, in her Henry the Eighth hat. Around him, on the blanket, lay his press-cuttings. Somebody had carefully underlined each mention of Werner's name with a red pencil.

Today, January 22nd, the Nazis held a demonstration on the Bülowplatz, in front of the Karl Liebknecht House. For the last week the communists have been trying to get the demonstration forbidden: they say it is simply intended as a provocation—as, of course, it was. I went along to watch it with Frank, the newspaper correspondent.

As Frank himself said afterwards, this wasn't really a Nazi

demonstration at all, but a Police demonstration—there were at least two policemen to every Nazi present. Perhaps General Schleicher only allowed the march to take place in order to show who are the real masters of Berlin. Everybody says he's going to proclaim a military dictatorship.

But the real masters of Berlin are not the Police, or the Army, and certainly not the Nazis. The masters of Berlin are the workers—despite all the propaganda I've heard and read, all the demonstrations I've attended, I only realized this for the first time today. Comparatively few of the hundreds of people in the streets round the Bülowplatz can have been organized communists, yet you had the feeling that every single one of them was united against this march. Somebody began to sing the "International," and, in a moment, everyone had joined in—even the women with their babies, watching from top-storey windows. The Nazis slunk past, marching as fast as they knew how, between their double rows of protectors. Most of them kept their eyes on the ground, or glared glassily ahead: a few attempted sickly, furtive grins. When the procession had passed, an elderly fat little S.A. man, who had somehow got left behind, came panting along at the double, desperately scared of finding himself alone, and trying vainly to catch up with the rest. The whole crowd roared with laughter.

During the demonstration nobody was allowed on the Bülowplatz itself. So the crowd surged uneasily about, and things began to look nasty. The police, brandishing their rifles, ordered us back; some of the less experienced ones, getting rattled, made as if to shoot. Then an armoured car appeared, and started to turn its machine-gun slowly in our direction. There was a stampede into house doorways and cafés; but no sooner had the car moved on, than everybody rushed out into the street again, shouting and singing. It was too much like a naughty schoolboy's game to be seriously alarming. Frank enjoyed himself enormously, grinning from ear to ear, and hopping about, in his flapping overcoat and huge owlish spectacles, like a mocking, ungainly bird.

•

Only a week since I wrote the above. Schleicher has resigned. The monocles did their stuff. Hitler has formed a cabinet with Hugenberg. Nobody thinks it can last till the spring.

The newspapers are becoming more and more like copies of a school magazine. There is nothing in them but new rules, new punishments, and lists of people who have been "kept in." This morning, Göring has invented three fresh varieties of high treason.

Every evening, I sit in the big half-empty artists' café by the Memorial Church, where the Jews and left-wing intellectuals bend their heads together over the marble tables, speaking in low, scared voices. Many of them know that they will certainly be arrested—if not today, then tomorrow or next week. So they are polite and mild with each other, and raise their hats and inquire after their colleagues' families. Notorious literary tiffs of several years' standing are forgotten.

Almost every evening, the S.A. men come into the café. Sometimes they are only collecting money; everybody is compelled to give something. Sometimes they have come to make an arrest. One evening a Jewish writer, who was present, ran into the telephone-box to ring up the Police. The Nazis dragged him out, and he was taken away. Nobody moved a finger. You could have heard a pin drop, till they were gone.

The foreign newspaper correspondents dine every night at the same little Italian restaurant, at a big round table, in the corner. Everybody else in the restaurant is watching them and trying to overhear what they are saying. If you have a piece of news to bring them—the details of an arrest, or the address of a victim whose relatives might be interviewed—then one of the journalists leaves the table and walks up and down with you outside, in the street.

A young communist I know was arrested by the S.A. men, taken to a Nazi barracks, and badly knocked about. After three or four days, he was released and went home. Next morning there was a knock at the door. The communist hobbled over to open it, his arm in a sling—and there stood a Nazi with a collecting-box. At the sight of him the communist completely lost his temper. "Isn't it enough," he yelled, "that you beat me up? And you dare to come and ask me for money?"

But the Nazi only grinned. "Now, now, comrade! No political squabbling! Remember, we're living in the Third Reich! We're all brothers! You must try and drive that silly political hatred from your heart!"

This evening I went into the Russian tea-shop in the Kleiststrasse, and there was D. For a moment I really thought I must be dreaming. He greeted me quite as usual, beaming all over his face.

"Good God!" I whispered. "What on earth are you doing here?"

D. beamed. "You thought I might have gone abroad?"

"Well, naturally ..."

"But the situation nowadays is so interesting ..."

I laughed. "That's one way of looking at it, certainly ... But isn't it awfully dangerous for you?"

D. merely smiled. Then he turned to the girl he was sitting with and said, "This is Mr Isherwood ... You can speak quite openly to him. He hates the Nazis as much as we do. Oh, yes! Mr Isherwood is a confirmed anti-fascist!"

He laughed very heartily and slapped me on the back. Several people who were sitting near us overheard him. Their reactions were curious. Either they simply couldn't believe their ears, or they were so scared that they pretended to hear nothing, and went on sipping their tea in a state of deaf horror. I have seldom felt so uncomfortable in my whole life.

(D.'s technique appears to have had its points, all the same. He was never arrested. Two months later, he successfully crossed the frontier into Holland.)

This morning, as I was walking down the Bülowstrasse, the Nazis were raiding the house of a small liberal pacifist publisher. They had brought a lorry and were piling it with the publisher's books. The driver of the lorry mockingly read out the titles of the books to the crowd:

"*Nie Wieder Krieg!*" he shouted, holding up one of them by the corner of the cover, disgustedly, as though it were a nasty kind of reptile. Everybody roared with laughter.

"'No More War!'" echoed a fat, well-dressed woman, with a scornful, savage laugh. "What an idea!"

At present, one of my regular pupils is Herr N., a police chief under the Weimar régime. He comes to me every day. He wants to brush up his English, for he is leaving very soon to take up a job in the United States. The curious thing about these lessons is that they are all given while we are driving about the streets in Herr N.'s enormous closed car. Herr N. himself never comes into our house: he sends up his chauffeur to fetch me, and the car moves off at once. Sometimes we stop for a few minutes at the edge of the Tiergarten, and stroll up and down the paths—the chauffeur always following us at a respectful distance.

Herr N. talks to me chiefly about his family. He is worried about his son, who is very delicate, and whom he is obliged to leave behind, to undergo an operation. His wife is delicate, too. He hopes the journey won't tire her. He describes her symptoms, and the kind of medicine she is taking. He tells me stories about his son as a little boy. In a tactful, impersonal way we have become quite intimate. Herr N. is always charmingly polite, and listens gravely and carefully to my explanations of grammatical points. Behind everything he says I am aware of an immense sadness.

We never discuss politics; but I know that Herr N. must be an enemy of the Nazis, and, perhaps, even in hourly danger of arrest. One morning, when we were driving along the Unter den Linden, we passed a group of self-important S.A. men, chatting to each other and blocking the whole pavement. Passers-by were obliged to walk in the gutter. Herr N. smiled faintly and sadly: "One sees some queer sights in the streets nowadays." That was his only comment.

Sometimes he will bend forward to the window and regard a building or a square with a mournful fixity, as if to impress its image upon his memory and to bid it goodbye.

Tomorrow I am going to England. In a few weeks I shall return, but only to pick up my things, before leaving Berlin altogether.

Poor Frl. Schroeder is inconsolable: "I shall never find another gentleman like you, Herr Issyvoo—always so punctual with the rent ... I'm sure I don't know what makes you want to leave Berlin, all of a sudden, like this ..."

It's no use trying to explain to her, or talking politics. Already she is adapting herself, as she will adapt herself to every new régime. This morning I even heard her talking reverently about "Der Führer" to the porter's wife. If anybody were to remind her that, at the elections last November, she voted communist, she would probably deny it hotly, and in perfect good faith. She is merely acclimatizing herself, in accordance with a natural law, like an animal which changes its coat for the winter. Thousands of people like Frl. Schroeder are acclimatizing themselves. After all, whatever government is in power, they are doomed to live in this town.

Today the sun is brilliantly shining; it is quite mild and warm. I go out for my last morning walk, without an overcoat or hat. The sun shines, and Hitler is master of this city. The sun shines, and dozens of my friends—my pupils at the Workers' School, the men and women I met at the I.A.H.—are in prison, possibly dead. But it isn't of them I am thinking—the clear-headed ones, the purposeful, the heroic; they recognized and accepted the risks. I am thinking of poor Rudi, in his absurd Russian blouse. Rudi's make-believe, story-book game has become earnest; the Nazis will play it with him. The Nazis won't laugh at him; they'll take him on trust for what he pretended to be. Perhaps at this very moment Rudi is being tortured to death.

I catch sight of my face in the mirror of a shop, and am horrified to see that I am smiling. You can't help smiling, in such beautiful weather. The trams are going up and down the Kleiststrasse, just as usual. They, and the people on the pavement, and the tea-cosy dome of the Nollendorfplatz station have an air of curious familiarity, of striking resemblance to something one remembers as normal and pleasant in the past—like a very good photograph.

No. Even now I can't altogether believe that any of this has really happened ...